WHERE THE
HILLS REPLY

What could she do, she wondered in despair. She had no money left, nowhere else to go . . .

A ruthless idea, born of desperation, took root in her mind and she returned to the kitchen quickly, before her courage failed her. Hendrik was applying black-lead to the top of the range where she had accidentally spilt water. He looked up when she entered.

"I have come to ask you," she said bluntly, "to marry me."

There was no mistaking the look of shocked distaste on his face, and it was not merely caused by her brazen proposal. "I have no interest in marrying anyone," he said.

"Neither have I. I am desperate to keep my family together, and this appears to be the only way."

**Also by the same author
and available from Coronet**

FAR FORBIDDEN PLAINS

About the author

Christina Laffeaty, the author of many romantic stories, has now written the second historical novel to use her stories and experiences of her youth in South Africa. Her first was the very successful *Far Forbidden Plains*. She came to England after marrying her husband at the age of nineteen, and they have lived in Cornwall for many years.

CHRISTINA LAFFEATY

WHERE THE HILLS REPLY

CORONET BOOKS
Hodder and Stoughton

First published in Great Britain in
1991 by Hodder & Stoughton Ltd

Coronet paperback edition 1992

Printed and bound in Great Britain
for Hodder and Stoughton Paper-
backs, a division of Hodder and
Stoughton Ltd, Mill Road, Dunton
Green, Sevenoaks, Kent TN13 2YA
(Editorial Office: 47 Bedford
Square, London WC1B 3DP) by
Clays Ltd, St Ives plc. Typeset by
Hewer Text Composition Services,
Edinburgh.

British Library C.I.P.
Laffeaty, Christina
Where the hills reply.
I. Title
823[F]

ISBN 0–340–56630–2

This book is for my husband,
David Laffeaty,
with my love

Acknowledgements

I want to thank 'Auntie' Laura Botes for having shared her experiences of life at the Lichtenburg diamond diggings with me, and for other anecdotes she passed on to me. I also owe a debt of gratitude to my journalist friend, Ronnie Hoyle, who has always been more than helpful to me since I moved to Cornwall and became a 'local author'. Last but not least, I want to thank my husband for appointing himself my publicity manager and succeeding so brilliantly in getting maximum exposure for my novels from the most unlikely sources.

Author's Note

The Rand Revolt of 1922 had many diverse causes, but most of the contributary issues are irrelevant to the story told in this novel, and would have been too lengthy, confusing and cumbersome to go into. I have confined myself to one of the bitter grievances of the Afrikaans mine-workers.

Prologue

1905

The baboon-mother sat alone on a rocky ledge as she grieved. Her heartrending lament was magnified by the echoing hills of Mooikrantz, and Wilhelmina wished desperately that the animal would stop, wished her wailing sob of pain and loss didn't sound so uncannily human.

During the past few years Wilhelmina had studied the troop of grey dog-faced baboons and come to know them well; at times she had even taken comfort from their many almost-human qualities, but not today.

Her arms tightened about her son Bastian, who was squirming to get down from her lap and complaining that he wasn't a baby, he was almost four years old, and that he wanted to go and play by the river with his small black friend Ezekiel.

"*Why* do I have to sit on your lap, Mama?" he demanded, his indignation growing. "I'm too old to sit on laps. I'm a big boy. Big boys don't sit on laps when they haven't even fallen over or anything. Why can't I get down?"

She answered with deliberate sharpness, "Because I say so."

"That's not a proper reason," Bastian objected. He paused, and then added accusingly, "And you made me have an all-over wash when it wasn't even bedtime! Why did you, Mama? You didn't make Hendrik have an all-over wash. It isn't fair!"

"Hendrik wasn't dirty." As she spoke she glanced at her eldest son who was standing apart from them and leaning against the rail of the farmhouse stoep. Eight-year-old

3

Hendrik was never dirty. He went to what she felt were unnatural lengths to keep himself clean, because to him being clean was part of being good.

"But why do I have to be clean in the middle of the day?" Bastian persisted with his grievances. "I'm *never* made to be clean in the middle of the day. Am I, Hendrik?" he appealed to his brother.

Before Wilhelmina could think up a convincing excuse, Hendrik supplied the answer. "It's because we're expecting callers." He gave her a look that said: *you* can go on lying if you want to, but I am a Good Boy and Good Boys don't lie.

"Oh." Bastian considered for a moment, his complaints put aside. Then he looked solemnly at her. "What are callers, Mama?"

Dear Jesus Christ. Wilhelmina thought with wrenching, agonising despair. Four words that sum up my past, my present and my future. "What are callers, Mama?"

She glared at Hendrik over Bastian's head, making it clear that if he gave away any more information he would be doing so at his peril. "They are just other people," she answered Bastian, trying to make it sound as if other people were unimportant, and that there was nothing unto-ward about the fact that other people would be calling at Mooikrantz for the first time in his life.

But he was frowning at her, and she steeled herself for another barrage of questions. Would he make the link between his recent all-over wash and the expected visitors? She had purposely not dressed him in his best clothes or put on his only pair of scuffed shoes, for that would have told him that something very unusual was in the wind.

He opened his mouth to ask another probing question but at that moment the baboon-mother rent the air with a lament of renewed anguish, and he asked instead, "Why is the baboon crying like that, Mama? Is it because the others won't let it sit with them?"

She looked at the main body of the troop, outlined high against the sky as they sat in what amounted to a wake.

She hadn't expected to feel grateful to the baboon-mother, but now she recounted what she knew, spinning it out and making a story of it.

"Can you see that young male baboon, sitting a little apart from the rest of the troop? He is her 'husband'. Baboons are much like human beings, you know. I used to watch him take her presents of oranges before they 'married' each other – "

"Baboons are pests and thieves," Hendrik broke in flatly.

"So are some people. A month or so ago, Bastian, the baboon 'wife' had her first baby. You've seen the way the babies hang on by all fours to the long hairs on their mothers' chests?"

He nodded, his eyes wide. She had often reflected that fate had played a mocking joke on him by giving him those eyes. As if there weren't already enough about him to set him apart, his eyes didn't match each other and one was green while the other was light brown with yellow flecks.

"Go on, Mama," he prodded her to continue the story.

"Last night a leopard pounced on the baboons' sleeping-place. Perhaps you heard the noise – the male baboons barking, the females screaming. No? Well, I heard it. I don't think the leopard managed to get a grown baboon before they scattered to the high peaks, so it must have grabbed the baby instead. The mother is crying for it."

"The poor baby." Tears of sympathy glistened in Bastian's eyes.

And the poor, poor mother, Wilhelmina thought.

She tried to make her mind a blank then, but because it proved impossible she consciously forced herself to reflect instead on the visual beauty of the farm. Mooikrantz was shaped like a triangle, one of its boundaries formed by a river which had its source somewhere in the hills; that range of hills itself consisted of no more than rocky out-crops elsewhere but here on Mooikrantz masqueraded as mountains, the sides of the krantzes or cliffs overgrown with tree ferns, with sugar-bush and massive wild-fig and

5

marula trees. In other places bare rocky ledges jutted out, and etched against the skyline were jagged peaks which only the baboons could scale and where eagles sometimes nested.

The lush, unspoilt beauty of Mooikrantz, she knew, was an added bitter affront to her neighbours, because all of *their* farms had been razed to the ground by the British during the Anglo-Boer War and had not yet recovered three years after its end, so that the verdant growth stopped abruptly along the edge of the rutted road that formed the third part of Mooikrantz's triangular border. If she turned her head away from the hills she could see the farm of her nearest neighbours, the van der Walts, with their austerely rebuilt home nestling against a slope clothed only in sparse new growth of stunted thorn scrub which had sprung up among the scattered boulders.

Their harvest had been a poor one of pumpkins and a field or so of maize, while Mooikrantz had yielded an abundance of wheat, and the orchards had been heavy with oranges and lemons and *nartjies*. Of course, nobody at any market within a reachable radius would buy any of it, because the produce was tainted by association with herself, and so Wilhelmina had fallen back on the means she had established in order for them to continue subsisting. The black labour force who'd shared Mooikrantz with their families had judged her no less harshly than did everyone else and had abandoned her, so that she'd been forced to take on uncommitted workers in their place. These workers, neither knowing nor caring about the details of her downfall, were happy to sell Mooikrantz's surplus produce at greatly reduced prices to black communities and share the proceeds with her.

"*Oh, poor me!*" came the self-pitying call of one of the many different kinds of weaver birds which nested along the river, and almost at the same moment Wilhelmina spotted the elegant carriage crossing the bridge spanning the river, on its way to Mooikrantz.

Involuntarily her arms tightened about Bastian, so

that he made a sound of protest. Her mouth dry, her heart hammering sickly in her breast, she glanced at the neighbours' house. Yes, there was Paulus van der Walt clambering on the flat zinc roof of their house, trying to hide himself among the pumpkins which were stored there and also served to stop the makeshift roof from blowing away in a high wind. His binoculars would be trained upon Mooikrantz and afterwards he would broadcast the unprecedented news of visitors to the farm.

Bastian was too intrigued, too over-awed by the opulence of the approaching carriage to ask questions. He simply stared at it with his mouth slightly open. Hendrik moved a little further away, as if he wanted to make it clear that *he* was in no way involved in what was to happen next.

The carriage, drawn by splendidly matching bay horses, drew up outside the house. The man who had been driving dropped the reins and sprang down lightly, then opened the door of the carriage and helped a woman to get out. She was smartly dressed, in a style of clothes Wilhelmina had never seen before and guessed must be in the height of modern fashion. Around her shoulders was draped a fox pelt complete with head and beady glass eyes, as if she had been warned that it might be cold here in the hills at the beginning of autumn.

"Why," Wilhelmina heard Bastian ask shrilly, with a mixture of horror and fascination in his voice, "is the lady wearing a dead dog around her neck, Mama?"

"Don't be rude," she reproved automatically, even though the woman clearly did not understand a word of Afrikaans.

Wilhelmina's gaze fixed upon the man, recognising the shock in his expression as he took in the change in her appearance. Nearly four years of total isolation and ostracism had not, she acknowledged bleakly, encouraged her to make the best of herself, and she knew she looked older and less prepossessing than any woman still in her twenties ought to.

7

He also looked quite different, now that he was no longer wearing British Army uniform; more remote, more – *alien*. In other circumstances, she wondered, would it have caused her pain to see him here with his wife, this man who had taught her that what she'd previously submitted to as an unpleasant duty could be transformed into a joyous celebration of love? Did he ever think of those years during the Boer War when he had suspended his role as the enemy and become her secret lover instead, her protector, her world? Did he know or care that their love had been the cause of her abandonment by friends, family and neighbours?

"I've come for my son," he said in English, the tone of his voice and the expression in his eyes softening the bluntness of his words.

She had thought she'd prepared herself mentally and emotionally for this moment, but now that it had come she was frightened to move or to speak in case it led to a wild outburst of grief. Desperately, she tried to force a protective numbness upon her senses but it was no use. Instead, she focused her attention upon Hendrik, standing so ostentatiously apart, and remembered how he had said to her one day, "People hate us and won't speak to us or visit us because you were Bad. *I* am going to be very, very Good to make them like us again."

For some reason this reminded her of Ewart le Roux, Hendrik's grown-up half-brother, who had resented her from the moment she had become his step-mother and whose last words to her had been, "You have stolen my birthright, Mooikrantz!"

"Did the lady," Bastian's awed voice brought her back to the present, "kill the dog on purpose, Mama, so that she could wear it around her neck? Or did it die, and she wanted to keep it and not bury it because she loved it?"

"Shh!" she whispered against his unruly fair hair. Hendrik had never seen his half-brother, Ewart, and now his other half-brother, Bastian, was to disappear from his life. Would the paths of the three of them ever cross in the future?

8

The thought brought a hollow reminder that *she* had never expected to lay eyes on her lover again after he had left to return to England. "I've come for my son," he repeated, his voice more insistent this time.

Hendrik, who was taught English at school, stared studiedly into the distance. Bastian had never heard the language spoken before, and was quite unaware of what was going on. Wilhelmina herself had been taught to understand a little English by the man during the years when they were lovers, but she couldn't speak more than a few words of it.

His letter, on notepaper embossed with a picture of a large ship, had conveyed nothing more to her than that it had been composed while at sea. But its accompanying translation in High Dutch, written by a lawyer in Cape Town, had torn open old wounds and inflicted new ones.

The gist of her former lover's letter had been that he'd felt unsettled after the war and had wished to emigrate and live – and invest in – the new prosperity of Johannesburg. His plans had had to be shelved because of his wife's medical problems which had culminated in an operation, leaving her barren. Because she was desperate to adopt a child and he did not believe he could feel towards a stranger's child as he should, he had confessed his wartime adultery to his wife. She had forgiven him and had agreed that he should ask Wilhelmina whether she would consider giving up to them the son he had fathered by her.

Among the chaos of emotion into which the letter had flung her, a thought had sneaked into Wilhelmina's mind: had he taken a gamble, and used as bait his son in South Africa to persuade his wife to uproot herself and make a new life in Johannesburg?

Wherever the truth lay, his letter had required a response. She could read High Dutch, because the Afrikaans language which Lord Milner was determined to stamp out was partly derived from it. But she could no more write in the cumbersome High Dutch than she could in English, and so Wilhelmina had simply penned the word "yes" at the foot of his letter and returned it to the address of the lawyer in Cape Town. A week ago she had received the final piece of correspondence between them, a brief note accompanied by a translation, telling her when the man would be arriving to collect their son.

But there was so much else they needed to discuss. If his wife had not been present, if there had been time, she could have used mime as in the old days to make him understand that he was her only hope, the only human being in the world to whom she could turn for help, and why. Surely he *would* help her? Surely the memory of what had once been between them would move him to come to her aid, now that fate had caused their paths to cross once more? He was a wealthy man and it would mean no great sacrifice to him.

But since they were no longer able to communicate in the way they used to, and his attitude made it plain that he was impatient to accomplish his mission and leave for the new life in Johannesburg he was planning, she could only say hesitantly, in rusty English, "Please – give money?"

She heard his wife gasp, and saw his mouth tighten. "How much?" he asked tersely.

She lowered her head in shock and bitter mortification. *He thought she was demanding money in exchange for Bastian.* Enmeshed in the trap of their inability to communicate, she could not explain that there was no connection, that she was simply grasping the God-sent opportunity of asking his help because she was in desperate need of money; that Hendrik had been seriously ill last year and that if she continued putting off the settlement of his outstanding hospital bills she would lose Mooikrantz.

Because she could not explain, she swallowed her humiliation, shifted Bastian's weight to one side of her lap and reached into the pocket of her dress for the scrap of paper on which she had written the exact amount she needed. The man looked at it, removed a roll of banknotes from his pocket and dropped it on her lap. "I'll send the rest by post," he said, his voice cold with distaste.

She stuffed the money inside her pocket and rose unsteadily, fighting to make her own voice come out calm and strong. "This is your Pa, Bastian, and your new Mama. You are to go and live with them in Johannesburg."

He gave her a baffled look and she knew he thought she'd made a grown-up joke and that he was searching for the humour in it. But then the man took a step forward, a smile on his face, and at the same time the woman moved closer to the stoep, her arms wide open in a receiving gesture, her eyes bright with emotion.

Bastian screamed. It was a sound filled with panic, fear and dimly-glimpsed understanding. Both his arms locked about Wilhelmina's neck in a stranglehold, and the screams turned into a wild, piteous plea. "No, Mama, no! Don't make me go! Please, please, Mama – I'll be good. I don't like the dead-dog lady or the man!"

Oh God, she thought. Oh God. You'd like it even less, my baby, my darling, if I let you stay and they start calling you not only "whore's son", "traitor's son" as they do to Hendrik at school, but also "English bastard". Letting you go is the best, the only good thing I shall ever be able to do for you . . .

Aloud, drawing on all her reserves of strength, she said sternly, "Now stop your noise and show everyone what a good boy you can be. You'll soon get used to your Pa and your new Ma and you'll enjoy living with them."

"No, I won't! I'm sorry I was naughty, Mama! Let me stay – "

His words ended in another piercing scream as the man uncurled his small fingers from around Wilhelmina's neck and scooped him up. He was still screaming as the man carried him towards the vehicle, and when the woman tried to give him a consoling pat he kicked out at her. Wilhelmina's hands grasped the stoep railing in a grip that brought physical pain, and part of her mind registered the fact that Hendrik had remained an unmoving and apparently unmoved spectator throughout the scene.

Would it have helped if she'd tried to prepare Bastian? No . . . Nothing would have helped, nothing would have made things easier.

"*My monkey!*" Bastian sobbed from inside the carriage, where the woman was trying her best to console and to confine him with an embrace. "I have to find my monkey first, Mama! You know I can't go away and leave my monkey behind!"

He was trying to scramble out of the carriage, but the man pushed him back inside. "My monkey!" Bastian screamed again.

Wilhelmina swallowed hard. "I'll search for it and send it on to you," she lied. She had hidden the home-made, stuffed toy monkey in the hope that he would be more likely to forget his real mother if he didn't take with him any treasured relic from home. Besides, his new "mother" would be showering expensive toys upon him.

The carriage began to move away from the house, and Bastian's screams fell like whiplashes on Wilhelmina's soul. "Please, Mama, don't make me go with the dead-dog lady . . . I want my monkey, Mama! I'll never be bad again or make a mess or get myself dirty . . . *Mama, let me come home!*" And finally, piteously, as all his other pleas failed he cried out to her, "You didn't kiss me goodbye, Mama! Make them bring me back so you can kiss me goodbye . . ."

Sounds echoed and carried here in the hills. Paulus van der Walt, spying on them from the top of his roof among the pumpkins, would have heard Bastian's cries. Soon the neighbourhood would seethe with the news that Wilhelmina le Roux had sold her bastard son to her former lover and his wife, had forced the poor child to leave her without even a farewell kiss. Her isolation would increase, the wall of hatred against her grow, if such a thing were possible.

She turned and stumbled inside the farmhouse, where she retrieved Bastian's toy monkey from its hiding place. Picking up his pair of scuffed shoes which he would never

12

again be wearing, she clutched the three objects to her breast.

The tears she had been repressing with such superhuman effort almost blinded her as she blundered outside, towards the ledge where the lone baboon-mother had resumed her lament of grief for her own lost baby.

Part One

Spring 1922

1

Today was to be special, a day of reunion and rejoicing, but also a very busy one, and so Sabella gave the stoep floor a mere lick-and-a-promise. It was still early morning, but the sun was already scorching down from a hard blue sky. It was going to be the kind of day, Ma would have said, to make even the crows yawn.

Crows had more sense than to flock to the Johannesburg suburb of Westdene, where even self-respecting mice would not find the average household pickings worth the bother of setting up home, and so Sabella didn't know whether or not it was true that crows yawned in the heat.

Ma had died three years ago, within a week of giving birth to the last of her five children, but remembering her favourite sayings was one way in which Sabella kept her memory alive. What would Ma have said about recent events? "It's enough to shame one's eyes from one's head," perhaps. Or, more philosophically, "The grass will grow over it," meaning that time would hide what had happened.

Sabella paused, leaning on the handle of the broom. All the houses in this and most other streets of the run-down suburb were of basically similar design. They stretched away into the distance, one-storeyed with corrugated-iron roofs splashed with various sizes of rust patches, and with a stoep running along three of their sides. Everything looked so ordinary and drab and almost boringly peaceful now, but only six months ago women and children had barricaded themselves inside those houses while their

17

menfolk fought pitched battles against the Union Defence Force. Everywhere on the Rand shops and stores and public buildings had been boarded up, tanks had rolled in the streets, the sound of gunfire had filled the air and hundreds had been killed in what was already being called the Rand Revolt.

Sabella was glad that Ma had been spared what happened next. Along with hundreds of others, Pa had been flung into gaol for his part in the revolt. But today he would be set free; let off with a fine. Dominee Roelof, who was their family parson, had been following the case against Pa in court and he'd said so with utter confidence, because the defence lawyer had repeatedly assured him of it.

The thought reminded Sabella that the parson would be calling in an hour's time, and she and the children would have to be ready when he arrived. She hurried to finish sweeping the stoep. Another of Ma's favourite sayings had been that one could tell the kind of people who lived in a house merely by looking at their stoep, and Sabella had to agree that there was a good deal of truth in this as she glanced at the house next door.

The Goosens never cleaned their stoep at all, and practically lived on it. The floor was caked with mud when it rained and covered in dust from the mine dumps when the weather was dry, and littered with all kinds of junk which their many children played with or fought over. Mevrou Goosen spent most of the day sitting in a corner on a sagging, ancient armchair which dripped horse-hair and doing nothing more strenuous than occasionally fanning herself with a fly-swat. Her husband lolled against a stack of grubby pillows, wearing an under-vest pocked with holes and more often than not drinking beer out of a bottle.

During her lifetime Ma had not allowed her children to have anything to do with the Goosens, and Sabella had seen no reason to lift that ban after her death. The Goosens were not respectable, and Ma used to say that their daughters would end in the gutter and their sons on the gallows.

As usual this morning they displayed a cheerful indifference to their role as social pariahs, and the parents smiled amiably at Sabella while their children stuck their tongues out at her or made rude gestures. She pretended not to have noticed, but it suddenly struck her that *they* could have sat in judgement on their van Renselaar neighbours if they'd wanted to. After all, it was Pa who had been in gaol for the past six months, and not Meneer Goosen.

Then she smiled wryly at the thought. Since Meneer Goosen had never been known to have a job of any kind, he'd not been called upon to join the escalating strikes which had crippled Johannesburg, and he was far too lazy to have joined, for its own sake, in the fighting which had followed. People said he supported his family by gambling, and the only part he could have played in the Rand Revolt was gambling on its outcome.

Sabella went inside the house and put the broom away in the scullery. She could hear her younger brothers and sister playing in the back yard and she hurried to put pans of water on the kitchen range so that she could wash them. Nantes, who was ten, and Anton, two years his junior, would leave for school as usual. The three-year-old baby of the family, Daan, and Ria, who was thirteen but what Ma used to call "slow", would be delivered into the care of Mevrou Roelof. This had been arranged so that Sabella would be able to accompany the Dominee to court and be present when they set Pa free.

Her heart began to beat with excitement, and she had to admit to herself that it was not purely because Pa would once again be back with his family. No, a good deal of her excitement lay in the fact that for the very first time in her life she would be riding in a motor car, she would be travelling beyond the perimeters of Westdene, and she would actually see what the city looked like. She had built up a picture of it in her mind from the newspapers and it seemed to her to be so different from Westdene that it might be an entirely alien and infinitely more enviable planet.

Even though Ma's death had forced Sabella to leave

school at fourteen, her voracious appetite for reading, her fascination with words and the construction of sentences had meant that she was far ahead of other pupils of her age by the time she took over Ma's domestic responsibilities. And because the only reading matter she'd been able to lay hands upon since leaving school were newspapers, she was aware that she knew more about most subjects than many adults of her acquaintance.

It had been a long time since they had been able to afford to buy newspapers, but each afternoon when the two older boys returned from school she left Nantes in charge and went to the Portuguese shop to buy three-farthings' worth of soup greens for supper. The vegetables would normally be wrapped in a couple of sheets of newspaper from a supply of second-hand papers which the Portuguese owner obtained from somewhere, but because Sabella always asked after his wife and baby, Meneer da Freitas would let her have a whole newspaper whenever he could spare one.

At home, she would devour each line of print before putting the newspaper to practical use. The most interesting articles were cut into squares which were then threaded on a piece of string and hung from a nail in the privy at the rear of the back yard. With what remained of the paper, she lined the shelves of the kitchen dresser, first folding it carefully and cutting it so that a filigreed frill would overhang each shelf. Ma had taught her how to do it and she had automatically carried on the custom without thinking about it.

But this morning Sabella found herself staring at the newspaper frills with a fresh and detached eye. For all her efforts, she realised, there was no possible way in which newspaper frills could be made to look pretty. Instead, it struck her for the first time that they looked downright pathetic. And yet she knew that every other woman in Westdene – with the undoubted exception of Mevrou Goosen – lined her dresser shelves with similar lacy newspaper frills. It wasn't even as if the newspaper helped to

20

keep the shelves clean, for the print rubbed off on them so that they had to be scrubbed whenever the frills were changed.

Now if only . . . Yes, it might well be possible – something stirred inside her, an ebullient, effervescent feeling transcending excitement. *She had just thought of a way of making money!*

Even though Pa would be set free today, the knowledge had been nagging at her mind that he was unlikely to be given back his old job as a power-station worker. The strikes had started because the Transvaal Chamber of Mines had decided to replace many of the Afrikaans miners with cheap, non-union black labour, and after the crushing of the revolt into which the strikes had escalated, the Afrikaans work-force in the mines had not only been cut far more drastically than had at first been proposed, but those who still had jobs had been forced to accept a sharp drop in wages. With unemployment so widespread, Pa was going to face a hard struggle to find another job, and his savings wouldn't last forever. And now she, Sabella, had just hit upon the solution as to how they were all to live!

As soon as she was able to have a private word with Pa, she would persuade him to invest most of his savings in buying American cloth. Sabella would then fold strips of it and cut it in the same way she cut the newspaper, and she would go from door to door, selling them. Good Lord, who wouldn't sooner pay to have permanent, washable and pretty covers for their shelves than go through the laborious periodic business of cutting newspaper into frilly covers which would never be anything but ugly and weren't even labour-saving? She burnt to go on making mental plans for selling shelf-covers, but it was time to call the children into the scullery to wash them.

Nantes, who had been named Ferdinantes after Pa, just as Sabella had been named Isabella after Ma, carried a jugful of hot water into the bedroom to wash in private. He could be trusted with his own ablutions because he had an inherent dislike of anything ugly, and to him dirt had always been

21

ugly. He was not tough and aggressive like most boys, but a quiet dreamer who saw beauty in the most unexpected objects and would come home from school with a speckled pebble he had picked up or a bunch of flowering weeds picked on wasteland.

Anton, at eight, was big for his age and always the aggressor in any squabble with his elder brother. He loved rough games and Sabella worried that he might develop into the kind of bully under whom Nantes so often suffered at school. His sensitive nature, coupled with the stammer from which he suffered, inevitably made Nantes a target for persecution by other boys.

She forced Anton's head over the stone sink and scrubbed his neck with blue household soap which was all she bought now because it was cheap. When I start selling my American cloth shelf-covers, she thought with excitement, I'll buy some of that scented Ivory soap.

Just before the two older boys set off for school, she handed them packets of beetroot sandwiches. "Pa and I will almost certainly be at home when you get back from school," she told them, "but if we should be delayed while picking up Ria and Daan, just wait here for us. Won't it be wonderful to have Pa back again?"

Nantes stammered fervent agreement, but Anton said, "There's a boy in my class whose Pa was shot dead by the soldiers." His tone seemed to imply that Pa had somehow caused the family to lose face by not suffering a similar fate.

"Will Pa bring sweeties?" Daan demanded.

"Sweeties!" Ria echoed. "Sweeties for Ria!"

"Perhaps," Sabella half-promised rashly. They *did* have something to celebrate, after all, and spending money on sweets no longer seemed a foolish extravagance when she thought of the profits she would be making from the sale of shelf-covers.

She washed Daan, who squirmed and complained that she was getting soap in his eyes, and then Ria automatically copied her baby brother by making the same complaint.

Ria was as beautiful as a doll, with round but empty blue eyes, pink cheeks, a rosebud mouth and fair curly hair.

At school she had been able to learn nothing, let alone the English which pupils were required to use at all times. Sabella used to shoulder the many cruelties directed at her, smarting under the jeers and taunts Ria herself could not understand, and fighting the children who tried to bully her sister physically. When Sabella was forced to leave school after Ma's death she had marched defiantly into the headmaster's office and announced that Ria would be leaving too. He must have been relieved to have the problem of Ria taken out of his hands, for no one in authority had come to force her to return to school.

When Sabella had washed her and Daan and dressed them in clean clothes she sent them to the front room to wait while she used the rest of the hot water to wash herself.

Afterwards, in the bedroom which she shared with Ria, Sabella changed out of her house-dress. Her wardrobe was limited to the clothes which had belonged to Ma who had, fortunately, been of slight build. With the boys in particular constantly needing new clothes there had never been anything left over to spare for Sabella, but she had been planning for a long while to make Ma's dresses over into more modern styles for herself. But in between looking after the children and doing the household chores and bringing up Daan there had simply never been time. And then the madness of the mass revolt had swept their world into chaos, and with Pa in gaol anything as frivolous as modern-styled dresses had fled from her thoughts.

The navy-blue dress she chose fastened high at the neck and reached to just above her ankles, and was going to be uncomfortably hot. So, too, were the old-fashioned buttoned boots which had also belonged to Ma, but it couldn't be helped. They were all she had that would be suitable for the occasion.

She brushed her dark brown hair, with more than a suggestion of red in it, and pulled it away from her face, twisting it into a knot in the nape of her neck. It was the

23

way Pa liked her to wear it and after he had been sent to gaol it had seemed to her that she would be taking unfair advantage if she carried out her rebellious threat to cut it short. Now that he was to be set free, however, she had every intention of doing so.

She made a face at her reflection, and then thought with a thrill: once I've built up a steady market for my shelf-covers I'll buy myself one of those modern dresses in a floating material, the kind they show in the newspaper illustrations . . .

The corners of her wide, full mouth turned down and her grey eyes took on a bleak look as reality threw cold water on her plans. Of what earthly use would it be to make herself more attractive? She was seventeen, and by the time Daan was old enough to fend for himself she would be in her late twenties and on the shelf. But even in the unlikely event of someone showing a romantic interest in her then, it would still be impossible for it to lead anywhere. Ria would be needing her for the rest of her life, and so would Pa. He had never shown any inclination to marry again, or perhaps he, too, had accepted reality and acknowledged that no woman was likely to want to become stepmother to so many orphans, one of whom was "slow". No, the day Sabella had taken on the legacy of responsibility left to her by Ma, she had also had a lifetime of spinsterhood thrust upon her.

The chugging sound of a motor car dispersed her gloomy thoughts. It would be Dominee Roelof, come to collect her with his wife, who was to take Ria and Daan back to the manse with her.

Sabella fetched her brother and sister from the front room, and by the time they reached the stoep Dominee Roelof had stopped his car outside. He remained in the driving seat because he knew as well as Sabella did that if he left the motor unattended the Goosen children would swoop on it like a destructive horde. Mevrou Roelof's matronly figure was climbing the steps to meet them, and after kissing Sabella's cheek she made a fuss of Daan. She

24

had never had any children of her own and Daan had been a favourite of hers since his babyhood. She tried hard to make an equal fuss of Ria, but it was clear to Sabella that she found it something of a strain. Sabella could hardly blame her. It *was* difficult to behave naturally towards a thirteen-year-old whose mind was that of a child of three.

"You're to be good," Sabella warned the children after she had kissed them goodbye, "or there'll be no sweets for you when I come home with Pa."

Once she was sitting beside Dominee Roelof and the car was turning the first corner Sabella discovered with a let-down feeling that she did not enjoy motoring at all, and that a queasiness was threatening to overcome her. At first she tried to fight it by concentrating on the novelty of leaving Westdene behind. But the other suburbs through which they drove, she realised, looked very much like their own. The only difference was that, as they drew closer to the city with its tall buildings dominating the skyline, there were visible signs still remaining of the near-revolution which had convulsed the Rand six months ago. Part of a slogan which had been painted on a wall and had not yet been completely scrubbed off exhorted workers to unite and fight for something-or-other; an outlawed Republican flag once defiantly hoisted to a roof now lay torn in the gutter of a side street; bullet holes pocked several wooden doors and fences and they passed the remains of a charred building – probably a police station, because she knew that police stations had been set on fire during the revolt.

Her feeling of nausea increased, and she guessed that she was making herself feel worse by constantly turning her head to look out of the windows. She lay back in the seat and closed her eyes, and gradually began to feel better.

She opened her eyes when Dominee Roelof stopped his car. Occupying almost an entire block was a large, forbidding-looking building with pillars flanking wide steps. She realised they had reached the city, but where were the sights with which her imagination had always filled the heart of Johannesburg? The bustling crowds, the

25

elegant women in their modern short dresses spilling from multitudes of shops? The only people to be seen were as poor-looking as she herself, their destination clearly the large building with its many different court rooms of which Dominee Roelof had told her.

As they entered the building together he said, "You'll see – there'll be a fine to pay, and Ferdinantes van Renselaar will be driving home to Westdene with us, a free man."

She nodded. After the bright, hard sunshine, her eyes did not immediately adjust to the gloom inside the building. As she entered one of the rooms with Dominee Roelof her nostrils were met by a strange, musty smell; the smell of old papers and old human despairs, she thought. The one high window was so small and inadequate that electric bulbs were burning in sconces, showing her the public benches and the raised platform, on one side of which the Union flag hung limply. There were words etched in the wall above the platform which she guessed were in Latin. Three ornate, unoccupied chairs stood behind a long leather-topped desk on the platform and facing it was something that reminded her of the pulpit from which Dominee Roelof delivered his sermons on Sundays. There were several other desks below the raised platform, and at one of them three men were sitting with notebooks and pencils neatly laid out in front of them. At one end of the room was a crescent-shaped cubicle, and as they found seats for themselves upon the already-crowded public benches, Dominee Roelof gestured towards the cubicle and said, "That's the dock. It's where your Pa will be appearing for the summing up."

Before she could respond the voice of the official who had let them into the court room boomed, "All rise!" She stumbled to her feet with everyone else. Several men in sober dark suits entered and three of them mounted the platform and sat down behind the desk.

Two of the men who had entered were carrying sheafs of papers. They put these down on neighbouring desks, and bowed towards the platform. From Dominee Roelof,

26

Sabella knew that the one with tufts of grey hair at his temples was the defence lawyer acting for Pa among others, while the bald man was acting for the prosecution. She also knew that the man who occupied the middle seat behind the desk was the presiding magistrate and the other two his colleagues who helped him to reach his verdicts.

Suddenly, as if by magic, two men had appeared inside the dock and one of them wore a policeman's uniform. "There's a cell below," Dominee Roelof whispered in Sabella's ear, "with steps leading up to the dock."

The policeman moved aside, and she was disappointed to see that it was not Pa who had appeared in the dock. The parson had told her that this particular court was dealing with cases similar to that against Pa, which were all connected with events during the Rand Revolt, and that several were to be summed up that morning. The parson had also warned her that they wouldn't know in advance when it would be Pa's turn, but she had still hoped he would be dealt with first.

Fortunately, the summing up of this case and the one following was brief. Sabella did learn something, however, which she had previously dismissed as wild rumour. Even before the first strike started, certain Afrikaans workers had styled themselves as "generals" and had secretly recruited "commandos" among fellow-workers, and there had been a plot to whip up support among rural Afrikaners and foment a mass revolution which would lead to the Transvaal once again being proclaimed a free republic.

The first two men to appear in the dock were freed after being fined, the money to be paid to the court in instalments. "You see?" Dominee Roelof whispered triumphantly in her ear, as if he had been personally responsible for the verdicts. But she was glad that the fines did not have to be paid in one lump sum, for it meant that Pa would be able to spare the capital she would need to buy American cloth.

The summing up of the next case took longer than would have been necessary, because the defendant insisted on the proceedings being conducted in Afrikaans. It was clearly an attitude he had taken from the beginning of his case, for the presiding magistrate said with weary resignation, "You have already made your point, Mr Joubert, and since you are perfectly familiar with English the court would be obliged if you would stop wasting its time by insisting on an interpreter."

"Afrikaans is my mother-tongue," the defendant responded inflexibly in that language. "The fact that I was forced to learn English in order to survive under the enemy who overran my country is immaterial. I have the same right as a Zulu or a Shangaan or a Sotho to have my case conducted in my mother-tongue."

An interpreter was duly called, and Sabella wondered if the man would have stuck so obstinately to his principles if he hadn't felt confident of also being let off with a fine. But having to listen to the same details translated from English into Afrikaans became boring, and she shut her mind to what was going on and thought instead of her plan for making shelf-covers.

Something struck her for the first time. What had she been about, planning to use American cloth? Apart from the fact that it was bound to be expensive to buy, its use would be economically unsound. American cloth was practically indestructible and once people had bought shelf-covers made of it her market would be exhausted.

Frowning, she considered alternatives, and gradually the answer came to her. *Wallpaper!* She knew about wallpaper because she had read about it in newspaper advertisements. "As used to decorate the best homes in London," they said, obviously aiming at wealthy English residents in Johannesburg. She knew that it came in many different colours and designs and could be bought by the roll. She could offer customers as large a choice as she would be able to afford to buy rolls, and since her finished products would be far cheaper than if she'd used American cloth, women would be quite happy to re-order from time to time, tempted by new designs and colours . . .

Her mental plans were immediately suspended when she saw that it was Pa who had now appeared in the dock. But oh, how changed he looked! Was it only because they had forced him to shave off his moustache and his side-whiskers that his face seemed so gaunt and grey? But no, he had definitely lost weight, and he looked as if he had been ill. While she made her shelf-covers she would concentrate equally on nursing him back to health . . .

Then she cleared her mind of everything else and fixed it upon the voice of the defence lawyer as he began to sum up Pa's case. "Several witnesses, Your Worships, have testified to the fact that the defendant has always been a mild-mannered man who deplored violence. We have established beyond doubt that he did not wish to go on strike in the first place, but was forced to do so when his fellow power-station workers voted to join the growing series of strikes."

Sabella tried to catch Pa's eye, but he was staring fixedly at the presiding magistrate. "Ferdinantes van Renselaar," the defence attorney went on, "can best be described as a victim of circumstance, a man who found himself in the wrong place at the wrong time. He did not go to the strikers' headquarters in Fordsburg when it was under siege because he had any intention of taking part in the fighting. He went out of simple, misguided but very human curiosity. He has admitted quite freely that he picked up a brick and threw it at a member of the Union Defence Force, hitting him on the head and rendering him unconscious and in need of medical aid. But, Your Worships, it has been proved by the testimony of several witnesses that he did so because the man was about to fire his gun at someone recognised by van Renselaar as an old friend."

The attorney's voice rose dramatically. "Who of us could truthfully say, Your Worships, that faced with similar circumstances we would not have reacted, instinctively and without thinking, in the same way?"

The presiding magistrate's nod was slight, and almost

certainly involuntary, but it caused Dominee Roelof to give Sabella an I-told-you-so smile.

"The defendant, Your Worships," the defence lawyer continued, "has already spent some six months in gaol. He was never one of the violent trouble-makers, never remotely connected with the revolutionary plotters. He has been little more than yet another victim of the Rand Revolt. I am asking you to allow him to walk free from this court."

The defence lawyer bowed politely to the three magistrates and sat down. The flanking magistrates turned to their colleague in the centre to confer together, but at that moment the prosecutor stood up.

"If it please Your Worships," he said, "I would like the court's permission to call a late witness."

The defence lawyer was on his feet. "This is most irregular, Your Worships!" he protested. "The prosecution has completed its summing up and if my learned friend had wished to call a further witness he should have done so at the proper time – "

"This particular witness, Your Worships," the prosecutor cut in, "has only come forward within the past half-hour. An usher handed me a note from him which I have been perusing while the defence summed up its case, and the note makes it quite clear that there is evidence to prove that Ferdinantes van Renselaar was far more than the innocent victim of circumstance he has been made out to be."

Sabella had been listening in bewilderment, and then with growing anxiety. She felt Dominee Roelof's hand on her arm in a reassuring gesture. She found a measure of reassurance, instead, in the irritation with which the three magistrates were regarding the prosecutor because he had introduced a complication in what had been a straight-forward case.

Then every vestige of reassurance fled as the prosecutor said with emphasis, "The evidence which I wish to bring before the court will almost certainly lead to the defendant's case being referred to the Supreme Court, where he would stand trial on charges of a serious nature. Sedition and conspiracy to overthrow the Government by armed revolution are but two that spring to mind."

A gasp rose from the public benches, and almost automatically the official's voice called out, "Silence in court!" Sabella's palms had turned clammy and her mouth dry. Who was there who could possibly have evidence that could lead Pa to stand trial on such serious charges? How could everything have gone so dreadfully wrong, just when Pa had been within moments of being set free?

The three magistrates discussed the matter in whispers, and after a few minutes the presiding spokesman announced, "The court will take a short recess."

"All rise!" the official called out, and obediently the public stood up and began to file out of court. Sabella remained where she was and now, for the first time, Pa did catch her eye. Don't worry, his expression said. It will turn out to be a mistake. There *can't be* such a witness.

The policeman who had been hovering at the back of the dock stepped forward and took Pa by the arm, leading him down the stairs to the cell below. Sabella found that she and Dominee Roelof were now the only members of the public still inside the court room, and they were politely but inexorably ushered out by the official.

"What – what happens to people who are found guilty of sedition or armed revolution, Dominee?" Sabella asked anxiously when they stood in the corridor.

He hesitated for a moment before responding. "Sabella, I've told you not to worry. Trust in God."

It was as impossible for her to do one as the other. Ma and Pa had spent their lives trusting in God, and where had it got them? Ma had died painfully and prematurely, and Pa was sitting in a cell waiting to be told whether some malicious witness would be allowed to give false evidence which could lead him to face trial on serious charges in the Supreme Court.

"What is the punishment, Dominee?" she persisted.

31

"I – well, I'm not sure . . ." He cleared his throat. "I'm not sure whether it's the gallows, or a firing squad. But Sabella – "

At that moment the official threw open the door to the court room as a signal that they were allowed to return to their seats, and she half-ran, half-stumbled to take her place on the public bench.

Pa stood in the dock again. Sabella closed her eyes, and prayed to a God in whom she had no trust that the magistrates had decided not to hear further evidence against Pa. Instead, like an obscenity falling on her ears, the official cried in ringing tones, "Call Mr Sebastian Grant!"

Many different reactions and emotions meshed inside Sabella, but the first to register in her mind was the fairly superficial one of surprise. It was an *English* name, and not one she had ever heard before. It was certainly not one of Pa's former bosses at the power-station who might have had a grudge against him. Pa used to complain to her about a Mr Elliot, who was a slave-driver, and a Mr Herbert, who sneered at the Afrikaans workers and said they were "only a degree or so more advanced than the kaffirs". Pa had mentioned a Mr Collins and a Mr Jenkins, but never a Mr Sebastian Grant.

The next moment Sabella abandoned the puzzle, because a man was making his way along the aisle towards the object that looked like a pulpit and must obviously be the witness box. All she could tell about him at first was that he was tall, and smartly dressed in dark trousers and jacket. He walked with a loose-limbed, arrogant stride, his broad shoulders very straight, and in the dimly-lit room it was difficult to make out the colour of his hair from behind. Then he took the witness stand and she stifled a gasp of surprise as the light from two electric bulbs in their sconces showed his face to the court room.

He was little more than a boy! Why, he couldn't be older than twenty or so. How could someone so young possibly possess damaging evidence against Pa? Relief flowed through Sabella. Whatever lies he might tell would soon be nailed by the far older, experienced defence lawyer.

He was swearing on the Bible to tell the truth and nothing but the truth. Her sense of relief was shaken by the calm assurance in his oh-so-English voice. She stared at him with hostility, and noticed against her will that he was striking-looking in an odd sort of way, because nothing about him appeared to match. She couldn't see the colour of his eyes from this distance, but his hair ranged in colour from khaki at the temples to every conceivable shade of blond, while his eyebrows and lashes were dark. Instead of the pale or fresh complexion which should have accompanied his fair hair, his clean-shaven face gave the impression of an outdoor worker. This was clearly not possible, and then she remembered reading that rich young Englishmen and girls spent a good deal of their time in playing tennis or boating or riding horses at special clubs to which they belonged.

A freak, she tried to dismiss him contemptuously. A rich, bored, spoilt society drone who had probably embarked on this for a dare. She had read that his sort liked to amuse themselves by challenging each other to stupid dares. But even as she thought it she had a horrible instinct that it wasn't true.

The prosecutor began to question him. "You are, I believe, the son of the Right Honourable Peregrine Grant, Member of Parliament. Would you please tell the court your age and your occupation?"

He answered with total self-possession which bordered on unconscious arrogance. "I am twenty-one years old. The nature of my occupation cannot be defined in one or two words. One day control of the corporation will pass to me, but at present I act as a kind of personal assistant to members of the board and heads of department in the Grant Mining Corporation. The purpose of this is to learn, at first hand, every aspect of the corporation's activities."

"Is it therefore a fact that very little, if anything, goes

on in the Grant Mining Corporation of which you are ignorant?"

"I would say so, yes."

"Including any decision made by the Transvaal Chamber of Mines, of which the Grant Mining Corporation is a member?"

"That is correct."

Anyone else, Sabella thought with illogical rage, would have added "sir" to his responses. But not this arrogant Englishman whose work had nothing whatsoever to do with Pa, and who could never have laid eyes on him in his privileged young life . . .

The next moment the prosecutor was voicing her thoughts in the form of a question. "Do you recognise the defendant in the dock, Mr Grant?"

"I do."

"Please tell the court about your association with him."

"The term 'association' is incorrect." Sebastian Grant glanced at Pa, and then dismissed him with a shrug. "I had one meeting with him, a somewhat bizarre one, towards the end of October last year."

"Do you believe there is some significance about the time of your meeting with the defendant, Mr Grant?"

"I believe it to be highly significant. On October 24th, 1921, the Executive Committee of the Transvaal Chamber of Mines held a crucial meeting – "

"A meeting," the prosecutor cut in, "at which we subsequently learnt that the decision was taken to force a confrontation with the trade unions, and gain complete control of industry."

And to impose large cuts in wages and manpower among the Afrikaans workforce, Sabella thought. That meeting had played a significant part in sparking off the Rand Revolt, but what on earth could it have to do with Pa?

The prosecutor seemed to be debating what question to put next. At last he said, "Mr Grant, you described your encounter with the defendant as having been bizarre. Will you please tell the court what happened."

In the witness box, Sebastian Grant paused to push back a wing of hair which had fallen over his forehead. An uninvolved part of Sabella's mind noted that he did not slick his hair down with scented oil, which she knew to be the fashion among well-to-do men, and the light shining on the fringes of his hair made it appear to be touched with silver-gilt. Then she dismissed these irrelevant thoughts angrily, and leant forward to listen to his reply.

"The defendant waylaid me as I left the Grant building in the afternoon of October 24th, 1921. He introduced himself to me in a way which seemed to suggest that I would instantly know who he was; that his was a household name." The glance of amused contempt which he flicked in Pa's direction added, almost as clearly as words would have done, *Presumably it's a household name among other Afrikaans nobodies.*

Such fury gathered inside Sabella that she wanted to hurl herself across the court to the witness box and do something violent to this over-privileged, supercilious, lying young man.

"The defendant spoke to me in Afrikaans," Sebastian Grant went on, "again as if he assumed that I would understand the language. As a matter of fact I have picked up a basic knowledge of it. He had the effrontery to ask me to call him uncle, in the way I've been told Afrikaners expect all younger people to address their elders as uncle and aunt to show respect, whether or not they are related."

Sabella sucked in a sharp breath. Oh, but he was lying quite blatantly now, for never in a hundred years would Pa have approached an Englishman and spoken to him in Afrikaans, because it was a well-known fact that Englishmen did not trouble to learn as much as a few words of Afrikaans, and Pa's English was perfectly adequate. It was true, of course, that young Afrikaners addressed all older people as uncle or aunt, and that fact lent a clever touch of credibility to Grant's story. But just wait until the defence attorney ordered the interpreter to speak to him

35

in Afrikaans! The puzzling question remained, however: *why* was Grant telling these pointless lies?

"How did you respond, Mr Grant?" she heard the prosecutor asking.

Sebastian Grant shrugged. "I told him he wasn't an uncle of mine and asked him to state his business because I had better things to do than speak bad Afrikaans to a stranger in the street."

"And did he state his business?"

"I didn't think so at the time. Admittedly my knowledge of Afrikaans is limited but I gained the general impression that he was rambling on about the many injustices suffered by the Afrikaans workers. His attitude implied that he expected me to sympathise with them. At that stage I was impatient to be rid of him, for he was beginning to seem more than a little unbalanced to me. He was actually asking me to tell him what I knew of the Chamber of Mines' future plans."

"And did you answer his questions, Mr Grant?"

"Indeed not! I pushed my way past him and I put him, and our strange encounter, from my mind until I chanced to see his name in the newspaper this morning. Ferdinantes van Renselaar is not a common name, and I couldn't remember at first where I had previously encountered it. The newspaper report simply included his name in the list of defendants appearing in court on charges relating to the recent revolt."

"Do you still consider the defendant to be unbalanced, Mr Grant?"

"No, I don't. I think he was trying to get information from me about the details of the decisions taken during the meeting of the Executive Committee of the Transvaal Chamber of Mines last year."

"The court has heard him described as being a humble power-station worker. Can you think of any reason why such a man should have concerned himself with decisions taken by the Chamber of Mines?"

"Only one reason suggests itself to me," Sebastian Grant

replied. "If he was one of the Afrikaans 'generals' he could have used anything I might have told him as propaganda to whip up support among rural Afrikaners for the revolution which we know was being plotted."

There was a murmur of shock and protest from the public benches, and the official called out, "Silence in court!"

The defence attorney rose, and said angrily, "I object, Your Worships! The witness has been invited and encouraged to speculate – "

"There is no jury present to be influenced by speculation," the presiding magistrate said. "In the interests of justice, the prosecution must be allowed to continue its line of questioning. You will have the opportunity to redress the balance when you cross-examine the witness." He waved his hand at the prosecutor, signalling to him to ask any further questions he wished to.

The invitation was promptly accepted. "Mr Grant, why do you suppose the defendant chose to approach *you*, and spoke to you in Afrikaans? He couldn't reasonably have assumed that you would understand that language, could he?"

"No. I think he must have found out in advance that I understood it to a degree. I believe he chose to approach me because he reasoned that, being young, I would automatically show him the respect Afrikaners are accustomed to expect from people of my age, and give him the information he wanted."

"I have no further questions, Your Worships," the prosecuting lawyer said, and after thanking Sebastian Grant, he sat down.

There was an electrifying silence in the room, a collective holding of breath, before the presiding magistrate spoke. "The defence attorney may now cross-examine the witness."

Pa's lawyer began to rise, but Pa said something to him in an undertone. He sat down again, and the entire court room was aware that they were carrying on an inaudible argument, inflexible on Pa's side, urgent on that of the man who represented him. Then, slowly, the lawyer's face began to reflect the anger and frustration and disbelief Sabella was experiencing, for she had guessed what was happening.

Pa was refusing to allow Sebastian Grant to be cross-examined. Why? What was he afraid of? He could have nothing to lose, and everything to gain by having the Englishman's lies exposed. Sabella fought back tears of hopelessness and incomprehension as the defence lawyer stood up and said in a wooden voice, "I have no questions to put to the witness."

A collective gasp rose from the public, and for once the official himself was too astonished to call out his usual command for silence. Sebastian Grant was asked to leave the witness box, and then Sabella listened with a sick weight in the pit of her stomach as the defence lawyer did his best to rescue Pa from his own incredible folly.

He made as much as he could about the point that Sebastian Grant had admitted his knowledge of Afrikaans was limited, and that he could therefore have been mistaken about what the defendant had said to him – if, in fact, the meeting between them had taken place at all. But everyone knew that in being prevented from cross-examining Grant the lawyer's case was damned, just as Pa was damned.

At last the man sat down, the slump of his shoulders signalling defeat. The three magistrates went into a huddle to confer together in undertones. Oh dear God, Sabella prayed again silently but hopelessly, don't let it be true. It *couldn't* be true. The very idea of Pa plotting revolution was ludicrous. He had never even been particularly interested in politics. Oh, he would sometimes say bitterly that the English bosses in Johannesburg made the Afrikaners feel like despised, unwanted foreigners in their own country, but that didn't mean that he had been one of the so-called "generals" who had plotted revolution . . .

But why hadn't he allowed Sebastian Grant to be cross-examined?

A moment later she heard the presiding magistrate putting that same question to the court. "We cannot escape the conclusion," he went on, "that it was because the defendant feared even more damning evidence against him would emerge if Mr Grant were cross-examined. The defence has made much of the fact that the witness's knowledge of Afrikaans, by his own admission, was limited. How simple it would have been to *demonstrate* the extent of that limitation by keeping Mr Grant in the witness box and asking the interpreter to address him in Afrikaans. We feel sure the thought must have occurred to the defence, and we feel equally sure that the defendant would not allow that to be done either." He paused to sip from a glass of water before continuing.

"If the defendant were no more than a victim caught up by events, then how did he know that in one of the companies making up the Transvaal Chamber of Mines there was a very young man privy to much important information? A young man who might have been sufficiently naive and vulnerable to pass on such information? How did he know that Mr Grant possessed a limited knowledge of Afrikaans unless he had first embarked on extensive research? Would a humble power-station worker have had the resources for such research? Did the defendant argue that the young man was more likely to keep his head if their conversation was conducted in English, whereas in groping for the correct Afrikaans words he might blurt out information of value to a revolutionary cause?"

The magistrate looked directly at Pa as he went on, "All these questions, we feel, should be pursued in a higher court. Ferdinantes van Renselaar, my colleagues and I are unanimous in our decision that you should remain in custody, and that your case should be referred to the Supreme Court."

Minor pandemonium broke out among the public then, and none of the official's orders could stem it. Sabella sat rigidly on her bench, feeling as if someone had dealt her a paralysing blow. She was dimly aware but not at all curious about the fact that Dominee Roelof had risen and was approaching the platform on which the magistrates were sitting.

Disconnected thoughts twisted through her mind. How was she to explain to the children? They were expecting not only Pa's homecoming, but also celebratory sweets . . . The gallows, Dominee Roelof had said, or a firing squad . . . All the time she had been sitting there, whiling away boredom by thinking excited thoughts about making and selling shelf-covers, fate had been waiting to shatter their lives . . .

She looked up and noted dully that Pa had been removed from the dock and that a stranger now stood in his place. Dominee Roelof was hurrying back towards her, beckoning to her, and somehow her legs, which felt as if they had been made of string, allowed her to stumble to his side. He took her arm and left the courtroom with her, and when they had reached the corridor outside he said, "Sabella, child, I asked the magistrates to allow you to speak to your Pa before they return him to gaol. In the circumstances, they said they would allow it. He is alone in the cell below the court now, because the lunch recess will follow the summing up of the case of the man now in the dock, and no more prisoners will be brought in until this afternoon."

She stared stupidly at him, and he had to repeat the information. "A policeman is waiting to take you to your Pa," he added. "I'll wait here for you."

Numb in mind and body, she followed the policeman along a labyrinth of corridors and then down a spiralling staircase. At last they came to a heavy door guarded by two uniformed men. The policeman whispered something to one of them, and the door was unlocked.

"We won't hurry you too much, Miss," the policeman said with sympathy in his voice. "No more than necessary, that is."

She could only nod. Pa was sitting alone on a bench

40

inside the cell, and she saw that the bottom half of the walls were painted dark green, and the rest a kind of dirty beige. The cell reeked of stale tobacco and sweat and fear.

Pa had clearly been expecting her. He rose, coming towards her. She stood where she was, her glance going to the ceiling. Stairs led to a trapdoor which opened up into the dock. Pa must have climbed those stairs, believing they would lead him to freedom . . .

"Well, Sabella," he said quietly, "how are things at home? Are the children in good health?"

"Yes, Pa, they – " She abandoned her automatic, stilted response and threw herself into his arms. "Oh Pa, *why*? How could you be so stupid, such a fool?"

"Is that how you should speak to your Pa, child?" he asked with gentle reproach.

She made a sound that was half hysterical laughter, half a sob of despair. "Do you know what Ma would have said? She'd have said, 'Stop forcing that lawyer to stand there with his mouth full of teeth, and allow him to question the Englishman! Expose all his lies – ' "

"They weren't lies, Sabella," Pa said quietly.

"*What?*" She stepped away from him, staring at his gaunt, pale face. "Are you – are you saying that you *did* plot revolution – ?"

He took her hand and led her to the hard bench, gently forcing her to sit down beside him. "What I'm saying is that I did go to see Sebastian Grant, and I did speak to him."

"In Afrikaans?" she asked incredulously. "And trying to make someone like him call you Uncle? Someone *you'd* be expected to call Sir? You can't have been that – that daring, or foolish – "

"I spoke to him in Afrikaans because I thought it was possible that he might still remember it, or that it would come back to him and arouse his sympathy. And I invited him to call me Uncle because I *am* his uncle."

She stared at Pa. Could he really be trying to fob her

41

off with an unfunny pointless joke? "He's English – " she began weakly.

"Only half-English," Pa corrected. "His mother is my twin sister, Wilhelmina. Sebastian Grant is your cousin, Sabella."

2

"Pa," Sabella cried, angry now, "your sister Wilhelmina died when she was fifteen!"

"No, she didn't. Her son is twenty-one years old so how could she possibly have died at the age of fifteen? Use your head, Sabella!"

She caught her lower lip between her teeth. When she was much younger, before Ma's death, she had sometimes resented bitterly the burden of household tasks forced upon her by virtue of the fact that she was the eldest, and a girl. Open rebellion would have been useless and so she had escaped into fantasy instead. As she scrubbed floors or cleaned the kitchen range she wove a drama in which she wasn't really the daughter of Ma and Pa at all, but a princess who had been stolen in infancy but who would soon be rescued to enjoy her rightful life of luxury.

As she looked at Pa she could only come to the conclusion that the horrors of prison life had similarly forced him to escape into a world of fantasy. But whereas she, as a child, had always known that her fantasies had no real substance, it appeared that Pa had come to believe in the fact that Sebastian Grant, the only man who could give damning evidence against him, was closely related to him and would therefore keep his mouth shut. And that must mean that Pa really *was* guilty of plotting revolution.

"It's all there in the family Bible, Pa." She spoke to him as if to a child. "All the names and the dates and the causes of death as well as the births. Wilhelmina died of a fever when she was fifteen. Your younger sister Sarie and your mother died in a concentration camp during the Boer War and your father was killed while fighting in the same war. Your younger brother Wouter died of his wounds after the Battle of Delville Wood in 1916, and two years later his widow and both their children were victims of the great Spanish influenza epidemic. Just as Ma was the last of the Pienaars, you and I and the children are now the last of the van Renselaars."

"Wilhelmina did not die." Pa stood up and began to pace the small cell. Involuntarily, Sabella thought of the many other men – and perhaps women too – who had paced that same cell in the past, torn between hope and despair as they waited to be taken into the dock above. How many others had there been whose minds had also slipped over the edge of sanity? And then she wondered whether it might not turn out to be a blessing in disguise that Pa was no longer sane. Could they *really* execute a man who believed that his dead twin sister was married to an English Member of Parliament, an important, powerful figure in the country?

Abruptly, Pa stopped pacing the cell and sat down next to Sabella. "The original family Bible was destroyed during the Boer War, and I started to keep a new one, putting down all the dates and names I could remember. The entry recording Wilhelmina's death is false. My brother Wouter and I took the decision to declare her dead, and our wives agreed. None of us ever mentioned her name again, because to us she *was* dead. She had done something we could never forgive or forget."

Sabella stared at him with dawning comprehension. She remembered how her childish questions about Pa's twin sister had always been brushed aside, and she had assumed it was because her death was too painful a subject to be discussed. No, Pa was not insane after all, but was simply telling a family truth at last. "Are you saying," she asked in disbelief, "that all of you regarded your sister as being dead, simply because she married an Englishman?"

"She didn't marry an Englishman."

Temporarily, the terrible ramifications of Pa's future trial

44

in the Supreme Court were pushed to the background of Sabella's mind as she probed with fascination and bewilderment into old family secrets. "Then how – ?"

"She married a man called Joop le Roux and had a son by him whom they named Hendrik. Joop was killed during the Boer War but Wilhelmina and Hendrik are still living on the farm Mooikrantz, near the Transvaal village of Stilstroom, about seventy miles away."

Sabella opened her mouth, and shut it again. Within the space of a few minutes Pa had told her that she had two male cousins, and an aunt who was alive, and there were so many questions hurtling into her mind that she didn't know which to ask first. "Why," she demanded in the end, "did you and Uncle Wouter decide not to record this marriage in the family Bible? And why does the son, Hendrik, not appear in it at all? Why did you choose to pretend that she'd died at *fifteen*?"

Pa gave a weary shrug. "It wasn't fair to young Hendrik, I know, to ignore his existence. But if we'd included him, and the marriage between Wilhelmina and his father, it would have raised questions from our children which we didn't want to answer. Wouter and I talked it over, and we decided that fifteen was the appropriate age at which to record Wilhelmina's death."

"But why?" Sabella asked.

"I suppose because we felt ashamed, not of ourselves but of our father. You see, he as good as forced Wilhelmina to marry an old man when she was only sixteen. Joop le Roux was a widower whose son Ewart was two years older than his new step-mother, and he helped to make her life more miserable than it already was. The farm, Mooikrantz, had originally belonged to Ewart's mother's people and he was livid at the thought of having to share it one day with Wilhelmina and any children she had by Joop. Ewart finally went too far and his father threw him out and disinherited him completely."

"*Why* did your father force Wilhelmina to marry an old man against her will?" Sabella cut to the heart of the matter.

45

"Because Father owed Joop money. He wasn't in a position to repay it and when Joop began to drop heavy hints that the debt would be wiped out if he were to become 'family' by marrying Wilhelmina, Father bullied the poor girl into accepting him. So when Wouter and I decided to record Wilhelmina's death in the new family Bible, it seemed just and fair to put her age at fifteen when she was still young and innocent and free of sin."

"*Sin*," Sabella echoed. She had a sketchy idea of what happened between married people to result in the birth of babies. In his Sunday sermons Dominee Roelof often preached against the temptations of the flesh and against adultery, and she knew vaguely that the two were connected.

A half-forgotten incident stirred in her memory. While she was still attending school, one of the pupils had called another a bastard and had been punished for using the word. Sabella's thirst for extending her vocabulary had prompted her to look it up in a dictionary. At the time she hadn't seen how it could be possible for two people who were not married to each other to produce children at all.

But now she understood what the sin was that Wilhelmina had committed with the Englishman, Peregrine Grant; a sin which had resulted in the birth of Sebastian Grant. She knew that Pa would never dream of going into specific details about such a matter with her, and so she merely asked, "How did your sister meet a rich Englishman, and one who was a Member of Parliament?"

"He wasn't a Member of Parliament at the time. It was more than twenty years ago, remember, during the Boer War. Peregrine Grant was an officer serving with the British Army, and he and his men went to the Stilstroom district to carry out orders to set fire to the farms, slaughter all livestock and take the women and children to concentration camps. But he and Wilhelmina – well . . ."

Pa cleared his throat and made a vague gesture. "When the war ended, and neighbours began to trickle back to their own ruined farms, they believed Mooikrantz had

46

escaped because the British had felt sorry for someone as young as Wilhelmina and decided to leave her and Hendrik in peace on the farm. They also believed the new baby she'd just given birth to was the son of her husband Joop. It was quite common, during that war, for Boer burghers to visit their homes whenever they could be spared, and – " Again Pa broke off in embarrassment. "Then it came out," he continued, "that Joop had been killed a year before the baby's birth, and, well, servants began to talk about the handsome English officer who visited Wilhelmina regularly during the war and – "

"And people realised that the baby's father was one of the enemy," Sabella finished for him.

Pa looked away. "What she had done was unforgivable. The family disowned her and she became an outcast in the neighbourhood. I think people might have relented in time – Wouter and I certainly would have – if she hadn't done something else even worse a few years later. Peregrine Grant had decided to settle in South Africa with his wife after the war, and make more money by investing his wealth in the booming Johannesburg. Wilhelmina must have kept in touch with him and known that he and his wife remained childless, and when young Bastian – as he was then called – was not quite four years old she offered to sell him to his father and his English wife."

"*Sold!*" Sabella echoed, shocked.

"Money was seen to change hands when he and his wife came for the boy."

A brief silence settled between them, and then Sabella gave herself a mental shake. The revelation of old family dramas, of sin and scandal and skeletons in cupboards, had temporarily made her lose sight of the terrible trouble Pa had unwittingly brought upon himself by going to see Grant. "What did you hope for when you waylaid Wilhelmina's half-English son, Pa?" she asked.

He made a gesture, signifying regret and defeat. "Peregrine Grant became such an important man that it was impossible not to follow what your Ma would have called

47

the 'doings and dealings' of himself and his family, and I knew that the young man learning the ropes in the business his father had started was my nephew. In the ordinary way I would never have thought of approaching him. But Sabella, all the Afrikaans workers on the Rand had become more and more concerned about their jobs in recent years, and there were widespread rumours about cuts among mine workers. I knew that if mine workers lost their jobs today, the power-station workers could lose theirs tomorrow. So I took the decision to go and speak to Bastian *as his uncle*, hoping to hear reassuring news for all Afrikaans workers."

"But he denied that you were his uncle – " Sabella began.

"I know. At the time, I believed it was his way of saying: 'I don't want to recognise kinship with you. Keep out of my life.' Then, when he appeared in court and gave evidence against me, I understood the truth. He really has no memory at all of the fact that he has an Afrikaans mother, no suspicion that he isn't the son of both Peregrine Grant and his English wife. If he'd known the truth, he would never have appeared in court and risked being cross-examined."

Sabella jumped up in anger and disbelief. "And – and that's why you refused to have him cross-examined? *To protect him?*"

"Yes."

"Oh Pa, how utterly foolish of you! What about protecting yourself? If you'd allowed the truth to come out, it would have proved that you were no revolutionary, that you were only concerned about your job, and that you'd gone to seek reassurance from your sister's son – "

"It wouldn't have proved that, Sabella. Indeed, if I *had* been one of the 'generals', what would have been more likely than for me to try and exploit my kinship with a young man who has connections with the Chamber of Mines? A nephew who might have had valuable information which would have helped to spark off a revolution?"

48

"Is that what your lawyer said?" Sabella demanded.

Pa shook his head. "He knows nothing about our relationship, and I don't want him to find out about it."

It was more or less what she had expected. "You *must* tell him, Pa!" she urged vehemently. "You must allow him to have Grant cross-examined!"

"No, Sabella. If I allowed that to happen, the family scandal would become public. That young man did not ask to be born out of wedlock; he did not ask that his mother should sell him to his father, and he didn't ask that the truth about his birth should be kept secret from him. I won't allow his life to be ruined by having everything come out in court."

"*His life!*" she echoed with bitter despair. "What about your life, Pa, and mine, and those of the children?"

"I put my trust in God, child. He knows that I am innocent, and will see to it that justice is done."

Her brain pounded with so many corrosive, enraged and desperate thoughts that she was unable to voice any of them coherently. *She* did not believe in a just God who would ensure Pa would go free if he continued to protect Sebastian Grant. And protect him from what? Certainly not from the death penalty, which was what Pa stood to face. Oh, he might lose some of his society friends, and suffer a degree of disgrace, and be looked down upon for having an Afrikaans mother to whom he was born, moreover, out of wedlock, but he would still have his wealth and his privilege and, most importantly, his life.

There was no opportunity to put any of these arguments to Pa, for the door to the cell opened and the policeman who had escorted her to it said, "I'm afraid your time is up, Miss. The prisoner has to be returned to gaol now."

She wrapped her arms about poor, thin, gaunt Pa, tears blinding her. *The prisoner has to be returned to gaol now*. How impersonal and businesslike that sounded, as if it were no more than a detail in the policeman's day. And, of course, that's all it was . . .

"Sabella," Pa's voice followed her as she stumbled to

49

the door afterwards, "don't try to interfere and contact my lawyer, because you might make things worse for me instead of better."

She didn't see how things might possibly be made worse for him, but in any case she could only contact his lawyer through Dominee Roelof, and some deep instinct cautioned her not to tell him about the family scandal, and so she nodded a mute promise before the cell door clanged shut between herself and Pa.

The policeman accompanied her only as far as the top of the winding stairs. "Will you be able to find your way to the exit from here, Miss?" he asked. He was, she thought with bleak bitterness, in a hurry to return the prisoner to gaol and wanted to waste no further time on her.

But she nodded mutely, and began to walk along the endless, twisting corridor. As she was about to turn another corner she heard a man's voice saying, "I'm glad you decided to drop in while you were on the premises. But are you sure you won't join me for luncheon at my club?"

"Quite sure," a familiar voice drawled. "Since I knew I would have to waste a good part of the day by doing my civic duty, I promised to take a young lady out on a picnic, and I still have to pick up ice and champagne and some French cheese from Bozzoli & Ferguson before I collect her."

Sabella had tensed at the first sound of his voice, but as she digested what he had said she felt raw fury ripping through her. A waste of part of his day . . . That's what he called what he'd done to Pa, was it? And now the most important thing on his mind was a picnic with a young lady, lunching on luxuries bought from Johannesburg's most expensive purveyors of delicacies, with no concern for anything but his own pleasure. And he was the man Pa had sacrificed himself to protect!

She tore around the corner just as a door closed and Sebastian Grant, whistling a tune under his breath, began to stroll down the corridor. She ran to catch up with him and then hurled herself at him, drumming her fists upon his chest. "You murderer!" she shouted. "You lying, arrogant devil! You – you bastard!"

"What – ?" He was clearly completely taken aback, but that did not stop him from easily grabbing her fists in one of his hands and then holding her in a confining grip. "I don't even know who you are – " he began, studying her, and his voice trailed away as he took in her appearance.

He made no effort to hide his expression of shocked but slightly distasteful pity as his gaze examined her old-fashioned dress that had belonged to Ma, the buttoned boots one scarcely ever saw any more, her hair scragged back from her face in deference to Pa. She saw him shake his head slightly, as if he hadn't realised before that anyone quite so drab-looking existed in the same world as himself.

Her voice was disjointed with rage. "Remember the man for whom you – you *wasted part of your day*? The man your lying speculation in the witness box sent for trial in the Supreme Court? He's my father!"

"I see." He put her away from him, but still held her at arm's length to prevent her from attacking him physically again. "I'm sorry, Miss van Renselaar, but every word of my evidence was the truth."

"The truth!" she spat at him, her voice under deadly control now. "There are many kinds of truth, Mr High-and-mighty Grant, and I'm going to tell you one *truth* you won't find at all to your liking! My father approached you and asked you to call him Uncle because he *is* your uncle! Your true mother is his sister, a poor, scorned, outcast Afrikaans woman on a farm with whom your father carried on during the Boer War!"

He whipped back the hand with which he had been restraining her, as if to touch her were to contaminate himself. His eyes were narrowed in a look of contempt and distaste, and part of her mind registered the fact that they did not match each other. One was green, and the other light brown flecked with yellow.

"You evil-tongued, lying little bitch," he said with cold menace. "Repeat that scurrilous, filthy fabrication and

51

you'll find yourself in almost as deep trouble as your father!"

He walked past her, giving her a wide berth as if she had been a particularly repellent insect with which he did not want to come into physical contact, and she watched him walking away with his arrogant stride.

He was on his way to picnic on champagne and French cheese with some wealthy girl who would be wearing a dress of floating material and whose hair would be cut in a becomingly modern short style, and he did not for one moment doubt that he was who and what he had always believed himself to be. Sabella knew that his threat against herself had not been an idle one. If she spread the truth about him in an attempt to help Pa he would use his considerable power to see that she paid for it.

For many different mixed-up reasons, she hated him as she'd never imagined it possible to hate anyone.

Dominee Roelof tried to offer her what comfort and reassurance he could as they drove back to Westdene. She sat with her head resting against the seat, her eyes once again closed to ward off nausea, and only half-listened to him. "I'll go and see the defence lawyer, and explain to him that it was nothing more than an attack of nerves that made your Pa refuse to allow him to cross-examine someone with such important connections."

It had been the only plausible lie she'd been able to think up on the spur of the moment, because the parson had naturally wanted to know what had passed between Pa and herself on the subject. She murmured something vague and non-committal.

"In any case," Dominee Roelof went on, "your Pa will have someone different to defend him in the Supreme Court. I'm not quite sure of my facts, but I believe that for a trial on a serious charge he'll have what's called a King's Counsel. They are far more clever and experienced than lawyers. A man like that will probably cross-examine whether your Pa agrees to it or not."

That hadn't occurred to her, and it gave her new heart. Oh yes, Sebastian Grant, she thought vengefully, how I'll look forward to the day when you'll have to accept that you're not quite the superior English-through-and-through creature you'd always thought! But in the meantime, she decided, her instinct not to breathe a word of the truth to anyone had been right, not only because of the threat Grant had offered her but also because it would help Pa's case far more if the truth came as a bolt from the blue in the Supreme Court.

Her thoughts strayed to Grant's true mother. Now that Sabella knew she was alive, she supposed she ought to think of her as Tante Wilhelmina, even though it was hardly likely that they would ever meet. What kind of woman could sell her own child?

The kind of woman, perhaps, Sabella decided, who had herself been sold by her father. Because being made to marry an old man against one's will to cancel a debt owed to him by one's father surely amounted to being sold? Even so, her son had not been much older than Daan, and he must have suffered . . .

She forced him from her mind and thought, instead, of Tante Wilhelmina's other son, Hendrik. He would be a grown man now and probably married with children of his own. It felt very strange to know that she and her brothers and Ria had relatives of whose existence they had been kept totally in the dark.

The reminder of her brothers and Ria made her wonder whether she should not ask Dominee Roelof to stop at a café so that she could buy sweets for them after all – not in celebration, but to console them a little for the fact that Pa was not to be restored to them after all. She would also have to think of something to tell them to explain why he hadn't been set free.

She turned to the parson in the hope of guidance. "How long do you think we'll have to wait for Pa's trial in the Supreme Court, Dominee?"

"It's impossible to say. I had a word with your Pa's

lawyer while I waited for you, and he said it could be months, perhaps even as long as a year or possibly two, before a definite trial date is set."

"Oh, dear Lord . . ." She thought of poor Pa, languishing in unbearable suspense for so long in a filthy, unhealthy gaol. But after a while other practical considerations began to nag at her. Whatever remained of Pa's savings could not possibly last for a year or perhaps two. No, sweets for the children would be out of the question.

"I've had an idea for making money, Dominee," she confided, after a moment's thought. "I meant to ask Pa to invest some of his savings to finance it, but the matter flew out of my mind after things went so badly wrong in court." She explained in detail how she wanted to make and sell shelf-covers, and when she had finished she added, "Pa gave you his bank book and authorised you to draw money for our needs. Couldn't you set aside a sum to pay the rent on the house and other outgoings, and sufficient for us to live on sparingly, and advance me the rest so that I may use it to buy wallpaper? I'm sure my idea will work – "

"I'm afraid I couldn't do that, Sabella," he interrupted with regret.

"I'd take full responsibility when it comes to explaining to Pa!" she pleaded. "And if you doubt that my pretty shelf-covers would sell, just ask Mevrou Roelof what she thinks! Why do you imagine women will spend hours unravelling an old shawl, say, and then crocheting a fancy table runner which doesn't really have a useful purpose? It's because they long for pretty things, and my shelf-covers will not only be pretty, but useful as well!"

Dominee Roelof gave an embarrassed cough. "I didn't want to have to tell you this, Sabella, but your Pa's savings ran out the week before last, when Nantes needed new shoes. The congregation have agreed to contribute what they can to keep your family going until your Pa is in a position to earn again."

Shock and humiliation settled like an indigestible lump in her breast. What more could this awful, disastrous day have in store? If only Pa had been open with her and told her exactly what his savings amounted to. But no, she'd had to be treated as a child, and a mere female at that. "I – wish you'd told me, Dominee," she muttered shakily.

"You couldn't have done anything about it." He hesitated. "Except – well, it has occurred to Mevrou Roelof – and to myself also, of course – that it would lighten your load if Daan were to come and live with us."

She forced herself to stifle her immediate, violent reaction to the suggestion. *Let Daan go?* Daan, whom she had brought up since he was a new-born baby? Pluck him from his family and hand him, screaming and fighting, into the care of the Roelofs? She was suddenly and unwillingly reminded again of Tante Wilhelmina selling her own young son, and she wouldn't allow herself to wonder whether *he* had screamed and fought at the time.

Aloud, she said as calmly and reasonably as she could, "It's very kind of you and your wife, Dominee, but I'm sure Pa would want me to keep the family together. However, we can't go on living on the congregation's charity. I shall have to find a job of some kind to support us until Pa – well, during the immediate future."

"Sabella, what kind of work could you possibly find when there are so many men who are unemployed?" the parson reasoned with her.

She set her mouth in a stubborn line. "The kind of work to which men are not suited, or which they wouldn't consider doing. Work in one of the shops or cafés in Westdene, serving customers, displaying the goods for sale, or I could even help Mr Seligman in his pawnshop. I often call in to see if he has anything cheaply on sale that we need, and he is forever complaining about being run off his feet." Growing enthusiasm gave momentum to her speech. "Yes, I'm sure Mr Seligman would be glad to employ me as an assistant!"

"And what about the children? Even if you *were* to find work, you couldn't leave them on their own all day long!"

She had already anticipated that problem, but she was not about to give him advance warning of what she had in mind. "I'll think of something," was all she said.

Perhaps she had become accustomed to the motion of the car, for she was able to look out of the windows now without ill effect. They had reached Westdene and would shortly be picking up Ria and Daan.

Mevrou Roelof received them in the comparative luxury of the manse, with its linoleum floors and its matching suites of furniture. Sabella left the Dominee to tell his wife of the events which had overtaken Pa, and went outside into the neat, small garden where her brother and sister were playing a game which involved looking for pebbles and stacking them in rival heaps.

Daan was too young, and Ria too mentally limited, to remember that Pa should have been there as well, but Daan *did* remember about the sweets, and he began to cry when he learnt there were none. Ria promptly joined him.

Mevrou Roelof came hurrying outside, and scooped Daan up in her arms. "There, my darling," she crooned, mistaking the reason for his tears, "before you know it your Pa will be home with you again. Would a ginger cookie cheer you up?"

"Cookie for Ria too!" his sister insisted through her tears.

"Of course, my dear." As she led the way towards the kitchen with Daan still in her arms, Mevrou Roelof looked at Sabella, and said quietly, "I'm so very sorry about what happened, child. When I think of your excited face when you left here this morning – "

"Thank you," Sabella cut her short. She didn't want to think about this morning, when her world had still been relatively normal and even held out hope. She changed the subject. "Were the children any trouble, Mevrou?"

"Not at all! Daan became a little over-active once or twice, but the darling boy minded me as soon as I gave him a gentle talking-to."

"And Ria?" Sabella persisted. "Was she good as well?"

56

"Oh yes." Fleeting relief crossed Mevrou Roelof's face. "She just copies Daan in everything, doesn't she?"

The children were given ginger cookies, and their tears were forgotten as they bit into them. Dominee Roelof entered the kitchen to join them.

Sabella took a deep breath, and addressed his wife. "Mevrou Roelof, I need to find a job – "

"A job!" the parson's wife looked shocked. "Young girls do not go out to work, Sabella!"

"If they are the eldest of a large family, and the alternative is to live indefinitely on charity, they have no choice but to become the bread-winner. The thing is, Mevrou Roelof, Nantes is responsible enough to look after the younger ones when school is out, but I wondered – would you be prepared to have Daan and Ria during the mornings until he could collect them and take them home?"

Husband and wife exchanged brief glances, and then Mevrou Roelof's expression became one of yearning as her eyes fell upon Daan. "I can't really approve of a respectable young girl taking a job, Sabella," she answered, "but I'd be glad to look after Daan and Ria in the event that you should be able to find work."

"The very *unlikely* event," her husband contributed. "Indeed, I believe it to be an impossibility."

Nothing, Sabella thought with sour humour, is impossible. Only a matter of hours ago I'd have said it was impossible that I might have an aunt who is alive, and that one of my two living male cousins is an arrogant, over-privileged young bastard in every sense of the word, and that he would turn up to give damning evidence against Pa.

Aloud, she said calmly, "Thank you, Mevrou Roelof. I appreciate your willingness to help, even if it should turn out that you and the Dominee are right, and that I won't be able to get a job of any kind."

But I will, she added grimly to herself. Even if I have to sink my pride and beg, I'll find a job somewhere, somehow. Just you wait and see.

3

"You not find work yet?" young Meneer da Freitas asked
Sabella after she had enquired about his baby son, who was
teething and keeping him and his wife awake at night. Ma
used to keep a notebook in which she wrote down recipes
for all manner of home remedies, and Sabella had told the
shopkeeper about the soothing syrup she herself had made
up for Daan when he was a baby.

Meneer da Freitas knew perfectly well that Sabella had
not yet found work, or she would not be here at her usual
time to buy vegetables for their supper. Mr Seligman, it
had turned out, would a hundred times sooner be run off
his feet in the pawnshop and then complain about it than
pay an assistant. Meneer da Freitas himself, to whom she
had next applied for a job, had told her with genuine regret
that his younger brother was due to leave school soon and
would be coming to work for him.

But she shrugged a resigned "No" to his question, and
leant against the wooden counter, pretending not to notice
that instead of merely grabbing any old carrot, any old
turnip, the Portuguese was selecting very carefully only the
biggest and best of each item making up the three-farthings'
worth of soup greens she had come for. Meneer da Freitas
probably also knew the names of all the other traders in
Westdene whom she had vainly approached in the hope of
finding paid work.

The care with which he selected vegetables for her nowadays showed that he'd heard how fanatical she had become
about making as few demands on the charity of Dominee

Roelof's congregation as she possibly could. When it first became clear that finding a job was going to be much harder than she'd hoped, she had taken Daan and Ria to the manse one morning and after the children had been sent out to play in the garden she'd explained to Dominee Roelof and his wife the reason for her call.

"I don't want to go on as before, accepting a weekly cash allowance for our day-to-day needs and having all other bills sent to you to be paid. Until I can find work, I want us to be as little of a burden as possible on the generosity of the congregation. Apart from the rent, of course, which will have to be paid in full, I'm going to cut down drastically on everything else. I've worked out that we could make do with porridge and cheap brown sugar for breakfast, soup for supper and bread for lunch. I know a butcher who will let one have a whole lot of marrow bones for a farthing and I'll boil them up for stock for the soup and use the fat-skimmings to spread on our lunchtime bread. The children's appetite being what it is, I don't see that we'll be able to manage on less than one loaf a day, but the cheapest kind made of unsifted flour only costs a penny-ha'penny for a large loaf – "

She had been interrupted by Dominee Roelof and his wife speaking simultaneously. "This is taking things much too far, and quite unnecessary – "

"Sabella," Mevrou Roelof's voice held disapproval, "why do you *buy* bread when home-made loaves work out far cheaper and are so much more nutritious and tasty?"

"I don't know how to bake bread. Ma never got around to teaching me."

"Then I shall – "

"It wouldn't really work out cheaper, you know," Sabella had said with a wry smile. "There'd be the extra fuel for keeping the stove going all that time, but apart from that, I well remember how we used to fall like wolves on Ma's delicious bread so that she'd hardly finished baking one batch before she had to start on another. No, we'll stick to less tempting shop-bought bread. I've worked out that, including the rent and electricity and fuel for the stove, we could live on six shillings and ninepence three-farthings a week, and that is all I will accept until I can find work."

They hadn't been able to budge her from that position, and it took all her ingenuity to feed the five of them on a few pennies a week. Only for Sundays did she buy a pound of beef shin to turn the soup into the more nourishing broth it used to be every day before she'd learnt they were living on charity. But just as she was now pretending not to notice that Meneer da Freitas was being over-generous in his selection of vegetables for the soup greens, she also pretended that meat gave her indigestion, and she divided the once-a-week treat between her brothers and sister. She could barely remember what it felt like not to crave more food at the end of a meal. If only she could find work . . .

Last evening, in desperation, she had decided to follow Dominee Roelof's constant urging to put her trust in God. She had forced herself not to think of Ma dying painfully before her time, or of Pa rotting away in gaol while he waited to face a trial which might yet lead to his execution. She had prayed silently but fervently to God, admitting that she paid no more than lip-service to religion and that it was therefore doubly hard for her to accept charity from people who were devoutly religious. She had put her case frankly, explaining that she found it very difficult to believe in a just God when people like Sebastian Grant enjoyed so many privileges and she wasn't even able to find a humble job.

"Dominee Roelof is always saying you can work miracles, God," she'd ended her petition, "and if you would only work one for me by letting me find a job, I'll be able to believe that you will also see to it that Pa receives the justice he deserves. Amen."

She sighed. In the cold light of day she had very little expectation that a miracle might be forthcoming. She shook the thought aside, and accepted the parcel Meneer da Freitas had made of the soup greens. He picked up a whole newspaper from the pile underneath the counter,

60

holding it out to her with a smile. But when she proffered her three-farthings he shook his head.

"What you tell me we must use for when babies grow teeth is worth much more than three-farthings," he said. "You keep your money, Miss Sabella. Today the soup greens is a present."

She felt the blood rushing to her face. This was charity, and both of them knew it. Of course, the three-farthings she had offered him were themselves the fruit of charity and not hard work, but Meneer da Freitas's refusal to accept the money somehow made it all so much more humiliating. But the kind young Portuguese would be so hurt if she left the coppers on the counter, and tomorrow when she called to buy soup greens he might not go to the trouble of picking out the choicest vegetables for her.

Muttering her thanks, she turned and hurried out of the shop. A bitter smile crossed her face as the thought struck her that perhaps God considered the free vegetables a sufficient answer to last night's prayer. Her bitterness sharpened when she passed the Goosens' house. Feckless and dirty as their next-door neighbours were, God certainly showered undeserved blessings on *them*! There they all were on their filthy stoep, and they were eating slices of watermelon which she knew cost a sixpence each; an expensive, between-meals treat. And she was quite certain that none of *them* ever prayed to God for anything, least of all for the luxury of watermelon. What would they be having for supper later, she wondered. A roast of pork with all the trimmings, perhaps?

Still seething with the injustice of it all, Sabella entered the house and went into the kitchen to prepare the evening's soup. The children were in the back yard, playing under Nantes's supervision. Once the vegetables had been chopped and covered with stock and placed on the kitchen range, there was nothing much that needed to be done until it was time to wash Ria and Daan before supper. Sabella glanced at the newspaper Meneer da Freitas had given her and then she cast a jaundiced eye on the shelves of the kitchen dresser. She no longer wasted time and effort on making newspaper frills for them and pretending they were pretty. Instead, every scrap of newspaper which was not needed for the privy was twisted into tight coils and used to save on coal for the range.

While she waited for the soup to simmer Sabella opened the newspaper and began to read it. Nowadays she found herself searching compulsively for any references to Peregrine Grant and his family, and she was seldom disappointed. There was almost always something he had raised in Parliament, or else the papers mentioned charity work sponsored by his wife Eliza, and several times she had felt her own blood-pressure rising as she read of some smart social function at which Sebastian Grant had been one of the guests.

Searching for their names in the newspapers, she knew, was like constantly lifting up a scab covering a sore and so preventing it from healing, but she couldn't stop herself doing it. The thought had scarcely left her mind when she noticed to her astonishment that this newspaper wasn't an old one as usual, but bore today's date. Meneer da Freitas must have given her his own morning newspaper, consigned to the pile underneath the counter because he had finished reading it.

Heady inspiration struck her. She had always been aware that employers advertised jobs in the newspapers, but in the past those given to her by Meneer da Freitas had been days or weeks old. But with this one only having appeared this morning, there might be something suitable for herself; something that had not yet been snapped up.

In addition to vacancies for shorthand-and-typewriters – occupations which were a total mystery to Sabella – there were jobs advertised for girls to work as machinists in factories or for waitresses. But one in particular caught her eye, because it was an advertisement placed by the department store whose fashion illustrations she most admired. James Paradise & Company required someone called a lift girl at a monthly wage of one pound ten shillings. No experience was necessary and girls of good appearance were invited to apply in person to the Personnel Manager, Mr Hudson, without prior appointment.

Sabella read and reread the advertisement until the words were indelibly printed in her mind. A lift girl, she supposed, lifted things down from shelves and lifted them up on to others. Any fool could do that. And to be paid a whole thirty shillings a month for something so easy and simple! She decided to ignore the fact that it also sounded boring, and reminded herself that the wages would be enough to free them from dependence on charity.

Her heart began to pound with excitement and growing awe. James Paradise, even though known to her only by illustrated advertisements, was her favourite department store. The unprecedented good fortune of being given a copy of today's paper, and Meneer da Freitas's refusal to accept her three-farthings, could not possibly be considered a mere coincidence. Not when one added to it the fact that she knew the one-way tram fare between Westdene and the city was a farthing and that if she hadn't suddenly found herself possessing three spare farthings she would not have been able to afford to go and apply for the job.

No, God had clearly listened to her prayer last night and had offered her the miracle she'd asked for. With a mixture of humility and jubilation, she began to make her plans. As soon as Nantes and Anton had left for school in the morning she would deliver Daan and Ria to the manse and then hurry to apply for the job with James Paradise.

She would get it, of course, because God was helping her.

Sabella would have liked to do something different to her hair before she left for the city, but she would not cut it short against Pa's wishes, and so she simply brushed it and pulled it back again from her face into a severe knot in the nape of her neck. She wore one of Ma's church dresses of dark blue and white striped calico, and a hat of matching dark blue straw which had also belonged to

Ma. Then, with the three-farthings in her pocket – one in case of emergencies – she set out, her heart hammering, to where the trams stopped.

She did not have to wait long before a city-bound tram arrived. With growing excitement and tension, she stepped on the platform and fulfilled an old childhood dream by climbing the winding iron stairs to the top deck.

A bell rang tinnily, and the tram began to jerk along the rails. To her relief, she found that its motion did not make her feel at all queasy, as Dominee Roelof's car had, and she was able to stare out of the windows, catching brief glimpses of other people's lives as the tram went on its way.

A sharp breath of shock escaped her when she realised that they were passing alongside Sophiatown. Bordering upon Westdene, the black suburb had meant no more to her before than smoke along the horizon, constant distant noise and the sound of fighting on Saturday nights. She hadn't dreamt that it looked like *this*.

Crude shacks and hovels were crammed close together along narrow dusty streets which were further marred by open gutters. The smoke, she now realised, was caused by the fact that women had to cook over outdoor fires. Half-naked children with mangey dogs at their heels came running towards the tram, cupping their hands in begging gestures.

And their fathers, Sabella thought, were probably among the cheap black labour in the mines who had replaced the Afrikaners thrown out of their jobs. How desperately cheap that labour must be! Suddenly feeling over-privileged by comparison, she lowered the window and rashly threw out her emergency farthing, and watched with pity as the children scrambled for it.

At last Sophiatown had been left behind and after passing through other poor white suburbs the tram halted at a spot where Sabella, craning forward, could see the rails ended. The man with the machine which spewed out tickets in return for coppers shouted, "Ter-min-us!"

and Sabella dismounted with the remainder of the passengers.

This was more the kind of thing she had expected on that fateful day when Dominee Roelof had driven her to the city in his motor car. She felt both exhilarated and frightened by the sight. Even in her imagination she had not visualised that there would be quite so many people hurrying along, or so many vehicles passing, rushing and writhing in both directions. She wandered uneasily along the pavement, trying to spot someone who did not appear to be in a desperate hurry so that she could enquire the way to James Paradise. But the people in the city reminded her of ants. They all knew precisely where they were going, and could not be deflected or halted in their course.

Then, to her relief, she noticed someone who was neither in a hurry nor going anywhere. A man stood on the street corner, a tray suspended from supports around his neck, and with bootlaces for sale displayed on it.

She asked him for directions, and he supplied them. She felt quite certain that he was as Afrikaans as she herself was, and yet both of them obeyed the unwritten rule that English was the only language recognised by the city. Sabella wasn't sure if she knew this by instinct, or whether the knowledge had somehow been assimilated over the years by reading the newspapers. She found herself understanding what Pa had meant when he'd said that the English made Afrikaners feel like despised, unwelcome foreigners in their own country. This bustling, noisy city certainly seemed foreign to her.

She threw back her shoulders. As long as she didn't forget the rules and spoke Afrikaans, there was no reason why anyone should despise her or make her feel unwelcome.

Motor horns blared and bicycle bells shrilled as she followed the bootlace-seller's directions, and there was a continuous hum of voices and of footfalls on the pavement. At last, from across the street, she saw the sign in gold lettering that bore the name of the store, and her heart pumped as she crossed and entered through glass doors.

She stood still, totally overwhelmed. The place was full of shoppers, mostly female and looking just like the sketches in the advertisements she had seen with their soft, floating dresses, their short hair and silk bandeaux or ribbons tied across their foreheads. There was a bewildering number of counters at which girls in smart uniforms, looking almost as fashionable as their customers, were selling perfumed soap or scent or face powder and rouge, and too many other things for Sabella to take in fully. Overhead, a strange contraption of wires and pulleys criss-crossed, and after a while she realised that cash paid by customers was placed in containers which ran magically along the pulleys to some unknown destination, and returned with change and a receipt.

She stood around, wondering which of the uniformed girls to approach so that she could ask to see Mr Hudson. But they were all so briskly, efficiently busy, serving customers, that she felt daunted at the thought of bothering them.

She was aware, suddenly, that a man in uniform trimmed with gold braiding was approaching her. "May I help you, Miss?" he asked politely.

She swallowed against the nervous dryness in her throat. "I – I would like to see Mr Hudson, the Personnel Manager, please."

"If you would follow me, Miss."

She did so, threading her way through customers and past counters, to where several latticed iron doors adjoined one another. But when she peered through the lattices she could see nothing but hollows going down to somewhere below.

"One of the lifts will soon be down," the man said. "Just wait here, Miss. It's the fourth floor you want for Mr Hudson."

Mechanically, she thanked him, her thoughts scattering in panic. The hollows behind the latticed metal doors had something to do with lifts, and a lift had nothing whatever to do with the act of lifting objects up or down. What a fool she had been, to imagine anyone would be paid thirty shillings a month for doing something as simple as that. Why had none of the newspapers she'd read ever mentioned lifts, or explained what they were? She would have abandoned all ambition to become a mysterious lift girl if it had not been that the kindly uniformed man had decided to wait beside her.

Through the wrought-iron lattices, she could see something descending. A platform, on which were visible several elegantly-shod feet. This, Sabella soon realised, was a kind of cage designed to fit inside the hollow beyond the door. It came to a shaky halt, and a female voice announced from within, "Ground floor!"

Women wreathed in silks and perfume and carrying parcels surged past Sabella as they stepped from the cage. Only one girl remained inside it, the girl who had leant across and pushed to one side the latticed iron door. This girl had a jaunty little hat tilted to one side of her head, and instead of a uniform she wore a smart dress in the store's apricot and cream colours, made of some soft material cut on the bias and with the skirt considerably shorter than ankle-length.

"Going up!" the girl called out, and several customers moved past Sabella to enter the cage. The uniformed man touched her arm.

"The lift will take you to the fourth floor, Miss. As you step out, you'll see Mr Hudson's office." He gave her a sympathetic smile, as if he knew how frightened and ignorant she was, and felt sorry for her.

There was nothing to do but enter the cage. Sabella's stomach lurched as the girl in charge pulled the door shut and the cage began to rise in the air. It stopped again with a shudder.

"First floor!" the girl announced, and continued as if it were a recitation learnt by heart "Millinery, ladies' foundation garments, lingerie, gloves and hosiery. Going up!"

I should never have come, Sabella thought miserably. What is lingerie? I've never heard of it. They don't mention it in any of the advertisements. No, I should never have come. I'll just stay in this thing until it returns to the bottom again.

Then a spark of spirit stirred inside her, and flared into resolve. She could learn by heart all the recitations the lift girl reeled off at each floor, and what did it matter whether or not she knew what lingerie was? All she needed was to remember how to pronounce the word. And quite apart from the thirty shillings a month, and the financial independence it represented, there would be such heady excitement in wearing a pretty bias-cut dress and a jaunty little hat.

"Fourth floor!" the girl announced. "Accounts and Personnel."

Sabella saw Mr Hudson's name written on a door opposite as she stepped out of the lift. She knocked on it, and heard a female voice call, "Enter!" She opened the door, and then wished with all her heart that she hadn't. She had imagined that the female voice belonged to a chaperone, and that she would be stepping straight into the presence of Mr Hudson. Instead, she found herself inside a kind of waiting room. A girl sat behind a desk, and perched on comfortable chairs along the walls of the room were perhaps half a dozen girls and all of them stared simultaneously at Sabella as if she had suddenly dropped in from the moon.

"May I help you?" the girl behind the desk asked her.

"I – " Sabella swallowed nervously. "I came – about the advertisement. The one that said a lift girl . . ." Her voice died away as she recognised the amused, pitying contempt in the eyes resting upon her.

"You had better sit down," the girl told Sabella in a voice that was clearly struggling not to break into giggles. "Mr Hudson will see you when he has interviewed the applicants who arrived before you. May I have your name?"

Even her name, which she had to spell out for the girl behind the desk, seemed to be a source of amusement to everyone in the room. Sabella crept to a chair in the corner and sat down, staring at the floor. She had assumed that any other girl desperate enough for a job at thirty shillings a month would be more or less as poorly dressed as she herself, but she had been wrong.

Thank you, God, she thought bitterly. Thank you for playing such a fine trick on me. "Girls of good appearance," the advertisement said. It meant girls with short, modern hairstyles and up-to-date dresses and shoes and eyebrows that all look like thin stripes. It *hadn't* meant a figure of fun in high-buttoned boots that had belonged to Ma and had gone out with the Ark, and a drab long dress of dark blue and white striped calico, and hair parted in the middle and scragged back into an old-lady bun. It's all they can do to keep from laughing out loud at me, God, and you must have known very well how it would be when you tricked me into thinking you'd worked a miracle just for me. But I'll tell you something, God; if you thought I'd slink out like a kicked dog, you're wrong. I know I don't stand a chance of getting the job, but I'm going to stay and see Mr Hudson all the same.

Now that she had given God a piece of her mind, she had the courage to lift her head and outface the amused, staring eyes of the other girls. One by one they were called into another office and the door closed behind them. Mr Hudson, Sabella supposed, must make notes and decide later which of the girls he would employ. Well, it certainly wouldn't be herself, and she had nothing to gain by waiting her turn. Nothing apart from her defiant stand against God's cruel little joke.

Several other girls had come into the office after Sabella, all of them looking smart and modern and not at all as if they were in need of a job. They studied Sabella with the same astonished amusement as the others had.

At last the girl behind the desk announced that it was Sabella's turn. She rose and walked slowly, her back rigid, her head high, to the door of Mr Hudson's office and opened it. He was a middle-aged man, soberly but smartly dressed, and she recognised the astonished look in his eyes as he rose politely and asked her to sit down.

"No, Mr Hudson," she said, meeting his gaze squarely, and went on with the speech she had been rehearsing. "I won't sit down, because both of us know that I would be wasting your time. I only waited my turn because I wasn't going to give anyone the satisfaction of watching me creep away, humiliated and beaten, without even seeing you – "

"Miss van Renselaar," he tried to cut in.

She ignored him, her voice fierce. "I know I was a fool to waste a precious halfpenny on the tram fares between the city and Westdene. A halfpenny can't seem much to you, but to myself and my brothers and sister it means two thirds of what is spent on our supper. When I saw the advertisement for a lift girl I was stupid enough to believe I would get the job. And now I'll tell you something else, Mr Hudson, something that will make you laugh even harder after I have gone, something to tell the others who have been smirking at the way I look. I had never seen or heard of a lift in my life before. I thought the job was for someone to lift things down from shelves and lift them on to others. That's funny, isn't it?" Her voice cracked slightly. "I'll leave you now to enjoy the joke."

She had turned away and had almost reached the door when his voice halted her. "Miss van Renselaar, please come back and sit down. I have no wish at all to laugh. I want to talk to you."

She turned slowly, suspiciously. But there was compassion in his eyes, and something almost like admiration, and no ridicule at all. She moved towards the desk and sat down.

He asked her to tell him about her family circumstances. She had given the matter a great deal of thought last evening and finally decided not to risk jeopardising God's miracle by telling the truth about Pa, because it was unlikely that anyone would want to employ a girl whose father was in gaol, awaiting trial on serious charges. Now that any illusion of a miracle had been shattered she didn't see why she should tell this Englishman, no matter how kind he seemed, about Pa being in gaol and so she made it sound as if he, like Ma, was dead. She referred to him merely as one of the victims of the Rand Revolt and told Mr Hudson how humiliating she found it to have to depend on charity.

"My eldest brother is only ten years old," she added, "so you can see why it is up to me to find work and become the breadwinner."

He smiled at her. "You've found work, Miss van Renselaar. The job of lift girl is yours."

She stared at him in frank disbelief, which turned into suspicion. "Are you giving me the job because you feel sorry for me?" she asked bluntly, and then gave herself a mental kick. She couldn't afford the luxury of pride.

"I wouldn't be human if I didn't feel sorry for a girl of your years with so many burdens on her shoulders. But no matter how sorry I might feel, I would not offer you a job unless – " He broke off, and shook his head, his eyes twinkling. "This has been the most unusual, original interview I have ever conducted with an applicant. You have courage and character and initiative, Miss van Renselaar, and while I must observe form and see other applicants I can tell you now that I have already chosen you for the job because of the qualities I have sensed in you. I have a strong feeling that you will not remain a lift girl for long and that you have a successful future with James Paradise & Company ahead of you."

Her mouth slightly open, she stared at him, too astonished to speak for a moment. "Th-thank you," she stammered at last in a dazed voice.

"You may start at the beginning of next week. You will be issued with a lift girl's outfit, and taught how to do the job."

They shook hands, and she moved to the door, feeling as if she were floating. She couldn't remember making her way back to the tram terminus. She *did* remember to

71

thank God, adding mentally, "Now I know you will look after Pa."

All the way home to Westdene she rejoiced in her triumph. But the biggest triumph of all was one she couldn't quite put into words. In many ways, she felt as she had when she'd suddenly thought of making shelf-covers and selling them. Most of all the triumph had to do with the knowledge of her own worth on the market. At the moment she was worth thirty shillings a month but one day – oh, she was going to aim at becoming worth thirty shillings a week of someone's money. And why stop there? Why not go on to become worth thirty *pounds* a week? Even that need not be the limit of her ambition. Who could say that she might not, in the far-off future, become worth *thirty pounds a day* to someone?

Sabella found that she needed every ounce of stamina she could scrape together once she started working at James Paradise. It was necessary for her to rise at four each morning to do the household washing or ironing or mending and whatever housework had been left undone the previous evening. Then she made lunchtime sandwiches for herself, Nantes and Anton and prepared the breakfast porridge. She also peeled and chopped vegetables so that she could put on the soup for supper the moment she returned home from the city. She made shopping lists for Nantes, who would pick up whatever was needed before he and Anton went to the manse to collect Ria and Daan. By the time she had delivered the children into the care of Mevrou Roelof Sabella had to fight grimly against the day's first tide of exhaustion.

She had very quickly learnt how to operate a lift and had memorised what to say at each floor, but this had done nothing to endear her to any of the other girls working in the store. She was, and always would be, an outsider.

It wasn't simply because of the drab, old-fashioned clothes in which she arrived each morning. After all, once she had put on the bias-cut dress issued by the store, and modern shoes and stockings, and her hair had been hidden beneath the jaunty little hat she looked very much like everyone else.

But whenever she entered the staff room during a rest period she could sense the other girls closing ranks against her. It wasn't because they were all English, either, and she the only one with an Afrikaans background. Some of the girls had Afrikaans surnames, but pronounced them as if they were English, and it soon became obvious to Sabella that they were using their jobs with James Paradise & Company as a means of shedding their roots and "passing" as English, and their main ambition seemed to be to marry Englishmen.

Other girls were English only by virtue of the fact that their ancestors had been among the settlers sent from Britain in 1820; none of them had ever visited Britain but they talked of it as "home". There were a handful of genuine English girls among the staff, girls who had been born in England and whose fathers had emigrated to take up positions as mine bosses. These girls stuck together and openly despised everyone else as their inferiors, but to Sabella's astonishment they said things like "was you" and "don't he", which even Anton knew was incorrect. They claimed to be working for what they called "pin-money" and Sabella thought sourly that the pins they used must be made of solid gold.

She stuck out like a sore thumb among these contemporaries of hers, and so she remained friendless. It was just as well, perhaps, she told herself philosophically, because she had observed that friends treated each other to coffee or tea and cakes in the staff canteen. She couldn't afford to treat herself, let alone anyone else, and she always sat alone in a corner, eating her slices of bread sandwiched together with fat-skimming.

Being friendless also allowed her to put everything of herself into her work. She had devised calculating little ways of tempting customers to visit departments they'd had no intention of entering. Instead of reeling off a monotonous chant at each floor she would say, "Gloves and millinery – and perhaps I should mention that the new lace gloves are selling so fast that stocks won't last the week. We've also had a shipment of new hats from abroad but I don't know whether or not they'll be on display yet. Foundation garments – " By the time she had got that far most of the women shoppers had already left the lift and gone to look for the new hats and the lace gloves.

The way in which she was helping to increase business did not go unnoticed by the senior staff, and did nothing at all to make her more popular with the junior members. She didn't care. She had her sights set on the goal of earning thirty shillings each week, instead of each month.

One Saturday morning she thought up another way of tempting customers into one of the less-popular departments. She dawdled deliberately as she took the lift down, and after everyone had got out on the ground floor and the waiting customers began to get into the lift she said, "I'm so sorry you've been kept waiting. The trouble was that when we stopped at the second floor, all the customers getting in were so excited about our new range of curtaining fabrics that everyone inside the lift wanted to get out and see them, and that caused an inevitable – "

Her voice trailed off and for an instant she feared she might faint. Ushering a pretty, fair-haired and very smartly dressed young girl into the lift was Sebastian Grant. This time he wore a dashing checked jacket in blue and white, with long rounded revers and a single button which fastened at the waist. A blue scarf which she recognised as being of silk was tucked into the neck of his white shirt, and his grey trousers were smartly casual. He didn't even flick a glance in Sabella's direction, and there was no start of recognition from him when the lift reached the first floor and she reeled off, automatically, the list of departments.

She stood in her allotted corner, watching him, hating

him. Oh, how cocooned in prosperity he still looked, how arrogant, he with his unmatching hair and eyes and brows and complexion, as if nature had absentmindedly reached for unrelated bits and pieces to fashion him, not looking at what she was doing.

Notice me, Sabella directed a snarling thought at him, and when he remained absorbed in his companion she added mentally and furiously, *You bastard*!

Everyone but he and the girl stepped out of the lift when they reached the second floor. Sabella was too busy trying to contain the chaos of feelings inside her to remember at once that she had deliberately and successfully lured customers to go and look at the new drapery.

Now that the three of them were alone in the lift, Sabella would have thought he'd notice her at last. But she might have been part of the machinery that allowed the lift to function for all the interest he had in her. Of course, dressed in the store's colours, she was practically invisible as far as he and his companion were concerned, just another humble member of the staff employed to serve such as themselves.

She listened to the conversation he was carrying on with the girl. It appeared that she had come with him to help him choose a birthday present for his mother. "A string of pearls, perhaps, Sebastian?"

"Lord, she has more jewellery than she could wear in a lifetime! No, try to be more original, Annette."

An all but insane rage swept over Sabella. She wanted to open her mouth and scream that his mother, his true mother, was unlikely to own more in the way of jewellery than her wedding band. She wanted to yell at him that this humble little lift girl whose existence he hadn't even noticed was his cousin, that he was a half-Afrikaans bastard who had condemned his own uncle to an indefinite period in gaol and a trial which might yet cost him his life.

Instead, she clamped her lips tightly together and stared at the floor of the lift. Perhaps it was as well that he hadn't deigned to spare her a glance, because if he'd recognised her he might have seen to it that she lost her job. She was fairly certain, from his conversation with his pretty companion, that the Grant family were valuable and influential customers of James Paradise & Company.

She opened the gate of the lift and muttered, "Third floor." Even though she kept her head bent she sensed that he still didn't glance at her as he left the lift with the girl. She raised her head, and saw him tuck the girl's arm into his own, and a spasm tore through her. Hatred, she told herself. Not jealousy at all. Why on earth should she be jealous? Dear God, how I *detest* you, Sebastian Grant, she directed a parting thought at him.

She didn't see him again. He and the girl must have taken another lift down to the ground floor. But after that day she never closed the gate of her lift without scanning the customers in case he were among them, and she found herself dreaming formless, disturbing dreams about him at night.

She had been working at James Paradise & Company for almost two months when one of the supervisors told her that Mr Hudson wanted to see her. She nodded speechlessly, her heart thumping. *Advancement.*

Only last week Mr Hudson had stepped into her lift on the fourth floor, smiled at her and said, "You've been doing a very good job, Miss van Renselaar." Yes, without doubt he was going to offer her advancement. Not only would it mean the first rung on the ladder which would eventually lead to the thirty shillings a week she had set as her first goal, but advancement would also bring a small increase in salary. She and the children would be able to stop merely subsisting; there would be meat more than once a week, perhaps even the occasional treat . . .

"You're to go straight in," Mr Hudson's secretary told her when she had reached the outer office and Sabella smiled at her, deciding to bury the memory of how the girl had struggled not to laugh at her when she had come to apply for the job. Mr Hudson's secretary did not return the smile. Sabella shrugged. It didn't matter.

Mr Hudson didn't smile either when she entered his office, and that *did* matter. Panic seized her. Had she gone too far in her campaign to manoeuvre customers into visiting departments in which they'd had no previous interest? Had someone lodged a complaint against her?

"Sit down, Miss van Renselaar," Mr Hudson said quietly.

She obeyed, and waited in trepidation. Was he deliberately taking his time to come to the point because he wanted to increase her punishment? But at last he spoke, and for a moment she could only stare at him stupidly because what he had to say was not remotely connected with what she had been thinking.

"I received a telephone call from a man who I gather is your family parson, Miss van Renselaar." He glanced at a note on his desk. "Someone called – I don't suppose I'm pronouncing it correctly – Rolloff."

"Roelof," she corrected automatically, and the next moment she was swamped by cold dread. Dominee Roelof would not have telephoned the Personnel Manager unless something were very seriously wrong. Daan – or Ria . . .

"An – an accident?" she managed through dry lips.

"No. Well, in a way I suppose one could say it was . . . Your parson asked me to break the news to you, Miss van Renselaar. He is on his way here, and he thought it might be best if he saw you when the first shock had worn off a little. He could then offer you spiritual comfort, he said."

One of them was dead. Her voice sounded very far away as she muttered, "My sister – or my baby brother?"

"Neither. It's your father, Miss van Renselaar. He tried to stop a fight between two other prisoners, and was fatally stabbed in the chest by one of them. There's to be an inquiry to find out where the knife had come from – "

She could no longer hear his voice. The room was swaying crazily around her. Then she became aware that

Mr Hudson was not sitting opposite her any more but was touching her shoulder and offering her a glass of water. She drank it as if by doing so her world would somehow right itself again.

She choked on the last mouthful of water, coughed, and then began to weep. She bent her head over the desk, aware that her tears were marking its expensive leather top. It didn't matter. She would be dismissed in any case. Who would want to have working for them someone whose father had been stabbed by another prisoner in gaol? Then she remembered that she'd lied to Mr Hudson in the first place and pretended Pa was dead instead of in gaol. That didn't matter either.

Oh Pa, she thought brokenly, with angry grief, why could you never mind your own business? Why couldn't you have passed by on the other side? You landed in gaol in the first place because you felt you had to save a friend, and now you're dead because you tried to prevent another prisoner from being stabbed. Oh Pa, you brave, big-hearted fool . . .

After a long while she sat up and wiped her face with the back of her hand. In silence, Mr Hudson offered her a handkerchief and she nodded in gratitude. She looked at him through swollen eyelids. "I'm sorry. For lying to you – about Pa."

"It was wrong of you to lie," Mr Hudson said quietly, "but understandable. Your parson explained the situation to me. He is convinced your father was innocent and would have been set free but for the last-minute appearance of a witness who threw doubt on the case."

She bowed her head. *Your fault, Sebastian Grant*, she thought. You killed Pa as surely as if you'd murdered him with your own hands.

In the grip of a sudden, searing agony she opened her mouth to tell Mr Hudson the family secret so that it could be spread and lead to the downfall of the young man she hated. But before she could utter a word, Mr Hudson said, "Stay with your brothers and sister for as many days as you need to. Comfort them and do your own grieving. Your job will remain open."

"Th-thank you," she said inadequately. There was no question, now, of spreading scandal about people who were among the store's best customers.

Mr Hudson took his watch from his pocket and consulted it. "Your parson should be here soon. Go and change into your own clothes, Miss van Renselaar, and then come back here to wait for him."

But Dominee Roelof was already inside Mr Hudson's office when she returned. He embraced her, and said, "Let me take you home, Sabella."

In his motor car, she kept her eyes closed and listened to his conventional words of comfort without believing any of them. She had believed – *truly* believed – that God would look after Pa, and he hadn't. She would never believe in a merciful and just God again.

"I'll do what I can," she heard Dominee Roelof say, "to persuade the authorities to allow you to attend your Pa's funeral."

"Thank you. Mr Hudson said I could have some days away from work." Something struck her belatedly. "I should have asked him if my wages would be reduced because of it. We really couldn't manage without the full thirty shillings – "

"Sabella," the Dominee interrupted gently, "you won't have to manage the way you did before."

"Whatever do you mean?"

"Haven't you realised yet that everything has changed, child? Before, your Pa was in gaol and the authorities had no official reason to concern themselves with you and the other children. But now you are orphans."

"I am earning sufficient to keep us going – " she began.

"You're under age, Sabella. The courts would not allow you to assume responsibility for your brothers and your sister. Indeed, I have already contacted the proper authorities and will be meeting with them as soon as possible to help decide the future of all of you."

"I *am* responsible for my brothers and sister!" Her voice had risen. "No one can alter that – "

"They can, and they will. Ria will have to be sent to a mental institution, and the boys will have to be found places in an orphanage." He cleared his throat. "That is, places will have to be found for Nantes and Anton. As for Daan, Mevrou Roelof and I are eager to adopt him."

No! The silent scream filled Sabella's mind. I won't let any of it happen, Pa – Ma. I don't know how I'll manage it, but I'll keep them together. Somehow. I promise you both.

"As for yourself," she heard Dominee Roelof go on, "there are supervised hostels for older orphans and a place will be found for you in one of them. So you see, your thirty shillings a month need not to be spent on anyone but yourself from now on."

If it had been thirty pounds a day it would still have meant nothing without the children. Silently and with finality, she said farewell to the job with James Paradise & Company and to all her ambitions. From now on those ambitions would have to be channelled into outwitting Dominee Roelof and the authorities, and finding a place to which to flee with the children before they could be swallowed up in orphanages and a mental institution and Mevrou Roelof's smothering devotion. If, indeed, there existed a haven to which to flee . . .

Mooikrantz! The name of Tante Wilhelmina's farm entered her mind like a prayer being answered, as if God were trying to make amends. Surely Tante Wilhelmina and her son Hendrik would not hold it against Sabella and the children that their parents had ostracised them? Not when they learnt that Sabella had only been told of their existence a short while ago? Especially when she promised to work from morning to night for their keep?

But to be on the safe side and avoid possible rejection, Sabella decided, she would arrive on the farm with the children without giving them prior warning.

With her bolt-hole decided upon, she knew that there were still many pitfalls and difficulties which awaited her before she would be able to spirit the children away. But she would overcome them. She had made her mental but binding promise to Pa and Ma.

4

The mid-morning sun was fierce, turning the train compartment into an oven and creating a shimmering haze upon the horizon, like water rippling in the wind. Sabella opened the window wider, deciding that more soot and dust blowing in upon them was preferable to the baking heat. The countryside, after Johannesburg had been left behind them, had come as a shock to her, having never before seen such vast unbroken expanses devoid of any signs of humanity.

She had hoped that, because she had woken them up at four this morning and they had sat for hours waiting at Johannesburg station, Ria and the boys would have fallen asleep on the train. But at first they had been far too excited and agog with curiosity and now, Nantes apart, they were growing increasingly cross and querulous. Daan was grizzling that his head hurt and that he was hungry. Ria immediately copied him. "Ria's head sore," she whimpered. "Ria hungry."

"Very well," Sabella said. "We'll have some of the sandwiches Mevrou Goosen made for us. There's jam or condensed milk."

"There's probably dead flies in them as well," Anton predicted sullenly, unwilling to be appeased. "You weren't supposed to make friends with the dirty Goosens, Sabella."

If God were to be thanked for anything, she thought fervently, then it was for the Goosens. Pa's funeral had not yet taken place, for there was to be something called an inquest, as well as other legal procedures which would

82

take time, and meanwhile Dominee Roelof had hastened to find places in different institutions for all of them save Daan, whom he and his wife were applying to adopt.

"You're being allowed a week in which to grieve together, Sabella," he'd said, "and for you to get the younger ones used to the idea of separation."

She had glossed over the details of Pa's death to the children, and had done nothing at all to get them used to the idea of separation. In between grieving for Pa she had racked her brains for ways and means of spiriting the children away to Mooikrantz from under the nose of Dominee Roelof. The younger ones seemed to view Pa's death as an extension of his incarceration in gaol, for which she couldn't really blame them. Daan and Ria had all but forgotten his existence and he was a daily-fading memory to Anton. Even Nantes, she suspected, had shed tears which had more to do with his soft heart and gentle nature than any closeness he'd felt towards Pa.

As Sabella reached for the sandwiches she thought that Ma would have been far less harsh in her judgement of the Goosens if she could have foreseen what pillars of strength they would one day turn out to be to her eldest child. Sabella had still been frantically examining and discarding as impossible one idea after another for secretly running away with the children when Mevrou Goosen had called on them, bringing with her a tin of Fry's Biscuits. "Meneer Goosen and I," she'd said, "reckoned you kids could do with a little treat to cheer you up."

The unexpectedness, the generosity and sheer luxury of the gift had caught Sabella with her defences down. Others had been expressing their sympathy in more conventional, practical ways but fancy biscuits in a tin which must have cost goodness knew how much, and bought for them not to keep them from hunger but to cheer them up . . . She had burst into tears and the next moment she'd been gathered to Mevrou Goosen's huge, stained and somewhat malodorous bosom and was crying her heart out.

After that it had seemed natural for Sabella to confide

fully in Mevrou Goosen. Where others would have had scruples, the Goosens had none. Mevrou Goosen consulted with her husband, and the whole matter was soon arranged. Meneer Goosen found a buyer of second-hand furniture and household goods who agreed to pay in advance for their possessions and collect them after Sabella had left with the children. There was enough money to settle outstanding debts and pay the fares of Sabella and the children to Stilstroom Halt, the nearest place to Mooikrantz at which the trains stopped. One of Meneer Goosen's friends owned a truck and he arranged to borrow it and drive Sabella and the younger ones to Johannesburg station while it was still dark, so that no one would see them and hurry to alert Dominee Roelof. Even if the parson should think of questioning the Goosens about the matter of their disappearance, he would get nothing out of them.

Now, as she bit into her condensed milk sandwich, Sabella recalled Mevrou Goosen's parting words. "You will have to walk with care in the future, even when you've come of age. It will go against you that you've run away with the children when a court had ordered them to go into homes, so if you do something even slightly wrong or attract attention to yourself, they'll have those kids off you before you can turn around."

Sabella glanced out of the window, and saw that the landscape was no longer quite so flat and lonesome. There were rocky ridges on the horizon, and only a short distance away from the railway tracks a group of animals were performing the most peculiar leaps and bounds.

"They're s-s-springbuck," Nantes said with authority. "And what they're doing is called *p-p-p-pronking*. No one knows why, but they do it at certain seasons."

Sabella watched the animals shoot high into the air in elegantly arched positions, the sun glinting on their white underbellies, their feet barely touching the ground before they launched themselves into the air again. Then, with mysterious abruptness, they extended their necks and raced away at speed.

She looked at Nantes with curiosity. "How did you know what they were, and what they were doing?"

"From a book in the s-s-school library." His eyes shone. "I n-never thought I'd s-s-see them in real life!"

"I think what they were doing was stupid," Anton said disagreeably. "And I don't like all this *nothing*," he added, waving his hand out of the window. "I like places with shops. I want to go home. I don't want to live on a stupid farm."

"It will be w-wonderful living on a farm!" Nantes argued with such enthusiasm that he almost overcame his stammer. "There'll be all kinds of beautiful wild birds, and flowers – "

Anton interrupted with an angry, jeering sound. "What there'll be will be this Tante Wilhelmina we've never even seen. I bet she'll strap us for the tiniest thing."

Daan began to cry at this, and predictably Ria followed suit. Sabella put an arm about each, and assured them that Anton was talking nonsense. She hadn't attempted to explain about the family scandal but had merely told them, this morning, that they were to go and live with Pa's sister, pretending that their aunt lived too far away for there to have been contact between their families in the past.

"Tante Wilhelmina isn't going to strap anyone," she said. To herself, she added, but she might well shut her door in our faces. Would a woman who had sold her own young son be prepared to take in nieces and nephews who were strangers to her?

After a moment, Anton said, determined to make trouble, "Well, I bet her son Hendrik straps us, then."

"No, he won't! He'll be – well, he'll be nice." Sabella had been wondering more and more about their cousin Hendrik, Sebastian Grant's half-brother. Would he turn out to share those unmatching looks? Of one thing she felt certain. He would not share Grant's arrogance, for that was a by-product of believing himself to be wholly English.

The ridges which had been on the horizon before, Sabella saw, were now stretching away on either side of the railway track. Their slopes were covered in rocks among which short, scrubby bushes grew. Birds, some of them brilliantly coloured, flitted from bush to bush and Nantes pointed out with excitement several odd-looking animals which stood on their hind legs, staring at the train for all the world like inquisitive little men, and which he said were *meerkatte*.

The train slowed down and stopped and Sabella saw a signboard reading STILSTROOM HALT. "Quickly!" she cried in panic. "We have to get out!" It was only when all of them had safely gained the platform with their parcels of possessions that Sabella had time to stare about her. Apart from themselves, no other passengers had alighted here, and only parcels were being taken from the train and offloaded on to the platform.

She had been assuming that "halt" was simply another name for station. But there was nothing whatsoever here; no building, no railway staff; only the sign bearing the name of the halt. Running parallel to the railway tracks she could see a narrow road of red earth but it, too, was deserted. The train whistle blew and a few moments later their little group stood there in the middle of nowhere and with no sign of another human being in sight.

"How w-w-will we get to Tante W-W-Wilhelmina's farm, Sabella?" Nantes asked.

As well as expecting Stilstroom Halt to be a proper station, she had thought it would be situated in a town. But there were low ridges clothed in scrub and an occasional tree and not so much as a single house anywhere in sight at which to ask directions. "I'll think of a way," she said, trying to hide her dismay.

Then, to her immense relief, she heard the clip-clopping sound of hooves, and a little later a black man came in sight, driving a mule-cart. He had, it transpired, come to collect the parcels which had been offloaded from the train.

He agreed to give them a lift and drop them within walking distance of Mooikrantz. Sabella sat with Ria and the boys on the back of the cart, surrounded by parcels, and as they gained the crest of one of the ridges she saw a small settlement at the foot of it. This, it turned out, was the village of Stilstroom. Apart from a few dozen dwelling houses there was a general store, a church, what looked like warehouses and very little else. Sabella felt unexpectedly homesick for noisy, crowded, sprawling Westdene, and she made no comment when Anton grumbled, "I'm going to hate living where there's nothing."

Some of the parcels left at the Halt were for the general store. As they waited on the cart Sabella became aware that people had come out of their houses to stare at herself and the children. There was something more than curiosity in their faces, something she couldn't define. Then the driver resumed his seat and they drove on, the stares following them.

The dirt road became increasingly steep. In a dip between ridges they travelled over a bridge crossing a river and then the road turned sharply to the right at a spot where immense blue-gum trees obscured the view. The driver stopped and turned his head. "There Mooikrantz, Nonnie."

She followed his pointing finger, peering between two of the blue-gums, and drew a sharp breath. Pa had mentioned hills, and she had imagined something like the ridges over which they had been travelling. But on the horizon, towering in the air, were high jagged outcrops and some of their slopes were covered in trees and shrubs while others glinted bare and flint-like in the sun. If these were hills, she thought, then mountains must be unimaginably high.

She and the children got down from the cart, thanked the driver and picked up their belongings. A narrow track led between fields towards a cluster of buildings nestling at the foot of the high hills.

Sabella had no idea what kind of crops were growing in the fields, but as they drew closer to the house she recognised a citrus orchard by the ripening fruit on the trees. The hills loomed over them, with gaps in places along which rutted paths had been created. As they approached the buildings on Mooikrantz they were stopped in their

87

tracks by a raucous sound of barking echoing around the hills, and Nantes said it probably came from baboons.

More than ever missing Westdene, with its own reassuringly familiar background noises, Sabella took the lead and walked on. There were several outbuildings and beyond them was the farmhouse, which appeared to be completely deserted. It was large and sprawling and obviously old. They climbed the wooden steps to the stoep, and she stared at it in disapproval. It was filthier even than that of the Goosens, with not a speck of floor visible beneath the layers of ingrained, hard-packed dirt. The front door was in two sections, and both of them were shut. She knocked on the door but received no response, and after a moment she pulled back the bolt on the top section. But it had obviously been secured on the inside as well. She moved to one of the windows. It was so grimy that she could only just make out the ponderous, very old-fashioned furniture inside what must be the front room.

"I don't like this house," Anton said. "There's probably a ghost."

"Don't be so silly!" Sabella snapped, but anxiety was beginning to eat at her. The house gave the impression of having been long abandoned. Could Tante Wilhelmina and Hendrik have moved away from Mooikrantz? But there were all those crops growing in the fields . . .

The stoep ran along all four sides of the building, and as she followed it she was heartened to see that a narrow and very clean length of fibre matting led from the wooden back steps to what must be the kitchen door. This was also shut but not locked, and when she had opened it she stared inside, filled with bewilderment and a sense of unreality.

To have described the room as being clean would have been an understatement. The top of the wooden table had been scrubbed white, but the glowing yellow colour of the legs showed that the top had never been intended to be white. Chairs had been arranged around the table in perfect symmetry. The range had been scrupulously black-leaded, and neatly stacked beside it, in painstaking alignment, were magazines about farming which were obviously saved for firing kindling wood.

"Wipe your feet," Sabella told the children, and gingerly crossed the highly-polished floor made of timber. Objects on the dresser shelves had been arranged at distances from one another that did not appear to vary by as much as a fraction of an inch.

"I don't like it here," Anton said again, aggressively.

Sabella could not help sharing the sentiment. There was something disturbing, abnormal, about the contrast between the fanatically clean kitchen and the filthy stoep and the grimy windows. Not that the kitchen window was grimy, of course. It gleamed as if it received a daily cleaning. "Go and sit outside on the steps," she told the children, "and I'll see if I can find something to drink with what's left of our sandwiches."

They were only too ready to leave that dauntingly clean kitchen. But Sabella did not make an immediate search for something to drink. Instead, she decided to explore the rest of the house, and as she went from room to room her perplexity and unease grew. Most of the door-handles were stiff, as if they hadn't been touched in a long while, and the rooms beyond them were dirty. The furniture was covered in deep layers of dust, and the timber floors had not seen a broom, let alone some polish, in ages. Only one other room shared the obsessive cleanliness of the kitchen, and that was a bedroom. Nothing was out of place inside it and there was nothing visible to show who occupied it. The bed was a huge double one over which a patchwork quilt had been spread with perfect symmetry. Merely standing in the doorway made Sabella feel like a snooper, and she closed the door again and returned to the kitchen. Leading off from it was a pantry, also fastidiously clean, and here she found a large bowl of milk, protected from flies by a cover of cheesecloth. She took cups from their hooks in the kitchen, and scooped out milk for all of them.

As they sat on the steps and ate their sandwiches, washing them down with milk, Nantes asked anxiously, "W-where do you think Tante W-W-Wilhelmina and C-C-Cousin Hendrik are, Sabella?"

"Perhaps they drove to the village." What she *really* thought was that only one of them occupied the house, and the most likely one was Tante Wilhelmina. Hendrik must have married and moved away, and because Tante Wilhelmina wasn't able to keep the entire house cleaned to her phenomenally high standards she had decided to close and ignore the rooms she didn't use. If she was running the farm by herself it would explain why she didn't have time to clean unused rooms.

Sabella tried not to dwell on the fanaticism displayed in those rooms which *were* clean, and told herself that someone of Tante Wilhelmina's fastidious nature would heartily welcome help from her niece. She carried the dirty cups into the kitchen, and told Nantes to take the children to play in the orchard while she did some cleaning. She had seen what she was sure must be a water pump in the kitchen yard, but first she had to get a fire going in the range so that she could heat some water.

In one of the outbuildings she found stacks of chopped kindling wood but no coal. There was a huge mound of round, flattish objects she had never seen before and whose use she couldn't imagine, and so she carried armfuls of kindling wood inside the house with which to heat water on the range. While she waited she changed into her oldest dress.

She was aching with fatigue by the time she had finished in the house and could tackle the stoep floor. This defeated her utterly, and it wasn't until she was scrubbing it for the second time that the truth dawned on her. The floor itself was made of packed earth, and by attempting to scrub it she had reduced it to a morass of soapy mud which stubbornly refused to dry. She sat on the wooden steps and tried, for the children's sake, not to burst into tears. Somehow the stoep made of earth summed up the bleak strangeness of the new life to which she had fled with them, and where she had no idea whether or not they would receive a welcome.

Nantes had organised a game of hide-and-seek. The noise the children were making, together with the barking of the baboons on the peaks, the bleating of sheep grazing on the slopes, the lowing of cattle and the various cries of unfamiliar birds struck echoes from the hills, and at first masked the sound of approaching footsteps. Sabella only became aware of them when the man had almost reached the house.

She rose, and deciding he must be a neighbour, addressed him. "If you've called to see Mevrou le Roux, I'm afraid she isn't at home. I think she may be out somewhere in the fields – "

"I am Hendrik le Roux," he interrupted, "and *I* was out working in the fields when someone came to tell me I had visitors."

"Oh . . ." She was too taken aback to wonder who could have told him. Tante Wilhelmina must be dead, because only one person lived in the house. But what kind of man would go to such obsessive lengths to keep the rooms he used so ritually clean and flawless?

He held out his hand, and she studied him. No wonder she'd assumed he must be a neighbour, for he looked at least ten years older than the twenty-five she knew him to be. He was sparely built with a stoop which made him appear hollow-chested, and he did not resemble his half-brother Sebastian in any way, but had thinning dark hair and light grey eyes and a serious, almost brooding expression. To her astonishment, he went on, "You are the daughter of my Uncle Ferdinantes."

"How on earth did you know?"

"Everyone in the district knows. The – family resemblance, I'm told, is quite striking."

Had there been a note of distaste in his voice, Sabella wondered, or had she imagined it? A family resemblance would account for all the attention she and the children had attracted in the village. "My name is Sabella," she said, and cleared her throat nervously. "I want you to know that I learnt about your existence only a couple of months ago. Pa told me the whole story, and when we were made homeless by his death I couldn't think of anyone but Tante Wilhelmina to turn to."

"It is my Christian duty to offer my cousins a home." His gaze went beyond her to the children, who had approached warily, and he shook hands with them in turn with little warmth.

As Sabella thanked him she wondered why he had avoided mentioning his mother. If she were dead, why hadn't he said so? But perhaps she wasn't dead; perhaps she had married again and lived elsewhere. She was about to ask him about Tante Wilhelmina when he noticed the muddy stoep and he demanded sharply, "What on earth happened to it?"

"I'm afraid I scrubbed it," Sabella confessed.

"Why? What possessed you?" Disconcertingly, he seemed about to burst into tears. "I'd just got it to the point where it didn't need cow dung and I could keep the dust down with a sprinkling of water!"

She was as bewildered by the reference to cow dung as by his obvious distress, and decided that she ought to explain why she had taken it upon herself to clean the house and inadvertently turn the stoep into a sea of mud. "There was no one here, and I had time on my hands and – " She paused, and deliberately went on, "I thought Tante Wilhelmina would be more likely to give us a home if I showed her that I wasn't afraid of hard work. Where *is* she, Cousin Hendrik?"

Jerkily, unwillingly, he said, "She – is dead."

"Oh. I'm sorry . . ."

"Why should you be?" His voice had turned harsh. "She lived her life in scandal and she ended it in scandal. She took her own God-given life in a way that guaranteed the le Rouxs of Mooikrantz would go on being the subject of wagging tongues. Excuse me," he added abruptly, "I must go and wash my hands at the pump."

Uneasily, Sabella watched him skirting the house. His hands had been perfectly clean and she guessed he'd made an excuse to stop all conversation about his mother. He had spoken about her with condemnation and without a hint of grief or compassion. How was he likely to regard the news that Pa had been stabbed to death while awaiting trial in gaol? Most likely, instinct told Sabella, he would see it as a gift to the "wagging tongues" he'd spoken of with such bitterness. And yet she couldn't keep it a complete secret from him, because the children knew Pa had died in gaol, even though they were unaware of the manner of his death, and they might well mention the fact.

When Hendrik returned, she had her story ready. "Pa was among the many people who were arrested after the crushing of the Rand Revolt and he died before the trial which everyone knew would prove his innocence – "

Hendrik brushed Pa's death aside as if it were an irrelevance, and said in a voice pitched high with agitation, "You've scrubbed the back stoep as well! We can't go into the kitchen because of the mud we'd track inside!" He called the children and told them, "Come with me; we'll have to collect straw from the barn so that we can spread a path of it to the kitchen door."

As he hurried them away Sabella gave a troubled sigh. She wished with all her heart that there had been someone else to whom she could have taken her family for sanctuary. What kind of man was he that he was more concerned about a wretched stoep than human tragedies?

He was still in the barn with the children when she saw a plump, elderly woman approaching the house. She carried a covered pail and her small black eyes within their beds of fat were staring at Sabella with curiosity.

"I am the widow Bessie van der Walt," she introduced herself, "and Hendrik's nearest neighbour. You, of course, are his cousin. You have van Renselaar stamped all over you, but what is your first name?"

"Sabella." She hesitated. "Mevrou van der Walt, how and when did Tante Wilhelmina kill herself?"

"Someone else will surely tell you if I don't. It happened eighteen months ago, and she drank water mixed with caustic soda."

Sabella stared at her in horror. What an excruciatingly painful and probably slow way in which to die, and all Hendrik had said about it was that it had been a scandal that caused tongues to wag. She wanted to ask the widow more questions about Tante Wilhelmina, but Hendrik appeared, carrying armfuls of straw and followed by the children doing the same. "Afternoon, Tante Bessie," he greeted his neighbour.

"I've brought over some stew for your supper, Hendrik, because I knew you weren't likely to have much to offer your cousins at such short notice."

He thanked her, and began to throw handfuls of straw on the wet stoep, and when a trail had been spread between the steps and the back door he dismissed the children and invited Sabella and Mevrou van der Walt into the kitchen.

His eyes flickered everywhere. He was, Sabella knew, checking to see whether she had created any disorder, and she wasn't surprised when he stooped to line up the slightly disarranged pile of magazines next to the range. A little defiantly, she said, "Would you like to see what I've done to the other rooms?"

As she led the way, she heard Bessie van der Walt exclaiming at the difference Sabella's handiwork had made, but Hendrik said nothing. Instead, he moved knick-knacks, rearranging them so that they stood in meticulous straight lines. Only when they had completed their tour of inspection did he offer what might have been intended as grudging thanks. "I found it impossible to keep the whole house clean *and* attend to farm matters."

"I'll continue to work hard for my keep and that of the children," Sabella said. "I'll take on more than just the housework."

"So it's true that you've come in search of a home," Mevrou van der Walt mused.

"Yes," Hendrik answered for her, "and I've accepted that it's my Christian duty to feed and shelter my cousins."

Bessie van der Walt did not comment. But when they had returned to the kitchen, and were sitting down by the table, she shifted her bulk in the chair. "Has anyone told you, Hendrik, that Sabella is the very image of your mother when she was young?"

"Yes, Tante Bessie." His tone made it obvious that it wasn't something on which he cared to dwell.

"The whole countryside has already guessed, as I did, that your cousins must have been orphaned and so turned to their father's only living relative." The kitchen chair creaked alarmingly as she altered her position again. "At first everyone will agree that you did your Christian duty by your cousins. But human nature is human nature."

He stared at her, obviously as mystified as Sabella was feeling. "What are you talking about, Tante Bessie?"

"What others would be talking about. They would talk about you, Hendrik, and about Sabella, and wonder what went on here in the evenings after the children were asleep and you were alone together."

He gave a strange, strangled little laugh. "You think so, Tante Bessie? You know, when we were growing up together, Jan Booysens was the ringleader among those who called me – well, everyone knows the kind of names they called me. Today it was *he* who took the trouble to come and search for me in my fields and tell me that my van Renselaar cousins had been seen on their way to Mooikrantz. Then he gave that jeering laugh of his and he said, 'You'll be sorry to hear, Hendrik, that the eldest is a pretty girl instead of a boy.'"

Sabella was astounded to hear herself being described as being pretty, and then she frowned as she wondered what on earth Hendrik could be driving at, for he went on with outrage in his voice which seemed wholly unmerited.

"I asked Jan Booysens to explain what he meant by that remark. I wanted him to say it out loud, with my workmen as witnesses. But he just laughed again and said a grown boy would have been able to help me with the farm work, and asked me what else did I think he'd meant?"

"What else indeed!" Mevrou van der Walt gave him a perplexed look. "Can't you see that he was trying to warn you that Sabella being a girl would cause talk?"

"You don't understand." Hendrik's face wore a look of anger and frustration. "You didn't hear the *way* he said it all. I know that he and his friends have been calling me names again behind my back – "

"You're far too sensitive, Hendrik! Oh, I've heard the young people making fun of you because of your per-nickety little ways, but they'll do more than make fun of you if your cousins stay here. There are many who remember Wilhelmina when she was young and beautiful and reckless, and Sabella is the image of her. It will be assumed that she shares more than Wilhelmina's looks and there'll be a lot of talk about clean-living, finicking Hendrik le Roux whose only hobby until now has been singing in the church choir, and what he might be up to with his girl cousin!"

Sabella was torn between angry indignation and bewilderment. She sensed that the widow and Hendrik were somehow at cross-purposes, but he appeared to have abandoned whatever point he'd been trying to make. Bessie van der Walt went on with a note of sympathy in her voice, "If you turn your cousins away, people will call it a heartless scandal, and if you give them a home they'll spread scandal about you and Sabella. I'm afraid you're caught between the devil and the deep blue sea."

"The devil and *two* deep blue seas," Hendrik corrected, and gave that strangled little laugh again. "No, it's too much. I've borne too much."

Whatever that other blue sea might be to which he'd referred, Sabella knew she was beaten. She stood up, and said with as much dignity as she could muster, "I'll take the children and leave. Perhaps we could get a lift back to Johannesburg."

Hendrik threw up his hand, sudden relief shining in his eyes. "No. I've just thought of something. If you, Tante Bessie, would stay here tonight to stop the older tongues wagging, I'll take my cousins to Stilstroom in the morning. Between Dominee Botha and the magistrate, places would be found for them in an orphanage."

"No!" Sabella cried on a note of panic.

"You'd find life far more comfortable, Cousin Sabella, in an orphanage than on a farm with no modern conveniences, and you and the children would be together – "

"We wouldn't! We'd be separated! You've obviously not paid any attention to Ria, or you'd know that an orphanage wouldn't take her in. If you imagine that I'd allow her to be sent to a mental institution . . . And then there's Daan. He's young enough for an orphanage to put him up for adoption by strangers!"

Bessie van der Walt eased herself out of her chair and placed a comforting hand on Sabella's shoulder. "Don't be so ready to expect the worst. I'm sure Dominee Botha will be able to come up with a satisfactory answer to everything. In the meantime, Sabella, perhaps your brothers and sister might like to come with me to fetch my overnight things. My cat has just had kittens and I think they would enjoy seeing them."

"I'm sure they would," Sabella said mechanically.

"And try not to worry." At the door, Mevrou van der Walt stopped and turned. "It's a pity you're such a confirmed bachelor, Hendrik. Marriage to your cousin would have solved her problems and given you a house that's clean all over." She winked and smiled at her own joke.

A tide of weariness and defeat and fear of the future swept over Sabella. She went into the bedroom where she had left their possessions so that she could change out of her mud-streaked dress. What a fool she had been, she thought, to imagine that she and the children would find a haven at Mooikrantz.

Mentally, she cursed Bessie van der Walt for interfering, and for feeding Hendrik's already exaggerated horror of attracting scandal. Sabella had never heard such nonsense in her life. How could anyone in the district possibly imagine that she might be even slightly attracted to such an odd creature as Hendrik?

She dismissed the thought and gave her mind to the problems facing her. She could not, she dared not, allow Hendrik to take them to Stilstroom in the morning, because if she did she would be forced to admit to the magistrate – who would otherwise discover it for himself – that places had already been allocated for all of them except Daan, whom Dominee Roelof had applied to adopt. The children would be taken away, and it was highly unlikely that Sabella would be allowed to visit them in the future. The authorities – and the Roelofs – wouldn't trust her after the way she had defied everyone and run away with her sister and brothers.

But what could she do, she wondered in despair. She had no money left, nowhere else to go . . .

A ruthless idea, born of desperation, took root in her mind and she returned to the kitchen quickly, before her courage failed her. Hendrik was applying black-lead to the top of the range where she had accidentally spilt water. He looked up when she entered.

"I have come to ask you," she said bluntly, "to marry me."

There was no mistaking the look of shocked distaste on his face, and it was not merely caused by her brazen proposal. "I have no interest in marrying anyone," he said.

"Neither have I. I am desperate to keep my family together, and this appears to be the only way. There'd be no scandal if we married."

He drummed his fingers on the table, staring into the distance. At last he spoke abruptly. "There is something I'd like you to see." He moved to the dresser, opened a large biscuit tin and took from it a document which he handed to her. It was his last will and testament, very neatly penned and dated a few years ago.

"I, Hendrik le Roux," it read, "in the knowledge that I suffer from a defective heart, that my life's span is short and that I shall therefore never marry and leave direct heirs, hereby bequeath the farm Mooikrantz and all my personal possessions to my half-brother Ewart le Roux. In the event that he pre-deceases me, I direct that my estate be shared equally between his children."

Shaken, Sabella handed the document back to him. "How – how did you find out about your heart?"

"I've known since I was a child. I had rheumatic fever and the doctors told my mother it had affected my heart."

She swallowed. "Did they – do you know – how long?"

He shrugged. "If I am careful to avoid stress and strain, and don't over-exert myself, perhaps five years – ten. No more. So you see, I couldn't marry you."

In five years' time, she thought, she would be over twenty-one. Old enough to be allowed to become the legal guardian of her sister and brothers. She could not afford pity for Hendrik to sway her from the battle of her own which had to be fought. "With a wife to clean the house for you and take on other tasks," she pointed out, "you would have to exert yourself less than you do at present."

A look of repugnance crossed his face. "I was referring to – to the strain that my – physical duty as a husband – would place upon my heart."

It was a moment before she understood. With relief, she assured him, "Oh, a marriage in name only would more than suit me! All I want is a home where I can keep my family together, and in return I'll take over all the household duties a proper wife would have done."

"No! I won't enter into such an arrangement! In the morning I shall take you and the children to Stilstroom."

She thought swiftly, and the audacity of the bluff that occurred to her almost took her breath away. But she forced herself to speak with calm assurance. "If you do

99

that, Hendrik, I shall have to tell the magistrate that we have other kin who might be willing to offer us a home. I'm talking about your younger half-brother. He is called Sebastian Grant now. I'll ask the magistrate to write to his father, explaining our desperate situation. Because we are his son's cousins, Mr Grant may be persuaded to help me keep my family together."

Hendrik's face had taken on a mottled colour. "That Englishman! He wouldn't lift a finger to help you!"

"He is a Member of Parliament now, and he wouldn't want to risk it being known that he'd behaved unsympathetically towards his son's cousins. I imagine temporary homes would be found for us in Stilstroom while the magistrate waits for Mr Peregrine Grant to come up with some kind of plan." She gave him a look of wide-eyed innocence. "I only hope it won't set the people here talking, Hendrik. Naturally they aren't going to admit to themselves or to others that they would have gossiped about you and me living under the same roof. People can be such hypocrites. They're bound to say that you turned us out and forced us to beg for help instead from the man who was responsible for your mother's downfall."

The desperate look in his eyes gave her hope that she might have won. He began to prowl around the room, and went into the pantry as if he were seeking refuge. He emerged again, seeming more glad than angry about the fact that she and the children had drunk from the dish of milk, as if it had offered him a straw at which to clutch. "You should have skimmed the cream from the top first and set it aside, because it has to go towards making butter. You have no idea of what farm life involves!"

"I would soon learn," Sabella said.

The next moment he was making a fearful issue of the fact that she had used kindling wood to boil water on the kitchen range. "On a farm it's important not to waste anything! What was wrong with the *miskoeke* in the fuel store?"

"*Miskoeke?*" she echoed, never having heard of it before.

100

"The stack of dry cow dung. Why didn't you burn that instead?"

She shrugged an apology. Cow dung, it appeared, played a large part in farm life. If she could put up with being married to Hendrik, she could put up with cow dung. "Now that I know what it's for, I'd do so in future."

He gave her a hunted look, and said, "I have to go and wash my hands." He didn't return afterwards, and she supposed he wanted to be alone while he weighed up which would be worse – marriage to her or the scandal she had hinted she would stir up for him. Mevrou van der Walt returned with the children. The kitchen range was stoked, Ria and the boys washed and the stew heated up.

At sundown they all sat around the kitchen table and after Hendrik had said grace they ate in near-silence. When the meal came to an end Bessie van der Walt volunteered to put Ria to bed in the room which she was to share with Sabella, while she herself took the three boys to the room in which they were to sleep together in a large double bed. She refused their request that a candle should be left burning in the room.

"It would be dangerous," Sabella told them, "and besides – well, I think Cousin Hendrik would say it was wasteful." She kissed them good night and went into the kitchen, where she was not surprised to find Hendrik meticulously drying the supper dishes and putting them away.

He refused her offer of help, and then said abruptly, "If I agree to marry you, Sabella, would you agree to abide by *my* terms?"

"What are they?"

"That we act the part of a devoted couple in public. Of course, we wouldn't be able to disguise the fact that the marriage was entered into in the first place for the sake of mutual convenience, but I want an assurance from you that no one will ever suspect it is not a true marriage in every sense of the word. For example, you will stop sharing a bed with your sister after we marry and move into the room that used to be my mother's, but you will do so discreetly, in such a way that no one will ever suspect you and I don't share a bed."

She stared at him. "Why is that so important to you?"

"Because, for the first time ever, I want my life to appear to be normal. What do you suppose people would say about me if they found out that our marriage was in name only? They would say that I'm not a proper man, that I am, after all, a – " He stopped.

Without really understanding the matter, she sensed that his terms had something to do with what he had told Mevrou van der Walt earlier, about being called names by the young people with whom he had grown up. She also sensed, very strongly, that it had more to do with his decision to marry her after all than had any of her own blackmailing threats.

"I also want your promise," she heard him go on, "that you won't, at some future date, demand one of those modern separations or divorce. You're very young, and many men would consider you pretty, and most of all I want your promise that you won't plunge me into another scandal by going off with someone else." Before she could respond he added, "Think it over carefully and if, in the morning, you still wish to go ahead, I shall see Dominee Botha and explain the reason for such a hasty marriage, and make the arrangements."

He handed her a bedtime candle and nodded good night. She went to bed, slipping quietly under the covers beside the sleeping Ria. Instead of relief that she would be able to keep the children together, she was filled with doom and despair at the prospect of having to pretend to be a true and devoted wife to someone as strange and uncomfortable as Hendrik. She didn't even like him, so how was she to sustain the elaborate charade that they enjoyed a normal marriage?

She felt Ria turning over in her sleep. Ria, Sabella thought, didn't remember anything for long. Provided she was kindly treated, she would settle down quite happily inside an institution. And what would be so terrible about

Daan being adopted by the Roelofs, who would shower him with love? Nantes and Anton, it was true, would be unhappy in an orphanage at first, but they would gradually make friends and forget Sabella, just as they had already almost forgotten Pa.

Was it really so unthinkable to let them go? She hadn't had time yet to write to Mr Hudson and tell him about her changed circumstances, and her job at James Paradise was still open. She could go back and pursue her ambitions, become the thirty-shillings-a-week person on which she had set her immediate sights. And in the supervised hostel where she would have to live, she might well make friends among the other inmates. Surely she owed at least as much to herself as she did to the children?

She was still turning the matter over in her mind when the boys burst into the bedroom, bumping into furniture and making so much noise that Ria woke up and promptly joined Daan in weeping. Sabella leaned out of bed, striking a match to light the candle. "What's the matter? What happened?"

In the flickering light of the candle, Anton's face looked ashen. "Th-there's a ghost in our room." His stammer was almost as pronounced as that of Nantes. "It w-woke us up."

"It was m-m-mice in the c-c-cupboard," Nantes corrected, but he didn't sound entirely convinced.

Daan clambered on to the bed and wriggled underneath the bedclothes. "Don't want you to go away again, Sabella," he sobbed, setting off Ria again. Anton forgot about the ghost in their room, and said in a trembling voice, "It was horrible when you went away."

"But I didn't go away," she protested, bewildered and guilty. It was uncannily as if they had been reading her mind.

Daan clutched her so tightly around the neck that she had difficulty in breathing. "You did! Every day, you did! And Tante Roelof made me kiss her all the time."

"Made Ria too – "

103

"No, she didn't," Daan contradicted, and his tone said that that had made it so much worse.

"When you came home in the evening," Anton accused, "you didn't want to hear what happened at school, not even when I got a star for sums."

Why, Sabella wondered as she gently disengaged herself from Daan's strangling embrace, had the children waited until tonight to reveal that they'd felt unhappy and neglected while she worked at James Paradise? Was it because they had sensed undercurrents, sensed that she was flirting with the thought of abandoning them altogether? And how *could* she have contemplated such a thing for an instant, after the promise she had made to the memory of Pa and Ma?

"I'll never leave you again," she said.

"We'll all l-l-live here with C-C-Cousin Hendrik," Nantes tried to comfort the younger ones.

"No, we won't," Anton said, giving up the battle he had been fighting against the weakness of tears. "He doesn't like us. I listened outside the window and I heard him say he was taking us away tomorrow."

"We're staying," Sabella contradicted emphatically. "You mis-heard, and it serves you right for listening at windows." Her voice softened. "Come into my bed. You too, Nantes. You and Anton can sleep at the foot of it – but only for tonight, mind."

They scrambled gratefully into the large bed and the weeping stopped as they jostled one another for space. But in a short while all of them were asleep and only Sabella lay wakefully among them.

She had finally committed herself to marrying Hendrik on his terms, finally abandoned all personal ambition. Dear God, what a bleak, barren future stretched before her . . .

Then she remembered something. She was ashamed of herself, but at the same time she couldn't help taking comfort from the fact that Hendrik had a weak heart. It was no use pretending to herself that she was not already looking forward to being his widow, even before she had become his bride.

5

On the morning before the wedding day Mevrou van der Walt, who had asked Sabella and the children to call her Tante Bessie, prepared potato yeast from a plant she had brought with her the previous evening, and explained to Sabella how she was to go about baking a batch of currant loaves which were to be offered to wedding guests the next day.

Tante Bessie set off for her own home to bake sweet cookies and bring them over with her that evening, the last one she would have to spend at Mooikrantz as chaperone. Goodnaturedly, she gave in to Daan's demand, instantly reinforced by Ria, to be allowed to accompany her home and play with her cat's kittens.

Hendrik had left long ago for his wheat fields where, with his two labourers, he did work whose nature was still a complete mystery to Sabella. She turned her attention to her two eldest brothers. Nantes had finished his breakfast and was looking pensive and subdued. Anton dawdled over his porridge in a way that Sabella knew was deliberate. She suppressed a sigh, studying them.

Nantes's scars did not show, for they were mental and emotional. But Anton bore fading bruises and fresh grazes on parts of his face and arms. In the beginning he had blamed them on the undergrowth through which he and his elder brother had to push their way as they took the short cut to the farm school on the other side of the lower hills. But after close questioning by Sabella he had admitted that he was being forced into fights with other boys.

"*You?* Nantes is usually the one they try to force into fights!"

"They call me and him English *rooinekke*," Anton said fiercely. "It's because we'd gone to an English school and we understand all the lessons."

Why, Sabella wondered again with exasperation, did there have to be this wide, hostile and enduring gulf between English and Afrikaner? She broke the silence, ordering her brothers, "Hurry up and fetch your book-bags, or you'll be late for school."

She wanted to harden her heart against the anguished look in Nantes's eyes and Anton's mutinous mutterings. I have troubles of my own, she wanted to yell at them; battles to fight as well! I shall have to take a sack and go and search for *miskoeke* to stoke the range, and take the dirty clothes to the river and wash them in ice-cold water the way Tante Bessie showed me, and cope with other farm things like lizards crawling into the house, and, oh God, tomorrow I have to marry Hendrik . . .

Instead, she hugged first Anton, who squirmed away, and then Nantes, who clung tightly to her. "The boys will soon grow tired of calling you names," she said. "In the meantime, Anton, you can't tell me you don't enjoy fighting, and for once you won't get into trouble for it at home because I know you're fighting Nantes's battles as well as your own." She turned to Nantes. "You could fight in your own way. Pretend the other boys don't exist, and think of the beautiful wild honeysuckle and ferns you've told me grow everywhere on the way to school. We must all try and look on the bright side of things."

She found her own advice hard to take later that morning as she squatted by the river, soaping and then rubbing dirty clothes against stones and, after rinsing them, spreading them out on bushes to dry. She had kneaded a great batch of dough and left it in a dish to double in bulk before dividing it between baking-tins and putting it into the oven.

With the washing done, she returned to the house and found that for some reason her dough had refused to rise at all. She went on stoking the range with dry cow dung and rechecked the dough but it continued to lie there in the dish, a flat, obstinately inert blob. By the time Nantes and Anton returned home from school she realised with despair that she had wasted all that flour, sugar and currants and her dough was never going to rise. Hendrik, she thought with panic, must not see the extent of such wastefulness.

She thought of throwing the dough out for the chickens to eat but there was no guarantee that they would have disposed of all the evidence before Hendrik came home. Instead, she wrote a note to Tante Bessie, telling her that the yeast had failed to ferment, and asking if *she* could possibly produce a batch of currant loaves in time to offer the wedding guests. She sent Anton and Nantes over to Tante Bessie's house with the note and the ingredients for currant loaves, and when she was safely alone she dug a shallow hole just beyond the front stoep and buried the dough. All evidence of her wastefulness had been removed by the time Hendrik came home, and he paid no attention when Tante Bessie arrived later and puzzled aloud about the mystery of why her yeast had not fermented.

Sabella could not help feeling like a human sacrifice the next morning as she set out for Stilstroom, wearing a new but plain skirt and blouse and sturdy, sensible shoes for which Hendrik had paid. Beside her in the driving seat of the mule cart, Hendrik did not look much like a bridegroom either, dressed in an ill-made matching coat and trousers. Tante Bessie had stayed behind with the children to prepare for the few guests who were expected after the wedding.

A mental image of Sebastian Grant entered Sabella's mind. Oh, she'd had to fight the temptation to send *him* an invitation to the wedding! She knew, from the short time she had spent with James Paradise, that mail sent to a business address was invariably opened and read by secretaries. How it would have shattered Sebastian Grant's smug, feather-bedded world if underlings at the Grant Mining Corporation had read that his half-brother, Hendrik le

Roux, was inviting him to the wedding of himself and their mutual cousin, Sabella van Renselaar.

Sebastian Grant, she thought bitterly, you with your superior manner and your unmatching looks, are entirely to blame for the fact that I'm forced to go through with this marriage. Oh, how I hate you . . .

She saw that they had reached Stilstroom, and moments later she entered the church with Hendrik. Curiosity had prompted many villagers to attend the service. Sabella tried to block from her mind the fact that she was irrevocably becoming Hendrik's lawful wife by thinking of other things, such as her relief that no one had ever questioned the matter of the children's legal guardianship. Everyone had seemed to assume that she had every right to care for her brothers and sister, and that the right would be passed on to Hendrik after their wedding. Even the magistrate, to whom Sabella had had to apply for formal consent to the marriage, hadn't thought to query the matter, or perhaps he had simply decided to leave well enough alone.

"You may kiss the bride," she heard Dominee Botha say, and after a moment's hesitation Hendrik bent his head and touched her mouth with tightly-pursed lips. It was over. They were man and wife.

Dominee Botha and his wife and a few selected guests accompanied them back to Mooikrantz where Tante Bessie had coffee brewing and freshly-baked currant bread sliced and buttered, flanked by platefuls of sweet cookies. Everyone ate and drank and toasted the newly-weds with coffee, and Sabella had to endure the weight of Hendrik's arm about her shoulder and force herself to smile warmly at him until the muscles of her face were aching.

The guests had gathered outside the house later, on the point of saying their goodbyes, when Dominee Botha remembered that he had brought his camera purposely to take a snapshot of the bride and groom. He began to pose Hendrik and Sabella in front of the house, fussily arranging and rearranging the attitudes he wanted them to strike.

"Hendrik, put your hand beneath Sabella's chin and then

smile at one another. Not too broadly; we want a mixture of happiness and a solemn awareness of the sacred vows you've just exchanged."

His wife was impatient for him to take the snapshot so that they could leave, but he said, "It is written, my dear: whatsoever thy hand findeth to do, do it with might, for there is no work in the *grave* . . ."

The last word come out in a shocked scream. Other screams filled the air as the spot on which Dominee Botha had been standing erupted like a volcano, scattering soil and pebbles at the guests. Dominee Botha lost his balance and fell, and when he had struggled to his feet again he was covered in an oozing, dripping white mess studded with currants.

Sabella's dough had at last risen in a most spectacular fashion in the heat of the sun. Tante Bessie, who guessed almost immediately what had happened, began to laugh helplessly, and in between her laughter she gasped out the truth to the others. People roared and giggled and chortled and wheezed and clung to one another in helpless mirth, and even Dominee Botha grinned ruefully as he tried to wipe dough from himself with his handkerchief. Sabella's own laughter died when she saw the expression of horror and repugnance stamped on Hendrik's face.

He tried to hide it, and said with awful, forced warmth, "My silly little wife! I'm so sorry, Dominee. Sabella, dearest, go and fetch towels and help to clean as much of the mess as possible from our poor parson."

Everyone was still laughing when she returned with the towels, and the false grin on Hendrik's face chilled her. She did what she could to help clean up the Dominee. She had to stop when someone gulped, "Exploding dough," and set everyone including the parson off into renewed paroxysms. Everyone apart from Hendrik. The guests were still laughing when they left, and the make-believe amusement slid from Hendrik's face like a mask. Ignoring the children who were rolling on the ground in their mirth he asked Sabella coldly to accompany him indoors.

Tight-lipped, he lectured her at length – about her deceit-fulness, her wastefulness and her lack of humility in not asking Tante Bessie's advice in the matter of making the dough rise. In addition, Hendrik condemned her total lack of shame, because she had laughed as unrestrainedly as all the others at the sight of the unfortunate Dominee Botha.

"But even he saw the funny side of it," Sabella pro-tested.

"He was trying to spare your feelings. There was noth-ing funny about it at all." Hendrik tore a sheet from one of the pile of old magazines, carefully lining them up in precise order again afterwards, and used the sheet to protect his hand from contact with the dry cow dung with which he began to stoke the range. Even Sabella had learnt that there was nothing to be squeamish about in handling dry cow dung; it didn't smell and felt like compacted straw, but Hendrik never touched it with his bare hands.

"Boil water," he commanded, "and then scrub away this horrible mess of dough and soil we've tracked into the kitchen." The "horrible mess" consisted of two small patches, but she knew he would not consider the job properly done unless she scrubbed the entire floor. And afterwards he would expect her to go and wash her hands under the pump, just as he had gone out to wash his own because only a sheet of paper had been between them and the dry cow dung he'd handled.

That evening as she lay alone in the bed which used to be Tante Wilhelmina's, Sabella remembered how desper-ately Hendrik wanted to be regarded as "normal". He didn't seem to understand that normality extended beyond being regarded as a "proper husband". In some way which she sensed but couldn't define his early years had warped him so that he would never be capable of normal feel-ings or reactions or expectations about anything. Their life together promised to be even bleaker than she had feared.

The farce of the exploding dough, she thought, had been a far more fitting memento of their wedding day than the snapshot which Dominee Botha had intended to take would have been. A snapshot showing a mixture of happiness and solemn awareness of the sacred vows she and Hendrik had exchanged would only have recorded for posterity an empty, miserable lie.

In the weeks and months that followed, Sabella often found herself wishing that her marriage had been actively unhappy, so that she would have had something to fight against, something to provide her with stimulus. But Hendrik offered her neither stimulus nor a reason for fighting, and her periodic acts of defiance were not enough to ease her frustrations. He did not even pay sufficient attention to the children to punish them for petty misdemeanours, so that she could have flared up in their defence, and Hendrik's austere, aloof manner daunted them so much that even Anton was careful to hide more serious transgressions from him.

On Sundays, when they went to church, Hendrik strove so desperately to present a show of marital intimacy between them that Sabella cringed, and at the same time it made her feel sorry for him. He held her arm awkwardly and called her "dearest" for the benefit of Dominee Botha and the congregation, and she hid her feelings and tried to appear to be a "normal" wife.

At home the two of them were rarely alone together, because he spent most evenings in Stilstroom, practising with the church choir. When he was at home he inspected the house minutely to make sure she had cleaned everything to his own obsessive standards, but he never failed to find something to criticise. At times like those she found herself thinking guiltily but longingly about his weak heart. Ten years at most . . .

She would shut the thought off in her mind, and concentrate her inner attention on something else instead, like the children. They had settled down quite well on the farm.

111

The boys at school no longer called Nantes and Anton "English" and picked fights. True, Nantes was still being taunted at school for other reasons, but no more than he had been in Westdene. "It's his own fault," Anton said with scorn. "It's not just his stammer, Sabella; it's because he *likes* learning recitations!"

"That's hardly a fault! Why don't you force the other boys to stop calling him names, and in return he could help you to learn your own recitations?"

"And have everyone call me a sissy too?" Anton reacted with horror.

Sabella sighed and gave up. At least on the credit side, Nantes had the pleasure of being surrounded by the beauties of nature to which he had always been drawn. Anton had forgotten the lure of living where there were shops in the excitement of waging war against the baboons from the hills. They would come down to the citrus orchard to steal the ripe oranges and he would scare them with blood-curdling screams and a barrage of stones that sent them loping back into the hills, from where they barked at him in echoing, empty defiance.

Because Hendrik would not entertain the thought of anything as "dirty" as a pet in the house, Daan and Ria often wandered off by themselves to visit Tante Bessie on her farm and play with her many cats. Daan was outstripping Ria mentally and in a rather touching way they now complemented one another.

"Mind the thorns, Ria," he would warn as they skirted a bush. "Thorns hurt. Don't step on the ant-nest. They get cross and bite you."

In return, she used her superior strength to give him piggy-back rides when he became tired. Sabella would watch them until they had disappeared from sight, knowing that Tante Bessie would be watching out for them in turn at her end, so that they were quite safe.

Tante Bessie had become an important part of all their lives, and it was she who schooled Sabella in farm ways. "This stoep," she remarked when she called at the house

112

and found Sabella sweeping it for the dozenth time, "needs to be smeared with fresh cow dung."

Sabella remembered Hendrik saying something about cow dung in relation to the stoep, and under her questioning Tante Bessie explained that cow dung mixed with a little water and spread on the surface of the stoep would dry to a hard, clean finish instead of producing endless clouds of dust. "Hendrik never found time to do it after his mother's death," she added.

Hendrik, Sabella knew by now, hadn't done it because he couldn't bring himself to touch fresh cow dung. She would not allow herself to be squeamish if this was the only way to solve the problem of the stoep.

Taking a pail and a spade, she walked to the dry-stone enclosure into which the cows were driven at night, and filled her pail with dung. After she had added water to it and stirred it with a stick she carried it to the stoep. I'll pretend to myself, she decided, that it's clay, and that I'm a sculptor about to create a work of art.

And indeed, as she spread the mixture on the stoep and used the heel of her hand to make spiralling patterns she entirely forgot the nature of the material she was using. Later, when the floor had dried and Nantes and Anton were home from school they exclaimed over it in admiration. Sabella felt flushed with achievement, but when Hendrik arrived moments later from the fields to refill his water flask he studied her handiwork with repugnance. "You must have wasted a great deal of time on it, time which could have been better spent on something else!" he said.

She gave him a challenging look. "Like sweeping the dust from the stoep about a dozen times?" She knew perfectly well what lay behind his reaction. It was disgust that she had apparently thrown herself with enthusiasm into doing something that filled him with revulsion.

He said nothing more, but she knew he would stand over her later and make sure that she scrubbed her hands raw in almost-boiling water before she would be allowed to prepare their supper.

But in the event, it was not she who prepared the supper that evening. Hendrik had gone back to the fields when a pony-cart arrived, driven by Tante Bessie. Ria sat next to her, smiling her beautiful, empty smile but there was no sign of Daan. This, and the expression on Tante Bessie's face, swamped Sabella with immediate terror.

"Where's Daan?" she cried.

"Daan sleeping," Ria sang out, and jumped from the cart.

"He's unconscious in the back, Sabella," Tante Bessie corrected with urgency in her voice. "We have to get him to the doctor. There's been an accident."

Sabella removed her apron, flinging it on the stoep floor, and ordered Nantes to look after Anton and Ria. Then she was flying to the cart, scrambling on to the back where Daan lay on pillows, covered with a blanket. His eyes were closed and his face was the colour of chalk.

Sabella curled herself up next to Daan and held him steady as Tante Bessie whipped up the pony. While she drove she explained what had happened. One of the cats had clambered on to the roof of her house, and Daan and Ria had decided to follow. The first Tante Bessie had known about it was when she heard Daan screaming and when she ran outside she found him lying on the ground, and Ria on top of the roof with the cat.

Sabella's imagination had already leapt to Daan's funeral when she felt him stir. Joyous relief whipped through her when his eyes opened. "My head hurts," he wailed.

"The doctor will make it stop hurting, my darling." She kissed his cheek and prayed to God, even though she had no trust in him, that it would prove to be true, and that her baby brother had not been seriously injured.

But after they had reached Stilstroom and Doctor Pelzer had examined Daan thoroughly, he said he could find no evidence of serious injury but thought the child might be suffering from a degree of concussion. "I'd like him to stay here tonight, Mevrou le Roux. My wife will put him to bed after he has had something to eat, and I'll keep looking in on him every few hours. I'm only doing this as a precaution. I'm sure he'll be able to go home tomorrow."

Tante Bessie expelled a heavy breath of relief, kissed Daan and announced that she would take the opportunity of picking up mail from the post office while they were in the village. Sabella watched Daan being carried out, looking very self-important, by the doctor's wife, and thanked the man fervently.

But Daan's accident had brought home to her the fact that she and the children would be in a very vulnerable position indeed if Hendrik should die much earlier than he had been given to expect. There was that will he had shown her, leaving everything to his Afrikaans half-brother, Ewart le Roux. If Hendrik died before Sabella's twenty-first birthday she would not even have the money with which to leave Mooikrantz with the children, and the authorities would take them away from her.

"While I'm here, Doctor," she said, "I want to ask you about my husband."

"Yes, Mevrou le Roux?"

If there was any possibility at all that Hendrik might die suddenly, she thought, she would have to ask him to make some provision for herself in his will. Aloud, she said, "In your opinion, might the end be quite sudden after all? As the result of an unexpected shock, for instance?"

He frowned. "I'm afraid I don't follow – "

"Surely Hendrik has consulted you about his heart?"

"Ah!" The doctor's frown cleared. "He didn't consult me, but about a year ago I had to treat him for a minor complaint, and then he informed me that he suffered from a weak heart caused by rheumatic fever when he was a child. I examined him thoroughly, and I could find no evidence of a weak heart. I told him that in his case rheumatic fever had not left a legacy of heart trouble, as it sometimes does. I could see that he was not entirely convinced and so I sent him, at my own expense, to a friend of mine who specialises in ailments of the heart and my diagnosis

115

was confirmed. Your husband's heart is perfectly sound and he has the same chance as any fit man to live to be ninety."

"I – see," she managed.

"It's a pity that you didn't speak to your husband frankly about the matter," she heard Doctor Pelzer go on. "You must have suffered a great deal of anxiety on his behalf. I know that his late mother was totally convinced her son would die young of heart failure and she'd passed that conviction on to him. Since you and he are first cousins I suppose she must have mentioned it in letters to your parents. But Hendrik has known for more than a year that his health is excellent."

Somehow, Sabella must have succeeded in preserving the facade of a relieved, devoted wife, for the doctor gave her a particularly warm smile and a handshake when Tante Bessie returned from the post office to collect her.

During the drive home too, she did or said nothing that caused Tante Bessie to suspect that she was suffering from more than delayed shock caused by Daan's accident. The numbness in which she was wrapped was momentarily pierced when Tante Bessie began to talk about Tante Wilhelmina, a subject which she normally side-stepped.

". . . should have shown more Christian charity," Sabella heard her say. "Poor woman, she paid heavily for what she did, and when she felt unable to pay any more she ended her life. But the way in which she did it made all of us feel guilty, and I suppose that's why we condemned her even more, because suicide is after all a sin only one step less grave than murder."

"I feel sorry for her," Sabella said mechanically.

Tante Bessie changed the subject to that of Daan's accident, and expressed the wistful hope that Sabella would not forbid the two children to visit her in future, and Sabella made all the appropriate, automatic responses.

The sun was setting when Tante Bessie dropped her at Mooikrantz. Hendrik had laid the table for supper, which was to be bread and butter and preserves and coffee.

Everyone wanted to know how Daan was and Sabella told them briefly.

"Such a fall could have caused him lasting damage in later life," Hendrik said.

She looked at him. Such as a weak heart? she wanted to ask with bitter mockery, but she didn't. What was the point in bringing the subject up? She knew perfectly well why he had offered her the lie about his own early death. It had been an excuse for avoiding marriage and more particularly what he called "the duties of a husband", something he obviously regarded as the epitome of dirtiness.

She thought of the will he had shown her. It had been made, she'd noticed, when he was twenty-one; probably on the day he gained his majority. At the time he'd made it he had believed he would die young, but why hadn't he destroyed it once he learnt there was nothing wrong with his heart? Perhaps because he'd wanted the farm and the rest of his estate to go to his half-brother Ewart, no matter when or from what cause Hendrik himself eventually died.

Well, he would have to change that will, Sabella thought. He would have to make adequate provision for herself and the children. But there was no hurry, she thought, with the taste of gall in her mouth. No hurry at all. She had just passed her eighteenth birthday and Hendrik could live until he was ninety and she eighty-two.

That night, when everyone else was asleep, she left the house whose walls seemed to be closing in around her as if it were a prison, and went outside. She had never gone out in the dark before and even in daylight she kept to the rutted tracks, but tonight her fear of the rural unknown was buried beneath the agony and the rage that possessed her.

Picking her way by the light of the stars, she wandered into the hills. Night insects chirped and somewhere a dog, or perhaps a baboon, barked. Sabella tripped over a boulder and didn't trouble to get up again. "Oh God," she cried aloud, and heard the hills echoing the anguish in her voice, as if they were mocking her. "That's my last hope gone!"

"Last hope gone, last hope gone, last hope gone," the hills replied.

She hadn't realised, until today, just how desperately she'd been clinging to the promise of early widowhood.

She wept with anger and despair and a complete lack of guilt, and the hills threw her misery back at her.

6

Life on Mooikrantz continued in its usual pattern. Autumn had set in, their second on the farm, and Hendrik was spending each day at Stilstroom, having their wheat milled, and Ria and Daan hurried away after breakfast to go and help Tante Bessie "harvest" the showers of mulberries which fell from the tree as they ripened.

Sabella had watched them on their way and returned to the kitchen to wash the dishes when she realised that Nantes had forgotten to take his lunchtime sandwiches with him to school. Resignedly, she picked up the tin and set off along the hill track to deliver it as quickly as possible.

She had never used the short-cut before. On her previous visits to the school she had walked along the rutted road which had been cleared and carved into the hills at their lowest point. Now she found that in places along this rough hill track which sometimes petered out into a scarcely visible footpath, thick verdant growth met overhead to form a tunnel. And just as Nantes had told her, there were ferns and wild honeysuckle vying for position with thorny scrub and bushes laden with berries and huge trees pregnant with wild figs on which the baboons feasted.

She often studied the troop and was amazed by their social behaviour. They clung to one partner for life and whereas the males seemed to be remarkably faithful, occasionally a female would commit adultery with an unattached young male. When found out, she would be punished just once by her partner and then forgiven, and her status within the troop would be restored. If animals could

119

behave with such charity, Sabella often thought, her mind straying to Tante Wilhelmina, why did human beings have to be so unforgiving?

She dismissed the baboons from her mind and continued on her way. There were places where water cascaded down in thin streams, fed from some higher source hidden from her view and running to join Mooikrantz's river boundary. Birdsong echoed all around her but the most insistent of them all, the one that evoked in her feelings of loneliness and a longing for more than life had offered her or ever would, belonged to the turtle dove.

She didn't stop to rest after she had reached the school and handed over the lunch-tin to Nantes. There were too many other tasks awaiting her attention at home. By the time she approached the house she felt hot and bedraggled, and her hair was coming down because the knot at the base of her neck had been caught in the overhanging branch of a tree.

She pushed the hair away from her face and saw for the first time that a very smart, expensive-looking but dust-covered motor car stood outside the front stoep. She was still staring at it in astonishment when a tall figure appeared from around the side of the house.

Slowly, they recognised one another. The sun glinted on Sebastian Grant's streaked fair hair and his eyes that didn't match had shadows around them. His sun-browned face was set in a grim expression as he came towards her. His smart suit looked crumpled, as if he had slept in it. Not that that gave her any moral advantage, she realised, thinking of her hair tumbling untidily around her face and the house-dress which she was wearing that had once been Ma's.

"What," Sebastian Grant demanded aggressively, "are *you* doing here?"

She flung up her head. "I have a perfect right to be here, which is more than could be said for you! How dare you snoop around as if you owned the place? I'm married to the man who *does* own it, and if I had a mind to do so, I could order you to leave!"

The dislike – the rage, almost – which had leapt into his eyes when he'd first recognised her, disappeared as he studied her. "Are you going to order me to leave?"

"No." For some reason her fingers were clumsy and unsteady as she gathered together her wayward hair and braided it into a plait which swung down one shoulder. It was because he was watching so intently what she was doing, she decided, as if – as if he were witnessing some previously undreamt-of female ritual. Of course, she remembered, girls in *his* world all had short, modern, fashionable hairstyles. "You may think I look a freak," she said pugnaciously, "but you needn't show it so – "

"No," he interrupted. "I don't think you look a freak. It was just – I didn't notice, that first time, how very pretty you were."

Colour crept into her cheeks and she felt as if something inside her were melting. Hendrik was the only other man who had ever said to her face that she was pretty, but he'd said it as if it were a regrettable defect from which she suffered. She also found it hard to cope with Sebastian Grant's abrupt change in attitude towards herself.

"Come inside," she invited gruffly. "I'll make coffee."

He followed her into the kitchen and sat down, and she busied herself at the range. "What has brought you here?" she asked unnecessarily, knowing that he must have come to find out whether it could possibly be true that his roots were on Mooikrantz.

But as he began to speak it became clear that his visit had had a far more definite purpose. She turned her head and saw the hard, self-mocking twist of his lips as he said, "I came to see what she was like, the mother who didn't want me and sold me to my father, who did. Instead, I saw *you*, and I wanted to strangle you for being the one who told me about her in the first place and turned my life upside-down."

"Poor you!" Sabella said scathingly. "I don't suppose for a moment that you've been broadcasting to the world what I told you, so you've obviously been brooding and

121

wallowing in self-pity. You should be thankful, instead, that your mother didn't bring you up to share her own hard, isolated life, but handed you over to your wealthy father. And why should you, with all your privileges, judge her for making herself a little money at the same time – "

"*You bitch!*" he cut in, his voice a savage growl.

She confronted him, her hands on her hips. "You called me that once before! But you are on my territory now, so apologise at once!"

"I do apologise," he brought out between gritted teeth, "but only because the insult demeaned myself, and not you!"

He might never have called her pretty and produced a melting feeling inside her. She restrained the desire to pick up a heavy pan and hurl it at his head. Instead, she mimicked with enraged scorn, " 'Turned your life upside-down . . .' At least you *have* a life to be turned upside-down! My father doesn't. He was stabbed to death by another prisoner while awaiting trial in gaol!"

Sebastian Grant's anger and disdain melted away and in their place was a look of shocked remorse. "And you blame me . . ."

"Of course I blame you!" she hurled at him. It was too late for shock and remorse. "If it hadn't been for you, he wouldn't have been in gaol!"

He stared into the distance, and when he spoke again his voice held a tone of forced neutrality, neither inviting forgiveness nor apportioning blame elsewhere. "When I read the item about your father in the newspaper on the morning of the trial, I mentioned that I'd recognised his name. We were at the breakfast table, my father and I. Naturally I told him of my meeting with Ferdinantes van Renselaar and he pointed out to me that it was my duty to give such vital evidence to the court. I was reluctant – for purely selfish reasons – to get involved. I had better things to do than hang around a court room for perhaps an entire day. My father reminded me of his own position as a Member of Parliament, sworn to uphold the law. Once *he* knew the facts it would have been a grave dereliction of duty on his part if he hadn't made certain that they were put before the court. Whether voluntarily or because I had been subpoenaed to do so at a later stage, he explained, I would have to make known the details of my meeting with Ferdinantes van Renselaar."

Sabella was silent for a while, digesting what he had said. If his father had known that Pa was Tante Wilhelmina's brother he would have found ways of easing his conscience, and would never have pressed his son to appear in court where he could have been exposed to cross-examination. She was about to transfer the blame for Pa's death to Peregrine Grant when, reluctantly, she saw where the truth really lay.

"I take back what I said," she forced herself to tell Sebastian Grant. "Pa died because of the kind of man he was. He wouldn't allow you to be cross-examined in court because he said if the family scandal became public it would ruin your life. He never thought of himself first. He didn't think of himself when he tried to stop a fight between two other prisoners, and that's how he came to be stabbed. You are not to blame for his death."

"*You* may not blame me," Sebastian said in a low voice, "but I blame myself. If I hadn't rejected what you told me, pushed it all to the back of my mind and convinced myself it was a vindictive lie, I would have tackled my parents and once they'd confirmed that you had told the truth, I would have had your father set free by testifying that I had been mistaken about his motives during our meeting. He would still have been alive."

"The most pointless two words in any language," Sabella said, shrugging and sighing, "must be: *if only*." She poured out two cups of coffee and handed one to him, joining him at the table. "What made you accept, after all this time, that I'd told you the truth about your birth?"

He laughed with no hint of mirth. "It didn't really take all this time. As much as I wanted to go on disbelieving it, I began to realise that what I'd previously thought were

123

no more than recurring dreams were rooted in memory. Gradually fragments of another life came back to me – a baboon-mother grieving for a baby which a leopard had taken; something about a toy monkey and a nonsensical but vivid image of a lady who wore a dead dog around her neck, and myself being made to go with her. I also thought about the way I seemed to pick up Afrikaans as soon as I first heard it spoken by one of our servants. I tried to push all the evidence away but it remained just below the surface. Last evening I was idly picking through some jumble Mother had decided to throw out and I found a fox-fur pelt, and recognised it as the 'dead dog' of my early memory. I waited up until she and Father returned from a dinner party, and after stalling for as long as they could they admitted the truth."

"They should have told you themselves when you were growing up," Sabella commented critically.

"They'd meant to, they said. But they found they'd been so successful in making me forget my true roots that it became more and more difficult to tell me. To complicate matters, they settled in Johannesburg immediately after they had formally adopted me and people they met socially took it for granted that I was the son of both of them. Apart from the fact that they wanted me to learn the truth before others did, it would have been more than a little awkward to explain that I was Father's true son but not Mother's. They still hadn't found the right moment to tell me the truth about my roots, when Father entered politics, and after that it would have ruined him if the truth came out. So – they were trapped."

Sabella studied him. The shadows around his eyes and the crumpled suit told her that when the confrontation between himself and his parents had come to an end in the early hours of the morning he had driven straight to Mooikrantz.

"You'd better know," she broke the silence, "that your mother is dead. She took her own life by swallowing caustic soda."

"Good God!" He stared at her, appalled. Then he shook his head. "It was a terrible way to die, but I can't pretend to a grief I don't feel. I have only the haziest memory of her. And you may dress it up as much as you like, but the fact remains that she didn't want me. I was just a saleable commodity to her." He changed the subject with an air of finality. "You and I have insulted one another and almost come to blows, and I've just realised that I don't even know your first name."

"Sabella. From Isabella, after my mother." She added deliberately, "*Your* mother's pet name for you was Bastian."

He did not react at all, but drained his cup of coffee. "I won't take up more of your time, Sabella. You must have work to do."

"The cows have to be milked," she agreed. "But – won't you stay and see Hendrik? He is your half-brother, after all."

"My half-brother – your husband. And all three of us cousins." He frowned at the thought, and then shook his head. "I'd better leave now and stay away. Father was right when he said it would be disastrous for me to establish ties with my Afrikaans family."

"One wouldn't want people to talk, would one?" Sabella sneered, mimicking the snobbish tones of some of the female customers who'd used her lift at James Paradise. "One would face social ruin if it were to come out that one had close connections with inferior Afrikaners – "

"Shut up!" he snarled. "I didn't mean that at all!"

"No?" she put in nastily. "In that case it must be the slur of having had an uncle who was stabbed to death in gaol!"

Sebastian's head jerked up. "That was a vicious thing to say," he managed through stiff lips.

"Yes," she acknowledged, and looked away. Under all the circumstances, why couldn't she accept with grace, if not indifference, his decision not to establish ties with his half-brother and cousins?

He began to speak more quietly, but with no less conviction. "What do you imagine it would do to my father's political career if my relationship to all on Mooikrantz should become public knowledge? If it came out that he committed adultery, in wartime, with the wife of one of the enemy? And while he was in a position of command, at that? As for Mother – who never gave me the slightest cause to suspect that I wasn't her true, deeply-loved son – does she deserve to be dragged down by a scandal?"

"No," Sabella agreed. She gave him a puzzled look. "Why do you and I want to fight all the time?"

His smile was rueful. "I don't know. Perhaps because we're cousins, and share the same hot blood?"

She made no comment. In a moment he would leave and her life would continue on its dull, uneventful, hopeless course. If she had been questioned just over an hour ago she would have sworn that he was the person she most hated in the world, so why did the thought of his leaving make her feel so – so – Her mind shied away like a nervous horse from the search for the right word. Instead, she told herself with a rough mental shake that quarrelling with him, exchanging insults, had made her feel alive for a few minutes, and that was all.

She stood up and said, "I really have to go and milk the cows now."

He seemed to have forgotten his decision to leave immediately, but followed her to the barn, where he watched as she tied the hind legs of a cow together and then sat down on a stool to begin milking.

"How did you come to marry Hendrik?" he asked.

She told him how she had fled from Westdene with the children, and why, and added ambiguously, "And then, well, one thing led to another and Hendrik and I decided to marry."

"For a city-bred girl you've adapted amazingly well!"

She shook her head ruefully. "Don't be fooled. After almost two years, I've only just mastered the milking."

126

"What do you miss most here on Mooikrantz?" he wanted to know.

She considered. "Reading. Hendrik subscribes to a farming magazine but it's deadly dull, all about crop-rotation and animal diseases. Yes, I miss the *Rand Daily Mail*. A shopkeeper in Westdene used to give me old copies."

"And you *enjoyed* reading them?" Sebastian asked with amazement. "Every other girl I know finds newspapers as deadly dull as you find Hendrik's farming magazines!"

"How can it be dull to read news reports from all over the world, and interesting articles, and about the social doings and dealings of the rich, not to mention the descriptions of new fashions . . ." She looked up, giving him a taunting smile. "Oh yes, even poor Afrikaans girls forced to wear their late mothers' old-fashioned dresses and high-buttoned boots can still dream about pretty, modern clothes. And of course, it was through an advertisement in the *Rand Daily Mail* that I found myself a job with James Paradise & Company."

He gazed at her in astonishment. "They gave you a job?" He stopped, looking contrite. "I'm sorry; I didn't mean – "

She laughed. "Oh, don't worry, my appearance caused exactly the kind of reaction you're imagining." As she continued the milking she told him the whole story, and sometimes he laughed but mostly he made sounds of admiration and respect.

"You stepped into my lift one day," she added. "You were with a very pretty, smartly-dressed young lady."

"I didn't notice you – "

"I know. How I hated you! I'm surprised you didn't sense it, and have me dismissed for what I believe is called dumb insolence. But then, I suppose you were too absorbed in your companion. Is she your fiancée?"

"No, just a friend. I'm not thinking of settling down yet."

Sabella leant sideways to untie the cow's hind legs, gave the animal a slap on the rump and rose, lifting up the pailful of milk. "Let me," Sebastian said, his hand closing over hers upon the handle.

Acutely aware of his touch, she said unsteadily, "How can I – let go – while you're trapping my hand? This is silly . . ."

"Yes." Their eyes met and locked, and she felt as vibrantly, physically stirred as if they had come together in an intimate embrace. An eternity seemed to pass before he moved his hand to free hers. Neither of them spoke as he carried the pailful of milk into the kitchen.

He set it down on the table and turned to her. "Goodbye, Sabella." It seemed entirely natural that he should bend his head and kiss her mouth. But it was not natural at all, part of her mind warned, even as she responded. It was not the way two cousins kissed, and certainly not the way in which a man should kiss his sister-in-law.

Sebastian drew away from her. She attempted a weak joke. "Well, so we've stopped fighting, and made friends . . ."

He didn't respond. He looked at her for a moment and then he turned away towards the kitchen door. She followed, and a few moments later she watched him walk to the front where he had left his car. He did not look back, and she told herself it was a good thing he would not be paying future visits to Mooikrantz.

But the thought of him filled her mind as she carried out her chores in a mechanical way. Several times she became angry with herself and put matters savagely into perspective. Sebastian might have been pressured by his father into giving evidence against Pa, but the fact remained that her own life had been permanently blighted because of his evidence. Had it not been for Sebastian, Pa would not have remained in gaol, he would not have been stabbed to death, she would not have been forced to flee with the children and make the sacrifice of marrying Hendrik.

To relieve her feelings she tried to pick quarrels with

Hendrik but he refused to quarrel. He lectured and preached and condemned, and if she tried to retaliate he walked away, looking grim and censorious. She banged pots and pans angrily about in the kitchen and told herself: Sebastian's visit was a diversion, that's all, and if my life hadn't been so predictable and utterly boring I would have forgotten all about it by now.

But the memory refused to fade, and as if to make sure that it would be kept alive Hendrik returned from Stilstroom a few days later with several rolled-up packages addressed to her, and which turned out to be copies of the *Rand Daily Mail*. Fortunately she had told him all about Sebastian's visit – apart, of course, from any mention of undercurrents – and she was able to explain the reason why he had sent the papers to her.

Hendrik chose to create an issue about it, and wanted to make a bonfire of the gift. English newspapers only printed lies, he said, and in any case reading them would waste time Sabella ought to give to other matters. She knew what the real reason was for his displeasure. No matter how one might fold the newspapers, they would never be capable of being arranged in perfect alignment with the old farming magazines after they had been read and their only use was for lighting fires.

She said acidly, "You have your farming magazines to read, so why should I be deprived of something that gives me pleasure?"

"We were not put on this earth for pleasure," Hendrik ended the argument dourly, and walked away.

She squirrelled the newspapers into her bedroom, almost as if they were love-letters. The first sour note was struck when she read about a ball to which Sebastian Grant had escorted Miss Annette Hunter. Her father, it appeared, was a shareholder in the Grant Mining Corporation and friends expected them to announce wedding plans before too long.

Why on earth should it concern me who he decides to marry, Sabella asked herself, but deep down inside

129

where guilty secrets and sorrows lay buried she knew the answer.

She suffered further disillusionment when the rolled packages continued to arrive for her, and she realised that the newspapers were not personal gifts from Sebastian which he posted to her himself. He had simply arranged – probably through his secretary – for her name to be added to the newspaper's subscribers. Sabella began to twist the newspapers into compact rolls for use as fuel, but before she did so she cut a small column from each issue to keep as a memento. A memento of what, she jeered at herself. Sebastian had probably forgotten already that he'd arranged for the newspapers to be sent to her, so why was she behaving like a fool?

But she continued to behave like a fool, and slightly more than a week after his first visit Sebastian himself gave the lie to the thought that there had been nothing personal about the sending of the newspapers, because he arrived on Mooikrantz one morning in his expensive car. As she left the house and they walked towards one another their eyes spoke a language which did not match in any way the formality of their greeting.

"How are you, Sabella?"

"I am very well, thank you. And you?"

"Fine. I had a business call to make in the area, and thought I'd drop by."

"I see." She pretended to believe the lie, but her heart was beating a joyful tattoo. He must have set out from Johannesburg in the small hours of the morning in the hope that she would once again be alone on Mooikrantz. By chance she *was* alone, but would not be so for long. The schools were on holiday and Nantes and Anton had taken Ria and Daan with them to the river, where they were building a dam. Hunger, boredom or a squabble might bring them home at any moment.

Sabella roused herself and invited Sebastian inside for coffee. He was carrying a small leather case; he had obviously brought it along, she thought, to back up his story

130

about having business in the area if Hendrik happened to be home. But Hendrik was still busy with the milling of the wheat harvest in Stilstroom.

Once she and Sebastian were inside the kitchen he put the case down on the table and opened it. Pushing aside tissue paper, he took out the most beautiful, most frivolous dress in soft, pale apricot Sabella could ever have imagined.

" 'Even poor Afrikaans girls,' " Sebastian quoted softly, " 'forced to wear their mothers' old-fashioned dresses and boots can still dream about pretty, modern clothes.' It's for you, Sabella. Underneath the tissue paper you'll find a pair of modern shoes and silk stockings. I hope it will all fit."

"I – You – I can't – " She swallowed, and forced herself to stop floundering. "Sebastian, are you out of your mind? I couldn't possibly accept it!"

"Why not? What's wrong with giving one's cousin a present?"

He knew perfectly well what was wrong with it, but she dared not bring out into the open what had to remain unsaid between them. "And when would you expect me to wear it?" she asked instead, her voice deliberately abrasive. "While milking the cows, perhaps?"

"I thought you could wear it to church on Sundays."

Hysterical laughter rose in her throat at the suggestion. The dress had one of the new short skirts which would reveal her knees to the world, and she might as well walk into church with a placard bearing the word HARLOT around her neck. And as to what Hendrik would say about it – "I couldn't wear any of it – ever," she said flatly.

He moved towards her so that they almost touched. "You could wear it now," he suggested in a half-whisper. "Just for me."

"N-no." Her legs had turned weak, as if they would no longer support her weight. Desperately, she tried to reduce the situation to a joke. "Unless – unless there's a wig underneath the tissue as well."

"A wig?" he frowned.

"A dress like this one would look ridiculous without

131

a short, modern hairstyle. Or are you suggesting that I should cut my hair off as well – just for you?"

"No!" he said with unnecessary vehemence. His hands went to the knot in her neck, scattering pins on the floor, until her hair was tumbling about her face. He buried both hands in it and began to draw her closer to him, and she was incapable of resisting.

But the sound of the children's approaching, quarrelsome voices broke the spell and galvanised her into action. She pulled herself free, began scrabbling on the floor for hairpins, and somehow she had managed to secure her hair in a semblance of its normal state by the time the children came into the kitchen.

The tales they had come to tell about one another were forgotten as they stared at Sebastian. Sabella introduced him without telling them that he was their cousin. Because Nantes and Anton had almost forgotten the English they'd learnt in Westdene, Sebastian spoke to them in halting Afrikaans, and offered to show them his motor car.

As soon as they had gone outside she scooped up the contents of the leather case and hurried to hide it. Hendrik only ever entered her bedroom to check that she had cleaned it properly, but to be on the safe side she stuffed the clothes inside a large chest which still held garments which had belonged to his mother. Even though his hatred of waste would not allow him to have the contents destroyed, he would never touch the chest, let alone look inside it.

Half an hour later, Sebastian left Mooikrantz. The children could not stop talking about his wonderful motor car and when Hendrik came home it was impossible to keep Sebastian's second visit a secret from him.

"I wish you wouldn't encourage him, Sabella."

"I don't."

"Obviously you must do, or he wouldn't have paid a second visit so soon after the first!"

"He only dropped by because he happened to be in the area on business."

"Visits from someone driving the kind of car the children

132

have been describing," Hendrik said in a brooding voice, "won't have gone unnoticed in the neighbourhood. I don't want the scandal-mongers wagging their tongues again."

"What do you mean?" she asked sharply, guiltily. "Why should there be scandal – "

"People would soon put two and two together and realise who he is! They'll start talking about the son my mother sold coming back to search for his beginnings. All those old, dead cows of years ago would be raked out of the ditch."

Hendrik was proved right about one thing. Sebastian's first visit had passed unnoticed, but his second one had attracted attention, and Tante Bessie had only to question the children to discover his name. "I knew immediately that it must have been Bastian," she told Sabella. "What did he want?"

"He – well, he had only just found out that Tante Wilhelmina was his true mother," Sabella embroidered, "and he called, hoping to see her. He feels very bitter towards her."

"Poor soul," Tante Bessie said. "Who could blame him?"

That was more or less what everyone in the neighbourhood said, and the scandal Hendrik had feared settled into a general feeling of sympathy for the young man they still referred to as Bastian.

The clothes hidden in her bedroom continued to draw Sabella like a magnet. She dared not try them on for fear of discovery, but she took them out of hiding whenever she could, thinking of Sebastian and how he had remembered what she'd said about yearning for pretty, modern clothes.

She was horrified when she realised that these exquisite, secret treasures of hers were becoming affected by the musty smell which clung to Tante Wilhelmina's clothes in the chest. She decided to burn the old clothes while Hendrik was safely away in Stilstroom.

She had taken most of the garments from the chest when

she saw the small wooden box at the bottom. Inside the box she found, among other assorted objects, a cheap notebook filled with faded writing.

Her eyes were wet with tears by the time she had finished reading the contents of the notebook. She replaced all the clothes inside the chest, found another hiding place for her own treasured garments, and then set out with Ria and Daan for Tante Bessie's house, carrying the wooden box.

While the children played outside with the cats, Sabella gave Tante Bessie the notebook to read. When she had finished she touched the hem of her apron to her eyes. "If only we'd known," she kept saying.

"The point is, I think Bastian should know, don't you?"

"Oh yes, he has the right."

"I know where to contact him," Sabella said, "but Hendrik doesn't approve of his visiting Mooikrantz."

Tante Bessie looked thoughtful. "I wouldn't normally encourage a wife to go against her husband's wishes, but in this case I feel Hendrik is wrong. When will he finish milling in Stilstroom?"

"On Wednesday next week, he told me."

"Hmm. Write a note to Bastian, Sabella, asking him to call on Monday. I'll drive to Stilstroom to post it, and I'll also collect Daan and Ria on Monday morning so that Bastian will be able to read undisturbed what his mother had written."

Sabella thanked her, and waited for Monday with many mixed feelings. Her note to Bastian — as she was increasingly thinking of him — had been brief and to the point. She had found something which it was important for him to see, so important that she would be expecting him on Mooikrantz on Monday morning.

She was waiting on the front stoep when his car drew up. She didn't go to meet him, but watched him approaching, her expression sober. He had obviously caught her mood for he made no attempt to touch her, but said quietly, "Good morning, Sabella."

"I'm glad you could come, Bastian."

His head jerked back. "Don't call me that! It's what *she* called me."

Sabella merely said, "Please come inside."

He followed her into the house and she threw open the door of her bedroom. "This used to be your mother's room." She moved towards the chest. "I was going through her clothes which are stored in here when I found *this*." She took the wooden box from the chest and handed it to him. "Open it."

He sat down on the bed and slowly, with obvious reluctance, pushed back the lid of the box. He took out a pair of small, scuffed shoes and looked at them without expression. She watched him closely as he picked up a stuffed toy monkey, and saw a spasm cross his face. Several minutes went by before he spoke, and then his voice was not quite steady. "I remember this. I remember crying because it had been left behind." He gave a sour, self-mocking smile. "Stupid, isn't it, the kind of rubbish a child will grieve over. But she wouldn't even let me take it with me when she sold me."

"Read the notebook," Sabella commanded.

"I don't want to." His voice had turned stony. "I suppose it's full of excuses for what she did."

"It wasn't meant to be read by anyone. It's a diary which she kept from time to time. Read it."

Slowly, unwillingly, he opened the notebook and then said with relief, "It's in Afrikaans. I can speak and understand the language adequately, but I can't read or write it at all."

Sabella went to sit next to him, and took the notebook from his hands. "Then I'll tell you what it says. It tells of her total isolation at the end of the Boer War. Not only would nobody have anything to do with her, but they wouldn't even buy the produce of Mooikrantz. Let me translate some of the entries for you. 'Hendrik came home from school today and asked me why the other children called him a whore's son. Oh God, what are they likely to call my darling Bastian one day?' I'll skip the next few years' entries," Sabella said quickly, before he could react. "There is a gap during which she didn't write anything, and it's explained when she started again. Listen! 'Hendrik has been allowed to leave hospital, and is slowly growing stronger. I tried to raise the money to pay the medical bills by sending some of the cattle to market. No one would bid for them, because they are mine. Ewart le Roux has written to me again, an abusive letter demanding a share of Mooikrantz's profits. He won't accept that I'm unable to make a profit. Should I hand over the farm to him if he would agree to pay Hendrik's hospital bills? But if I did, where would we go? There is no one in the entire world to whom I could turn. No, I will not feel sorry for myself. I will not regret the birth of my beloved Bastian, or the brief joy I experienced with his father."

"Who," Bastian interrupted, his voice gruff, "is Ewart le Roux?"

"Wilhelmina's stepson. According to the diary, he was constantly bombarding her with letters, accusing her of stealing his inheritance, Mooikrantz, by marrying his father."

"Go on reading the diary," Bastian commanded.

Sabella turned a page. " 'Dear God, what am I to do? Bastian's father wants to bring him up as his own. It seems his wife is unable to have children. My natural instinct is to cleave to my baby at all cost, but would he thank me for it one day? How could he grow up here as anything but a misfit? Not only illegitimate, but the son of an Englishman, a son of one of the enemy? Here, he faces life as an outcast. In Johannesburg, with his father, his life would be one of advantage and prestige. Dear God, please give me the strength to make what my mind tells me is the right decision, the unselfish decision.' "

Sabella looked up. "There is only one more entry. 'They came for my baby today. I was forced to ask Peregrine for money, and I didn't have the English to explain about Hendrik's illness and medical bills. So now it will be believed that I sold my beloved Bastian. All I have left of him are his poor, scuffed little shoes and the toy monkey I made for him. Perhaps I am luckier than the baboon-mother. She has nothing. The Lord giveth, and He taketh away.'"

As Sabella put the notebook back inside the wooden box she saw that Bastian was turning the toy monkey over in his hands. "The baboon-mother – " he began, his voice sounding rusty.

"I know. You told me about her. A leopard had taken her baby."

"Yes." He dropped the toy monkey and his hand went up, covering his face. She sat down beside him, putting a comforting arm around his shoulder.

He groped blindly for her, in the way of a child seeking comfort. "If only I'd known," he muttered thickly. "If only I'd had the chance to come and see her, help her, give her comfort . . ."

Sabella stroked his hair. "Wherever she is, she'll know what you're thinking and feeling."

"Do you really believe that?" he asked, again like a child desperately seeking assurance.

"I do, Bastian."

"*Bastian*. I no longer mind being called that."

"I think it would have pleased her. It would have shown that she hadn't lost her Bastian for good, that he hadn't permanently turned into Sebastian Grant."

He clung to Sabella and gradually, imperceptibly, the grieving child blurred into a man of passion, and she felt herself being swept along in a tumult of answering need and hunger. Unthinkingly, with unreasoning urgency, they helped each other to undress.

With three younger brothers, she'd thought a naked man would hold no secrets for her. But as she recognised the obvious difference between the body of a boy and that of a man in the grip of pulsating passion, she was checked by a feeling of conscious alarm and underlying arousal. Then he moved towards her, and nothing in her previous experience had prepared her for the exquisite delight of such close bodily contact.

"I love you, Cousin Sabella," he whispered against her mouth, his hand stroking the inside of her thigh, and every trace of her alarm fled.

A shred of common sense still remaining told her that now was the time to check what would otherwise soon be completely beyond their control. Instead, she allowed him to pull her down on to the bed and twined her naked legs around his, and slid her hands along the length of his back. The common sense voice reminded her of the promises she had made Hendrik, and the awakened, abandoned one countered recklessly, *He didn't make me promise that I wouldn't commit adultery.*

But she *had* promised him that no one would ever know their marriage was not "normal" and she owed it to him not to allow Bastian to guess that she was a virgin. When he parted her lips with his own she forced herself not to show surprise, and then she wondered delightedly why the darting of his tongue inside her mouth should send such a trembling warmth throughout her being. Her fear of the unknown was suspended as he began to gentle her with kisses which sent her senses into a state of delirium.

His fingers and his lips and his tongue created tingling impulses which seemed to set her on fire, and she began to copy him, instinctively knowing that what pleasured her would do the same for him. When the moment came and he lowered his body to hers and entered her, the cry she gave was more of ecstacy than of pain and she locked her arms about him as if to bond him permanently to herself. They began to move together in a rhythm that she knew must be as old as time itself, for it came to her quite naturally. The most unimaginable, the most sensational convulsions tore through her, overwhelming her with exquisite fulfilment.

He held her close afterwards as they lay, sated for the moment. "Do you love me, Cousin Sabella?" he asked softly.

"You know I do." With her fingertip, she traced the lines of his eyebrows.

"We belong together. We're right for each other." He moved his head to kiss her shoulder.

Reality came crowding in upon her and she began to weep. "What is it, my love?" he asked, stroking her loose hair.

"We can't belong together. You'll have to leave – and never come back."

He jumped up and pulled her to her feet. "I'll be taking you with me when I leave."

"You're insane! I have three brothers and a mentally retarded sister – "

"Naturally they'll come with us, Sabella!"

She pushed him away from her and reached for her clothes. "I'm married to Hendrik. Don't pretend to have forgotten."

"You don't love him," Bastian said, pulling on his own clothes, "and there's such a thing as divorce."

She finished struggling into her clothes. "I couldn't ask Hendrik to divorce me," she said tonelessly. "I promised him that the marriage would be for life."

"*Every* married couple makes that promise – "

"This was different. It was a special promise I made him beforehand."

"And you're so moral, so upright, so *spineless* that you wouldn't break a promise under any circumstances?" Bastian demanded angrily.

"I'm *not* spineless!" she cried with matching anger. "I may not love Hendrik, but I owe him a debt. He took us in when we were homeless and penniless. In any case, what you're suggesting is madness! What do you suppose your parents and all your English friends would think if you suddenly turned up in Johannesburg with the children and myself?"

"They can damned well think what they like!"

"Your father is a Member of Parliament," she reminded him. "We wouldn't just be some anonymous couple running away together to live in sin! The newspapers would dig into the past. They would find out about your birth,

139

about your father's abuse of his position during the Boer War. As you once pointed out yourself, he would be ruined!"

"That was before I'd heard my true mother's side of the story! He would have brought his ruin upon himself. What a cold, callous creature he must have been, to have ignored both my mother and myself until he suddenly found he couldn't get an heir by any other means than by taking me away from her!"

"And if his political career is ruined through you," Sabella countered, "do you suppose you would still have a secure future with the Grant Mining Corporation?"

"No." Bastian shrugged as if it were of no consequence. "The shares my father settled on me are held in trust until my thirtieth birthday, and he'll revoke the trust. But I am quite capable of providing for all of us by my own efforts."

Their arguments continued as the morning wore on, and to all hers he had an answer. Sometimes he raged at her and called her a coward, at others he tried to seduce her into agreeing with him. But about one thing he remained adamant; he would not leave Mooikrantz unless she and the children went with him.

When Nantes and Anton returned home from school he switched his attention to them instead, talking to them in his mangled Afrikaans, taking them for spins in his motor car and generally proving to Sabella his genuine wish to share her responsibility for the children. He used the same tactics when Ria and Daan arrived home, and Sabella's heart contracted with love for him when she saw the tender sensitivity with which he behaved towards Ria.

But he was wasting his time, she thought bleakly. The lives of too many people would be ruined if she were ruthless enough to put love before everything else. The life of his father, of the woman who had brought him up as her son, of Hendrik . . .

Another thought struck her. The same publicity which would ruin Peregrine Grant would also draw the attention of the authorities to the children. It was quite inconceivable that they would allow the children to remain in the care of a sister who had run away from her husband to live in sin with another man. But she knew in advance that Bastian would sweep this argument aside as he had all the others.

She looked at the lengthening shadows thrown by the hills. Hendrik would soon be returning home. She hurried outside and ordered the children to go and tidy themselves. When they had reluctantly left Bastian's side and she was alone with him she said with agitation, "Please, please go now! Hendrik will be home soon and he doesn't know that I'd sent for you. It would be very difficult to explain to him – "

A reckless light leapt into Bastian's eyes. "If I told him that I'd taken you to bed, would he throw you out?"

"No, he wouldn't," she said quietly. "He is terrified of attracting scandal, and it would seem like his mother's story all over again. He would keep the knowledge to himself, but it would strain our life together unbearably and I would never forgive you."

Bastian sighed. "Very well. I'll hide the truth from him – for the time being. But I'm not leaving. I shall tell Hendrik that I'd decided it was high time I met my half-brother."

There was an immediate mutual antipathy between Hendrik and Bastian when they met a short while later. Sabella realised that there was more to it than the fact that, as far as Bastian was concerned, Hendrik was the one who stood between the two of them, and Hendrik's hostility could not have been explained away simply by the fact that Bastian's very existence had been the cause of the scandal under whose shadow he had grown up. They would, she sensed, have disliked one another under any circumstances.

Outwardly, Hendrik was polite to his half-brother and invited him to stay for as long as he liked. Bastian thanked him in his fractured Afrikaans and they sat in the kitchen, making stilted conversation while Sabella prepared supper.

Hendrik suddenly cut through something Bastian was

141

saying by exclaiming sharply, "Sabella, you didn't wash your hands before peeling those potatoes!"

She went outside to the water pump, wishing Hendrik hadn't revealed his obsession in the presence of Bastian, who would only use it as further ammunition in his battle to persuade her to run away with him.

She squirmed again after supper, when Hendrik began to dry and then polish the dishes and cutlery as he usually did, and returned several utensils to her with the comment, "This is not what I would call *clean*, my dear."

When the children had been washed and the kitchen had been made as spotless as Hendrik demanded it should be, he said, "Sabella, my dear, I should like a word in private with you in our bedroom."

She had never been with him in his bedroom before. The only occasions on which she entered it was when she changed the sheets, because he chose to clean the room himself. Now, she stood stiffly in the centre of the room while he lit candles. "You will," he said, his voice expressionless, "share this bed with me while Bastian Grant is on Mooikrantz."

"But – but surely – I'd thought of letting him have Ria's room, and she could share with me – "

"And risk him finding out, and encouraging him to jeer at me in secret? Oh no!" Hendrik's voice brooked no argument. "While I keep him company you'll move your things in here so that he may have your room."

Sabella chewed at her lower lip. It would not suit her, either, to have Bastian discover that she did not share Hendrik's bed, because it would give him so much more scope for putting pressure on her. She nodded, and went to prepare her room for Bastian's use.

Dressed in her enveloping nightgown, she lay rigidly on the edge of Hendrik's bed later, waiting for him to join her and at the same time blessing the fact that the old-fashioned bed was large enough for three adults. Hendrik snuffed out the candles before he undressed, and she could hear him grunting as he put on a nightshirt. Panic suddenly

142

swept over her. What if their close proximity should overcome his distaste for what he called "husbandly duty"? She would not be able to bear it if he made an intimate approach to her, especially not after what had happened this morning, with Bastian. She felt Hendrik climbing into bed, and relaxed slowly as she realised that he, too, was keeping as far away as possible on his own side of the bed.

Poor Hendrik, she couldn't help thinking. So repressed, so emotionally warped. The bed-springs creaked as he turned over, still hugging the extreme edge of the bed.

Her mind strayed to Bastian as she too changed position with a creaking of springs. Only a wall separated them and she fought an overwhelming desire to creep out of bed when Hendrik fell asleep and join him.

But Hendrik was so tightly strung that she could tell he was only pretending to be asleep, and she too lay awake. Oh God, she thought, what if Bastian stays and stays, as he is quite capable of doing? We couldn't go on like this night after night . . .

She greeted the dawn with a gratitude which she felt certain Hendrik fully shared. She pretended to be asleep as he rose and pulled on his clothes and went outside to wash at the pump. She got up too, lighting the range in the kitchen, feeling tired and tense and apprehensive.

When Hendrik had left for the fields and Nantes and Anton for school, Bastian told Daan, "Why don't you take Ria and go and sit in my motor car? You could take it in turns to pretend to drive."

No objection Sabella could have thought up would have kept Daan and Ria from running to take advantage of such an offer. Alone together in the kitchen, Bastian turned to Sabella, looking at her with angry frustration. "I'm leaving this morning," he said in a way that made it clear he was flinging down an ultimatum. "I can't spend another sleepless night under this roof, listening to the creaking of the springs of the bed you share with another man."

"Oh . . ." The relief she felt was heavily tainted with desolation.

But he had not admitted defeat after all. He tilted her chin with his forefinger. "Let us go and fetch Nantes and Anton from school," he urged, "and leave for Johannesburg with the children."

"No."

"Give me a reason I can accept, Sabella, for refusing even to consider it!"

She had already told him of her fears of having the children taken away from her, but he had dismissed them. His English blood and upbringing had given him the kind of arrogance that convinced him he would be able to fight the authorities and win custody of the children. Her own Afrikaans instincts told her that the authorities would rigidly enforce the decisions they had made after Pa's death. But Bastian would never entertain the possibility of defeat, and it was useless to go over the same ground once again.

He cupped her face between his palms. "You can't think of a convincing reason! I love you, Sabella, and you love me. We belong together. Please come away with me, you and the children."

"I can't. You'll never understand." The stark, fundamental truth was that she had to make a choice between Bastian and the children, and how could she spell out to him that she *had* to put the children before him when he wouldn't accept that she needed to make a choice?

"You'll never understand," she repeated deliberately, "because of the way you've been brought up. The sacrifice would be too great."

"There's no sacrifice I wouldn't gladly make – "

"*Your* sacrifice?" she echoed brutally. "I'm talking about the sacrifices *I* would have to make! Here on Mooikrantz the children and I have security. I can't throw that away and go off with you into some uncertain future."

He stared at her. "I've told you, I'm perfectly capable of earning a living for all of us – "

She interrupted him with a derisive sound. "You may

144

think you are, Bastian! It's because you've never known what it is to be poor. Look at you, with your expensive clothes and your gold watch and the diamond pin in your tie! Look at your nice, smooth hands and your well-trimmed fingernails. What kind of work do you think you'd find once your father has disinherited you and your English friends have turned their backs on you?"

"I'll find something, damn you!" he ground out, clearly flicked on the raw.

She forced herself to arrange a look of scorn on her face. "As a labourer with a road-making gang, perhaps? I've known what it's like to be hungry all the time. I'm not prepared to face that kind of life again, or plunge my family into it. With Hendrik we have security; with you we'd face starvation."

"Thank you so much," Bastian said tautly, his eyes glittering with cold rage, "for your touching faith in me." He turned and strode to the door, where he stopped. "Go on playing safe and stay here, buried alive with my warped half-brother. I'll think of you sometimes, washing your hands before you're allowed to peel potatoes. But we won't meet again."

Moments later she heard his car speeding away from Mooikrantz. Daan and Ria came into the kitchen, weeping their disappointment at the abrupt departure of the fascinating new-found friend and his fascinating car. Sabella dried her own eyes and gathered the children to her in an automatic gesture of comfort.

Just like Tante Wilhelmina all those years ago when she'd let Bastian go, there wasn't a mortal soul to whom Sabella could have turned for comfort in her own grief and loss.

As the weeks slipped by the cheerless aridity of life on Mooikrantz was altered by two developments, one of them so cataclysmic that Sabella became swamped by growing despair at its many implications.

She was pregnant. She hadn't realised it at first, never having been told the symptoms of early pregnancy. Ma,

145

of course, would never have dreamt of discussing such a subject with her, and it was from other girls at school that she'd learnt how babies were conceived. But what happened between conception and birth had been a mystery to all of them, and not sufficiently exciting to be researched. On one thing the more knowledgeable girls had been agreed. One couldn't possibly become pregnant "the first time".

So, when her monthly flow failed to appear, Sabella thought it was probably because she felt so drained and wretched from longing for Bastian. Then, one morning, the smell of the breakfast coffee sent her, gagging and heaving, at a run towards the crude corrugated iron structure which enclosed a hole in the ground and was Mooikrantz's lavatory.

A mental picture formed in her mind after she had been sick. A picture of Ma, almost six years ago, turning pale at breakfast-time each morning and hurrying to the privy. This had gone on until her spare, thin body began to acquire a distinctive bump at the front.

Inconsequentially, Sabella remembered the first time she had ever consciously seen a pregnant woman. She had been about ten years old at the time, and when she asked Ma why the lady had such a fat stomach when she was otherwise quite thin, Ma had explained that it was a hernia, caused by lifting heavy objects. Sabella had been surprised after that to discover how many women there were in Westdene who suffered from hernias – until an older girl at school told her the truth.

Wild laughter bubbled in her throat. If only Hendrik might be persuaded that she, too, suffered from a hernia once her pregnancy became obvious . . . Then terror flowed through her. How would Hendrik react when he found out that she was expecting a baby? It would indeed be like his mother's adultery all over again. In all probability, his fear of scandal would cause him to pass the child off as his own, but oh God, he would make her pay in so many ways for what she had done. And he would not be indifferent to the baby as he was indifferent to her brothers and sister. He would be unable to stop himself from regarding it as unclean; he would hate it and make it suffer in the years to come, pretending to himself and others that he was "disciplining" it.

She would have tried to seduce him by slipping into his bed and inviting intimacy, so that she could make him believe he was the father of the child growing inside her. But she knew in advance how hopeless that idea was. She only had to remember how he had lain, tense and awake, as far away from her as possible on the one night they had shared a bed.

One morning something happened that took her mind, temporarily, from her growing problems. Hendrik had left for the fields and Nantes and Anton for school and Sabella was clearing away the breakfast dishes when she heard the unfamiliar sound of a motor vehicle approaching. Her first heady, heart-stopping thought was that it was Bastian. But when she hurried out to the stoep, Daan and Ria following her, she saw that the vehicle drawing up outside the house was a motor van. A stranger stepped from the cab and approached. He wore a city suit and a trilby hat, which he removed to reveal heavily oiled hair slicked back from his forehead. His upper lip was outlined by a pencil-thin moustache which lent a slightly sinister air to the smile he offered Sabella. He greeted her in fumbling, groping Afrikaans and introduced himself as Mr Steedman.

"I am fluent in English," Sabella said. "My name is Mrs le Roux. How may I help you?"

The man looked both disconcerted and puzzled. "Pierre's sister-in-law, perhaps?" he asked.

"Pierre?" she echoed blankly.

"Pierre le Roux. I'm a friend of his."

She was on the point of disclaiming any connection with a Pierre le Roux when it struck her that he might well be the son of Hendrik's other half-brother, Ewart. "I think you could be referring to my husband's half-nephew, if there is such a thing," she said.

For some reason Mr Steedman's face fell, but he recovered his poise quickly. "May I ask, Mrs le Roux, for how long you have been married and living here?"

"Two years," she answered, frowning at the intrusive question.

"It's just that I was surprised," Mr Steedman explained quickly, smoothly. "Pierre didn't mention you. The only Mrs le Roux I expected to find here was his grandmother. Obviously, he hasn't visited Mooikrantz since your marriage. I know that he used to call as often as he could to see his grandmother."

"I see." Sabella made her expression inscrutable. Either Pierre le Roux was a liar, or this man was. "What brings you here, Mr Steedman?"

"I'm looking for a small farm to buy as an investment for when I retire one day. Pierre said his grandmother might be prepared to sell Mooikrantz."

"She was his step-grandmother, Mr Steedman, and she died almost four years ago. If he did pay visits to her while she was alive, Pierre le Roux must have done so in great secrecy."

To her astonishment, Mr Steedman seemed to miss the sarcasm in her suggestion and accepted it almost with relief, as if it had added credibility to his story. "That was probably it! There had been some kind of falling out in the family, hadn't there?"

Sabella said nothing. This man, instinct told her, was not to be trusted.

"The farm has passed to your husband?" he wanted to know.

She nodded. "I'm quite sure he wouldn't be interested in selling it."

"He might be persuaded if the price was right." The man's eyes scanned the hills. "Would you mind if I took a walk out there, and had a look at the potential of the farm?"

"I'm sorry, but my husband is the person you should approach. You would find him in the fields, busy with the

148

last of the harvest." She gave him directions to the fields and he set off in his van to follow the track for as far as he could before completing the journey on foot.

That evening, during supper, Hendrik had the most astonishing story to impart about their meeting. "The man finally admitted, after I'd made it clear Mooikrantz was not for sale at any price and I'd asked him some blunt questions, that he doesn't know Pierre le Roux at all. Steedman buys and sells second-hand furniture and it turned out that he'd bought an old desk from my half-brother Ewart. Stuck between two of its drawers were some letters which gave him the names of my mother, of this farm, and also letters written home to his family by Pierre le Roux. Steedman would have thrown the letters away if he hadn't come across another document also trapped between the drawers. Have you heard of the Kruger millions, Sabella?"

"No . . ."

"It's gold in half-minted form, said to have been hidden on behalf of President Kruger in the last stages of the Boer War. It has never been found and it may not even exist at all. But this man Steedman says he found a document dated a year before the war ended which suggests it is buried somewhere on Mooikrantz. He offered to share the treasure with me if I would give him permission to dig wherever he pleased!" Hendrik made a sound of contempt. "As if I would have my land laid waste in search of fools' gold! I sent him on his way, but I'm afraid we haven't seen the last of him."

And indeed they hadn't. While Sabella worried and agonised and suffered every kind of torment about the baby she was expecting, not only did Steedman return to Mooikrantz with bribes and promises in exchange for permission to dig on the farm, but somehow the story about the Kruger millions spread and daily other men arrived at the house, with picks and shovels packed on carts or wagons or mules, also begging to be allowed to dig. Hendrik became increasingly angry as he sent them away.

The lure of gold affected Anton too, and Nantes to

a lesser degree. They came home later than usual from school each day, and Sabella knew that it was because they had been upending boulders and scooping out earth with improvised implements. She lectured them angrily, because she couldn't believe that the Kruger millions would have been hidden on Mooikrantz. Of all the farms in the district, it was the only one which had remained occupied by its owner during the Boer War, with servants tending livestock in the hills and an English officer paying regular visits to the house. Was it likely that anyone would have chosen it as a hiding place when there had been so many other, derelict farms where the gold – if it existed at all – could have been hidden with no fear of anyone secretly watching?

If only, Sabella thought wanly, she had been able to believe in the possibility that there was buried treasure on Mooikrantz. She would have clawed and scrabbled in the earth herself until she had found it, and solved her problems by taking the children and running as far away as she could.

One morning Tante Bessie called on her so early that Sabella was forced to offer her coffee and in spite of the iron control she had learnt to force upon herself to hide her nausea Tante Bessie's sharp eyes weren't fooled. "When are you going to tell Hendrik about the baby?" she asked bluntly.

"I – " Sabella swallowed, trying to think of a believable excuse. "Tante Bessie, I want to be quite sure there's no chance of my losing the baby. Ma," she lied wildly, "lost several babies during the first months of pregnancy and I – I'm afraid I might have inherited the weakness from her. So please, *please* say nothing to Hendrik to – raise his hopes – before all danger has passed. Besides, I want to tell him myself."

"Yes, he deserves to hear it from you, but he should hear it *now*." Tante Bessie leant forward, an intense expression in her small black eyes. "Sabella, I also lost every single one of the three babies I conceived during my marriage. I believe I lost them for the same reason your Ma lost hers. I wasn't brave or wise enough to stop my husband from bothering me in bed. You *must* tell Hendrik, and explain to him that it's important he gives up his marital rights for a few months."

Sabella fought the hysterical laughter rising in her throat. Instead she said with as much conviction as she could muster, "Tante Bessie, I can't help it but I'm superstitious. I've got it fixed in my mind that if I say anything before the baby starts to show, I'll lose it. Please promise to keep my secret!"

Tanté Bessie gave her a long, strange look. "I won't *tell* Hendrik," she said at last, with an emphasis Sabella could not understand but which worried her.

She soon realised that she had cause to worry. Tante Bessie became a far more regular visitor than usual, and stayed until Hendrik returned from the fields, and every day she brought with her some knitting. She had, she'd explained, unravelled a white woollen shawl of hers for which she no longer had any use, and when Nantes asked with interest what she was knitting she told him, "It's a secret, but it's for someone very small."

So that, Sabella thought with doom, was how she meant to tell Hendrik about the coming baby. Not in words, but by letting him see a baby garment taking shape as she wielded her knitting needles.

I might as well tell him and get it done with, Sabella thought dully. He'll have to know some time, so what am I achieving by putting off the moment?

One afternoon she was staring at the lacy pattern forming in whatever garment Tante Bessie was knitting when she heard the sound of a motor vehicle approaching. It had become a familiar sound and she recognised it immediately as Mr Steedman's van. All her worry and despair became channelled into anger instead, and she leapt from her chair and hurried out to the stoep.

"My husband has told you again and again," she screamed at Mr Steedman, "to keep away from his land!

151

You may *not* dig anywhere on Mooikrantz! There's a loaded gun in the parlour and if you don't remove yourself at once I'll fetch it and – "

"You – you don't understand." Mr Steedman was twisting his hat in his hands so that it almost resembled a wrung-out washing rag. He was not wearing city clothes this time, but an old pair of trousers and an open-necked shirt, and she noticed that he looked very pale. "There's been – I'm afraid something very bad has happened."

"What do you mean?" Sabella asked sharply.

Mr Steedman moistened his lips. "I've brought your husband home." He half-turned to indicate his van, and for the first time Sabella noticed the humped shape in the back, covered by a khaki blanket. She ran past Mr Steedman and he tried to stop her as she clambered on to the van but she brushed him aside and pulled the blanket away.

A scream rose in her throat but turned into bile instead. Her hand clapped to her mouth, she sprang from the van and then Tante Bessie was at her side, holding her head as she retched violently but drily.

Sabella straightened up. "All that – blood," she whispered jerkily. Her eyes fastened upon Mr Steedman. "You – battered him to death. You murderer . . ."

"No, Missus!" he protested, jamming his hat on his head and then wiping his face with a handkerchief. "He was killed by a baboon."

"You liar!" Hysterical rage had strengthened her voice. "Hendrik grew up among the baboons! He knew how to handle them! *And the blood came from the back of his head!* If a baboon did attack, it wouldn't do so from behind!"

"He wasn't attacked, Missus. A big, male baboon fell on him."

"*Fell!*" she shouted. "Baboons leap, and scramble, and swing themselves from rock to rock! *They do not fall!*"

"They bloody do!" Steedman roared, his own self-control deserting him. "When they're pissed as a fiddler's bitch, they bloody do!"

Sabella was silenced, staring at him. She hadn't understood what he'd meant. The sight of Hendrik's head lying in a pool of his own blood haunted her, and part of her mind gave thanks for the fact that the children were all playing by the river and she would be able to spare them the worst horror of what had happened.

Tante Bessie decided to take control of the situation. "Do you know any Afrikaans?" she addressed Steedman in that language.

"A little."

"Right. Now tell us, as well as you can, exactly what happened."

He did so, haltingly, groping for the right words. In defiance of Hendrik's refusal to allow him to dig on his land, Mr Steedman had drawn his van off the road and camouflaged it with tree branches, and for the past week he had been camping among the hills, searching for the Kruger millions. But Hendrik's suspicions had obviously been aroused for today Mr Steedman had seen him leave the fields and walk towards the hills, carrying his binoculars.

"I watched him climb a marula tree to get a better view," Steedman said, and shuddered. "It never struck me that he might be in danger. I'd seen the baboon climb the same tree earlier. First it had eaten what berries it could find on the ground, and I could tell it was pretty drunk by the time it swung itself clumsily up into the tree to look for more berries at the top – "

"Drunk?" Sabella interrupted incredulously. "That's nonsense – "

"No," Tante Bessie assured her. "Now that the harvest has been gathered and food is scarce, a baboon *would* scavenge for something like marula berries. Those lying on the ground would have been fermenting. Marula is highly intoxicating, Sabella, and with the baboon drunk and Hendrik frightening it by climbing the same tree, it's quite true that it could have fallen like a dead weight on Hendrik instead of leaping clear."

153

"The beast knocked him down," Mr Steedman confirmed, looking vastly relieved that Tante Bessie had accepted his story. "He fell heavily on a rock and the baboon staggered away. By the time I'd managed to get Mr le Roux on to the back of my van I could tell he was dying. He never had a chance, not with his skull split open like that."

"You'll have to drive the body to Stilstroom," Tante Bessie directed. "Take him to Doctor Pelzer, who'll deal with everything and call in the proper authorities." She turned to Sabella. "And you, my dear, had better go and lie down. I'll heat some milk for you."

Poor Hendrik, Sabella thought as she allowed Tante Bessie to lead her inside the house. Poor Hendrik. All he had wanted of life was to be considered normal, but nothing had ever been normal for him, and his death had been bizarre in the extreme. Killed by having a drunken baboon fall on him . . .

But later that night as she lay in bed, unable to sleep, other reactions began to set in. Guilt was the uppermost, and it gnawed away at her. The timing of Hendrik's death had been so convenient for herself, so opportune, so in-the-nick-of-time. She couldn't rid herself of the morbid feeling that she had somehow, subconsciously, wished Hendrik's death on him.

She turned over in bed, longing for sleep. Because of her pregnancy and because of the grief she innocently expected Sabella to be feeling, Tante Bessie had insisted on taking over the practical arrangements for the funeral. Tomorrow she intended driving to Stilstroom in her pony and trap and buying black-bordered cards so that one could be sent to every neighbour. Everyone in the district would know by now that Hendrik had been killed, and how, and would swiftly learn by word of mouth when the funeral was to be, but still Tante Bessie insisted that things had to be done in the proper way and the black-bordered cards sent out.

I must remember, Sabella told herself, to ask her to post

a card to Ewart le Roux. I wonder if he knows that Hendrik had left Mooikrantz to him in his will?

Her heart lifted, at the same time deepening her feeling of guilt. It didn't matter at all that Ewart would be inheriting Mooikrantz, because she would be sending a black-bordered card to Bastian, Hendrik's other half-brother. It would contain nothing more than the news that Hendrik was dead and the announcement of the time and date of his funeral.

But in spite of the quarrel with which they had parted, Bastian would hurry to Mooikrantz, because the black-bordered note would also tell him that she was now free, and that there was no reason remaining in the world why the two of them should not marry once a reasonable time had elapsed to show respect to Hendrik's memory.

She smiled with guilty joy as she imagined Bastian's face when she told him about his baby she was expecting.

Part Two

Winter 1924

7

Pierre le Roux sat on the top deck of the tram as it rattled its way through the Johannesburg suburbs. The tin box on his lap, which had held his lunch-time sandwiches, was now filled with a selection of the most expensive Continental chocolates imported and sold by Bozzoli & Ferguson. It was intended for his landlady, and should be worth at least a ten-shilling cut in next month's board and lodging. The chocolates were worth far more than that on the market, and his landlady knew it. Unfortunately, she also knew that he had helped himself to them, and so he would just have to be grateful for the saving of ten shillings towards the fulfilment of his Big Dream.

Pierre grinned sourly to himself. A drop in the ocean! He might as well stop fooling himself. Petty pilfering from Bozzoli & Ferguson was never going to provide him with the capital he needed. And if he didn't find that capital in time, Ernest Trump would give up the idea of a partnership and go it alone.

With genuine respect, Pierre thought of Ernest Trump. He, too, worked for Bozzoli & Ferguson and he, too, had been milking the luxury food emporium but in a systematic, visionary way, with an eye to the future.

It was Pierre's job, as stores manager, to make sure that orders were filled and packed up so that Ernest could drive them for delivery to wealthy customers in out-of-the-way places like Pretoria. And it was Pierre who had spotted, some time ago, that something odd was afoot regarding those orders.

"Look here," he'd challenged Ernest, "these invoices show that customers you deliver to, who used to place regular orders for certain items like Continental sausages and potted pâtés from France, now only want them very occasionally. I ought to know, because I've made up the orders more times than I care to remember. I think Mr Ferguson might be interested to find out what jaded the appetites of the customers for those particular goodies."

"Mr Ferguson," Ernest Trump had returned calmly, "might be just as interested to find out why so many perishables which had reached their prime and remained unsold were never donated to the Salvation Army as they should have been."

It hadn't been lost on Pierre that Ernest Trump had done his homework in advance, anticipating that if anyone were to spot the inexplicable dropping off of sales of certain lines it would be the stores manager. As well as his good looks and charm, Pierre's most valuable asset was his ability to present an image of himself most likely to appeal to any particular individual, and so he'd said with a rueful shrug, "There was another army in as great a need of those perishables – my army of starving relatives on their worked-out smallholding outside Johannesburg."

It was true that the smallholding was worked out, but there was no army of relatives starving on it. Pierre's father Ewart had died of drink a year ago; his mother had run off with another man when Pierre was eleven and he didn't even know if she was still alive. His sister was married and living in a Johannesburg suburb and only his younger brother Louis remained on the smallholding, scratching a living by keeping chickens and the odd turkey.

But the lie, aimed to appeal to the devoted family man in Ernest Trump, had not really been necessary, because it turned out that Trump had realised a long time ago that he had a potential ally in Pierre. "Between the two of us," he'd said, "we could build up a business that would give Bozzoli & Ferguson a run for their money."

"How?" Pierre asked, curious and excited.

"I'd better start at the beginning. As we both know, Bozzoli & Ferguson ship most of their stock from Britain and the Continent. Not only does that make the merchandise very expensive, but it means that by the time things like German or Italian sausages and salamis reach Johannesburg they've lost much of their flavour through spending so long in transit. So I started thinking about all the foreigners living right here in Johannesburg; the Italians and French and Germans and Greeks – "

"Now you come to mention them," Pierre broke in, "those people don't buy from Bozzoli & Ferguson. Most of them probably couldn't afford to do so on a regular basis, but you'd think that just occasionally, as a special treat, they would buy one of their imported national delicacies."

"Exactly! And the reason, I've discovered, why they don't buy from Bozzoli & Ferguson is because they make their own national delicacies! By doing some very thorough research I found several French families who make their own pâtés; I befriended Germans whose women-folk make traditional smoked sausages and Italians who make salamis and also their own fresh pasta. And that is just to mention a few. To begin with I asked the women to make, at my expense, samples of their national specialities and when I next made my delivery to customers of Bozzoli & Ferguson, I said to them: 'Look, I'm sorry, but our shipment of potted galantines from France, or Italian or German sausage – or whatever – has been held up, but Bozzoli & Ferguson managed to get supplies of similar products elsewhere and they want you to accept them with their compliments.'"

"But you must have lost a lot of money on the deal," Pierre exclaimed, "because the invoices would still have shown that Bozzoli & Ferguson *had* supplied the complete orders!" To Pierre, accustomed to exploiting any situation for profit, no matter how small, it seemed to be a shocking waste. "Unless, of course, you sold the Bozzoli & Ferguson imports to other markets?"

"What my family couldn't eat, I destroyed." Ernest

Trump gave him a sharp look. "And if you're to come in with me, *you'll* have to stop selling pilfered produce to other markets. Your greed would lead to our downfall." He returned to the original subject. "My gamble paid off because – as I'd expected – when I next made a visit to the customers who'd tried out the locally-made delicacies they all raved about them. In future, they said, they wanted them instead of the imported stuff. So I opened a bank account in the name of Quality Victuals, had some invoices printed, and every time I delivered to these customers, the home-made Italian or German sausages, the French pâtés and the Scottish haggis were all separately invoiced to Quality Victuals. Well, no, not every time," he corrected himself. "As you know from the invoices, I had to take an occasional loss by ordering those products from Bozzoli & Ferguson in the customers' names and giving them to my family to eat. I implied to the customers, without saying so, that Quality Victuals was an offshoot of Bozzoli & Ferguson, operating from the address on the invoices – my own – so that orders for goods from Quality Victuals were never sent to Bozzoli & Ferguson. But now the time is coming for me to expand. I want to leave the firm and take on more outworkers to supply more customers. And I want you to come in with me as a partner."

"Why me?" Pierre asked, highly flattered.

"Not because of your honesty," Ernest returned drily. "Because you have access to the names and addresses of all of Bozzoli & Ferguson's customers, and we could sell to them direct. How much capital do you have?"

"Well – a pound or two."

"You'd need at least three hundred. I'll give you nine months to raise it. I can't wait any longer than that, because I want to employ more outworkers to make such things as game pies and handmade chocolates and Continental patis-serie. Besides, the longer we delay the more chance there'll be of Bozzoli & Ferguson getting wind of what's going on. They could easily offer the outworkers a higher price for their produce and Quality Victuals would not only go out of business, but you and I would find ourselves without jobs – myself for having poached the firm's customers and you for having turned a blind eye to it."

That had been several weeks ago. Pierre gazed unseeingly out of the tram window as he recalled the ultimatum. Apart from paying the outworkers, cash was needed for renting a warehouse and installing refrigeration, and for buying at least one delivery van. He reflected with bitterness that it was beginning to look more and more as if he would have to say goodbye to the chance of attaining his Big Dream which Trump had offered him.

Eleven years he had spent in chasing the Big Dream which was, simply, to become very, very rich. Since running away from the wretched family smallholding at fourteen he had done anything, tried every way. There had been a period spent in prospecting for diamonds at Hopetown and when that failed he'd sold water to other diggers. At one stage he had even tried his hand at professional gambling at the diggings, but he'd lost more often than he'd won, and then he had decided to see what Johannesburg could offer. But in this city he had come up against the exclusive English wall which denied him, as an Afrikaner, anything but dead-end, poorly-paid jobs in the gold mines or in factories. So he had deliberately set out to improve his English to a high standard but even that had not been enough. The best it had offered him was the job as stores manager with Bozzoli & Ferguson, heading a team of black packers and sorters.

He thought with frustration of the elaborate scheme he had first dreamt up for raising the capital he needed. He had taken an eight-carat diamond he'd found years ago at Hopetown and had kept as a bitter memento, and visited Mr Hill-Carstairs, one of Johannesburg's most eminent diamond dealers who also happened to be a geologist.

"Would you please take a look at this," Pierre had said, affecting a barely-contained inner excitement mixed with doubt as he unwrapped his handkerchief in which he had folded the diamond. "I picked it up a short while ago and

163

I just wondered . . . No, it's silly; I'm just wasting your time and making a fool of myself . . . It couldn't possibly be a diamond – could it?"

Hill-Carstairs examined the stone and then, with regret tingeing his professionalism, confirmed what Pierre had known from the outset. "It is, but I'm afraid it's not a gem diamond but one that would only have industrial use and is of very little value."

"Oh." Pierre allowed himself a visible swallow of bitter disappointment. Then, with the air of a man unwilling to relinquish a dream, he asked, "Tell me, sir – am I right in thinking that where there are industrial diamonds, there are also likely to be valuable gems?"

"That's right, yes." Hill-Carstairs looked at him with curiosity. "Where did you find this stone?"

"I – Well, I'd rather not say." Pierre's expression was an appeal for understanding. "I don't want to start a rush to the place, because if I can raise some capital I want to prospect there myself." Then, as if it had been something that had only just occurred to him, he came out with the true reason for consulting the expert. "What you said a moment ago, sir – about it being likely there are valuable diamonds where an industrial one was found – well . . . I just wondered if you'd be willing to put it in writing for me. It may help, you see, to persuade someone to back me financially and make it possible for me to go prospecting."

Hill-Carstairs looked at him and his expression said that he was seeing what Pierre wanted him to see – some poor naive innocent who couldn't even identify a diamond for certain when he saw one, let alone tell an industrial stone from a valuable gem, and who desperately needed a dream to which to cling. "Very well," Hill-Carstairs said, picking up a pen. "I'll put it in writing for you, and wish you the best of luck."

Pierre's next port of call was a firm of money-lenders, Steedman Brothers, from whom he'd been forced to borrow small sums in the past. There were three of them but the brother he saw was Harry Steedman. To him Pierre showed the industrial diamond and Hill–Carstairs's note and asked for a loan of three hundred pounds. "And where's your collateral?" Harry Steedman demanded bluntly.

For once Pierre didn't need to play a part. His surprise and bewilderment were genuine as he indicated the geologist's note. "Here, of course. It *proves* there are diamonds where I picked up the industrial stone."

"It doesn't prove that you picked it up. Someone could have given it to you or sold it to you as the real thing. If you did pick it up, the note doesn't prove you're going to find a stone worth three hundred pounds plus interest. It doesn't prove, either, that you would get permission to prospect wherever it is you say you found the industrial diamond."

Inspiration struck Pierre. "I found it on my grandmother's farm, so there'll be no problems about getting permission to prospect."

Steedman's eyes narrowed. "Hmm . . . If it's your grandmother's farm, why do you need such a large loan? You could live with your grandmother, and all you'd need would be a pick and shovel, a sieve and water. If you found diamond-bearing kimberlite *then* I'd consider lending you three hundred pounds."

Pierre had been thinking quickly. There was no point in confusing the issue by mentioning Hendrik le Roux, he'd decided. Pretending to be putting all his cards on the table, he said, "There's a bit of a problem. My father fell out, years ago, with my grandmother, and since his death I've been healing the breach by paying visits to her. It was during such a visit that I picked up the industrial diamond. She has made a will, leaving the farm between myself and my brother and sister. I won't be doing any prospecting until my grandmother dies, and the real reason why I need the loan is because I want to buy out their share of the inheritance from my brother and sister."

"Words," Steedman responded succinctly. "That's all you've offered me. No proof, no collateral. Therefore, no loan."

English bastard, Pierre thought with rage. He didn't attempt to hide the rage as he snarled, "I'm sorry, but I can hardly hop on a train to Stilstroom and visit Mooikrantz to ask my grandmother to lend me her will, so that I can get hold of the money to buy out my brother and sister before they discover there are diamonds on the farm!"

He had the malicious satisfaction of seeing that Harry Steedman was rapidly writing down the information he had deliberately allowed to slip. Let him go and waste his time and efforts by sniffing around Mooikrantz for diamonds that didn't exist, Pierre thought vengefully.

It had afforded him considerable amusement since then to learn that Steedman had, indeed, departed for Mooikrantz. His story that he was searching for the Kruger millions had fooled only the naive, and every prospector with diamond-fever burning in his blood had followed him there, adopting the same alibi Steedman had so conveniently handed them.

Pierre picked up his lunch tin and got off the tram, beginning to walk towards his lodgings, Oh, it was funny all right, thinking of all those prospectors scrambling over Mooikrantz on a fool's errand, but it wasn't going to do a single damned thing to bring him closer to finding a way of raising capital. The irony was that any bank manager would have lent him the money if he'd explained the true reason why he wanted it, but for the fact that he'd have to disclose the way he and Ernest Trump planned to cream off the best customers of their employers.

As he entered the house where he lodged, his landlady came scuttling out of the kitchen. Before he could show her the contents of his lunch tin and begin haggling about the size of the discount the chocolates were worth, she fished inside her apron pocket and brought out a telegram.

"This came for you," she said, her expression avid.

He ripped open the seal and read the telegram. "Not bad news, I hope," he heard his landlady say, in a tone that made it clear bad news was no more than could be

166

expected from a telegram, and would he hurry up and share it with her.

"The most wonderful news in the whole damned world!" Pierre responded with a whoop of joy, and catching hold of her, danced a little jig in the hall. She protested angrily, pulled herself free, and then asked with blunt inquisitiveness what his good news had been.

He was on the point of telling her, but stopped. She saw him as a bit of a scalliwag with a fondness for women and gambling, someone who financed his proclivities by pilfering from his employers who, in her opinion, could well afford the loss and had it coming to them anyway, them with their fancy foods for which they charged sums an ordinary person could live on for a month. He never knew when he might need her goodwill again, and there was no point in shocking her by telling her what the telegram had said.

So he smiled mysteriously, shook his head, and read again the magic words telegraphed to him by his brother Louis. *"Hendrik le Roux dead. Funeral Friday afternoon."*

Two brief sentences that meant he was about to get his hands on the capital he needed to go into partnership with Ernest Trump. Who would have thought his salvation would come from that direction? Hendrik le Roux's heart, according to the man's late mother, should have been sound for at least another three years and more probably for eight or nine.

Tomorrow, Pierre told himself with a broad grin, he would ask for compassionate leave and make the arrangements to travel to Mooikrantz.

On the morning of Hendrik's funeral the earth was covered by the blanket of the winter's first frost, which produced a crunching sound as Tante Bessie set out from Mooikrantz in her pony and trap to drive to Stilstroom and collect the mail. It was all part of the ritual of burial, for there would be more black-bordered envelopes addressed to Sabella by neighbours, expressing their condolences, and people reading these notes after the funeral would be mortally offended if they did not find their own among them.

As Sabella busied herself with other practical tasks which formed part of the burial ritual, such as roasting a leg of lamb of which cold slices would be offered to the mourners later, she tried not to think of the most macabre part of the whole ritual.

Hendrik's body lay on display in the parlour, inside an open coffin. The lid would not be screwed down until everyone had had a last look at his remains, and his widow had pressed her lips to his cold, dead ones which had never invited a kiss from her while he was alive. She dreaded the thought of it, just as she dreaded the silent condemnation from the neighbours when she failed to appear prostrate with grief. But how *could* she put on a show of grief when Bastian would be coming today, and they would be married after a token period of respect for Hendrik's memory?

She had just taken the roast lamb out of the oven when she heard the sound of Tante Bessie returning. The old woman placed a pile of letters on the table and reached for an apron so that she could help with the preparations for the mourning feast.

Sabella sat down and began to slit open the black-bordered envelopes which had been ritually posted by neighbours at Stilstroom, then franked, and then collected from the same place by Tante Bessie. Sabella read the stilted messages of condolence and put them aside to join the pile of others already received.

Frowning slightly, she saw that one letter was conspicuously without a black border. She slit open the envelope and a moment later the words of the note it contained swam before her gaze in a chaos of disbelief and anguish.

The note was from Mrs Eliza Grant. "Since you had communicated with Sebastian at Grant Mining Corporation," she had written, "and marked the envelope both URGENT and PRIVATE, his secretary sent it on to me. I decided that in my son's absence from the country my wisest course would be to open it on his behalf. I am sure he will be very sorry to hear of your late husband's sudden death, and on his behalf I offer you my sincere condolences. While Sebastian cannot be present at the funeral, I am sure he will wish to visit your husband's grave and pay his last respects just as soon as he and his wife have returned from their honeymoon."

Sabella dropped the note on to her lap and some automatic compulsion forced her to go on opening the black-bordered envelopes and reading people's commiserations. Her mind ceased to connect the words of condolence with Hendrik who lay dead in his coffin in the parlour; it was Bastian they were describing as they wrote of her great loss and of the void in her life which would be hard to fill.

With the last of the black-bordered letters opened, she bent her head and gazed down at the note on her lap. The words were still there in all their cruel mockery; it hadn't been a nightmare conjured up by her own imagination. She studied the flourish with which Mrs Eliza Grant had signed the note and then she tortured herself again by rereading its message.

As soon as he and his wife have returned from their honeymoon. Oh God, Bastian, Sabella railed silently, how could you, how could you? When I'm expecting your child, and Hendrik's death has set me free? I know we parted in anger, but it was only a few weeks ago, so what happened to that love you said you felt for me? *On your honeymoon*. Oh, dear Jesus, is she Annette, this girl you married, this girl who is your wife, with whom you now share your life, your laughter, your mind and your body? I hate her, and I can't bear it . . .

A wail of anguish erupted from her and echoed around the room. She rested her forehead on the table and howled like an animal in pain. Tante Bessie was stroking her hair as she began to weep wildly, saying, "That's right, child, let it all out. I've been worried about you, taking your loss so calmly. Crying will do you good."

Nothing will do me good, Sabella thought with utter desolation. Bastian is married to someone else.

Two things forced her to check her abandoned grief. Her weeping had started off the children, too, and suddenly it seemed immoral to be mourning for the loss of another man when her husband lay in his open coffin in the parlour. She sat up, reaching in her pocket for a handkerchief and screwing up Eliza Grant's note.

"I'm – sorry," she said unevenly, and comforted the children, and then got up to help Tante Bessie, who looked at her with compassion and concern and whispered that she would have to try and be strong for the sake of her unborn baby.

"You will always have a part of Hendrik left alive in the baby," she said. And Sabella checked the indecent, hysterical laughter that bubbled in her throat, and went to change into the most funereal clothes she possessed. Tante Bessie had made black armbands for the children to wear. All the funeral rituals had to be observed.

When Sabella emerged from her bedroom it was to find that the first of the mourners had begun to arrive. Custom, Tante Bessie had explained, dictated that the widow should greet them at the front door, and invite them to gaze at Hendrik in his coffin before they drove to the church in Stilstroom for the funeral.

The pattern of this ritual was shattered when a dilapidated truck arrived and three people stepped from the cab. The other mourners looked at them with curiosity and it was obvious that they did not belong to the neighbourhood.

There was a tall, thin, plain young woman with shrewish lines beside her mouth, accompanied by a man who was obviously her husband. Flanking them was a young man in his late teens or early twenties with acne scars and a jubilant look in his eyes which was quite out of place on such an occasion.

The woman addressed Sabella. "I am Johanna Klopper, and this is my husband Andries, and my younger brother Louis. You must be one of the neighbours who kindly made themselves responsible for the funeral arrangements – "

"I'm Sabella le Roux, Hendrik's widow."

"*Hendrik's widow!*" Johanna Klopper echoed shrilly. "You can't be!"

Before Sabella could respond to such an astonishing, hostile reaction, Tante Bessie thrust herself forward. "I assure you, Mevrou Klopper, that Sabella married Hendrik quite legally almost two years ago. But what it has to do with you I can't imagine!"

The woman's eyes hardened. "Hendrik made a will in which he said he would never marry because of his weak heart, and that Mooikrantz would pass to us after his death!"

Tante Bessie began with scorn, "Weak heart, my foot – " but Sabella interrupted her.

"You – you must be the children of Ewart le Roux, my late husband's half-brother."

"Two of them. My elder brother Pierre arranged to travel by train."

"Your father?" Sabella began, still trying to gather her scattered thoughts. Was she about to meet Ewart le Roux,

171

the step-son who had never forgiven Tante Wilhelmina, the half-brother Hendrik had never seen?

"My father is dead. Just as we know Wilhelmina is dead. A friend of ours was visiting Stilstroom just after she killed herself. The point is," Johanna Klopper went on belligerently, "that she made a will, leaving Mooikrantz to our family if she should survive Hendrik, and he in turn made a will in our favour when he reached twenty-one."

"And we were sent copies of both wills!" her brother Louis le Roux chimed in. "If Hendrik had decided to change his will when he married you, he would have written to us and told us!"

Oh dear God, Sabella thought dully. She hadn't imagined that matters could possibly be made worse than they already were. Of course Hendrik hadn't changed his will, because he'd learnt that there was nothing wrong with his heart after all, and if he had thought of changing it he must have decided there was plenty of time – just as Sabella had done. And now – now these relatives of his had come to stake their claim to Mooikrantz and as well as being pregnant, as well as having lost Bastian, she and the children would be homeless and penniless . . .

"A man's property passes to his widow," Tante Bessie said flatly.

"Not if he had willed it to his half-brother's family!" Johanna Klopper claimed with force.

The pre-burial ritual was scattered to the wind as brother and sister and the latter's husband competed with one another to stake their claims and Sabella stood there, feeling drained and unreal as she listened to it all and heard neighbours chiming in and taking sides.

"If Hendrik had made a new will," Johanna Klopper challenged, "then let us see it!"

"This is hardly the time – " Tante Bessie began to protest angrily.

"Look, whatever else we may be, we're not hypocrites! We didn't come here to pay our respects to Hendrik le Roux. He might have been our father's half-brother but

172

none of us knew him. All we knew was that his mother had stolen our birth-right, and we're here to get it back!"

Sabella stood there numbly, the children gathered around her and with Daan and Ria clutching her skirt and crying. The funeral ritual had been turned into an ignoble charade, the body in the open coffin forgotten or ignored as the battle of greed and acrimony raged. Older neighbours who remembered Ewart le Roux as a youth took the side of his children and agreed that Hendrik's will should stand, while others argued that Ewart's children ought to do the decent thing and let Hendrik's widow have Mooikrantz.

Two ill-dressed men suddenly arrived in the room, the trousers of one of them held up by string, and the incongruous sight of them among people wearing mourning clothes created a temporary lull. One of the newcomers said with an oily, ingratiating smile, "We thought the funeral would be over by now. We'd heard the farm was going to be sold and my brother and I wanted to have a look – "

"No, you didn't!" Sabella cried, finding her voice at last. "You are here because you want to search for the Kruger millions! Get off my land!"

"It's not *your* land!" Louis le Roux bellowed. "And what's this about the Kruger millions?" Avarice sent his voice several octaves higher. "Johanna, if the Kruger gold is here on Mooikrantz we'll be worth a fortune!"

Sabella closed her eyes in despair. She should not have mentioned the Kruger millions. Nothing would now persuade Ewart's children to give up even a part of their claim to Mooikrantz.

With the attention of everyone riveted upon his brother and sister and the girl who was Hendrik's widow, no one had noticed Pierre's arrival and in the first shock of assessing the situation he'd decided to remain an anonymous background figure and collect his thoughts.

One of the many ways in which he'd tried to raise capital had been on the strength of Hendrik's will, and the legal position had been spelt out to him. Rage rose inside him

173

as he glanced at the coffin. Couldn't the man at least have had the decency to let them know that he'd changed his mind about not marrying? He, Pierre, had come on a fool's errand and for a moment he thought of leaving as unnoticed as he'd arrived, and try for a lift to the railway halt so that he could catch the next Johannesburg-bound train.

Then, gradually, he began to see that all might not be lost after all. He gazed around the room, making a mental inventory of the old-fashioned furniture, recognising yellow-wood and stinkwood. Sometimes during his lunch hour at Bozzoli & Ferguson, he would amuse himself by looking in at a nearby auction house and he'd learnt to spot the kind of things that would fetch high prices. There were several pieces of sought-after early Cape furniture in this room alone, and already he had thought of a way of persuading the widow to let him get his hands on them.

He shouldered his way through the crowd and faced his brother and sister. "You are not only fools, both of you," he said coldly, with distaste, "but fools without a scrap of human decency! I'm ashamed to be your brother!"

"Don't you sit in judgement, Pierre!" Johanna shrilled. "What brought *you* here, other than your third-share in Mooikrantz?"

"There'll be no third-share for any of us," he said flatly, ignoring her accusation. "The moment Hendrik married, that will he made in our favour became null and void, and his widow will inherit his estate."

"We'll see about that! We'll take the matter to court – "

"Any lawyer would tell you that you have no case." Pierre turned to the two ill-dressed strangers. "*You!* You're like a pair of vultures! Make yourselves scarce and don't try to come back! This farm is private property and there'll be no prospecting here."

As the two men scuttled outside, Louis echoed with a frown, "Prospecting? They wanted to search for the Kruger millions! Are you saying they're really after minerals, Pierre?"

174

Kicking himself mentally for that slip of the tongue, Pierre answered his brother in a curt voice. "Whatever is, or isn't, to be found on Mooikrantz doesn't affect the issue of the farm's ownership. Now, I suggest that we remember there is a man lying dead in his coffin in this room, and behave accordingly!" He moved towards the widow, holding out his hand. "I don't think I need to introduce myself to you, Mevrou le Roux," he said with compassion in his voice. "I offer you my condolences, and my apologies for the behaviour of my brother and sister. And may I say that I, for one, am glad Hendrik had a few years of happiness with you."

As she took his hand Sabella studied him. He seemed both young and at the same time older than his years, but not in the same way Hendrik had. *This* man looked as if he had packed a good deal of experience and adventure into his life. His hair was dark and his eyes light grey and although he was not particularly tall he held himself as if he were. And unlike his brother and sister, he had taken the trouble to wear a black armband for the occasion.

"Thank you," Sabella whispered. "Are you – are you sure about Hendrik's will?"

"Quite sure." He silenced her with a wry smile, and added, "I would like to pay my respects to Hendrik now."

He moved towards the coffin, and one by one the other mourners followed him and filed past it. Sabella's legs suddenly felt as if they were stuffed with sawdust and she fell into the nearest chair. Today, she thought, must surely be the most terrible one she would ever have to endure in her life.

Her entire body froze when she heard Tante Bessie say, "Sabella, it's time for you to make your last farewell to Hendrik, so that the lid may be put on the coffin."

She rose shakily, holding on to furniture as she began to move towards the coffin. Suddenly, Pierre le Roux was blocking her path, holding her by the upper arms. "The poor girl is on the point of collapse!" he said roughly to the room at large. "She has just been through a distressing, shameful ordeal and she faces that of the funeral itself. I'm sure she has already said her private farewell to her husband. Have the coffin lid screwed down."

Sabella looked at him with enormous gratitude, and his eyes told her that he'd guessed she had dreaded having to kiss her dead husband's lips in public. While the coffin was being carried outside, to where the funeral carriage drawn by a team of black horses was waiting, he made her sit down. She thought how different he was from his sister and brother, whose attitude made it clear that they felt they had been robbed of their rightful inheritance.

If she was aware of anyone during the funeral service later, and then the burial, it was Pierre le Roux. It was he who offered her a dry handkerchief when her own had become a sodden ball, he who supported her while she wept. It shamed her deeply that her tears were not for Hendrik at all, but for Bastian who was on his honeymoon somewhere with his bride.

Bastian, you betrayed me, Sabella mourned brokenly as Dominee Botha conducted the burial service. You betrayed both of us, and our unborn child. While I'm enduring this hell you're enjoying your honeymoon . . .

At last the funeral was over. Pierre was the only one of his family who joined the other mourners in returning to Mooikrantz afterwards, and while dear, kind, good Tante Bessie made sure that everyone had something to eat and drink he sat in a corner next to Sabella and stopped her from dwelling on her grief by forcing her to talk about her future, and make practical plans.

"I don't know what I'm going to do," she admitted wanly. "Hendrik's two black labourers have already hinted in a roundabout way that they would become a laughing stock if they stayed on to work for me. Tante Bessie says it's because I'm from the city, and know nothing about farming. I'd learn about farming if I could, but it would be impossible for me to help with the hard labour because – well, I'm expecting a baby."

As she said the words Sabella thought with a mixture of bitterness and guilty gratitude that the baby's legitimacy would never be questioned now. Neither Bastian nor anyone else would ever suspect Hendrik had not fathered it.

Pierre patted her hand sympathetically and said, "I might be able to help you raise a little money to tide you over for a while. There's far too much furniture in this house, and I know a man in Johannesburg who collects old-fashioned stuff and uses the wood for the new furniture he designs. I'm sure I could get him to pay you a few pounds for anything you have no use for."

"Thank you, but a few pounds are not going to solve my problems. I think I may have to sell Mooikrantz lock, stock and barrel." She added with a sour laugh, "There have certainly been enough offers to buy it, lately."

"Because of the supposed existence of the Kruger millions?"

Sabella nodded, and then narrowed her eyes. "But *you* said something about prospecting. I've never been able to understand how anyone could seriously believe the Kruger millions might have been hidden here. But if all those men were really after minerals, then it begins to make sense. And if there *are* minerals here – "

"Sabella." Pierre leant towards her, lowering his voice so that it would reach only her ears. "What those men have been after are diamonds. But apart from the landowner's permission one needs a Government licence to prospect for diamonds, and that's why the story of the Kruger millions was used instead."

"Diamonds?" Sabella repeated in a dazed whisper. "There are *diamonds* here?"

"No, there aren't. I've no idea how or why the rumour started, but rumour is all it is." He gave her a smile that reminded her of that of a naughty small boy. "I'll be honest and admit that the rumours sharpened my interest in inheriting a third-share of Mooikrantz. But I have experience of diamond mining, and there's nothing about the terrain here to suggest the presence of alluvial deposits or kimberlite."

Sabella thought deeply for a moment, and something began to stir inside her – something very much like the feeling she'd had when she thought of making and selling shelf-covers, and again when she'd gone to work for James Paradise & Company. *Here* was a focus for her thoughts and her energies, as well as a means of dulling her grief. "The rumours weren't started by me," she said, "but I'm going to take advantage of them, and sell the farm for far more than it would otherwise have fetched."

Pierre gave her a sharp look. "You mean you'll encourage people to believe there really *are* diamonds on the farm?"

"None of them has ever mentioned the word 'diamonds' to me," she returned coolly, "so why should *I* mention it? I will, however, make a point of telling everyone wishing to buy Mooikrantz that I don't believe the Kruger millions were hidden here. What could be more moral than that?"

Pierre whistled under his breath. "For a grieving young widow, you have a very shrewd business sense."

"If that's a criticism," she said, flushing, "let me remind you that I have to think of my family and of the baby I'm expecting!"

"It wasn't criticism; it was a compliment. In the meantime, Sabella, let me sell some of the furniture for you to keep you going – "

"No, I don't want it to seem that I'm so desperate that I'm selling off bits of shabby old furniture. From now on I'm going to tell everyone who comes here, pretending to be after the Kruger millions, that if they would like to make an offer for the farm I'd consider it. Then I'll accept the highest offer."

Pierre didn't comment, but changed the subject and asked if she could put him up for the night. Tante Bessie also elected to stay the night so that she could take Sabella's chores on her own shoulders.

"You go and sit and keep that nice young relative of

178

Hendrik's company," she told Sabella, after all the other mourners had left.

"I've had an idea, Sabella," Pierre said, excitement shining in his eyes. "I think you're right about selling Mooikrantz and taking advantage of the rumours about the diamonds. But not the way you're planning to do it. Judging by the two men I threw out today you've mostly been dealing with small-fry up to now. But in Johannesburg I could contact men with vast fortunes, and interest them in Mooikrantz by mentioning the persistent rumours about diamonds. If one of those men bought the farm you would make enough money for your family to live in considerable comfort on the invested interest."

She considered for a moment. What he had said made a good deal of sense, and in the world of business dominated by men, it would be to her advantage to hide behind a man in the matter of selling Mooikrantz. "Very well, Pierre," she said. "If you can find a buyer greedy and rich enough to gamble a fortune, I won't offer Mooikrantz to anyone else in the meantime."

"Fine! There's just one thing, Sabella — I hate to bring it up, but I'd have to ask for a commission to cover expenses. Does twenty per cent of the sale price sound unreasonable to you?" he asked, looking embarrassed. "I don't think I could operate on less."

She assured him that it sounded perfectly reasonable, but he was still anxious to make the position clear. "The remaining eighty per cent would be yours, and it would still be far, far more than you'd get if you sold the farm to one of the fly-by-nights who have been pestering you."

She nodded, thanked Pierre, and after she had said good night to him and to Tante Bessie she went to her room. As she lay in bed she thought of the three men who had been brothers by law or by birth, and yet had been so completely unalike. According to Pierre, Ewart had turned out to be a drunken failure; Hendrik had been emotionally crippled and yearned for a normality he was never destined to attain. Then she thought of Bastian —

It was impossible to think dispassionately about Bastian and sum him up as she had summed up his half-brother a·d step-brother Ewart. Helpless grief overwhelmed her oɪce again. She recalled the last words he had spoken to her before he left Mooikrantz. "*We won't meet again.*" He was as lost to her as if he were dead, like Hendrik. She wept, and if anyone heard the sound of her grief they would assume she was mourning her dead husband.

At noon the next day Pierre set out to walk to the road where he hoped to get a lift to the halt. "I'll be in touch with you soon," he told Sabella.

Because winter was upon them, and they could not expect to be hired by anyone else until spring was around the corner, the two labourers who had worked with Hendrik remained on Mooikrantz and looked after the livestock. One bleak, cold day followed another as Sabella tried to keep thoughts of Bastian from her mind by immersing herself in plans for the future. She would not settle down to live in idle comfort once Mooikrantz had been sold. She would, instead, find some way of making a fortune. Why not start off with shelf-covers, as she'd once planned to do?

In the meantime she sent away the men who still arrived daily to ask permission to search for "the Kruger millions" or offered to buy the farm. Then Pierre returned to Mooikrantz one Sunday afternoon in a very expensive-looking car driven by a man who was clearly wealthy and had no interest in Sabella or her family. His attention was concentrated entirely upon the farm and upon the question of whether it might be worth buying for its mineral rights. He and Pierre walked out into the hills and when they returned to the house they stopped only for long enough to drink the coffee Sabella offered them before they left again. As he climbed into the passenger seat of the car Pierre gave her a conspiratorial, reassuring wink.

After that, he returned to the farm every Sunday, each time bringing with him a different man in a different expensive motor car, but he never arrived empty-handed. There were gifts of luxury biscuits and tins of meat in jelly and chocolates which melted in the mouth. He explained to Sabella that Bozzoli & Ferguson allowed their staff to buy for next to nothing such merchandise as had passed its prime or whose tins were dented. She suspected that he paid the full price for the presents, because the dents in the tins looked as if they had been recently made on purpose, and she could find nothing at all stale about the biscuits and chocolates. But she accepted his generous gifts with gratitude, and shared them with Tante Bessie, who thoroughly approved both of Pierre and of what he was doing on Sabella's behalf.

"No doubt Hendrik would have thought what you're planning is dishonest," she said, "but the way I look at it is that these men, with their greedy hopes fixed on making yet more money, deserve everything they're likely to get."

With growing excitement, Pierre confirmed the extent of the greedy hopes being raised. "There are now a great many rich men after Mooikrantz, Sabella," he told her when he called as usual one Sunday and his latest prospective purchaser had wandered off to look at the farm by himself. "I feel we should put the property up for auction and let them fight it out between themselves," Pierre went on. "I have some leave due and I'll take it next week to come and arrange for the auction to be held in the church hall in Stilstroom. The farm is going to sell for many thousands of pounds!"

She was unable to visualise even one thousand pounds, let alone several. She felt his hand closing around hers. "What will you do with the money, Sabella?"

Fearing he would laugh if she told him she meant to use it to make a fortune, she told only part of the truth. "I'll invest it and rent a house for us in Johannesburg."

"In Westdene, where you have friends?"

"No." She hesitated, and then decided to trust him. "I dare not go back anywhere near Westdene. The court said my brothers had to go to an orphanage after Pa died, and

181

Ria to a mental institution, and the Dominee applied to adopt Daan. I ran away with them to Mooikrantz, and when we leave here we'll have to live where we're not known, or the children would be taken away from me. I'm not twenty-one yet, and so I couldn't apply to be made their guardian."

"I see." He gave her hand a squeeze, and unexpectedly dropped a light kiss on her mouth. He stood up. "I can hear the latest hooked fish returning. I'll see you next week, Sabella, when I come to set up the auction."

But the following week, when yet another expensive car drew up outside the house, only one man stepped from it, a well-dressed one with an authoritative manner, and not one who had previously paid a visit to the farm with Pierre.

"I do hope you speak and understand a little English, ma'am," he greeted her courteously and slowly.

"I speak it fluently," she said, and introduced herself.

He offered her his hand. "My name is Hill-Carstairs. Since the farm is up for sale a group of companies with interests in the diamond industry appointed me to act on their behalf. I'm a geologist, Mrs le Roux, and I've been asked to come and take samples for signs of diamond-bearing alluvial deposits or kimberlite on the farm."

"I see." She hoped he would not read her inner dismay. Greed fed by rumour was one thing; tests made by an expert quite another. Politeness forced her to invite him inside for a cup of coffee.

He accepted, and followed her into the kitchen. As she busied herself at the range, she said, "You mentioned something about diamonds, Mr Hill-Carstairs. Men have been coming here in droves, wanting to buy the farm because they believe the Kruger millions were hidden here."

"I've heard of that ingenious red herring," Hill-Carstairs began, and at that moment Pierre walked into the kitchen. She introduced the two men and noticed that Pierre shared her sense of shock at the visit from a geologist.

"Mr Hill-Carstairs wants to take samples of soil for testing — " Sabella began to go on.

"No," the geologist interrupted her. "That won't be necessary. Thank you for the coffee, Mrs le Roux." He stood up. "I don't need to take samples to know there are no diamonds here, that the rumours are just that and no more. I have to return to Johannesburg now to submit my report."

To Sabella's stunned disbelief, he nodded and saw himself out. Pierre's expression showed defeat. "I'm afraid that's the end of all our hopes and plans. Within twenty-four hours his report will become public knowledge. I'll have to call off the auction."

"I simply don't understand! How could he have made up his mind so suddenly, when he'd told me he'd come to take samples? Why didn't he even trouble to take those samples?"

"He didn't need to," Pierre said. "Just by looking at the terrain he could tell, as I could, that this isn't diamond-bearing land."

"All that hard work of yours," she said miserably, "and for nothing . . ."

He came to stand behind her and put his hands on her shoulders. "All I care about is the fact that you and your family now face an uncertain future."

She sighed. "As a farm, Mooikrantz won't fetch much now, so we'll have to stay here. At least it gives us a roof over our heads, and if the labourers leave I'll simply let the wheat fields lie fallow, and sell most of the livestock, and grow vegetables and keep chickens and a couple of cows for milk and butter."

"I hate to think of you, subsisting like that!" he said in a rough voice. The pressure of his hands on her shoulders increased as he pulled her to her feet, forcing her to face him. There was tenderness and sincerity in his grey eyes as he went on, "Let me tell you something, Sabella. For purely selfish reasons I'm *glad* that you won't become a rich woman after all. If you had been rich, I would never have been able to tell you that I've grown to love you, and that I want to take care of you and of your family and the baby you're expecting."

"Oh . . ." She felt the colour flooding into her cheeks. "I – hadn't guessed."

"I made sure that you wouldn't. I was afraid you might suspect I was after your money." He touched her cheek in a brief caress. "Well, now there won't be money standing between us, and I can tell you how I feel."

"I – I'm sorry. You're making me feel so humble – and so guilty – because I can't think of you as any more than Hendrik's relative, and a good, kind friend."

He smiled. "Hendrik has only been dead a few weeks, and you're expecting his baby. Naturally, romantic thoughts couldn't have been further from your mind. I'm prepared to wait as long as I have to for those romantic thoughts to begin stirring, but what I'm not prepared to do is leave you here pregnant and without help and struggling to keep yourself and your family – "

"Pierre," she interrupted desperately, "as you said yourself, Hendrik has only been dead a few weeks and people would be outraged – "

"I don't believe you're the kind of girl who'd give a fig for what people said! In any case, you wouldn't be here to be affected by what they're saying. I'll rent a house in Johannesburg for us to begin with. Sabella, I won't be working as a stores manager for much longer. A friend and I are going into partnership and starting our own business. Even if you were to decide that you could never love me, I'd still want you to share my life and I'd still want to take care of you and shoulder your heavy burdens."

"You're – very good, very understanding, but – "

"Sabella," he cut in, his voice extremely serious now, "from what you've told me, Hendrik never legally adopted your brothers and your sister, and the authorities could have taken them away from you at any time. Even if you won't consider anyone else, consider them. They're in a very vulnerable position."

"Not as long as we continue to live here quietly," she argued.

"Yes, but *could* you? What if one of the newspapers gets hold of this Kruger millions nonsense, and decides to publicise it? It would immediately draw official attention to the children's position. One of the things I want to do as soon as you've agreed to marry me is to adopt all the children – including the baby you're expecting. Then no one would ever be able to take any of them away. No, don't say anything now. I'll give you six weeks in which to think it over."

Life seemed totally empty to Sabella now. There was nothing to look forward to; no excitement at the thought of Mooikrantz being auctioned for a high price, no new life of security awaiting them, and no prospect of sublimating her wasted love for Bastian into the building of a fortune. There was only worry about the future and the renewed fear that the children might be taken away from her. How could she not have worked out for herself that the wretched story about the Kruger millions might well reach the newspapers and result in a blaze of calamitous publicity?

Sabella also found herself facing the approach of Sunday with a sense of loss. There would be no visit from Pierre and she would miss his lively company, his enthusiasm, his many different forms of generosity. It took an extraordinary man to want to support so many children who were not his own, simply for love of her. And he wished to go even further, and adopt them . . .

Could she, should she, marry once again a man she did not love, purely for security for the children? At least Pierre was more interesting and attractive than Hendrik had been, and perhaps she would learn to love him in time . . .

And then Bastian arrived on Mooikrantz, and as she gazed at him with his unmatching looks and his differently-coloured eyes and the unconscious arrogance with which he held himself, the blending of pain and joy that surged through her told her she would never grow to love anyone but him.

9

At first Sabella had thought the sound of an approaching motor car meant that Dominee Botha was paying her a visit. Nantes and Anton had left for school, and she was in the kitchen, straining the morning's bucket of milk through cheesecloth while Daan and Ria hugged the range for warmth. Then Bastian walked in, wearing a city suit. Ria was the first to react.

"Pretty-car uncle!" she cried, jumping up and down with excitement. "Ria drive car!"

"Yes," Bastian said without taking his unmatching eyes from Sabella's face. "You and Daan go and pretend to drive my car."

"Put your coats on first," Sabella ordered automatically.

They ran to fetch the coats she had made for them and Sabella found herself alone with Bastian. "I believe," she said in a tone as blank as she could make it, "that I have to congratulate you on your marriage."

He gave a sour laugh. "Congratulate me on making the biggest fool of myself? I arrived back in Johannesburg late last evening from my farce of a honeymoon, and when I'd seen the notice of Hendrik's death you'd sent me I understood the message behind it. I left straight away for Mooikrantz."

"That must have enchanted your bride!" Sabella flung at him, angry because it was all too late, and her own joy at seeing him was a total waste of emotion.

"My bride's indifference is matched by my own." He

186

began to move towards her but she warded him off, flinging up her chin as well as her hands.

"Just what do you think you'll accomplish by coming here, Bastian? So your marriage was a mistake, according to what you've said. That doesn't make you any the less a married man, and I'm no more prepared to run away with you now than I was when *I* was the married one!"

His mood changed and he looked at her with tender, amused mockery. "I know. That's why I've come, instead, to live with you."

She stared at him with a tumult of conflicting feelings threading through her, but in the end outrage won. "You're out of your mind! If you think I'm going to become the new Tante Wilhelmina, with you as the new Peregrine Grant, and recreate that long-ago scandal in the neighbourhood – "

"There'll be no scandal." Bastian cut her short with another swift change of mood. "I shouldn't have teased you like that. I'm here with my father's knowledge and blessing, and when I reached Stilstroom I dropped into the post office with the excuse of buying stamps but in reality to make everyone aware of the fact that I'd come, as soon as I'd heard of my half-brother's death, to be with my sister-in-law and help and support her in the care of my cousins, and generally do what I can to secure their future. Country people don't say much, I've noticed, but what those inside the post office *did* say made it plain that they approved."

"And did they also approve," Sabella demanded tartly, "of the fact that you'd deserted your newly-married wife in order to pay a lengthy visit to your sister-in-law?"

"I didn't desert Annette. She was the one who walked out of the marriage. There's no need for anyone to know about her existence, Sabella."

She gazed helplessly at him. "Why did you do it, Bastian?"

"I was drunk," he said simply. "I was so angry with you, so maddened by the thought that I could never have you, that I deliberately set out to get drunk at a party and asked Annette to marry me right away. I don't believe I was entirely sober from then onwards until I found myself on honeymoon with her." His lips curled in a smile of self-derision. "Would you like to hear something really stupid? The thought of you reading about the wedding in the *Rand Daily Mail* was the spur of my drunken reasoning. I wanted to hurt you as badly as you'd hurt me."

Sabella shook her head at the waste and the folly of it all. "After you'd left Mooikrantz, Bastian, I wrote to the *Rand Daily Mail* offices and cancelled the subscription. It would have been too painful if the papers had continued to arrive."

He gave a crack of humourless laughter. "Which makes my lunatic act doubly pathetic! I concentrated so hard, posing for the *Mail*'s photographs with Annette beside me, straining to look the picture of happiness to punish you for your lack of faith in me . . . And you never even saw the newspaper."

"Oh Bastian," she confessed too late, "it wasn't true that I lacked faith in you. It was the only way I could think of to protect my brothers and sister. If I'd run away with you, as you'd insisted, they would have been taken from me and placed in institutions."

"I still don't believe that, but I accept that *you* believe it, and because of it I've made certain there'll be no scandal. Annette doesn't even know of your existence, and your name won't be mentioned when we divorce. We went our different ways as soon as our so-called honeymoon cruise ended and our ship docked at Cape Town. She stormed off to stay with friends in the Cape and I made for Johannesburg – "

"From what you've said," Sabella put in critically, "Annette is an injured, innocent party. You didn't love her; you proposed to her when you were drunk and you weren't completely sober until your honeymoon, which you've described as a farce. It seems to me that you must have made it so!"

188

"Once I faced what I'd let myself in for," he returned with force, "I did my damnedest to make the marriage work! Annette didn't love me either; she knew I was drunk when I proposed to her and she accepted because her parents had dinned it into her head for years that I would make the ideal husband for her. Her father owns shares in Grant Mining Corporation and our marriage would square everything off so neatly. So you needn't feel sorry for Annette! She's with friends in the Cape, where she chose to be, and I – " He broke off, gazing at her with eyes made soft by love, "am where I most want to be in the world. You look wonderful, Sabella. You've grown a little more rounded, and it suits you."

Before she could tell him the reason why she had grown more rounded he pulled her into his arms and then he was kissing her with almost violent hunger. She responded with all the ardour of pent-up longing, but part of her mind remained self-protectively alert. If Bastian knew that she was expecting his child there was nothing he wouldn't do, no reckless folly he wouldn't commit, in an effort to end his marriage quickly so that the child could be born in wedlock. She had only to remember that he himself bore the stigma of illegitimacy to realise how extreme his reaction would be.

Footsteps from outside reached them, and she pushed Bastian hurriedly away. She was stoking the kitchen range when Tante Bessie came in, hugging her arms against the cold.

"Well, well," she said with approval, studying Bastian. "You've grown into a fine young man. You probably won't remember it, but you used to wander over to my farm when you were little. You had those odd eyes even then."

Sabella introduced them formally, and Bastian said with a laugh, "My odd eyes gave me many fights when I at school was."

"So you can still speak Afrikaans," Tante Bessie commented, "even though it comes out a bit crooked. Never mind; it will improve with practice. It's all over the neighbourhood that you've come to see what you can do to help Sabella, and your concern for your brother's widow does you credit. The first thing you could do is try and talk some sense into her labourers, who are threatening to leave."

The swiftness with which news travelled in the neighbourhood never ceased to surprise Sabella, and the fact that Tante Bessie had not warned her – as she had warned Hendrik – that Bastian's presence under the same roof would cause talk, meant that everyone else shared her approval of his concern for the young widow they all thought of as no more than his pregnant sister-in-law.

Sabella drew a sharp breath of startled enlightenment at the thought. *Pregnant!* That was the key, the reason why no one would suspect anything improper between herself and Bastian. She waited tensely – "on heated coals", as Ma would have said – for Tante Bessie to mention the coming baby, because Sabella had not yet decided how to solve the dilemma of what to tell Bastian about its parentage. On the one hand she felt he had a right to know he was the father, but on the other she was terrified of the possible consequences if she did.

But she ought to have known that a woman of Tante Bessie's generation would never have dreamt of referring to such a delicate subject in a man's company. After she had drunk the coffee Sabella had made she left, and Daan and Ria, who had grown tired of playing at driving Bastian's car, decided to go with her. Once alone together, Bastian reached for Sabella again but she evaded him and said firmly, "No! You have convinced everyone that you're here only as my caring brother-in-law, and I'm not prepared to betray trusting people like Tante Bessie behind their backs!"

She felt a little dashed by the fact that he put up no cajoling arguments but accepted her decision with a shrug. "I'll go and bring in my suitcase and then I'll round up the labourers and have a chat with them."

The two labourers, Ezekiel and M'dala, had been children living on Mooikrantz when Bastian was small and they remembered him. Ezekiel, Sabella learnt, had been his special friend. They gathered around the warmth of the kitchen range, sipping mugs of coffee which Sabella had poured for them, and grinned with delight and unmalicious amusement as Bastian spoke to them in his fractured Afrikaans. Sabella had never felt at ease with them, believing that they despised her for her city background and ignorance of farming. But as they conversed with Bastian she learnt more about their lives and their attitudes than she had before.

It wasn't because she was city-bred, she discovered, that they had signalled their wish to leave. They had feared she would give them orders in matters of which she knew nothing. They were perfectly capable of carrying out all the work on the farm for which she did not already take responsibility; Hendrik, they intimated, had only taken the lighter tasks from their shoulders – initially, no doubt, because of his belief in his weak heart and later from habit. He could be replaced by Ezekiel's young nephew, who would work for his keep alone.

With the problem of the labourers settled, Bastian turned his attention to other matters. All the children were delighted that he would be staying and it struck Sabella with force that the boys in particular suffered from the lack of a father-figure in their lives. Hendrik had never tried to fulfil that role, but Bastian wanted to know all about their activities at school; he explained to them how his motor car engine worked, and listened with interest as Anton and Nantes expressed their views about the baboons in the hills. To Anton they were adversaries who had to be sent running and barking to their own fastness on the jagged peaks, while Nantes almost lost his stammer as he described how the young baboons played just like human children, pulling each other by the tail or throwing stones at *dassies*, the small rock-rabbits which lived in the hills.

Sabella listened to the conversation as they ate supper,

and thought of the drunken baboon that had fallen on Hendrik. Afraid that one of the boys might blurt out this bizarre fact, she changed the subject, and soon they were talking about the day when they had first arrived on Mooikrantz.

"We had c-condensed-milk sandwiches for our lunch," Nantes remembered. "And you thought the s-stoep was made of cement, and you s-s-scrubbed it, Sabella."

"There was a ghost in our bedroom," Anton contributed, "and you let all of us sleep with you that night."

"There are no such things as ghosts," Sabella said, and pushed her chair back. "Time to get you washed before bed. Stoke the range for me, Nantes, so that I can boil water."

Even though the evening followed the pattern of routine, Bastian's presence somehow altered it and gave it an almost festive atmosphere. There was, Sabella knew, a great deal that still had to be said between them, not least the matter of her pregnancy. But not tonight, she thought; not yet. It is all still too new, too sudden. I need time to think and prepare . . .

"I'm sure you must be tired," she told Bastian, when the children had said their good nights. "I'll show you the room I've prepared for you."

It was the one Hendrik used to occupy, and in deference to his memory she felt obliged to say, "I couldn't bring myself to go on sleeping here after his death. Good night, Bastian."

"Good night, Sabella." He took the candle she'd lit for him and made no attempt to kiss her, not even lightly on the cheek.

She returned to the kitchen and did a few necessary chores before she, too, retired to her room. Distantly in the hills, she heard a commotion among the baboons. A leopard-attack, or perhaps two males squabbling and the rest of the troop taking sides. *Boomsingertjies*, small insects which inhabited the trees and bushes, snapped and chirruped their nocturnal songs and there came a flapping of wings as birds flew over the house, probably night-owls on their way to search for prey. From the direction of the river came the croaking of frogs.

As she undressed Sabella thought how familiar all these sounds had become to her; sounds which had once made her uneasy or afraid. Then she realised that she was deliberately concentrating on the sounds of the night so that she would not think of Bastian, separated from her only by a wall . . .

At almost the same moment her door opened and he entered, wearing nothing but dark blue pyjama trousers. "There's a ghost in my room, Sabella," he said softly, with mock-fright, his eyes deliberately rounded and contrasting sharply with the hunger in their depths. "Please may I come into your bed?"

"Bastian – " Her voice caught as she followed his gaze travelling over her. She was dressed only in an under-shift which she'd made herself from the kind of cheap muslin usually sold as cheesecloth, and in the flickering light of the candles she knew that it concealed very little.

He set his own candle down and crossed the space between them. His arms closed about her, and he murmured against her hair. "You wouldn't be so cruel as to banish me to a room with a ghost?"

"There are no such things – " she began idiotically, and stopped. "Oh Bastian," she went on with a helpless sigh, "we shouldn't – "

"I know. It's wrong, it's immoral, it's a scandal and a sin." But even as he whispered the words he was unhooking her under-shift so that it finally fell to the floor. He drew in his breath. "You've become – voluptuous."

Tell him, a voice inside her head insisted. But tell him what? another countered. That the baby is his – or Hendrik's? The part of her that had nothing to do with any of those voices was responding to Bastian's mouth on her own, and then on her breasts, and without protest she allowed him to ease her on to the bed.

She wanted him to drown himself in her, fuse the two of

them together so that they became one. But he teased her, drove her mad, intensified her hunger with delicate kisses and feathery caresses until a wild tempest had been built up inside her, and only then did he part her thighs with his hand and she discovered that the tempest was consuming him equally.

She bit his shoulder to muffle the cry of fulfilment which rose in her throat and which would have awakened the children. He held her close afterwards so that they were locked together as one.

"Sabella," he said, and simultaneously she began, "Bastian – "

"Yes, my love?" His forefinger trailed along her cheek.

"No, you first."

"I wanted to tell you about Annette. I don't want you to waste a moment in the future on any feelings of jealousy where she is concerned. She and I never shared anything like *this*." His arms tightened about Sabella to make his meaning clear.

"Are you saying that you never – " she began.

"No, I'm not saying that. But physical intimacy was quite unimportant to her. It was just some inconvenient duty she accepted she would have to endure from time to time. But – and this was what made me realise we could have no future together – I discovered that as soon as I'd asked her to marry me she'd gone to a doctor and armed herself with contraceptives. Every barrier modern science has invented to prevent pregnancy had to be erected before she would allow me near her. And children are important to me, Sabella. Perhaps because I grew up as an only child I have a need that's almost like an ache for a child or children of my own. Annette simply doesn't want children at all. To her, they're something that ruins a woman's figure and gets in the way of her social life. She graciously told me that she might consider adoption, provided that nurses and nannies were hired to bring up the child."

Mental alarm bells began to ring in Sabella's head. She hadn't realised quite how strongly Bastian felt about a child of his own. If he knew the baby she was expecting was his he would fight tooth and claw for his rights as its father, no matter what the circumstances. And there were so many ways in which circumstances could change . . .

If Tante Wilhelmina, Sabella thought, had been able to pass *her* illegitimate child off as having been fathered by her husband, his true father would never have wanted him. She would not have been forced to hand him over and sever all ties with him. He would not have become lost to her . . .

Sabella broke the long silence. "So it was about children that you and Annette quarrelled, and this led to her leaving you?"

"It was part of it. But we quarrelled about so many things – about the fact that I refused to buy for her every expensive trinket that caught her fancy at our various ports of call, and about the arrogant way in which she treated the ship's stewards, reporting them for the smallest oversight. We quarrelled because of her habit of dragging my father's status into every conversation with others. She never referred to him simply as her father-in-law; she always added, 'The Right Honourable Peregrine Grant,' as if it were a hereditary title that belonged to the family. I called her a grasping snob and she called me selfish and tight-fisted. By the time the ship docked at Cape Town we were barely on speaking terms."

"I see." Circumstances might change, Sabella thought again. Unlikely, even impossible as it may seem, instead of a divorce there could be a reconciliation between them, and if Bastian knew that he had fathered a child he would be totally ruthless in his determination to adopt that child. It would be Tante Wilhelmina's story all over again . . .

"And now," Sabella went on, her mind resolutely made up, "now it's my turn to tell you something, Bastian."

"Yes, my love?"

"You said I had become voluptuous, more rounded. The reason for it is that I'm expecting Hendrik's baby."

"Oh." He withdrew from her and lay on his back with his arms folded underneath his head.

The instinct to fight against any possibility of ever losing her unborn child helped Sabella to whip up a convincing show of anger. "What did you expect?" she demanded. "Hendrik was my husband!"

"I know." Bastian's voice was very quiet. "It's just – I'm jealous. I can't help it. He had everything I wanted."

She could not afford to allow herself to be moved by the admission, any more than she could afford to tell him that her marriage to Hendrik had never been consummated. Instead, she said, "You once called Hendrik warped, and it was the truth. All he'd ever wanted in his life was to be normal, like other people, but even death cheated him of normality. Poor Hendrik . . . Do you know how he died?"

"They told me, in Stilstroom, that he'd had a fatal fall."

"A baboon drunk on fermenting marula berries knocked him out of a tree and his skull was smashed against a rock. So don't you, ever again, feel sorry for yourself and jealous of poor Hendrik!"

Bastian turned on his side and reached for her once more. "I won't. I'm going to stay here until your baby is born, and by that time Annette will have started divorce proceedings against me." He cupped his hands about her breasts. "In the meantime I'm going to help Ezekiel and M'dala with the farm work."

He was offering her the moon, but something would not allow her to believe in the reality of it. "Surely your father will object to you staying away so long," she said.

"No. He knows the situation regarding Annette, and he also knows that I feel responsible for my relatives. The Grant Mining Corporation can get along very well without me. I'll write to my father tomorrow and tell him of my decision."

He silenced any further objection she might have made by kissing her, and within moments a new wildfire had been kindled between them and they made love with heightened urgency.

Neither of them slept at all that night. When they were not losing themselves in one another, they talked and planned for the future. But it was a future Sabella could not allow herself to fully believe in. When dawn began to wash the sky with pink colour, she said, "Bastian, from tonight you must stay in your own room. There are three intelligent, inquisitive boys in the house and we couldn't hope to hide from them for long the fact that we're lovers. Even Ria is a threat because she'll sometimes wake up and come to my room, and she'd innocently prattle to others about what she'd seen."

He sighed, and begged a compromise. "Just now and again – when there's a ghost in my room?"

"There are no such things as ghosts," she returned primly, and then smiled. "Just now and again – when Nantes and Anton are at school and Ria and Daan are visiting Tante Bessie. But only when we are quite sure that it's safe."

With that compromise they had to content themselves, and the occasions became fewer as the children grew more and more attached to Bastian. They accompanied him when he drove to Stilstroom to buy provisions and knitting wool and other materials so that Sabella could make a layette for the coming baby, and in the evenings he would sit and watch her as she knitted and sewed.

During his first week on the farm Bastian had received a letter from his father. "He doesn't quarrel with my decision to stay on here for as long as I want to," Bastian told Sabella. "He accepts that I have a duty towards my pregnant, widowed cousin and her brothers and sister."

Their lives had fallen into a cosy pattern and it was very comforting to think of Bastian remaining on Mooikrantz for the birth of the baby, and quite wonderful to contemplate their marriage once Annette had divorced him. But Sabella still refused to relax her instinctive caution. She would wait until she and Bastian were truly man and wife before she told him that *he* had fathered the child she was expecting.

197

One day, when he seemed to have been on Mooikrantz for ever, he set out with Daan and Ria to drive to Stilstroom to buy farming equipment Ezekiel said they needed. They had scarcely left when Sabella heard footsteps approaching and a moment later Pierre le Roux stood in the kitchen doorway, carrying a suitcase and smiling at her.

"Hullo, Sabella," he said.

Since Bastian's arrival on Mooikrantz, she had given Pierre only a few fleeting thoughts before dismissing him from her mind. She hadn't even told Bastian about him because the intimate moments they shared together had always been crammed with more personal and important matters to discuss. When she *had* consciously thought of Pierre's proposal of marriage she had pushed the matter aside as something which would have to be dealt with in the distant future. Now, she realised with a shock that the six weeks he had given her to consider his proposal had passed, and that he had come for her answer.

Belatedly, trying to hide her dismay at his arrival, she said, "Hullo, Pierre. How – how nice to see you."

"The black driver who collects parcels at the halt gave me a lift." He crossed to the kitchen table, kissed her cheek and placed his suitcase on a chair. As he opened it and brought out chocolates, tinned galantines and biscuits he asked, "Have you kept well, Sabella? Or has the baby been causing you much discomfort?"

"No, I'm fine," she answered abstractedly, and then went on to thank him for the gifts he had brought with him.

"It's my pleasure. And the children? How have they been?"

"Fine," she repeated, but her chest felt tight with anxiety. They could not go on making meaningless small-talk indefinitely. Soon he would demand her answer to his proposal, and there was no uncomplicated way in which she could turn him down.

He snapped shut the lid of his suitcase, but not before she had noticed it contained items of clothing. Her glance

198

had not been lost on him, for he explained, "I've taken a couple of days off work, Sabella, so that I'd be able to stay the night. I hope I'm welcome?" He smiled as he asked the question, and her heart sank because he was so totally confident of her answer. And that meant that he was just as confident that she would agree to marry him . . .

"Of course," she said aloud, and because it offered her a breathing space she added, "I may have to borrow blankets from Tante Bessie because I've cut up some of the spare ones to make winter coats for the children. Pour yourself some coffee, Pierre, and make yourself at home while I check on the blanket supply."

She hurried out of the kitchen before he could respond. Her excuse had been based on truth, because although she intended giving him Ria's room she didn't want to share her own bed with her sister, who had only just been weaned of her old habit of creeping in next to Sabella if she woke up in the night, a habit which could be dangerous once the bed had to be shared with a baby. So Ria would have to sleep on the front room sofa tonight, and Sabella found there were only two thin spare blankets for her. Because she didn't really want to deprive Tante Bessie of any of her own much-needed blankets during a cold winter's night, Sabella decided to raid all the other beds and take at least one blanket from each.

This was not at all a simple manoeuvre when it came to Bastian's bed. He had insisted, from the start, on making it himself so that it would not be yet another chore to add to her existing ones. But he made his bed in the way he'd said they had taught him at boarding school. The corners of the sheets and blankets were mitred and tucked in tightly underneath the mattress, and as she was carefully removing the top blanket her hand encountered paper. She frowned as she pulled out an envelope which had been hidden underneath the mattress.

With an unpleasant shock, she discovered that the envelope bore her own typewritten name and address. Bastian must have collected it from the post office during one of his

199

past visits to Stilstroom, but why hadn't he given it to her? Its seal was still intact so that he couldn't possibly know what the letter said or who the sender was, which made his motive for hiding it under his mattress all the more mystifying and disturbing.

She sat down on the bed and opened the envelope. The letter she withdrew from it consisted of several handwritten pages and she turned first of all to the signature. It was that of Peregrine Grant.

With an ominous feeling in her heart, she began to read the letter.

I am writing to you and asking my secretary to type your name and address on the envelope so that Sebastian will not be able to guess who your correspondent is and destroy this letter.

When he returned from his troubled honeymoon and learnt of your husband's death my wife and I made no objection to his decision to leave right away and visit you and offer you support. We know that you, your late husband and your brothers and sister represent to him the family of which he feels he has been cheated. The understanding between him and ourselves was that he should visit you and spend a day or two on the farm while he assessed the needs of yourself and the children.

A day or two on the farm. The thought hammered in Sabella's brain as she put the letter down, afraid to go on reading. Bastian had been lying to her. She had to prepare herself, mentally and emotionally, before discovering the full extent of his lies. Sabella forced herself to continue reading the letter.

I am writing to you because of subsequent events of which I think you might be ignorant, and because Sebastian has been ignoring all of my letters to him, and also because I dare not take the risk of arriving at Mooikrantz in person to confront him. As a public figure, it's all but impossible to keep my movements secret.

Shortly after he left for your farm two things happened almost simultaneously. I received a letter from Sebastian, tendering his resignation from the Grant Mining Corporation. You may imagine my shock and surprise, since he has been groomed to take control of the corporation one day. But now he informed me that he intended to devote himself, instead, to farming Mooikrantz in the future! This is total madness and a complete waste of his skills and training. I had barely finished reading his letter when Annette arrived at our home.

According to her the honeymoon had not been the disaster Sebastian described, and their tiff on disembarkation had been because he'd been unwilling to join her in visiting friends in the Cape, and so she had flounced off to do so alone. But she'd soon regretted it and come to make peace. I need hardly tell you that her conciliatory mood has undergone severe changes as time has passed without sight or sound of Sebastian, and she has had to endure the humiliation of attending functions without him and trying to fob off questions from their friends. I dare not tell her where he is because she is unaware of the secret of his birth. I've done my best by pretending that urgent business had taken him to Rhodesia, but I'm afraid she no longer believes me, since if it were true he would have written to her by now at the very least.

She would never entertain the thought of divorce, as Sebastian had led us to believe, but she *is* talking of a legal separation. Rightly suspecting that I know where he may be reached, she has asked me to deliver an ultimatum to him. She will give him until the end of the month, she says, to join her in the home they bought before their wedding. If he has not returned to her by then she will apply through the courts for an order of Restitution of Conjugal Rights, and if he fails to respond to it she will start proceedings for a legal separation.

I have repeatedly written to tell Sebastian this but I

suspect that after reading my first letter he has destroyed the others unopened. I can understand, if not condone, his quixotic decision to work the farm on which he was born, and to support the only blood-kin he has, but he is not and never will be a farmer. It would make more practical sense for him to pay you a regular allowance and return to what he is best fitted to do. Indeed, he *must* return before Annette carries out her threat to file for Restitution of Conjugal Rights. The newspapers would seize upon it and hunt out Sebastian's whereabouts, and it would not be long before the whole story, including the circumstances surrounding his birth, became a public sensation. It would plunge my family into scandal and spell the end of my political career. I dare say you would not care very much about my own downfall, but please remember that once the newspapers start to dig into the many facets of the scandal it will be discovered that your own father died in gaol, while awaiting trial for what might have been tantamount to treason.

For the sake of his memory, for the sake of the family affection I've no doubt you have for Sebastian, please do all in your power to persuade him to return home as soon as possible and certainly not later than the end of the month.

Sabella replaced the letter in its envelope and sat there, a roaring sound filling her ears, her mouth dry, her hands trembling violently. Bastian had not only lied to her but he had taken reckless, ruthless risks with the futures of so many people.

And oh God, she thought with terror, others – and particularly newspapermen – would be unlikely to share Peregrine Grant's innocent view of her relationship with Bastian. She would be involved in the scandal too, and Ria and the boys would immediately be taken out of her care.

For a moment the room spun around her in renewed shock as she realised that Bastian had precisely three days left before Annette would put her threat into action. Sabella *had* to speak to him alone, persuade him to go home. Oh Lord, why had Pierre chosen today to arrive at Mooikrantz? Then she remembered that if he hadn't arrived, she wouldn't have had to search for blankets and wouldn't have found the hidden letter.

Sabella began to pace the room, trying to think what to do. Until Pierre left tomorrow she would be unable to start arguing with Bastian. He wouldn't give in easily, if at all, and unless he left for Johannesburg by the day after tomorrow Annette would carry out her threat and plunge all of them into disaster.

The sound of an approaching car told her that Bastian was returning home, and she felt dazed as yet another dilemma struck her. Pierre knew about Tante Wilhelmina's disgrace, but he did not know the name of the Englishman involved. If Sabella introduced Bastian to him as her cousin, he would be bound to make the connection. He might be too polite to bombard Bastian with personal questions, but he would certainly ask questions in Johannesburg and discover that Bastian's father was the Member of Parliament, Peregrine Grant. How ironic it would be if Sabella were to succeed in persuading Bastian to leave Mooikrantz in order to avert a scandal, only for Pierre to create unwittingly that self-same scandal by asking too many questions and leading others to put two and two together. And, she thought with despair, if she turned down his proposal he would guess that it had to do with Bastian, and might he not, in his anger and hurt, add a modern scandal about her relationship with her cousin as well as resurrecting the old one between Tante Wilhelmina and Peregrine Grant?

Slowly, painfully, inexorably, it came to her what she had to do. She had no other choice. She took a deep breath, straightened her shoulders, picked up the letter and left the room. Then she went to join Pierre in the kitchen, knowing that Bastian would soon enter it with the children.

"I've decided to accept your proposal of marriage,

Pierre," she said as evenly as she could. "I can't pretend that I love you – "

"My dear Sabella," he interrupted, taking her hand. "I've told you, I'm prepared to wait patiently for your love."

At that moment Bastian and the children entered the kitchen. As soon as she saw Pierre, Ria hurled herself enthusiastically at him. "Chocolate-uncle!" she cried with delight.

Sabella saw that Bastian's eyebrows were raised. She gave him a warning look, and said in English so that the children wouldn't understand, "Pierre, allow me to introduce Mr Grant. He is connected with the Chamber of Mines, and had a theory that there might well be diamonds on Mooikrantz after all. But he has decided any further prospecting would be a waste of time and he's leaving tomorrow."

Bastian was clearly taken aback, but her warning look had had its effect and he did and said nothing to contradict her story. She hurried to press home her advantage. "Mr Grant, allow me to present Pierre le Roux, who will be staying the night. I had to raid all the beds for blankets to make up a spare one, and I found *this*." She pressed his father's letter into his hand, and with a stunned look his fingers closed over it. "You must have mislaid it. Now, if you'll excuse me," she added, her voice no longer steady, "I – have to make up a bed in the front room for Ria tonight."

She hurried out of the kitchen. Daan and Ria would keep Pierre from following her, she knew, but Bastian would come looking for her once he had read his father's letter. As she smoothed sheets over the sofa in the front room tears rolled down her cheeks. She didn't turn her head when she heard the door opening.

"Yes, Sabella," Bastian said quietly, "I admit that I'd lied, to my parents and to you. I didn't want to waste time in arguing with them about my decision. I told the literal truth when I said I had come to live with you. Since you didn't trust me to be able to support you and the children

204

if I broke away from my father, the obvious answer was for me to learn to farm Mooikrantz." Something fluttered to the floor and she saw that it was the pages of Peregrine Grant's letter. "I realised who the sender was, but I couldn't bring myself to destroy it or even to read it." Bastian gave a humourless laugh. "A scruple of that kind doesn't make much sense, does it?"

"Such – such scruples as you *do* have are certainly odd." She turned to face him. "Oh Bastian, how could you have been so reckless, so foolish as to ignore your father's letters?"

He shrugged. "The first one simply set out all his arguments as to why I should leave Mooikrantz, and said Annette had returned and wanted a reconciliation. He was right; I did destroy the others unread because I assumed they were on the same lines."

"You wanted to remain in your fool's paradise," Sabella said bitterly. "You told so many lies . . ."

"I wanted to be with you," he explained simply, and added, "They weren't all lies. I told the truth about Annette, and I really did believe she would accept our marriage had been a disaster, and that she would have enough pride to divorce me quietly and without public fuss. I still can't understand why she wants the marriage to continue."

"If you really did tell the truth about her," Sabella said, "then it's obvious why she wants to remain your wife. Since she's not a passionate woman, according to you, and unlikely to fall in love with someone else, and she doesn't want children, why should she accept the stigma of divorce? As your father's heir you'll be very rich one day, and in the meantime she wants to continue being the daughter-in-law of the Right Honourable Peregrine Grant." Sabella swallowed hard before going on, "Does – does Restitution of Conjugal Rights mean – ?"

"It means that I have to go to bed with her," Bastian bluntly confirmed what Sabella had been suspecting. "I won't do it. I don't love her and she doesn't love me and she refuses to give me children. It would be a meaningless act."

"I'm not stupid!" Sabella lashed out in sudden anger. "I don't imagine for a moment that a lawyer would be present to make sure you obeyed the order to the letter! It's obviously a legal term which means that you have to go back and live with her. And you *must* go back."

"I won't do it," Bastian said implacably. "Let her cause a scandal if she wants to."

Sabella drew a long, ragged breath. "I knew you would say that. I knew it would be the attitude you'd take. And that's why I told Pierre, just a few moments before you came into the kitchen, that I would marry him."

Bastian's first reaction was to laugh, but as she gazed steadily at him she saw him grow pale beneath his tan, so that his face turned into a beige mask. "Who – who is he?" he asked jerkily. "I assumed – he was a relative."

"He is. His father was Hendrik's half-brother, and he was very kind to me after Hendrik's death." Briefly, she explained how Pierre had tried to help her sell Mooikrantz for a vastly inflated sum, and when that failed, asked her to marry him instead.

Bastian hurled angry, probing questions at her, and when she had answered them all he said with force, "The man's a crook! Couldn't you see that?"

"It was entirely *my* idea to take advantage of the rumours about diamonds, and sell Mooikrantz at an inflated price! Pierre simply offered to help me."

"In exchange for a large commission," Bastian reminded her bluntly.

"It would have been a mere bagatelle if we'd been able to get the price for Mooikrantz we were expecting!"

"And when the whole scheme blew up in your faces, he decided to marry you for what he could get out of it!"

"Which would be precious little! If Pierre had wanted to marry someone for what he could get out of it, he'd hardly have chosen a widow encumbered with four children and a fifth on the way! Someone who owned a small farm of little value! And far from telling me a pack of lies as you had done, and which risked me losing my brothers and sister, Pierre has promised to adopt them!"

"Has he, indeed! I wonder why? There has to be something in it for him . . ."

"He loves me," Sabella said, facing him with a challenge in her eyes. "Do you find that so impossible to believe?"

Bastian said nothing, but gazed into her eyes and she saw the anger and frustration and pain in his own. He broke the silence. "Why didn't you tell me about him before?"

"I was living in the fool's paradise you had created for us," she said with bitterness. "Pierre and his proposal no longer seemed important." Her mood changed and she sighed. "Please leave me alone now to get on with what I'm doing. I've hardly exchanged a dozen words with Pierre since he arrived and if he came looking for me he'd find it very suspicious that I'm having an obviously unbusinesslike conversation with you."

"I'm more than happy to risk him jilting you!" Bastian said with an abrasive laugh.

"You fool!" Sabella flung at him. "I'm not thinking of myself! Pierre would certainly wonder exactly who and what *you* are! Do you want to destroy the protective identity I gave you when I introduced you to him?"

Bastian watched her narrowly. "*Why* did you find it necessary to lie to him, Sabella?"

"It's obvious – " she began.

"You're right; it is! Obvious that, deep down, you don't trust him either. You fear he might blackmail me or my father if he knew the truth."

"It's no such thing!" she denied furiously, but Bastian gave her a grim smile and nodded slowly.

"I'll leave you in peace," he said, "because I want to get to know the saintly Pierre le Roux for myself."

A while later, when she looked out of the window, she saw the two of them walking outside, engaged in conversation, and her feeling of tension increased. Bastian was so reckless, so ruthless in his determination to share her life, no matter at what cost to himself or to others, that it terrified her to think of what he might be saying to Pierre.

Nantes and Anton returned home from school at almost the same time as Bastian and Pierre entered the house after their walk, and Sabella suddenly saw a new danger staring her in the face. Ria was too mentally limited to understand the complexities of relationships, and the fact that Daan had been referring to Bastian as "cousin" would have no significance for Pierre. Bastian was obviously not old enough to qualify for the Afrikaans courtesy of "uncle" and so he had become "cousin" instead. But what if Anton or Nantes were to blurt out the fact that the English visitor to whom they had apparently given the courtesy title of "cousin" *was* their cousin in truth?

Before she could decide whether or not to take her elder brothers aside and make up a reason why they should not do so, she realised that they were ignoring Bastian and greeting Pierre with the same delight Ria and Daan had displayed. Under Bastian's jaundiced gaze, Pierre hooked his arm through Sabella's and said, "Your sister and I are going to be married, and I'm going to become both your brother-in-law *and* your pa. What do you think about that?"

"You can't be both," Anton objected.

"W-would we have to c-c-call you Pa?" Nantes wanted to know.

He grinned at their cautious reaction. "I *can* be both, and you may go on calling me Cousin Pierre as you've been doing, or Pa – whichever you prefer."

Anton decided to change the subject to one of more immediate interest. "Did you bring chocolates again this time, Cousin?"

"I did indeed," Pierre smiled, indicating the presents displayed on the dresser.

Sabella doled out chocolates to the children, knowing they would disappear into a bedroom with them to exchange them to their own individual liking.

Bastian spoke for the first time after they had left.

"Bozzoli & Ferguson's Continental Mixture," he mused. "I know they cost a small fortune. And you bring such luxuries each time you call. A very expensive courtship, Mr le Roux." He added smoothly, "But then, you work for them, of course. No doubt there's a staff rule about buying from their competitors."

His tone of voice and his expression had carried the clear innuendo that Pierre had stolen the luxuries from his employers. But instead of taking offence, Pierre answered pleasantly in English, "Staff are able to buy certain items at very low cost. You obviously understand Afrikaans, since you were able to follow my conversation with the boys."

"I have a limited knowledge of the language," Bastian said shortly.

Still in that pleasant voice, but with lifted eyebrows, Pierre went on, "I'm a little surprised that the cost of my courtship should concern you, Mr Grant. I thought your interest was in diamonds."

"Ah yes, diamonds." The grin Bastian gave him was positively demonic. "I would be very interested to know who first started the rumour that there were diamonds on Mooikrantz. It would have had to be someone in Johannesburg, wouldn't it? Someone who knew the name of the farm and where it was located. Someone, perhaps, who expected to inherit it one day — or at least a share in it."

"And somehow knew in advance that Hendrik would soon be killed by a drunken baboon falling on him?" Pierre returned with a laugh.

"Or had wrongly been told that he had a weak heart and might die at any time," Bastian suggested. "I understand that there had been a will, leaving the farm to you and your brother and sister, a will which became null and void when Hendrik le Roux married."

Pierre frowned. "It's obvious what you're hinting at, but you're barking up the wrong tree! From what we had been told Hendrik could have lived for another eight or even ten years. It would have been pretty stupid of any of us to start those rumours so prematurely."

"It's strange, all the same," Bastian said reflectively, "that when the farm was visited by that geologist – what was his name? Mrs le Roux couldn't remember it – "

"Hilary – Higgins – something like that," Pierre responded. "What are you trying to suggest, Mr Grant?"

"Only that it was strange that as soon as the man laid eyes on you, according to Mrs le Roux, he decided there was no truth in the rumours about diamonds on Mooikrantz."

Pierre turned a look of astonishment and hurt on Sabella. "*Did* you say that?"

"I certainly didn't!" she answered with force, glaring at Bastian. "I can't remember exactly what I told Mr Grant about the geologist's visit, but he's twisting my words!"

"Or putting them into perspective," Bastian suggested.

"Or perhaps adding two and two together and deciding they make five," Pierre responded with a smile.

Sabella could stand no more of this verbal sparring, deliberately provocative and insulting on Bastian's side, and commendably restrained on Pierre's. "I'm going to milk the cows," she announced, and grabbed the milking bucket and stool and hurried outside to the corral.

Tears were rolling down her face almost as copiously as the milk spurting into the bucket. Oh God, it was looking more and more as if Bastian would refuse to leave Mooikrantz in time to avert a scandal, robbing her promise to marry Pierre of all point.

She heard a sound behind her but went on with what she was doing. "Sabella," Bastian asked in a challenging voice, "if I leave tomorrow, and stop Annette from carrying out her threat, will you promise not to marry Pierre le Roux?"

It was the last question she had been expecting, and astonishment as well as her tears prevented her from answering it.

"The man's a crook," she heard Bastian go on, "and you don't need him. I'd see to it that you and the children want for nothing." His voice softened. "As for the baby you're expecting – I'd provide for it as if it were my own."

Terror rushed in to join all her other emotions. What an ominous knell his words had struck. Unhappily bound in marriage to Annette, who refused to give him children, would he be prepared to go on providing from a distance for the baby "as if it were his own"? Not if Sabella knew him! He would want to *make* the baby his own by adopting it. Once he returned to his father's world he would be powerful and rich. If one added to that his authority as her cousin and her brother-in-law and therefore her closest male kin, it was easy to imagine him convincing a court that the baby was too great an added burden for a young widow to bear, and that he was acting in the best interests of both by applying to adopt the child. The instinct that had warned her not to let him know that he had fathered her baby now warned her that his already-proprietorial interest in the unborn child would sharpen and that she dared not remain a vulnerable widow.

"Well?" his voice reached her. "What do you say?"

Bastian was a fighter, a ruthless fighter, and she could not risk him fighting her for their baby. "I say no." Sabella used her sleeve to wipe the tears from her face. "If I were stupid and weak enough to allow you to support us, Bastian, I would put myself completely in your power. I'm going to marry Pierre, and be as good a wife to him as I can." Her voice grew stronger as anger seized her. "And will you please stop calling him a crook, and making insulting insinuations to his face? You already have him wondering why someone who'd supposedly come here to see if there might be diamonds should take such a very personal and offensive interest in his affairs!"

"I don't care what he thinks! And if you insist on keeping that stupid promise to marry him, then I'm going to stay here and find out precisely what he is after!"

"Can't you accept that he wants to marry me because he loves me?" She rose, placing the bucketful of milk on top of the drystone wall. The sun had set; in a moment it would be

211

dark and already the first bright star was visible in the navy blue sky. In the hills, the troop of baboons were making their way towards their sleeping-place.

Bastian caught her in his arms and held her. "I can't let you marry someone else and place yet another barrier between us," he said with the harshness of pain in his voice. "And certainly not Pierre le Roux. I don't trust him, Sabella."

"And I don't trust you." She daren't even mention her unborn baby without arousing his suspicions, and so she went on, "Unless I'm safely married to someone else you'll go on dreaming up other reckless, ruthless schemes which would end in my brothers and sister being taken away from me."

"Sabella," Bastian said hoarsely, changing tack completely, "let Annette carry out her threat. Why should my father's political career stand between your happiness and mine? Let's stay here and defy the world. I won't allow anyone to take the children away from you."

She rested her forehead against his chest. It was not just a question of his father's political career being ruined. Both his parents would be plunged into scandal and disgrace; everyone in the district would condemn and ostracise herself and Bastian just as they had his mother, and the children *would* be taken away from a sister who was openly living in sin.

His hand came up to caress her face and she realised that he had taken her silence as a sign of capitulation. She tried to free herself, but his hold on her tightened. She would have to make her decision plain.

"I'm going to marry Pierre," she told him quietly, with determination.

He let her go. "And I'm going to try and stop you," he said uncompromisingly.

Supper that evening was a nightmare to Sabella. She had had no opportunity yet to be alone with Pierre so that she could invent a halfway plausible reason for the behaviour of the man she had been addressing as "Mr Grant" and now

212

she was being forced to listen as Bastian made things worse by stepping up his campaign of provocative, barely-veiled hostilities against Pierre. The children were unnaturally subdued but this was probably less because they sensed undercurrents than because the adults were speaking in English, which excluded them. Nantes and Anton, she guessed, were also mulling over the fact that she would be marrying Pierre.

As soon as the children had gone to bed Bastian gave Pierre a smile which held all the amiability of a tiger about to move in for the kill. "You must have been wondering why I've asked you so many personal questions. The answer is simple. Sabella lied when she introduced me to you. She did it to protect me, although I'm puzzled that she should have thought I needed protection from the man she says she means to marry. I'm her cousin, the illegitimate half-brother of her late husband."

"Wilhelmina's son by an English officer!" Pierre exclaimed.

"Precisely. My father is now a Member of Parliament, and if it became known that I'm his son by an Afrikaans woman with whom he'd had an adulterous affair while he was fighting in a war against her people – well, it would mean the ruin of his political career, and social disgrace for his family."

Sabella had been listening to him in bewilderment and disbelief, but slowly she began to understand the motive behind his frank disclosure to Pierre. Still obsessed with his totally unfounded belief that Pierre was a crook, Bastian was telling him almost in so many words: you would be better off forgetting about Sabella and blackmailing me instead.

It did not surprise her in the least that his insulting, unspoken message had passed completely over Pierre's head, and he told Bastian with sincerity, "Your family secret will always be safe with me."

Bastian looked less than enchanted at the promise. "As Sabella's cousin as well as her brother-in-law," he said,

"I'm naturally concerned that she should not marry the wrong man."

"And you believe that I *am* the wrong man," Pierre summed up without rancour. "I hope to prove to you that you're mistaken. And since all three of us are members of different branches of the same family, I hope you'll keep in contact with us after Sabella and I are married."

"*If* you ever marry!" Bastian snarled, his hostility nakedly displayed now.

Still Pierre refused to rise to the bait. "As to that, if Sabella were to change her mind, of course I'd try to accept defeat gracefully. *Have* you changed your mind, Sabella?"

"No," she answered in a strained voice.

"In that case," Bastian said, showing his teeth, "you may be damned certain that I shall stay in very close contact indeed! But don't count too much on that marriage, either of you. It has just occurred to me that Sabella is still only nineteen, and as her closest kin I might be able to claim guardianship of her."

Sabella rose, so violently that her chair fell over with a clatter. "I've had enough!" she cried furiously. "Get out of my sight, both of you! Go to bed and leave me to tidy the kitchen in peace!"

Pierre went to her and tried to place a comforting arm around her shoulder, but she flung it off. "*I want to be left alone!*" she all but screamed.

"She's overwrought," she heard Pierre say. "We must remember her condition. I think, old chap, we had better make ourselves scarce."

"I'm not your 'old chap'," Bastian said frostily, but when Pierre had left the kitchen he went too, throwing over his shoulder at Sabella, "We'll continue the discussion tomorrow."

Tomorrow, she thought with despair as she put away plates and cutlery. Another day of battle with Bastian and another day closer to the one when Annette would trigger off a scandal that was certain to send the lives of all of them hurtling into disaster.

Another point struck Sabella. It had already occurred to her that as her only close kin, and in view of the fact that she was not yet of age, Bastian could legally assert authority over her. But could he *really* have himself appointed her guardian? If it proved that he could then she would be powerless, for the next two years, to fight any decisions he might choose to make, not only regarding herself but also her baby – and his. The implications scarcely bore thinking about.

She was on her way to her bedroom later when Bastian's door opened silently and she was pulled into his room. He silenced her by kissing her.

When he raised his head the candles at each side of the bed showed the hopelessness, the anger and love in his differently-coloured eyes.

"I'm admitting defeat, Sabella," he muttered.

"This is another trick – " she began.

"No. I'll leave tomorrow."

"I don't believe you. All those threats you made – "

"Accomplished absolutely nothing," he finished for her, dourly. "Pierre le Roux didn't put a foot wrong. I'm even beginning to wonder if it's true that my instinct tells me he's a crook. Isn't it simply that I can't bear the thought of you marrying him, or anyone else? I don't know," he finished with a sigh.

"Then all that talk about claiming guardianship of me – " Sabella began.

"Bluff." He gave a mirthless laugh. "Even if a court were to decide that a girl who had been someone's wife for two years, was pregnant with her late husband's child, and had been offered marriage by someone else needed a guardian, they wouldn't appoint *me*! They would only have to see the two of us together to know that my interest in you is not in the least that of a guardian. And how could I risk them interrogating you, and forcing you to admit that we'd committed adultery? That *would* lead to your brothers and sister being taken away from you."

"Yes," was all she could think of saying.

He loosened the knot in her hair and spread it out, burying his face in it. "I'd sacrifice anything or anyone for you, Sabella," he muttered. "But since I can't stop you marrying le Roux it would be pointless to sacrifice my father's career and my mother's pride. So I'll leave tomorrow. But – let me have tonight?"

"It would be wrong – " she began in a trembling voice.

"It has always been wrong, and at the same time so very right." As he spoke he was undoing the buttons of her dress. It slipped over her shoulders and his hands explored her body with a lingering intensity that spoke of parting. She could no more have stopped him then than she could have stopped a volcano erupting.

I'll make it up to Pierre, she told herself. I don't love him, but I'll never betray him again after tonight . . .

Bastian led her towards the bed. "I'll leave tomorrow and stay out of your life, and make what I can of my own. So – this time it isn't adultery, Sabella. Call it our last goodbye."

It had been a fine speech, but she knew that Bastian had lied. Oh, he would leave in the morning, but he would never stay out of her life. For as long as there was breath in his body and blood in his veins he would scheme and manoeuvre for the two of them to have a life together eventually.

She didn't know whether to despair at the thought, or to rejoice.

10

As much a prisoner in his bed in the Johannesburg General Hospital as if he were in gaol, Pierre had plenty of time to brood bitterly on the death of his Big Dream. It had been a desperate gamble, marrying a frumpish widow with a brood of brats in tow, but at the time it had been his only hope of raising the capital he needed. Now, after only two years, he had to face the galling fact that the gamble had left him a loser.

Visiting times at the hospital, more often than not, only served to rub his nose in his defeat. Sabella, thankfully, wasn't able to visit him at all because she couldn't leave the children. The last thing he wanted was to see that look in her eyes that said: I told you so; I told you from the beginning it was a mistake to recruit cheaper outworkers because they would turn out inferior produce and you would lose customers and money.

So far, thank God, he had also been spared a visit from Ernest Trump. This was because his partner's wife was dying a painful, lingering death from a condition that made her totally dependent on him. It was because of his wife's condition that Trump had left Pierre in sole charge of running Quality Victuals during the last six months of its existence.

Some of Pierre's vistors were welcome, like old friends from his past who sympathised with his ill-luck and with the pain the complicated fracture of his leg must be causing him, but who smuggled in liquor with which to celebrate his escape from even worse injury or death.

Other visitors were not welcome at all, like the representative of the insurance company, outworkers who were owed money, and more particularly Police Sergeant Vorster who had called yet again to go over the facts for what seemed like the dozenth time.

The pretty ward sister who had taken a fancy to Pierre pushed a screen around his bed to give him some privacy and shield him from the curiosity of other patients.

"Now let me see, Mr le Roux," Sergeant Vorster began in that bland voice of his, consulting his notebook. "The van belonging to Quality Victuals was parked in the courtyard at the rear of the company's warehouse, and strewn all over the floor of the yard were cardboard packing-cases?"

"I'd been running the business single-handedly, Sergeant, and there were more urgent matters on my mind than clearing the yard of packing cases."

"And these urgent matters were also the reason why you didn't take the van to a petrol station earlier that day to have the tank filled?"

"That's right. I had an early delivery round to make the next morning and I realised I couldn't do it without a full tank."

"But surely it wouldn't have taken very long for you to have the van's petrol tank filled at a station the following morning?"

Pierre played for time by making a charade of settling himself more comfortably in the bed and drawing attention to his plaster-encased leg suspended in the air by means of weights and pulleys. "I knew I had cans of spare petrol stored in the yard and it seemed pointless to waste time in the morning by stopping at a filling station. Besides, that's what the spare petrol was *for*. To top up the tank when necessary."

"But surely not at ten o'clock at night, and in darkness?"

Pierre forced himself to relax by breathing in deep lungfuls of hospital air, a mixture of boiled cabbage and disinfectant and wax polish. "I didn't expect the yard to be in

218

darkness, Sergeant. It is normally well-lit by an electric light above the rear door of the warehouse. It wasn't until I flicked the switch that I realised the light bulb had fused."

The policeman consulted his notes again, and shook his head. "So you lit an *oil-lamp* to allow you to see what you were doing. Surely that must have struck you as a foolishly dangerous thing to do when working with petrol?"

"Not at the time, no." Pierre gave him a rueful smile which said: we all do stupid things sometimes without thinking, don't we? "I was impatient to get on with what I'd gone there to do," he went on, "and as I always kept an oil-lamp in the warehouse for emergency lighting, I decided to use it."

"It didn't occur to you to replace the fused light bulb with the one inside the warehouse?"

"No, it didn't. As I said, I was impatient to get the job over and done with so that I could go home to my family."

"Mmm . . . Have you been able to remember what it was that made you drop the oil-lamp at the same time as you spilt a considerable amount of petrol which immediately soaked into a cardboard packing-case on the floor?"

"As a matter of fact, I have." He cursed himself for not having come up with such a neat answer before. "I think that shock must have blanked what happened from my mind for a time. But I've been concentrating very hard, and slowly it came back to me. Something leapt on to my shoulder as I stooped over the van's petrol tank. It could only have been a stray cat. The next thing I knew there was a sudden *whoosh* of flames, and if I hadn't thought quickly enough to scale the wall of the yard and jump to the other side, I'd have been burnt to a crisp instead of just breaking my leg. I can only hope the stray cat reacted as swiftly as I did." The unspoken rider to his statement was: *would I have been stupid enough to do it deliberately when there was no guarantee that I'd climb the wall in time, before the petrol tank exploded?*

The policeman made no comment. It still amazed Pierre

219

that no one had considered the possibility that he might have scaled the wall *before* the fire started, that he had thrown the oil-lamp down on the petrol-soaked packing-cases lying close to the delivery van with its overflowing tank and with a trail of other packing-cases leading like a fuse to the wooden warehouse door.

"I understand," Sergeant Vorster went on, "that Quality Victuals was in financial difficulties at the time the fire started."

"I wouldn't say that, Sergeant. The business had suffered a slight setback but it was nothing I couldn't have put right within a very short while if the fire hadn't ruined everything."

"When I spoke to your wife I gained the impression that it was more than a slight setback," Sergeant Vorster commented.

The news that Sabella had been questioned jolted Pierre. She knew far more than was good for her, and if the little bitch wanted to get back at him for that business over Daan . . . He thrust the thought aside, fearing it might show in his face, and he gave Sergeant Vorster a man-to-man look. "My wife left school at fourteen, Sergeant, and the only things she knows anything about are bringing up children and keeping house."

"In that case, why did you trust her to do the bookkeeping for the business, Mr le Roux?"

Pierre laughed to cover the fact that he was seriously disturbed. "Is that how she described what she did? She simply kept a record of the names and addresses of customers."

"And this record, together with bookkeeping ledgers, was inside the warehouse when it burnt down?"

"That's right. I wanted to go thoroughly over them to see where I could improve the service to our customers. I found it hard to concentrate in a houseful of children, particularly with a toddler who is forever falling over and crying."

The policeman's nod could have meant anything. He went on with careful neutrality, "It's true, is it not, that your insurers have refused to pay claims under the policies covering the building and contents of the warehouse, and also the van and consequential loss of profits?"

"Yes." *Damn them to hell, the bastards*, Pierre thought viciously. Aloud, he went on with a smile, "I don't see how they can legally continue to refuse payment of the claims when there is no question of arson being involved."

"I wouldn't say there's never likely to be a charge of arson, Mr le Roux." Sergeant Vorster stood up, putting his notebook back in his pocket. "I think it's only fair to warn you – we've discovered that someone whose identity is being withheld from us has hired a private investigator to pursue the matter. The police do not have the manpower to concentrate exhaustively on one particular case, but the private investigator has been told to spare no expense. If he were to come to us with proof that arson *was* committed –" The policeman shrugged, making his meaning clear.

Pierre stared at his retreating back after the ward sister had removed the screen around his bed. He smiled at her, and even managed a flirtatious joke, but his thoughts were scrambling around in his brain. There was only one person with the means and the motive to have hired a private investigator to sniff out possible clues, and that was Bastian Grant, damn his miserable, misbegotten English soul. God, how Pierre had come to hate Sabella's cousin!

He couldn't even relieve his feelings by making his hatred plain. He had never allowed his façade of large-minded amiability mixed with injured innocence to slip in his dealings with Bastian Grant – not even when the bastard had been at his most offensive, pointing out to Sabella that the sale of Mooikrantz had furnished Pierre with more than enough capital to go into partnership with Ernest Trump. At the time, Sabella had defended her husband vigorously, and why shouldn't she have done so? He had totally convinced her that it was *her* idea that the money should be invested in the partnership, because she'd believed it would give him the major share in the business, and she had hoped to have a hand in running it once the baby was old enough not to need her constant attention.

Of course, she was no longer as trusting as she'd been in the beginning. Not that it mattered. Pierre had what Bastian Grant most wanted in the world, and *that* was his revenge against the man. But this private investigator business . . .

Pierre clenched his hands into impotent fists. The *helsem* wanted him in gaol, of course, so that he would be able to moon around Sabella even more than he had been doing until now. Oh, Pierre had never been fooled for a moment about the feeling between those two. It was like an electric charge in the air each time they met, and even when they sat yards apart and discussed the weather one got the feeling that invisible bands of steel bound them to one another.

To give her her due, Sabella had never done anything to encourage Grant's constant intrusion into their lives. No, to be accurate, there had been one occasion when she had shown her hand. It was when the baby was born. She had insisted that the child should be called Katrien, the second name of Wilhelmina, and that Grant should be Katrien's godfather. "Since Hendrik was his half-brother, he has the right," she'd said. It hadn't escaped Pierre that Wilhelmina Katrien le Roux had also been *Grant's* mother.

But he had smiled and agreed and pretended to welcome even more visits from Grant now that he had the excuse of wanting to see his god-daughter. The way Pierre looked at it, there was absolutely no advantage to be gained by him forcing a confrontation with the Englishman. Better to smile and be pleasant and store up every grievance until the right moment came, the moment when there would be something in it for himself.

In the meantime, it had caused him considerable satisfaction to witness the suppressed longing and frustration between his wife and her cousin. Grant's wife would obviously never divorce him. She was forever being featured in the newspapers, attending some la-di-da function or opening bazaars or fêtes, and usually with some reference to the fact that her father-in-law was the Right Honourable Peregrine Grant. She looked a cold, haughty bitch, for all her beauty, which went some way to explaining why her husband hankered after dowdy Sabella instead. Lady Nevershit, Pierre had nicknamed Annette Grant. Her husband was away in England on business, he knew from the newspapers.

But he'd hired a private investigator to sniff out proof of arson, Pierre thought, a red mist forming before his eyes.

And then something even worse happened to destroy his peace of mind. A lawyer came to see him in hospital, announcing that he represented Bozzoli & Ferguson.

"It has come to light," he said, "that you and your partner, Ernest Trump, have been deceiving customers of Bozzoli & Ferguson into believing that your business, Quality Victuals, was connected with their company. As a result of the fire which put you out of business, Bozzoli & Ferguson have been inundated with complaints from their customers about orders paid for but not delivered by Quality Victuals, as well as numerous complaints about the steady deterioration of the quality of the products supplied by their supposed sister company, the said Quality Victuals. The reputation of my clients has suffered seriously, and they don't want to harm that reputation any further by having a writ served on you while you are still in hospital. But I'm asking the hospital administration to inform me of the time and date of your discharge and then we shall proceed against you and your partner."

After he had left, and Pierre's first panic had subsided, bitterness began to eat at him. There was not a shred of hope left, now, of ever reviving his Big Dream. Even if the insurance company were to pay the claims he had been banking on when he started the fire, the money would be swallowed by legal fees and fines when Bozzoli & Ferguson took him and Trump to court. Then there was that damned private investigator digging away into his affairs, and the wrath of Ernest Trump to be faced . . .

What did he have to show for all his painstaking efforts

and his planning? A wife who was about as exciting as yesterday's cold mealie porridge, and five brats who had nothing at all to do with him.

As the days passed he was no longer confined to bed, but hopping around on crutches. The pretty ward sister said he would soon be able to go home, only returning to the hospital when it was time for the plaster to be removed from his leg, and his plans slowly began to take shape.

He wouldn't wait for the hospital to discharge him, and have someone hovering outside to slap a writ on him. He would discharge himself without any prior hint to anyone, and he would neither go home nor return to the hospital to have the plaster removed. He was going to disappear.

Let Sabella beg the money from her cousin to pay his hospital bills and all the other bills that had been piling up. He would collect the small, secret nest-egg he had prudently salted away, and go to ground somewhere when he left the hospital. There were any number of old friends who would be happy to have him stay, and would swallow whatever story he chose to tell them. Sabella's usefulness to him was over.

It occurred to him that now might be the time to apply to the Right Honourable Peregrine Grant for money in return for his silence about that old scandal concerning his son's birth. But on reflection Pierre discarded the idea. Blackmail was only worth the risk if one made the initial demand sufficiently reasonable not to spur the victim into calling in the police, and then afterwards dipped into the same fountain from time to time. The fact that he would have to lie low for an indefinite period ruled that out. More importantly, Bastian Bloody Grant would learn about it, and nothing would suit *him* better than to have Pierre arrested for blackmailing his father, and at the same time allow the truth to come out and set himself free. Lady Nevershit would divorce him *then*, without a question, and since Sabella would also have grounds to divorce Pierre, he would be giving those two the thing they most wanted – to be together. No, blackmail was out.

224

There was another reason why he shied away from blackmail, and it was the same reason which contributed to his unwillingness to expose the true feelings he nursed towards Bastian Grant. It was not a reason which Pierre cared to admit to himself, other than rarely and fleetingly as he did now. It had to do with his need to be admired, and no one would admire a convicted blackmailer. Achieving his Big Dream would have earned him the supreme accolade of admiration but since his Big Dream lay in ashes he would take admiration wherever else it might be found. For this reason he would never tell his friends the truth about his desertion of Sabella and the children. God, they all thought he was wonderful because he'd adopted the children, and he wanted to hold on to that. He would have to work out a story, favourable to himself, to explain why he couldn't go back to Sabella and his adopted children. It would have to be something that made it seem he was sacrificing himself for their sakes.

Still considering various ideas, he picked up his crutches and hopped into the hospital day-room. Several other patients from the men's surgical ward were sitting at tables and playing cards for small stakes, and because he was popular with them they urged him, as usual, to join them.

"No thanks," he grinned. "I've told you before – each blow-fly to its own turd, and mine doesn't happen to be whist played for ha'pennies." He sat down and picked up the hospital's copy of the morning newspaper. He never troubled to read the news but turned straight to the racing pages. Not that he could afford to place a bet, of course, even if there had been such a thing as a bookie's runner in the hospital, but the next best thing was to pick likely horses in different races and then check the next day to see whether or not they had been winners.

This morning, however, the word "diamond" leapt out at him from the front page, and as he studied the headline excitement gathered inside him. "CLAIM-PEGGING

225

RACE AT ELANDSPUTTE" they screamed, and underneath, in slightly less bold print, "*Lichtenburg Prepares for
Diamond Rush.*"

The newspaper report itself quickened Pierre's excitement, which surged like an electric current through his
blood. A diamond had been found on a farm named
Elandsputte, not far from the small town of Lichtenburg,
and now that it had been established that it had not been
a mere random find a public rush for claims was being
organised. Anyone with half-a-crown to pay for a digger's
licence would be free to run and stake a claim of not more
than 225 square feet on which to dig for diamonds.

A slow smile spread across Pierre's face. Thousands
would be taking part in the rush. What better place in which
to hide oneself from writs and the police and a beavering
private investigator and a partner with vengeance on his
mind? What better chance of shaking Bastian Grant off his
back for good?

Sabella and the brats were still of use to him after all. As
a man on crutches, with a wife and five children to support,
he would be given a headstart in the rush, and since he was
experienced in the business of diamond mining, he knew
exactly what to look for in a prospective claim.

Yes, instead of a liability Sabella and the brood of children
had been turned into an asset. Not only would they ensure
for him the sympathy he would need from other participants
in the diamond race, but they would provide him, gratis and
for nothing, with the labour he would otherwise have had
to hire once his claim had been staked. Only the toddler,
Katrien, would have no vital role to play in the search for
diamonds – *yet*. But in a year or so even she would be able
to help with the washing of gravel.

The Big Dream was beckoning Pierre once again.

11

The traffic streaming towards Lichtenburg had become a cavalcade, swelled by farmers ruined by the drought which had been blistering the land for almost two years now. The convoy was so dense that its pace was frustratingly slow and it made little difference whether one was travelling by motor car, truck, a wagon drawn by mules or oxen, by donkey cart or on foot. The pedestrians were joined by poor-white Afrikaans road-workers who abandoned their jobs there and then as diamond fever swept over them, and tagged along with their government-owned pickaxes and shovels, shouting to wives and children left weeping outside their shanties the promise that they would soon be back with fortunes.

"At a wage of five-and-six a day," Pierre commented, "who can blame them for walking out on their jobs?"

Sabella said nothing, but she thought that the five shillings and sixpence a day had at least been guaranteed. Those women outside their shanties had as little choice in the matter as she herself had had in taking the children and joining Pierre on the way to Lichtenburg.

She thought of his return from hospital, two weeks ago, when he'd been brought home by one of those many friends he kept in the background. With few illusions left about him, she had been far less than overjoyed at seeing him again. But she had learnt to play the game by his rules, and so she had lied when he asked how she had been managing financially. "I eked out the money you gave me before the night of the fire, and the only outstanding bill is for electricity."

The truth was that they would have starved if she hadn't accepted, with gratitude tainted by humiliation, the sum of money Bastian had pressed upon her before he left for England. She had refused it at first but he had looked at her with the familiar mixture of anger and pain in his eyes and growled, "Don't be so damned selfish, Sabella! How do you think *I* would feel, stuck in England and wondering whether you had food in the house or even a roof over your head?"

The money Pierre had given her hadn't lasted more than a few days, and he must have known it, but she had learnt by now that he had the ability to lie convincingly to himself, and she wasn't surprised when he said, "Good girl, Sabella. The electricity bill will have to remain unpaid. The little money I have left will have to be used to buy a wagon and mules and then we must leave immediately for Lichtenburg. We can't take with us anything but basic necessities."

Those basic necessities, Sabella thought now as she sat in the back of the wagon with Katrien on her lap, amounted to very little. The crockery brought from Mooikrantz when it was sold had been exchanged for tin mugs and plates and a primus stove at the first general store they'd reached after abandoning the rented, furnished house in Johannesburg. Apart from their clothing and bedding only a few pots and pans had been brought along. In vivid, incongruous contrast with such austerity she had smuggled on board her most treasured possessions – the dress and shoes and stockings Bastian had bought for her more than two years ago and which she had never worn. The only tangible reminder of his love for her, they were sewn inside her pillow, still wrapped in tissues and with the surrounding feathers concealing the parcel's shape. She had learnt just where to lay her head to avoid the sharp edges of the shoes.

She smiled wryly to herself. Their sleeping arrangements were so primitive and uncomfortable that the heels of the shoes digging into her neck would have made little difference. At the same general store Pierre had bought, along with picks and shovels, some mattress-covers made of ticking, and when they reached a native *stad* he had handed the covers to a group of enthusiastic black youngsters who, in return for a few coppers, had filled them with dry mealie-leaves. Sabella had sewn up the open ends. These crude, lumpy mattresses were what they slept on at night, on top of and underneath the wagon.

If there was one comfort to which Sabella could cling in their present circumstances – and for some considerable time to come – it was the fact that Pierre's plaster-encased leg as well as lack of privacy would rule out any physical intimacy between them.

In an ironic way she had found that she was able to understand Annette. The physical act, when not entered into with love, was something which, if it could not be avoided, became no better than a burden and a duty to be endured in the hope that it would soon be over and leave no legacy. How she envied Annette her access to contraceptives! Until Pierre had fractured his leg Sabella had lived in monthly dread of discovering herself to be pregnant again. Her few prayers to that God she had learnt could not be relied upon had been fervent pleas that he should save her from conceiving a child by Pierre, and in God's haphazard way he had chosen to answer them so far.

Katrien had fallen asleep on her lap and Sabella cradled her gently, an overwhelming tenderness flowing through her. How could she have thought of the clothes as the only tangible evidence of Bastian's love? His daughter had inherited his hair of different shades of blonde, and her eyes were the identical colour of his own green one, so that Sabella had often in the past waited, with her heart in her mouth, for him to question the paternity of the little god-daughter he loved so deeply. But he obviously accepted that the colouring was a family trait passed on by Tante Wilhelmina's side of the family and inherited from Hendrik.

Sabella's eyes felt gritty with unshed tears as she thought of Bastian, who was still in England and would have no idea where they were or how to find them once he returned to Johannesburg. Perhaps it was as well that they should at last lose touch with one another, and that he would no longer be able to make those poignant, intrusive, unbearable visits, fraught with tension, to see her and the children and menace Pierre with hostile questions and hawklike surveillance. But oh, how she missed him . . .

The cavalcade had ground to a halt and the almost permanent dust-cloud it swept up was slowly dispersing like drifts of red smoke. Pierre lowered himself from the driving seat, reached for his crutches and called to the children who had elected to walk alongside the wagon, "Which of you would like to come with me to see what the cause of the hold-up is?"

"Me, Daddy!" Daan and Anton responded simultaneously, and predictably their sister echoed, "Ria, Daddy!" After a moment Nantes also lifted a hand in a signal that was not quite so committed as the response of the others. His stammer had worsened so that, quite often, he did not try to speak at all.

Sabella watched them making their way with Daan, Anton and Ria competing to walk on either side of Pierre, and Nantes trailing behind the man they had decided in the end to call "Daddy". Sabella shook her head in bafflement. The children, with the exception of Nantes, had greeted Pierre with undiminished joy when he returned from hospital and it was as if they had washed the past from their minds.

Perhaps the instinct of the very young was a true one. It really was beginning to seem that physical pain and his period in hospital had changed Pierre. Certainly, no one watching him as he hopped along surrounded by the children could have doubted his complete devotion to them. She could hear people calling out sympathetic greetings to him, asking about his leg, and she knew he would be stopping frequently before he reached the head of the cavalcade with the children. Pierre had already made many friends among the other diamond seekers. But she sensed that Nantes, who kept his own counsel, shared her reservations about Pierre.

Perhaps the two of them were wrong. Perhaps the dark and secret side of him had been exorcised by his experience in hospital. Of course, it was far too much to hope that he would ever be entirely honest or truthful. Sabella shrugged resignedly. On the other hand, he was trying to do his best for his wife and his large family of children with whom he had no blood ties but had adopted and accepted as his responsibility. How many other men, virtually penniless and hopping on crutches, would have resisted the impulse to leave them to their fate? She knew that he must often be in pain but he never complained or lost his temper. Who was she, who had never been able to give him love and had married him for her own ends, to judge him for the flaws she had discovered in him? Especially when it was becoming apparent that he had conquered the worst of those flaws?

It seemed to have taken forever, but at last they had reached their destination, a shanty-town overspill of the small town of Lichtenburg. And what a bleak, barren place it was, Sabella thought, looking around her. The meagre shelter offered by an occasional wait-a-minute thorn tree or white stinkwood had been snapped up by earlier arrivals who had erected zinc shacks in their shade or put up tents. Now it didn't matter very much where, in that uncomfortable terrain, one chose to erect one's own shelter. Two of the many friends Pierre had made along the way were driving into the ground the four poles he had bought, and then suspending tarpaulin above them, lashing a corner to each pole. Sabella had already experienced so many indignities and humiliations along the way that she felt almost hardened to the crudeness of what was to be their future dwelling-place.

Pierre had already surveyed the ground, and now his voice cut into her thoughts. "Sabella, that corrugated iron building over there is the office where one has to buy a licence and get a digger's certificate. Leave Nantes here with Katrien to guard our belongings and bring the others and come with me while I buy my licence. I've been told there are buckets and sieves on sale at a stall nearby, and you and the children can help to carry them."

A long line of men were waiting to buy licences, and when at last it was Pierre's turn he addressed the official behind the makeshift desk. "As you can see, I'm on crutches and I'm sure everyone would agree that I should be given a head start – "

"No," the official interrupted impassively, "it's going to be every man for himself; the halt, the old and the lame on equal terms with the young and athletic."

"Damn it!" Pierre exploded. "How can I be expected to manage? It wouldn't just be the running, it would also be the driving in of the pegs and then struggling to get upright again, and my crutches are bound to get kicked beyond my reach in the rush!"

The man behind the counter shrugged. "The rules say that everyone runs when the starting pistol is fired. Do you want to buy a licence or don't you? There are others waiting their turn behind you."

"I can't see how – " Pierre began in defeat, but Sabella moved to stand in front of him. She hadn't come all this way, suffered hardship and indignity, just to have to return to Johannesburg again, penniless and homeless.

"Is there anything in the rules," she asked the man, "that says *I* couldn't run and stake a claim?"

He looked reflectively at her. "No, lady. But I have to tell you that you'd stick out like a sore thumb, and the men running are bound to have it in for a woman with the cheek to compete in what, after all, is their world."

"*I'll* worry about that," Sabella said, and turned to Pierre. "Agreed?" He nodded in a bemused way and handed over the coins he'd been holding, and the man behind the counter asked her name so that he could write it in his records before issuing her digger's licence.

As they moved away afterwards Pierre said in a worried voice, "He was right about you being a target, especially as there are many who'll be after the piece of ground I've picked out as likely diamond-bearing terrain."

"I have a plan," she assured him. "But I know nothing about staking a claim so you must explain it to me."

He did so as he took her to see the piece of ground he had his eye on; a dip in the surface of the earth which, he said, suggested an ancient water-course. "You'll be given four pegs, Sabella. When the starting pistol is fired you'll have to run as fast as you can and stake out an area no bigger than fifteen feet by fifteen. You drive in the pegs to mark out the square. Remember that an inspector will come round later to check on the measurements of your claim and if it's larger than it should be you'll forfeit it and have your licence taken away. So make your square smaller than it should be; you'll be allowed to move your pegs later and enlarge your claim to the permitted size."

They used the children as a cover, telling them to run ahead and play so that Pierre and Sabella would seem to be rounding them up as they went after them. In reality, he was showing her the spots in which she should drive in her four pegs. She committed them to memory and returned to the crude shelter which passed as their home.

"Pierre," Sabella said, "I want to borrow your sharp knife."

As he handed it to her he asked, "What do you want it for?" She calmly answered his question by loosening her long hair and chopping it off roughly at a level with her ear-lobes. She couldn't help thinking with a certain bitter humour how she used to yearn for short hair in the days when to be in fashion had seemed so very desirable.

"Deal with the back for me," she told Pierre, handing him the knife. "I can't reach. For the purpose of the rush I'm going to become a young man. I have a pair of trousers and some shirts I bought second-hand for Nantes but which he hasn't grown into yet. They'll fit me reasonably well and

I'll borrow his hat. Long hair would have come undone and given me away."

When her shorn hair had been gathered up and disposed of she rooted through the trunk holding their personal possessions and found a hand-mirror. Her roughly hacked-off hair would have looked terrible, she thought dispassionately, if it weren't for the fact that the ends had decided to curl. She looked prettier than she ever had before, at a time when to look pretty was the least important thing in her life.

While they waited for the rush to start Sabella concentrated on becoming as fit as it was possible to be while living on an inadequate diet of steadily-dwindling food. Her last pair of shoes had fallen to pieces during the journey to Lichtenburg, when she'd often had to walk miles to buy mealie meal or flour from farmers' wives; at the time she had been deeply humiliated by having to walk barefoot, but now she perceived it as having been a blessing in disguise, because the soles of her feet had toughened so much that she could cross the roughest terrain without pain, and if she'd had to wear a pair of Pierre's or Nantes's boots she would have found them a considerable handicap.

In preparation for the rush, she took two buckets several times a day and ran to where the water-pumps had been installed, filled them and hurried back to the shelter. If anyone noticed her with her shorn head covered by a sun bonnet they would have dismissed her as a harassed wife in a rush to get back to her family. In reality she was exercising her muscles and learning to control her breathing.

On the day of the rush she lined up with an army of others, dressed in trousers and shirt, with Nantes's hat jammed on her head and her four pegs clutched in palms that were sweaty with nervous anticipation.

The starting pistol went off with a crack. The people scrambling to stake their claims resembled frantically stampeding animals and the air was filled with the din made by relatives of the runners shouting encouragement. Someone tried to trip Sabella up; she staggered momentarily,

234

regained her balance and ran on. A burly man was also after the claim she was heading for and he made deliberate attempts to bring his hob-nailed boots down on her bare feet each time he succeeded in catching up with her. She put on a burst of speed to outstrip him once and for all and felt a searing pain shooting along her side. Ignoring it, she ran on, drove in one peg, straightened, measured the distance with her eyes, and reached the spot where the second peg should go a split-second before the man who had tried to trip her up. Then she zig-zagged between him and the runner with hob-nailed boots, the pain in her side excruciating now. By the time her third peg had gone in her competitors conceded defeat and she was able to catch her breath before driving in the final peg. Illogical tears coursed down her face as she limped away, to be caught in Pierre's arms.

"You did it!" he exulted. "By God, sweetheart, you did it! We're in business!"

In spite of her exhaustion and the pain in her side, she felt euphoria rising inside her to match his. "Yes, Pierre, we're in business."

Sabella often thought back to that moment later, and wondered whether she would have been quite so exultant if she'd known what "being in business" would turn out to be like. Life at the diggings was hard and crude and reduced one to the very basics of existence. Water had to be paid for at a farthing a gallon and since it was needed for washing the excavated gravel it could not be used regularly for keeping oneself clean. Sometimes Sabella was reduced to forcing the children to spit on a piece of rag so that she could remove the worst of the dirt from their faces and hands.

Shops had sprung up, constructed of corrugated iron, where one could buy almost anything at vastly inflated prices. Since the back-breaking work in which all of them had to take part could not be done on empty stomachs, Sabella had to buy mealie meal, coffee, milk and sugar on credit. Cooking a meal was another problem, because when fuel was available at all it was ruinously expensive, and any spare moment the boys had was spent in searching for dry dung.

But what dominated the lives of all of them was the grinding toil which started at dawn and didn't finish until darkness fell, and left them with bleeding palms and muscles which felt as if they were on fire. First of all the earth on their claim had to be loosened, and Sabella took it in turns with Pierre to wield the pickaxe and a spade to break up the ground. Since everyone around them was also engaged upon this preliminary task it was like living in the midst of a perpetual dust-storm, and visibility was often so poor that if the owners of motor vehicles had not switched on their headlights all work would have had to be abandoned. Anton and Daan shared the task of collecting the loosened earth in buckets and tipping it into a sieve which Nantes and Ria took in turns to shake in order to separate the gravel from the soil. While all this was going on Katrien played placidly by herself in the dirt.

When Pierre judged that the heap of sieved gravel was large enough to warrant it, he hired a washing-and-sorting machine. This had to be cranked by hand, and inside it was fitted a bobbin with pegs which broke up the gravel. Pierre cranked the machine; Sabella carried gravel in buckets to feed into it and the children worked in relays to fetch water from the pump and pour it onto the gravel. The heavy deposits were spewed out into a large pail by the machine and then thrown into a barrel containing three sieves. Each lot had to be sieved under water and the deposits examined for signs of diamonds, which meant squatting in mud for hours at a time. Accompanying the back-breaking work was the never-ending noise; the sound of machinery, of pick and shovel, of shouted oaths or cries of frustration or excitement from thousands burrowing for diamonds in the dirt.

Elation overcame weariness as the first washing yielded several modest gems on Sabella's claim. Even Ria was able to recognise a diamond after the first few had been found, for it wore a "jacket" like no other stone. At the end of the week Pierre took the diamonds to the tents set up by the buyers who arrived each Friday to examine and buy stones.

"All Englishmen, of course," Pierre reported afterwards with an angry laugh. "Not for them the squalor and toil of grubbing for diamonds. *They* merely buy them at a price set as low as possible."

Hardship, Sabella had noticed, had given Pierre an increasing grudge against the English. Inevitably her thoughts strayed to Bastian, but they were sad and resigned rather than raw with frustrated desire and loss as they used to be. But then, she would have defied any woman and all but perhaps a handful of men to experience physical desire or finer emotions in these conditions. The diggings had become a foretaste of hell with their tin shacks, their shelters made of canvas or sacking or old packing cases or sheets of rusty corrugated iron, and their growing atmosphere of desperation as so many other claims failed to yield any diamonds.

At least their own hard work was continuing to receive modest reward, for each washing brought to light more small diamonds, but even so it seemed like a vicious circle to Sabella, because most of the money they made had to pay for the hiring of the machine, for repayment of their debts at the shops, for firewood and water and fodder for the mules.

One day she straightened up from her back-breaking task of feeding gravel into the machine and stared at the water pumps. They were no more than crude, curved pipes embedded in the ground and fitted with canvas spouts. The spouts made it equally possible for a child to fill a pail with water as it did a man to fill barrels on the back of his donkey cart before driving it to his outlying claim.

"Pierre," Sabella said abruptly, "I've had an idea. Those mules of yours are eating their heads off to no useful purpose. The children and I could somehow manage here on our own while you take the wagon and mules and buy

237

water at a farthing a gallon and sell it to the diggers at their claims. They would find it as cheap and more convenient to buy from you at, say, tuppence a barrel instead of paying hired labour to carry it to them on foot. And it would mean a steady income for us during the weeks when we don't find diamonds."

Pierre stopped cranking the machine and leant his weight on one crutch. "*Allemagtig*, Sabella," he exclaimed with appreciation, "you're a man-and-a-half when it comes to bright ideas! But are you sure you and the children could manage without me?"

"Quite sure." She forebore to point out that they were already managing without him for long periods each day, because he was increasingly complaining that the plaster on his leg was driving him crazy through the itching it caused, and then he would sit on the ground and hack away at it with his sharp knife while Nantes took over the cranking of the machine. She gave Pierre a challenging look. "In return I want a proper home, built as soon as there's enough money, even if it is only a few rooms made out of zinc." One of the worst indignities of life at the diggings was the lack of privacy.

From that day their fortunes improved slowly, and modestly but surely. Sabella gained her home of zinc with four small rooms and a flat roof, and Pierre even bought her an old but serviceable kitchen range so that she no longer had to cook in the open, on the oil-guzzling primus or a smoking dung fire. His sharp knife had at last managed to hack off the last bits of plaster on his leg and only a slight limp still remained as evidence that it had ever been fractured. To Sabella's overwhelming relief, however, he made no sexual advances to her now that lack of privacy and the plaster cast no longer stood in the way.

As others also prospered at the diggings more zinc houses sprang up; cafés, bioscopes, lodging-houses and even churches constructed of corrugated iron established themselves, as well as a police station for dealing with fights among the diggers and the more serious crime of "walking diamonds" – gems stolen by hired labourers and bought illegally in secret deals.

What gave Sabella the greatest satisfaction of all was the day when a small school opened at the diggings. Fortunately, they could now afford to pay for hired labour so that the law could be complied with and all the boys, including Daan, sent to school. The building was so cramped and the number of pupils so large that a shift system had to be operated, and only Nantes regretted the fact that his schooling consisted of no more than three hours in the morning.

For some people at the diggings life continued to be hard and unrewarding and even those who were more prosperous had to share the same miserable conditions of almost permanent dust-storms, of wading through a morass of mud when it rained, of no electricity supply or sewage system. But those same conditions did not deter many young women of easy virtue from streaming into the diggings and taking up residence, and illicit she-beens, or drinking places, also began to operate in secret, their whereabouts carefully guarded by both owners and customers so that the police would not raid them.

Sabella was walking home from the shops one Friday afternoon. Their "score" for the week had been a good one and she'd felt justified in buying meat and vegetables for the rare luxury of a stew for supper.

As Sabella approached their house she could hear Pierre in conversation with another digger, although she couldn't see them because they were at the back of the zinc construction.

"You certainly struck lucky," she heard the other digger say in envious tones, "when you decided where to peg out your claim."

"*Luck!*" Pierre echoed. "It had nothing to do with luck, my friend! I spied out the land and decided where diamonds were most likely to be found. I was on crutches when the starting pistol went off, and I can tell you this – by the time I'd driven in all four of my pegs the blood was streaming from my armpits where the crutches had bitten into them."

Sabella came face to face with the two men as they emerged from the back of the house. Without stopping to think, she blurted out, "But *I* ran to stake the claim and the licence is in my name – "

Pierre went to her and put an arm around her, giving her a squeeze. "Don't throw a fit, my love," he said in a teasing voice. "I just wanted to see whether you would allow me to steal your thunder or not."

She forced herself to smile, and freed herself, hurrying inside the house. Daan and Anton were safely at school; their lessons were held in the afternoon shift. But Nantes was sitting on a mealie-leaf mattress next to Katrien, carefully cutting shapes from an old flannelette shirt while Ria looked on. "I'm m-m-making a d-doll for K-K-Katrien – " he began to stammer enthusiastically when he saw Sabella.

"Disappear," she ordered urgently, having decided to be on the safe side. "Take Katrien and get out. You too, Ria."

She had been too late. Pierre's voice came from behind her, quite pleasant in tone, contrasting shockingly with the obscenity he used towards Nantes and confirming what she had instinctively feared. "Playing like a girl again are you, *fokken* nancy-boy?" At the same moment Pierre was removing his belt with lightning speed and then he was holding Nantes with one hand and beating him mercilessly with the other. Katrien and Ria began to cry and Sabella hurled herself at Pierre, drumming at his chest with her fists, kicking at his shins. He stopped beating Nantes but didn't let him go. "Please, Sabella," he said reproachfully, "you know what happens when you interfere."

Her hands curled into useless fists and a sour taste filled her mouth. Oh, she knew well enough. The more she interfered, the more severely he would beat Nantes. Her brother was biting hard on his lips so that his whimpers of pain were muted, and tears rolled down his cheeks.

Sabella was weeping in silence too, but with helpless rage and self-blame. How could she have been so stupid? Hadn't she learnt, by now, that Pierre should be allowed to believe in his own lies? Hadn't she had the bitter lesson dinned into her sufficiently that if she did anything to anger him, he would take it out on one of the children?

Helplessly, she watched the calculated way in which Pierre used his belt on Nantes, beating him solely on parts of his body where the evidence would be hidden from others. Only fear for her brother's continued punishment prevented her from making other attempts to intervene. *Fool*, she raged at herself. You thought he'd changed. Why didn't you realise it was only lack of privacy that restrained him?

At last Pierre decided to stop beating Nantes, and put his belt on again. The boy made vain attempts to wipe his eyes and his nose on his sleeve. The scene had not yet played itself out, Sabella knew, rage and hatred almost choking her.

"You know why I beat you, don't you, Nantes?" Pierre asked so gently that the uninitiated would have thought their ears were betraying them.

"Y-Y-Y-Y . . ." Nantes had to abandon the effort to get the word out.

"Yes," Pierre supplied it for him, and added with that same deceptive gentleness, "Yes – *who?*"

Nantes knuckled his eyes and made a visibly desperate effort to bring his stammer under reasonable control. "D-Daddy."

"Good. Now why did I beat you?"

His face red as he struggled to make the required response, Nantes stammered, "B-b-because you l-l-love m-me."

Pierre nodded. "And?" he prompted.

After several abortive attempts, Nantes managed what only his family would have been able to identify as the ritual response: *I love you too, Daddy*.

Pierre smiled. Feeling physically sick, Sabella addressed

her brother. "Take Katrien and Ria with you and see if you can find fuel."

He lost no time in obeying. Sabella faced Pierre. "One day, when you least expect it," she said with a deadly menace of which she'd never before believed herself capable, "I'm going to pay you back in full for every beating you've given one of the children."

"My dear Sabella, I chastise them when they need it, and for their own good, just as any caring father would – "

She cut through the familiar self-lie, unable to stop herself. "Hadn't you better check your armpits?" she taunted scathingly. "The force you used on poor Nantes might have reopened those dreadful, bleeding wounds caused by running to stake the claim on crutches."

His eyes narrowed in his whitened face, and she knew she should have held her tongue. "Be careful, Sabella," was all he said quietly. "Be very, very careful."

After that day she felt as if she were being forced to walk on eggs without daring to break one of them. By some kind of unspoken communication Anton and young Daan had been made aware of the beating Nantes had received and only Anton remained untouched by the changed atmosphere. Pierre had only beaten Anton on one occasion and the boy had taken his punishment unflinchingly, without weeping or crying out, and there had been total conviction in his voice afterwards when he went through the required ritual of acknowledging and expressing love between himself and the man who had beaten him. Then, spontaneously, he had hugged Pierre. And because he *did* love Pierre and admire him he hadn't only escaped future punishment, but considered that when his "Daddy" gave one of the others a beating it had been fully deserved.

Sabella didn't know whether she ought to worry more about Anton's attitude than she did about those of the others. The beating of Nantes had awakened memories in Daan of the past punishment he himself had received at Pierre's hands, and he reacted by fawning on his "Daddy".

While Nantes was like a cowed dog that kept out of the way as much as possible or tried to make itself invisible, Daan behaved like a cur that creeps on its belly to lick its master's hands in the hope of escaping a whipping. Pierre had never beaten Ria or Katrien, but Sabella had no illusions that it was because they were girls. No, Ria was too mentally limited and Katrien too young to be able to go through that charade which seemed so necessary to Pierre in a warped way that Sabella didn't understand. Even so, the two of them reacted to the changed atmosphere inside the crude zinc-built house.

Sabella's one dismal comfort lay in the fact that Bastian was no longer part of their lives. Dear God, how it used to terrify her that he would find out about the beatings, and do something reckless and catastrophic. This fear had forced her to instil into the children, subtly and without putting it into words, that the beatings should be covered by a conspiracy of silence.

Pierre gave no indication that he noticed the way the children were behaving, but Sabella worried that he might seize an excuse for another beating. He certainly had good reason for wanting to punish her further, because the story that the digger's licence was in her name and that she had run to stake the claim had spread, and people would ask Pierre jokingly about the state of his "bleeding armpits".

So far he was taking the gibes in good part, still pretending that the story had been deliberately concocted to tease Sabella. Then he would counter by asking maliciously, "And how have you been scoring lately?" because he knew that few of their immediate neighbours were finding diamonds in sufficient quantities to do more than subsist.

As if fate were conspiring against Sabella and the children, their own claim began to yield fewer small diamonds and some weeks they didn't score at all. It would need very little for Pierre to take his frustration out on one of the children, and her inner tension became almost unbearable.

But one afternoon when the hired labourers were feeding gravel into the washing-and-sorting machine and cranking it while Pierre and Sabella squatted in the mud, each of them examining gravel thrown into the sieves by the machine, she expelled her breath in a sound of incredulity. Wearing its familiar "jacket" and lying right on top of the heap of gravel in her sieve was a diamond far larger than any they had found before.

She knew better than to draw public attention to the find. Bitter experience had taught her that anyone known to have made a considerable score could expect a flood of hard-luck stories from others, made all the more difficult to ignore because they were invariably genuine. There was precious little room for charity at the diggings, and so she waited until the afternoon's washing-and-sorting was over before she showed Pierre the diamond inside the privacy of their house.

"Sabella, you little marvel!" Pierre exulted. "It's a nice stone, but not quite of the first water."

"We should get enough for it on Friday to keep us going for – "

"I'm damned if I'm going to offer it to the licensed dealers on Friday," Pierre interrupted, a calculating look in his eyes. "They'd pay no more than their fixed price."

"But you have to sell to them, by law!"

"To hell with the law! I'm taking it to Johannesburg, where I know someone who'll give me a good price for it."

"I can't let you do that, Pierre," Sabella protested. "The penalties for illicit diamond dealing are very severe, and the licence is not only in my name, but *I* found the stone."

"Only you and I know about the diamond, and if we keep our mouths shut, who would be any the wiser? I'll leave in the morning, and you can tell people that I've decided to go and drive transport because our claim is failing."

"No," she dug in her heels. "We sell to one of the licensed dealers on Friday."

He gave her a long, intent look. "Be careful, Sabella," he said quietly, repeating the implicit threat that had been hanging in the air since the last time she'd displeased him. "Be very, very careful."

She tried not to let him see the shudder that passed through her, and turned away. The subject of illicit diamond dealing was not mentioned between them again.

Towards noon the next day he brought her five pound notes which he'd borrowed from one of the money-lenders who had set up business at the diggings. "I'll have to stay away for at least a week," he explained, "to make the story about trying to drive transport believable. This will tide you over until I return."

She nodded, her expression grim. If he were found out in what he was planning to do, she would be deemed equally guilty, if not more so. But the alternative was too stark to contemplate. She would be punished through one of the children. At least, she told herself as she helped him to pack his few clothes on the wagon, they would be granted a week in which the atmosphere would not be tainted by his presence.

But only three days had passed when Mr Kowalski, the money-lender, visited her claim and demanded the return of the loan he had made Pierre.

"My husband will be back in about four days' time, Mr Kowalski, and will repay you then as arranged," Sabella said.

"No, no, no! For three days only I make him a loan. See here, Missus – evidence!"

She stared at the scrap of paper. There it was in black and white, and bearing Pierre's signature. The loan was to be repaid in three days, and as collateral Pierre had pledged Sabella's most treasured possession, her kitchen range.

Deliberately, she kept her head bent over the note so that Mr Kowalski would not see her expression. Pierre had borrowed the money simply to prevent her from suspecting what he'd had in mind, and he had known from the outset that he would not be there to repay it.

He was not coming back. The diamond she had found must have been far more valuable than he had led her to believe, and the reason why he had decided to sell it illicitly was only too clear.

Not prepared to share the proceeds with anyone, he had stolen her diamond and left her and the children there in that squalid, merciless hell to fend for themselves.

12

Sabella looked up. Without meeting Mr Kowalski's eyes, she gazed around her at the harsh world in which she and the children had been abandoned, the maze of shoddy zinc and corrugated iron shacks on which the sun shone down without mercy, the mounds of excavated earth which created a blinding sand-storm whenever the wind blew. And she couldn't help remembering the beauty of Mooikrantz.

A crook, Bastian had called Pierre, and she hadn't believe him. Even though she had since accepted that he *was* a crook, among so many other things, it had never occurred to her that he might steal from her. Not blatantly, like this . . .

"The capital please, Missus, and the interest also," she heard Mr Kowalski say with weary patience.

"I – I can't repay it." A considerable portion of the five pounds had gone on the accumulated rental for the washing-and-sorting machine, and out of what was left of it she had to pay the labourers and keep a few shillings for food.

Mr Kowalski sighed. "Then your kitchen range I must take instead, and sell for what I can get."

"Please," she said desperately. "Give me a little time. Don't take the range."

He spread his hands. "You want I should become a *schnorer*, a miserable beggar? I give you time, Missus, and then everyone else want time also, and very soon poor Jacob Kowalski is finish, *kaput*."

Sabella had been thinking quickly. "Mr Kowalski, I could use the kitchen range to make money with which to repay you. A lot of the men at the diggings are here without their families. When they stop for a meal it's almost always a hunk of shop-bread, often stale, washed down with a swallow of water. If I kept the range I could make *vetkoeke* and coffee to sell to them instead. I would pitch my prices high because both the coffee and the *vetkoeke* would be fresh and hot, and besides – they're used to high prices at the diggings and in any case, people always think the more of something if it costs above the average. Don't you think it would be short-sighted of you to take the kitchen range away when it could earn both of us a profit?"

The hooded dark eyes that had been gazing at her with deliberate mournfulness suddenly gleamed with approval and amusement. "*Chutzpah* you've got, Missus, and that is something Jacob Kawolski likes. So, you keep the range and you come see me in a week."

"Thank you," she said fervently, and watched him leave, stroking his flowing grey beard and laughing to himself.

Bravado had allowed her to retain temporary possession of the kitchen range, but could she make her hastily devised plans work? She smiled bitterly at the memory of her old dreams of making a fortune by her own efforts. Now, she would have to use all her energy, all her wits and ingenuity simply to survive in this terrible world of the diggings.

She shrugged the thought aside and called the hired labourers together, and explained to them that her husband would have to be away for far longer than he'd first thought, and that she had no option but to pay them off in the meantime.

She looked at them, four sinewy black men squatting in a circle with nothing but sympathy and understanding in their eyes. "We go on working, Nonnie," one of them suggested, "and when you score, you pay us."

"*Ewé*," the others chorused agreement.

Her eyes filled with tears at their selfless generosity. "Thank you, but it wouldn't be possible. We haven't found a single stone during the past three days, and I couldn't go on paying for water, let alone the rental of the machine."

She left them and then, with Katrien in her arms and Ria dogging her footsteps, set out to call on men whose families were not with them at the diggings.

Her idea, plucked out of thin air, proved to have been an inspired one. Without exception the men to whom she spoke agreed enthusiastically to buy hot *vetkoeke* and coffee from her each day. They were to provide their own mugs and condensed milk and she would charge a farthing a mug for coffee and a penny for two *vetkoeke*.

Sabella returned to the house to check on the raw materials which were needed for herself and her family to survive. Fortunately, she had a good stock of flour, but her supply of coffee was low, and she sent Nantes to buy more.

She rose early the next day, because the sale of coffee and *vetkoeke* had to be staggered. The first batch was to be sold to diggers for breakfast, another for a mid-morning break, and after that she would have to go on supplying lunch until two in the afternoon.

Whichever of the children were not at school had to help her with the deliveries. She mixed flour, salt and baking powder in a large bowl, added an egg to the water for extra lightness and when a soft dough had been made she dropped tablespoonfuls into sizzling hot lard, turning the puffy balls so that they browned on all sides. At the same time a large potful of coffee was brewing on the side of the range.

Sabella herself carried the coffee-pot out to the diggers, and Anton, Daan and Ria took it in turns to carry the basket into which the *vetkoeke* had been packed with a cloth covering them to keep them clean as well as hot. Katrien toddled after them, doing her best to keep up, and whoever wasn't carrying the basket of *vetkoeke* had the task of going back for her.

As the morning sped by, Sabella thought wearily that they were like clockwork dolls. The novelty had very soon worn off for Anton and Daan and they had begun to complain about the pace which they were expected to keep up. "It's not boys' work," Anton grumbled. "Daddy wouldn't let you make us do it if he was here."

"Yes," Daan whimpered, "when is Daddy coming back? The other boys are going to laugh at us, Sabella, for helping you sell *vetkoeke*."

"Ria want Daddy," their sister wailed, understanding only the germ of their complaints.

"Well, Daddy isn't here," Sabella said curtly, "and if you want to go on eating you'll have to go on helping me."

But it was a relief when Nantes came home from school and he could take over from his younger brothers, for he understood the importance of what Sabella was doing, and threw himself with enthusiasm into helping her.

By late afternoon the smell of *vetkoeke* and coffee made her feel nauseous, and she ached in every limb. She sat down to count the farthings and pennies she had collected. If she were to pay Mr Kowalski the capital and the interest by the end of a week she would have to make more *vetkoeke* and persuade the diggers to buy more.

The following days became a blur of standing by the range, hurrying out to sell coffee and *vetkoeke*, rushing home to make more, and even that was not going to be enough. Oh, she would be able to repay Mr Kowalski, but her supplies of raw materials were running short, and how was she going to support her family if she were unable to buy more?

She began to tout for other work to do in the afternoons and evenings. The same diggers who bought her *vetkoeke* and coffee had clothes that needed mending or darning and she took on these chores, charging from a farthing to a penny for sewing on buttons, mending seams or darning and patching. She functioned in a permanent haze of fatigue.

After a week of grinding, monotonous toil she went to see Mr Kowalski, carrying his loan plus interest in a heavy basket packed with farthings, halfpennies and pennies.

He paid her the compliment of not counting it, and offered her a glass of wine. "*L'chaim*," he said, raising his glass. "To life, Missus."

"To life," she echoed bleakly. Could this endless treadmill of work without any compensations whatever be called living?

The habitually inscrutable old eyes of the money-lender took on a look of warmth and compassion as he studied her. "A *schmuck* he is, that husband of yours, to leave such a wife. He's not coming back, am I right?"

She dropped her eyes. "He is driving transport. I don't know when he'll be able to return."

With an abrupt gesture, Mr Kowalski divided the pile of coppers she had spilt out on his desk into roughly two halves, and pushed one pile towards her. "Here, Missus, take and pay me back when you can, and not to worry about interest. A present I make you of the interest."

"I – I . . . Thank you," she whispered, overcome.

The indefinite loan made it possible for her to carry on. She bought more flour, lard, coffee and eggs and continued her catering service, and during the afternoons and evenings she did whatever other work she could get.

Now and again something happened to light up their grim existence like a shaft of sunlight piercing a dark cloud. Her lies that Pierre's absence was only temporary and that he was driving transport hadn't fooled anyone, and people performed small acts of kindness that warmed Sabella's spirits. But one day a family called Viljoen went much farther than mere kindness, and sent her a present of a generous-sized piece of beef. She was only on nodding acquaintance with them and couldn't understand the reason for such unexpected generosity, until Anton told her that one of the Viljoen boys was his best friend.

Having enjoyed the rare luxury of beef stewed with onions and carrots, Sabella felt that mere thanks were not enough to express their gratitude, and the following afternoon she fried a special batch of *vetkoeke* and carried it to the shack of the Viljoen family.

251

She was warmly thanked for the *vetkoeke* and invited inside for coffee. She should really have got on with her work, but politeness forced her to accept the invitation.

In many ways the Viljoen family reminded her of the Goosens in Westdene. There was a similar brood of unruly children, and instead of being outside working on his claim, Meneer Viljoen sat at the table in the crowded kitchen, aimlessly whittling away at a piece of wood. Even though shortage of water meant that hardly anyone at the diggings was entirely clean, Mevrou Viljoen gave the impression that, whatever their circumstances had been, her dress which stretched tightly over her ample bosom and stomach would still have been stained and spotted with grease . . .

Sabella started, hardly able to believe her eyes, her assessment of the Viljoens taking a different course. A spotted mongrel dog was chewing away in a corner of the filthy floor at a whole leg of mutton. How on earth, she wondered, did these people find it possible to afford to feed their pet on such expensive meat? Where could the money be coming from?

A boy whose apparent age suggested that he was Anton's friend entered the kitchen, and Mevrou Viljoen broke off what she had been saying to Sabella. "Ah, Buksie!" she exclaimed with relief. "Hurry, boy, or there'll be no supper for us tonight!"

The boy crossed the room, patted the dog's head and took the remainder of the leg of mutton from it. "The *bleddie* animal would have killed anyone else if we'd tried it," Mevrou Viljoen confided to the bemused Sabella, and rose, taking the meat from her son. Sabella tried to hide her shock as the woman went to the stove and dropped the meat, just as it was, into a pot from which the smell of stewing onions was drifting.

Mevrou Viljoen came to sit at the table again. "He don't like poultry, that dog," she told Sabella with regret. "Buksie tried and tried, but he could never get the *bleddie brak* to take a chicken from a butcher. Funny, really, 'cause he don't like bread much either, but he's quite good about *that.*" She brightened. "Still, Buksie is managing to get him to like the smell of pork. Tell you what, Mevrou le Roux, first time that dog brings home a nice piece of pork, I'll see you get a share."

Sabella managed to thank her politely, her own reaction carefully hidden. If the Viljoens *did* send over a piece of pork, she thought, necessity would force her to cook it and eat her share of it. But even so, knowing the meat's history, and no matter how thoroughly she'd washed it beforehand and how tastily she might have prepared it, she would eat it – as Ma would have said – "with long teeth" and only for the nourishment it would provide.

She left the Viljoens and returned home to prepare the next morning's batch of *vetkoeke* to be fried. It occurred to her to wonder why it was that people like the Goosens and the Viljoens seemed to get so much more out of life than those who worked hard to shift for themselves. She shook her head in bafflement. The Viljoens, who lived on the leftovers of what their son had trained his dog to steal, had exuded a happiness and contentment that Sabella envied and doubted if she could ever achieve for her own family.

She worried about the children as she worked. Katrien was not getting a fraction of the attention she deserved from her mother and was growing up any-old-how. Daan obviously felt neglected too, for she often surprised tears in his eyes for which there seemed no reason. Nantes was his old, good, sweet, sensitive self now that the cloud of fear had been lifted from him by Pierre's departure, and he was always thoughtful of others, but Anton was becoming more and more unwilling to do his share in earning the family's daily bread and he was also becoming more aggressive. But Ria worried her most of all. The girl might have the mental age of a child of three, but she had the well-developed body of a seventeen-year-old and if one ignored the empty look in her blue eyes and her toddler vocabulary, she was quite breathtakingly beautiful. Sabella had noticed more than one lonely digger watching her sister with expressions of lust. Somehow, she would have to try and find a way of protecting Ria in this cesspit in which they were forced to live . . .

But it was not Ria who caused the most alarming development in their family. Most evenings now, Sabella was far too exhausted by the time she had finished all the work she'd taken on to do more than fall into bed next to the sleeping Katrien. But late one evening she decided to check on the other children and give them extra blankets because the weather had turned unseasonably cold. It was then that she discovered Anton was missing, and all the indications were that he was not simply answering a call of nature.

She caught her breath with fear. This place was bad enough during the day, but after dark . . . She shuddered, and shook Nantes's shoulder until he woke up and sat upright, blinking at her in the light of the candle she was carrying.

"Where is Anton?" she demanded in an urgent whisper.

Nantes yawned, and then shivered. "I – I c-c-can't tell you, Sabella."

"You *can*, but you won't. Is that it?"

He nodded miserably. "Anton m-made me promise."

"Does that mean that he threatened you?"

"Yes. He – he s-said he would g-give me a b-b-black eye if I t-told."

"A promise forced from someone under a threat doesn't deserve to be honoured. I'll make sure that he doesn't lay a hand on you. But you *must* tell me where he is." Her blood froze at the thought of her twelve-year-old brother somewhere out in the dark, sinister world of the diggings at night. "Tell me, Nantes!" she repeated.

He began hesitantly at first, and then the story tumbled out in his relief at sharing with Sabella what had been troubling him deeply. It was a story to trouble anyone, she thought with dismay as she listened.

It seemed that Anton and some other boys had discovered an interesting and profitable feature of night-life at the diggings. Those men who had scored and consequently had money to burn frequented the many illegal shebeens at night; at some point or other a fight invariably erupted, and then the drinkers would spill out of the shebeen, jackets were shed and thrown down on the ground as the men squared up to one another, and in the ensuing drunken chaos no one noticed that the gang of young boys were going through the pockets of the discarded jackets lying on the ground.

"And Anton has been doing this for how long?" Sabella asked, trying to hide her shock and her feeling of guilty responsibility from Nantes.

"About a m-m-month, I think."

"Do you know where the shebeen is to which he went tonight?"

"They v-visit all of them, Sabella, l-looking for a f-f-fight to s-start."

"Will you try to keep awake, Nantes, in case Katrien wakes up and needs attention? I must go and look for Anton."

God, she thought as she let herself out into the night, how she hated this place where men leered at Ria and where Anton was being turned into a petty thief and where one had to work oneself into the ground merely to survive.

She had no torch or lamp, and a naked candle would have been useless. If the tin shanties, the tents and burlap shelters were a maze by day, they were a jungle by night and she was forced to feel her way. Being illegal, shebeens did not advertise themselves, and all she could do was set a course towards any place from which candlelight could be seen flickering, or which was lit by a carbide lamp. The first one she reached turned out to be a brothel, and she had to beat a swift and frightened retreat when a potential client decided that she would do as well as any of the harlots inside.

She leant against a zinc shack in the dark, catching her breath and waiting for her heartbeat to slow down. Chancing to look up, she was struck by the pure beauty of the night sky in contrast to the ugliness down below. The Milky Way shimmered like a trail of crushed diamonds and the stars seemed to gleam so low in the sky that one gained the illusion of being able to reach up and touch them.

Sabella shook herself. She hadn't come out into the cold to admire the exquisite beauty of the sky. She had to search this sewer of a place for her brother, who was a thief. *And it's my fault,* the thought thudded in her brain.

She became more adept at avoiding obstacles and picking her way. The next lighted shack she reached *was* a shebeen, for she could hear drunken singing coming from inside it. There was no sign of young boys outside, however. Only a thin, shivering woman wrapped in a threadbare coat hovered about.

"You come to try and bring your husband home too?" she asked Sabella.

"No."

"Pity. The two of us could have gone inside together. We'd have stood more chance." The woman gave a hopeless sigh. "The police try to close these places down, but as soon as one closes another opens. If only the shebeen owners didn't poison the wine, it wouldn't be so bad."

"*Poison?*" Sabella repeated, startled. "Surely not – "

"What else would you call it?" The woman's voice was bitter. "They add metal polish to the wine, or methylated spirits to give it more kick. Makes the men mad drunk."

Sabella shivered. And outside such places her brother spent the best part of each night, waiting to steal from some digger made drunk beyond caring about the contents of his jacket-pockets.

She wished the woman luck, said good night and picked her way to the next shebeen. The same debauched, unsavoury scenes met her eyes each time she peered through successive windows. The men, she thought, had probably come there mostly for company, but what they received instead was expensive and dangerous oblivion.

When she finally ran Anton to earth it was by sheer

256

chance. His gang had dispersed and he was on his way home, and the two of them literally almost ran into one another.

"Well, Anton," she said grimly, taking his arm in a firm hold.

He tried to bluster. "I remembered I'd left my catapult at school, and I went to look for it – "

"Don't lie. I know where you've been, and what you've been doing." She marched him inside their house and lit every candle she could find so that he was unable to make an unobtrusive move to hide his spoils. "Turn out your pockets," Sabella ordered.

Sullenly, he obeyed, placing their contents on the kitchen table. She was staggered and appalled to find that his night's haul, mostly in half-crowns and florins, amounted to almost two pounds. She wanted to weep, but instead she said cuttingly, "I suppose you couldn't be bothered to take tickeys or copper. What have you been doing with all the money you've stolen, Anton?"

"Saving it." He gave her a defiant stare.

"What for?"

"To start working our claim again!" he burst out. "Nantes would never do it; he's a nancy-boy – "

"*Don't use that word about your brother!*" she thundered.

"Well – *someone* should be keeping things going for Daddy. I almost have enough now to rent the washing-and-sorting machine again and hire men to work it, and I'm old enough to leave school – "

"You certainly are not! Go and fetch the rest of the money you've stolen."

He picked up a candle and began to leave the kitchen, but on second thoughts she decided to accompany him. The money had been hidden inside an old sock stuffed underneath the box-wood chest-of-drawers in the boys' bedroom. If I hadn't been so busy and unable to clean the house properly, Sabella thought, I would have found the money a long time ago.

When she returned with Anton to the kitchen and spilt

the coins out on the table she found that his ill-gotten gains amounted to almost ten pounds.

"Have you any idea from whom you've been stealing, and how much from each?" she asked.

"No," he said sullenly.

"Well, since we can't give it back to its rightful owners, I'm confiscating it."

"That's stealing!" Tears sprang to his eyes. "You thief, Sabella!"

"A fine word, coming from you!"

Anton began to cry in earnest then. "Daddy said – he said – a boy should learn to stand on his own feet – and be a man – "

A fine man your "Daddy" is, Sabella thought bitterly. She knelt at Anton's side and tried to embrace him but he squirmed away from her. "Listen, Anton," she said seriously, "if the police had caught you and the other boys they would have searched all their homes. They would have found this money and it would have told them that you had been stealing for a long time. Do you know what would have happened to you?"

"They'd have given me a hiding," he said in a surly voice.

"No. You would have been sent away to a reformatory."

"W-what's that?" he asked, uneasy now.

"It's a school which is also a prison. You wouldn't have been allowed to leave its grounds, you would have been severely punished if you broke any of its strict rules and you would have been locked up at night. And you wouldn't have been allowed to come home for years."

"Oh." His eyes widened with fear. He looked at the stolen money strewn on the table top and said in agitation, "Sabella, we'd better throw it away!"

"If we were seen throwing money away in *this* place," she returned with dour humour, "they'd lock us up in a lunatic asylum!" She put her arm around Anton, and this time he didn't shrug it off. "Will you promise not to go with the other boys again?"

"Yes, Sabella. It was Buksie Viljoen who told me how easy it was."

That didn't surprise her. She knew that Anton would lose face with his partners-in-crime if he told the truth about what had happened, and she feared the pressure to conform might lead him to join them again, and so she suggested, "I think it would be best if you told the other boys that a policeman stopped you tonight on your way home, and ordered you to turn out your pockets. Tell them he warned you that he would be watching you from now on, and so you daren't lead the policeman to them."

Anton accepted the face-saving suggestion with relief. Anxiety clouded his eyes again as he looked at the coins on the table. "What about the money, Sabella? The other boys spend theirs on sweets and stuff, so the police wouldn't send *them* to a prison school if they're caught and they tell on me."

"Don't worry about the money. I think it would be best if I visit all the churches and divide it between their poor-boxes." She kissed him. "Now go to bed."

She herself lay awake for a long time that night. She thought of the corrupting influence of the diggings, and then fretted about the time it would take to visit the many churches and surreptitiously slip donations from the stolen money into their poor-boxes. If anyone saw her, they would find it hard to believe that she could afford acts of charity.

Then her thoughts concentrated on those poor-boxes themselves. Their contents had to be very thinly spread among the needy, and made a barely perceptible difference to their lives. *She* ought to know; the most she had ever received from the Dutch Reformed Church's charity had been a pound of mealie meal, enough for one morning's breakfast.

And when it came to it, who at the diggings was more needy than her own family? She didn't know of any other woman whose husband had deserted her and left her to provide for five children. Anton was right, of course. If she kept the money he had stolen she, too, would be guilty of theft. But if the end justified the means?

Guilt was thrust into the background as excitement surged through her, the same electrifying exhilaration which she had experienced before when ambition had stirred inside her. Unable to sleep, she made mental plans for the business she meant to start with the money stolen by her brother from the pockets of unknown drunks.

Early the next morning Nantes, kept from school by Sabella, was left to watch over Katrien and Ria while Sabella set out for Mr Kowalski's office, the money confiscated from Anton weighing down her shopping basket. She and Anton shared secret glances, and guilt swept over her, because she knew he believed she was going to distribute the money he feared would incriminate him among the poor-boxes of the churches. But her feeling of guilt didn't last long and by the time she reached Mr Kowalski's office it had been overtaken by excitement.

The money-lender watched as she counted out three pounds. "That is what I owe you, including the interest. There's no reason why you should forfeit the interest, because I can afford to pay it."

"That *schmuck* of a man you married, he has come back?"

"No." She felt herself colouring, and gave him a straight look. "Just between the two of us, Mr Kowalski, he won't be coming back. And that's why I need your advice. You know all about the shebeens there are at the diggings?"

He nodded, his expression one of distaste. "I understand," she went on, "that the owners add stuff like metal polish and methylated spirits to the wine. Why do they do it?"

"To buy and sell strong spirit, Missus, they cannot afford, and when a man becomes drunk he has a wish to become more drunk still. Why, I do not know. But to put those things in wine is to make the men drunk, and a man who is drunk will spend much money and not count his change. So – more profit for the owner of the shebeen. What for do you want to know?"

She took a deep breath. "I – I've managed to raise a little capital, and I want to start a shebeen of my own, but one that is different. I believe that most of the men who visit shebeens do so because they are lonely; their families are far away and there's not much comfort to be had, sitting alone in a shack or a tent. My shebeen would have rules; no fighting or bad language, and no getting drunk, because the wine I sell won't be adulterated."

"It would make no profit, such a shebeen," Mr Kowalski observed.

"I believe it will. I'll offer something different, something no other shebeen provides – refinement, if you like, or discrimination. Visiting my shebeen will give men a sense of occasion. But my main problem is that I have no vehicle, no means of buying wine and smuggling it into the diggings, and you are the only person I know I can trust. Would you be prepared to act as my agent and buy the wine on my behalf?"

"Aai, aai, aai!" he laughed, slapping his palms on his desk. "Was it *chutzpah* I said you had? You have more, Missus, much more! To act outside the law is what you are asking Jacob Kowalski to do!" He paused. "For you, I will do it. Now tell me more about the shebeen you wish to run."

They spent most of the morning together, going over her plans. He made several suggestions which she accepted with gratitude and in the end he undertook to buy other things on her behalf which she would need to turn her kitchen into a shebeen.

In less than a week she was ready for business. Labourers had been hired to extend the kitchen of the house, making it more than twice its original size and laying a cement floor. A door had been constructed which led straight from the outside into the boys' bedroom so that the children would be kept apart from the shebeen.

Her brothers had been far too relieved to be freed from

the tyranny of helping her to sell *vetkoeke* and coffee to question her explanations, and Anton had made no connection between her plans and the money he had stolen.

"I'm going to turn the kitchen into a kind of café," she told them, "where diggers can come in the evenings and drink soup or coffee and have something to eat and talk among themselves."

"Will we have to help?" Anton had asked suspiciously.

"If you want to, you could clear up and wash the dirty dishes for me." Shrewdly, she had calculated that the suggestion would ensure they kept away from the shebeen.

"No thank you!" Anton had declined hurriedly, and Daan was quick to support him. Only Nantes offered his services.

"No, I'll need you to keep Ria and Katrien out of the kitchen," Sabella had said. The last thing diggers paying for an evening's relaxation would want was a toddler underfoot, and Ria had to be kept out of the way for her own good. Besides, Sabella did not want any of her brothers to find out that the "soup" she would be serving was really malmsey.

Mr Kowalski had taken care that word would be spread about the new and different shebeen that was opening that evening, and the diggers were made aware of the strict rules it would be imposing. The children had been fed an early supper and had gone outside to play before bedtime, and Sabella stood alone in the enlarged kitchen, gazing approvingly at what had been achieved between herself and Mr Kowalski.

Apart from the kitchen table and chairs, there were benches and stools for the customers. Red-and-white checked cloths had been spread over the table and the benches, and set out on the table, protected by a piece of muslin, were platefuls of elegant small sandwiches filled with sliced salt beef, a present from Mr Kowalski.

"You want they should buy much wine," he had said with a twinkle, "so you make them thirsty with salt beef!"

Sabella nodded with satisfaction and went to change in

time to receive her first customers. Even though she had earlier unpacked them to be aired and ironed, tears filled her eyes as she prepared to put on, for the first time, the dress of pale apricot shantung which Bastian had given her what seemed such a very long time ago. She eased on the silk stockings and stepped into the matching apricot shoes. They pinched and, like the dress, were no longer fashionable, but that didn't matter. If she and Bastian had been able to look into the future, she thought, neither of them would have believed that the clothes would make their debut at the opening night of an illegal shebeen in a nightmarish place like the diggings.

She was only able to examine her appearance in sections with the aid of a hand-mirror. The apricot shade was a perfect foil for her creamy complexion and her reddish-brown hair which she had continued to keep short, so that it curled around her face. Bastian should have been the one who first saw her wearing the clothes, and not a crowd of strange men . . .

She put the thought aside and went into the kitchen just as the first of the customers arrived, looking both excited and at the same time a little sheepish. But their eyes registered appreciation when they saw her. In her beautiful but outmoded clothes she was bringing a touch of glamour into their lives.

"Good evening, gentlemen," she smiled, and crossed to the kitchen range. Almost taking up its entire surface stood a large cauldron, and to anyone who was unaware that the range had been raked out and allowed to cool down it would have seemed that it was soup she was ladling out into mugs from the cauldron. She would have preferred to serve the malmsey in glasses, but there was always the risk that a policeman might peer through the window. At the diggings, she knew, there was an unwritten rule against informing on anyone, so that the risk she ran otherwise was very small.

The opening night was an enormous success. There was no mistaking the fact that her customers appreciated their surroundings, her service and her personal appearance. What she was giving them, in exchange for money, was not just mugfuls of malmsey and salt-beef sandwiches. She was making available to them something they had almost forgotten about in the crudeness of the diggings. Sipping their unadulterated malmsey, eating their sandwiches, watching her moving about the room in her lovely clothes, they could forget about the ugliness and complete lack of grace at the diggings. As she had promised Mr Kowalski she would, she was selling them refinement and a sense of occasion.

Her business thrived beyond her wildest dreams. She attracted the respectable but lonely element of men among the diggers, and they didn't mind paying the high prices she charged, because they appreciated the little touches she added as money became available, like soft cushions for the stools and pretty rugs scattered on the cement floor.

Illegal her business might be, even immoral, but as she continued to make a profit she felt the old, previously stifled ambition within herself soaring. If things went on as they were she would have saved enough, in a year's time, to take the children back to Johannesburg and start a business of another kind, a legitimate business instead of one outside the law. In the meantime she gave the money she was saving to Mr Kowalski to keep in his safe for her, because she was afraid that if she banked it, official attention would be drawn to her illegal shebeen.

Late one evening as she circulated among her customers, pausing at benches to chat pleasantly to them, she heard the door opening. The flickering candlelight was sufficient merely to show her that the man who had entered wore a suit, and her heart thumped in panic. Only an official would wear a suit at the diggings.

Trying to hide her fear, she moved towards him, a smile fixed on her face. She had had her story prepared for just such an eventuality. This was a private party given for

264

friends and no money had changed hands. Her customers, she knew, would back her to the hilt.

"Good evening," she began, and stopped, her breath catching in her throat and an almost-forgotten joy pounding in her veins.

"Sabella," Bastian said, and his expression tempered her joy. His gaze travelled over her. "You're wearing it at last, I see. I'm glad it came in useful." His voice was arctic.

"You – if you're criticising me – " she began in a whisper.

"You're damned right; I am. For flaunting yourself, wearing my gifts to attract customers to your illegal she-been." He changed the subject. "Now that I'm here, may I have a drink?"

She nodded and moved to the range, where her hands shook as she ladled malmsey into a mug for him. He took it, unsmiling, and asked, "How much?"

"Don't – be stupid," she said unevenly.

"It's you who are being stupid. All your customers are watching us. They would wonder why you didn't charge me for the drink." Again that frosty note came into his voice. "You don't want to make them jealous, do you, by making it appear that I'm someone special? It's obvious that your business thrives because you divide your charming attention evenly among your admirers and so preserve harmony."

"A shilling," she said curtly.

His eyebrows rose. "Your customers must obviously feel that they get their money's worth." He handed her the coin and watched as she pulled out the pan into which the ash from the range had been raked, and hid the shilling with the other coins underneath the cold clinkers and ash. "You've learnt all the tricks of running a shady operation, I see," he commented.

Only the presence of her customers prevented her from uttering the furious retort hovering on her tongue. He went to sit down, but didn't attempt to engage anyone in conversation, and his aloof, well-dressed presence soon created an inhibiting atmosphere among the men. One by one they said good night to Sabella and left.

"How dare you!" she rounded on Bastian in rage, as soon as the door had closed behind the last customer. "What do you know about – "

"*You* ask *me* how I dared?" he cut in, his rage matching hers. "I've been searching for you for months, but I didn't dream I would find you among the dregs of humanity, selling cheap wine and your provocative, teasing sexuality to poor fools who pay profiteering prices to sit and lust after you with their eyes! I'm ashamed of you, Sabella!"

"Oh, are you!" She moved towards him, her eyes glittering. "Then I'll give you cause to be even more ashamed of me! I started my business with money Anton stole from drunken diggers while they were too busy fighting to think about their jackets lying on the ground, and I confiscated his haul. So now, take your halo and get out of here, back to your own nice, cosy, sanitary life!"

Even in her rage she could see that she had shaken him. His own anger subsided. "Things were that bad?"

"They were worse. I won't bore you with the details."

He caught hold of her wrist. "Why didn't you get in touch with me when that crook you married deserted you?"

"He is away, driving transport – " she began.

"Don't lie. How do you think I knew where to find you? I've had a private investigator searching for clues to your whereabouts, and by chance he met a man in Johannesburg who was also looking for Pierre le Roux, who owed him money. Your husband's creditor supplied the information that he'd abandoned you and the children at the diggings." Bastian drew her against him, and his touch awakened feelings she had thought had permanently withered inside her. He asked hoarsely, "Why didn't you contact me and ask for help?"

"You were in England – "

"You must have known that I returned months ago!"

She leant her forehead against his chest. "It would only

have started all over again – you pressing me to divorce Pierre and live with you, not caring about other lives that would be ruined."

He was silent for a moment. His hand cupped her chin, raising her face to his. "You were right," he admitted. "Oh, Sabella – "

She knew that if he kissed her, she would be lost. Freeing herself, she said prosaically, "I have to collect the mugs and clear up the room. Where are you staying, Bastian?"

"I paid a week's advance rent for a room in a lodging-house in Lichtenburg." He laughed shortly. "I was advised not to drive my car to the diggings, so I left it there, and hired a black driver to bring me here in a pony trap. I've been at these cursed diggings since the afternoon, trying to find you among thousands of shacks that all look alike. It was only when I went inside one of the shebeens tonight that I learnt you were a competitor of the owner and I was given directions to your place. I have no way of getting back to Lichtenburg tonight. Could you give me a bed?"

She directed a mirthless laugh at him over her shoulder. "I couldn't give you a *bed*, Bastian. We don't possess such luxuries. All I can offer you is a mattress stuffed with dry mealie leaves, spread out on the kitchen floor."

"That would do," he said, his voice deliberately expressionless.

It was the mattress she used to share with Pierre, until he'd left her and she'd moved in to share Katrien's. Bastian went with her to fetch it, while she lit the way with a branch of candles. He kept her waiting as he knelt down, studying the sleeping Katrien. She busied herself, finding sheets and spare blankets.

In the kitchen, they moved benches to make space for the mattress. Suddenly ashamed of its crudeness, Sabella collected the cushions from the stools and spread them out on the mattress before she covered the whole with a sheet. When she had finished making up his bed she said goodnight, but he caught her by the wrist.

"*Stay*," he said hoarsely.

267

The look in his eyes was that of a starving man, and every instinct urged her to appease his hunger and her own. But she shook her head. "No. Good night, Bastian."

He pulled her against him. "Please, Sabella. It has been so long." And then he kissed her, and she felt her defences beginning to crumble. She made no resistance when he drew her down on to the mattress. With his mouth still locked on hers, he began to unfasten the buttons of the apricot shantung dress and when he had slipped it over her shoulders his lips moved to her throat and then to her breasts. She felt as if she were about to drown in their mutual need and longing, and knew that if she did not save herself now it would be too late. She hooked her fingers into his hair and forced him to lift his head. "No, Bastian. *No!*"

He removed her hands, imprisoning them in his. "Why not?"

There were so many excuses she could have offered him. That the children might walk in and find them together – which she knew was highly unlikely, because they had become accustomed to sleeping through noise. Or she could have used the moral argument against committing adultery. Instead, she decided to tell him the naked truth. "I'm afraid of becoming pregnant." And this time, she added mentally with bitter amusement, there would not be a conveniently dead husband to cite as the father. This time it really *would* be Wilhelmina's story all over again.

Bastian's hand went to her breast, tightening over it. "God, Sabella," he said with frightening intensity, "there is nothing I would wish for more – that you should bear a child of mine."

She pushed him away with force, and sat up. "Oh, I believe you!" She uttered a corrosive laugh. "You would have me in your power then, wouldn't you, Bastian? You would use the child as a weapon. If I refused to agree that we should ride roughshod over everyone else and live together in scandal, you would take our child away from me just as your father took you away from Wilhelmina!"

"That isn't fair – " he began.

"But it's true. You would want a child of yours to have the best that money could buy."

"Damn it, yes!" he exploded. "Is that so unnatural?"

And of course it was not unnatural at all. If Bastian knew that Katrien was his daughter he would not allow her to spend another night here at the diggings. Indeed, at times when life had been at its hardest it had occurred to Sabella that if she had been truly selfless, she would voluntarily have given their daughter up to Bastian so that Katrien might have a better future. And every time her heart had cried out in response: *No, she is mine! I could never let her go!*

An anger whose existence she had never suspected before erupted inside her. "How easy life is for men! They want to father children but they don't expect those children to take over their entire existence! It's so different for women. Children make a woman totally vulnerable; they make her compromise, accept second-best for herself. Because she loves them, she is robbed of the right to be a *person*."

"Sabella – " Bastian tried to stem her impassioned flow.

She went on, ignoring his interruption. "And let me tell you something else. You complain about Annette's refusal to give you children. Why the devil *should* she? She knows you don't love her. By expecting her to give you children you want to reduce her to the level of a brood-hen. And you're aggrieved because she refuses to let you!"

His answering laughter was harsh. "You're crediting Annette with more sensitivity than she possesses! It's her figure she's concerned about, and her social life – not her rights as a person." His mood changed suddenly. "But I do understand your fears about becoming pregnant, Sabella. It would complicate the situation, and you're right, I *would* fight you for any child of ours if I had to."

There was little comfort to be derived from the confirmation that her instinct had, from the beginning, told her the truth. "I'll go to bed now," she said, starting to rise.

He reached for her. "Sabella," he said with quiet intensity in his voice, "I love you in a way that is far stronger than the mere need for sex. Stay with me, let me hold you and feel your body close to mine. Let us comfort one another just by being together. *Please?* I won't press you or trick you into anything more."

A long sigh shook her. Her life had been so lonely, in spite of the admiring presence of her nightly customers. Silently, she began to undress, aware that he was doing the same. They had slipped underneath the bedclothes and lay on the mattress, embracing. He moved away slightly, stroking her hair. "Oh, Sabella, I've missed you. And I've been half out of my mind with worry about you. I can't leave you in this terrible place."

"And I won't leave with you, and live with you in a blaze of scandal that will hurt others."

"Perhaps," he said, "we could reach a compromise. We're compromising now, aren't we?"

She was unable to answer, for his fingers were stroking her skin, sending shudders of delight through her, and when she became aware of his own arousal she turned instinctively towards him to offer herself. He held her off, saying, "I promised, remember?"

It was a unique and humbling experience to discover that a man was capable of loving her sufficiently to be strong for her as well as for himself. His kisses and caresses were the more poignant for the knowledge that he would allow them to lead no further, and after a long while she fell asleep in his arms, as trusting as a child.

She woke up with a start and saw that dawn was about to break. Bastian was asleep, lying on his side and with one arm about her waist, his streaked hair tousled, his dark lashes surprising her with their thickness and length. They were so like Katrien's . . .

She lifted his arm gently and eased herself from the mattress, picked up her clothes and tiptoed to the room she shared with Katrien. She had dressed in her ordinary day clothes by the time the little girl woke up.

Sabella went and roused the boys and Ria, and told them that Bastian was visiting them and had spent the night sleeping in the kitchen. Her brothers were excited at the news, but later when they sat at the kitchen table and he shared their breakfast they were tongue-tied and ill at ease in his presence. Sabella guessed it was because the boys were older now, and more aware of the gulf between them and this cousin who was rich and wore a smart suit and drove an expensive car, far too expensive for him to have risked driving it to the diggings which the boys had accepted as their world. Bastian did not fit in there. As usual, Ria's reaction was to copy her brothers, and only Katrien abandoned reserve and hauled herself up on to his lap and offered him wet, generous kisses. Sabella turned towards the range, unable to bear the look of wistful longing and love as he responded to the daughter he had no suspicion was his.

Bastian refused to return to Johannesburg and leave them at the diggings. He made arrangements to be picked up each evening and driven back to his lodgings in Lichtenburg, but the days he spent with Sabella, trying to persuade her to sell the shebeen and leave.

"I won't do anything to cause so much as a single tongue to wag," he promised at last. "I'll buy a house in Johannesburg for you – oh, very well, rent one, if you'd find that easier to accept. I won't leave Annette and I won't spend any nights with you. I'd pay the bills for anything you and the children need, and I'd even find a way of disguising the payments as a business expense so that you needn't fear anyone would find out."

"No," Sabella said uncompromisingly.

He gave her an angry, baffled look. "Why not? You can't *want* to spend the rest of your days in this sewer of a place, running an illegal shebeen!"

"Not the rest of my life. In about a year's time, I should have saved enough to be able to take the children and rent a house in Johannesburg. And then I want to start a business."

271

"What kind of business?" Frustration made him cruel. "Another illegal drinking den, a suburban one this time?"

She brushed the taunt aside, and said passionately, "Bastian, you don't know what it's like to be a woman with children; a wife or a widow or even a spinster, as I used to be, and to see those children go hungry because there's no man to provide for them or because he can't earn enough to cover their needs. You don't know what it's like to feel useless, powerless. I want to start a business which will give women like that both help and hope – and, yes, pride in themselves as *persons*."

"How?" His interest had been stirred.

"Do you remember how Pierre used to employ out-workers? Well, I want to do something similar. I want to give women work to do in their own homes, using whatever individual skills they possess. Knitting, sewing, crocheting, embroidering, making lace . . . And I want to provide a shop in the city where the articles they make can be displayed and sold."

Bastian looked startled as well as rueful. "I should have known that there would never be anything uncomplicated about you, my darling cousin." Then he shook his head. "But another *year* spent in this place? I can't bear the thought of that."

His hired driver arrived at that moment with the pony cart, and there was no time to continue the argument. Bastian touched her face, and said softly, "You know why I won't spend another night here, don't you?"

"Yes." She looked into his differently-coloured eyes, and their mutual gaze held perfect understanding. The discomfort of a mattress stuffed with mealie leaves spread on the cement floor had nothing to do with it. He couldn't bear to watch her customers looking at her with desire in their eyes, and most of all he didn't trust himself to maintain the restraint he'd imposed on both of them that night when they had slept in each other's arms.

The following morning he was back at the diggings, earlier than usual. As soon as he was able to be alone with

Sabella, he said, "I have a proposition to make you. Put the shebeen up for sale and let me lend you the money to start that business you were talking about. No, Sabella," he stopped her as she opened her mouth to protest, "this isn't charity, or something that would give me undue power over you. I'll have documents properly drawn up by lawyers. As far as I'm concerned it will be a business investment and, knowing you, I expect to make a profit out of it. What do you say?"

It was certainly a tempting offer, she thought. And she *would* make a profit, because the years during which she had studied newspaper advertisements had given her a sense of style, and she would see to it that her outworkers made the kind of articles rich women would want to buy . . .

"If you won't consider yourself," she heard Bastian go on, "then think of the effect another year at the diggings will have on the children. You told me yourself that Anton had been corrupted into stealing. Why shouldn't it happen again, when he sees his friends doing it and getting away scot-free? And I've watched the way men look at Ria. Then there's Katrien – " His voice roughened. "She's starting to talk. Do you want her to learn the obscenities in common usage here?"

"No," Sabella said, her mind made up. She smiled at him. "I accept your offer, Bastian. Have the documents drawn up."

During the next two days, whenever she was free, they discussed how much capital she would need, the best way to attract the right kind of outworkers, the location of the retail outlet, a wage for whoever was employed to manage it, and what seemed like dozens of related subjects. Any lingering fear Sabella had had that Bastian might be tricking her into putting herself in his power was dispersed.

They had just settled the last of the major points of their discussion when Anton and Daan arrived home from the afternoon school shift. But this time they were running, and Anton's face was aglow. "Daddy is back!" he shouted jubilantly. "He didn't see us, but I saw him! He's on his way home, and driving a truck!"

"*What?*" Dismay mixed with foreboding twisted Sabella's stomach into a knot. "You – you must have seen someone who looked a little like him." She wouldn't believe it. If she didn't believe it, it wouldn't turn out to be true.

"It *was* him!" Anton insisted. And even as he spoke, the sound of a heavy vehicle was coming towards them.

Under his breath Bastian said, "I'd guess that he's heard about your shebeen."

Yes, she thought bitterly. Oh yes, that would certainly have been enough to send Pierre hurrying home. Particularly since he would probably have spent the money from the proceeds of the diamond he had stolen from her.

Nantes, Ria and Katrien had come into the kitchen to join the others. The battered-looking truck churned up a dust-cloud as it approached the shack. It came to a halt, and Pierre jumped from the cab.

Then something happened that stabbed Sabella to the heart. With a sense of betrayal she watched the children run outside to greet Pierre, shouting, "Daddy! Daddy!" Not just Anton, who had always looked up to him and for whom he could do no wrong, but Daan as well, and Ria, and finally Nantes and Katrien. Pierre embraced the boys, kissed Ria and swung Katrien into his arms. The final betrayal came when Katrien tried out a new word: "Dellie!" she cried in imitation of her young uncles and aunt. "Dellie, Dellie, Dellie!"

Oh God, Sabella thought, oh God, how could *all* of them have forgotten the past? Even Nantes?

It didn't help much to realise, on reflection, that Nantes had run to join the others because he hadn't wanted to be noticed by Pierre as the only one who hadn't done so. But to watch Pierre acting out, for the benefit of an audience of neighbours, a scene of emotional reunion with the children he'd abandoned so cold-bloodedly filled Sabella's mouth with bile.

The children hanging on to his arms and with Katrien hoisted on to his shoulders, Pierre entered the kitchen. "My dear Sabella," he smiled, moving towards her. "It's wonderful to be home at last!"

"I want to talk to you," she said stonily. "Alone."

"Of course, my love. We have a great deal of catching up to do, haven't we?" He held out his hand to Bastian, and said, "Nice to see you, but you *will* excuse us, won't you? I'm sure you'll understand."

"Only too well," Bastian said shortly, ignoring the offered hand.

Pierre swung Katrien down from her perch on his shoulders and took Sabella's arm. She shook off his hand, and he said reproachfully, "It wasn't my fault that I couldn't return earlier. You know how uncertain the transport business is – "

"The children and Bastian can no longer hear you," she silenced him as she shut the door of the bedroom, "so drop the pretence. You came back because you'd learnt about the shebeen I was running."

"I'd heard that it was making far more than I ever could, driving transport. You've always had clever ideas, Sabella," he congratulated her. "But with my help the shebeen could make even more money."

"I'm putting the shebeen up for sale," she told him bluntly. "Bastian is giving us transport to Johannesburg, where I'll rent a house for myself and the children. I'm going to start proceedings to divorce you."

"Divorce me?" he echoed. "On what grounds?"

"Desertion, for one – "

"But I didn't desert you, Sabella. I told you that I was going away to drive transport, and you've been telling people at the diggings the same thing!"

"Only to hide the fact, at the beginning, that you'd stolen the diamond I'd found and gone off with it – "

"*What* diamond, Sabella?" he interrupted, frowning.

Chill swept through her. It was impossible to tell whether Pierre was mocking her, or was lying to himself and believing his own lies. She tried to make her voice hard and steady. "You know perfectly well what I'm talking about. I know I can't use the theft of the diamond against you in a divorce court, because it would make me an accomplice to illicit diamond dealing, but you've left us here alone for months, Pierre, without caring that we might be starving to death, and I'll certainly use *that* evidence against you!"

"Sabella!" he cried angrily. "How dare you! I've been sending you money regularly! How dare you suggest that I'd allow you and the children to starve?"

This time she *knew* he had convinced himself of his own lie. It struck her for the first time that Pierre needed to convince himself of such lies, because deep down, at a level of which he was probably not conscious, he disliked what he was and wanted to deny it.

"Well, I didn't receive a penny from you," she said, "and there are more than enough people here who would confirm the fact that I had to sell coffee and *vetkoeke* and take in mending just to survive. I'm divorcing you, Pierre, whether you want to accept the fact or not."

"In that case," he said, folding his arms across his chest, "*you* had better accept, Sabella, that you'll be losing the children."

"I won't lose them – " she began in some bewilderment.

"Oh yes, you would. I'm their legal father, remember? You are merely the sister who defied the courts and ran away with them. And since I've also adopted Katrien, what court would decide that she'd be morally safe with a mother who took the money I'd sent home, and used it to finance the running of an illegal shebeen?" He shook his head. "Oh my, Sabella, what *is* it going to sound like when I describe my horror at returning home to find that you've been entertaining drunken riff-raff night after night under the same roof as those innocent children?"

"It wasn't like that." Her thoughts were running in a desperate circle through her brain.

"No? Then how will you explain what you did with

the children while men were getting drunk on the premises?"

This, Sabella thought numbly, must be how a fly felt when it was being wrapped in a spider's web. "I'll tell the court how you beat the children," she played the only card left to her.

"And who would you call as witnesses? Name one, Sabella," he invited in a pained voice.

There *were* no witnesses, she acknowledged to herself in despair. He had always beaten the children on parts of their bodies where no bruises would be visible, and all of them had maintained a conspiracy of silence about the beatings.

"On the other hand," she heard Pierre point out, "*I* could call several witnesses to testify to the children's joy when they saw that I was back. *My* children," he added with emphasis, "whom I adopted."

Now, for the first time, she understood why he had insisted on adopting the children. It had given him a permanent hold over her. Just as he beat them to punish her when she angered him, he had planned from the start to use his position as their adoptive father as a weapon against her if and when it was needed. And dear sweet Jesus, how she had played into his hands by encouraging a conspiracy of silence about the beatings, and by allowing her pride to hide the fact that he had abandoned her and the children.

Yes, she was as firmly wrapped as that fly with which she had been comparing herself. "Well, Sabella?" she heard him ask. "What have you decided? To sell the shebeen and sue me for divorce – which I'll fight, and which will end with you losing the children?"

"God, how I hate you," she whispered.

He beamed, as if that had answered his question. And he was right, of course; it had. She turned away and he followed her from the bedroom into the kitchen, where the children swooped on him again – all but Nantes, who had made himself scarce.

277

"Bastian," Sabella said tonelessly, "shall we walk outside for a while? I need to talk to you."

Pierre grinned expansively, as if his permission had been sought and he was granting it. Scowling, Bastian took Sabella's arm and swept her from the house. "What happened?" he demanded.

She dared not tell him the whole truth. He mustn't know about the beatings, or the cold-blooded reason why Pierre had adopted the children. Bastian's immediate reaction would be violence against Pierre, and that would only make matters worse and solve nothing.

"We – talked things over," was all Sabella could think of saying, "and decided to stay together as a family."

Bastian swore under his breath. "You're lying! He threatened you. How?"

Wearily, she told him as much of the truth as she dared. "If I start proceedings to divorce him, he'll fight me and claim custody of all the children – including Katrien."

"He'd never succeed!"

"Yes, he would. As their adoptive father, he'll claim that I'm unfit to have care and control of them." She smiled bitterly. "Because I kept up the fiction that he'd gone to drive transport, I doubt if I'd be able to prove desertion, especially as he claims to have sent money home regularly. I certainly didn't receive a penny, but again I couldn't prove it. So what would you suggest I do, Bastian? Tell the court the real truth – that I'd used money my brother had stolen, and I'd confiscated, to finance my illegal shebeen? That would make me seem the ideal person to have custody of the children, wouldn't it?"

Bastian muttered an obscenity under his breath. "Your husband is a crook, Sabella, and there's nothing straightforward about him, is there? He's after the shebeen, of course, and yet . . . If I hadn't witnessed the scene between him and the children with my own eyes, I wouldn't have believed he cared a rap about them."

Sabella maintained a careful silence. After a moment Bastian went on with a frown, "Claiming custody of them would be going to incredible extremes, however he might feel about them. How would he be able to care for Katrien, for instance?"

He wouldn't bother, was the simple answer. He would leave Nantes to manage as best he could. "Believe me, Bastian," Sabella said with quiet despair, "Pierre *would* claim custody of the children." He would do it to punish her. And dear God, how she would be punished by imagining what he was putting them through, beating them and exploiting them in any way that would be to his advantage. And when it suited him, he would simply abandon them, and she wouldn't even know about it. And then he would lie about it to others, and to himself . . .

"Fight him, Sabella! Call his bluff!" Bastian urged. "I'll help you; I'd engage the best lawyers. I wasn't able to collect proof that he'd committed arson, but the circumstantial evidence could be brought out in court to show the kind of man he is!"

"Even if a clever lawyer were to discredit Pierre in court," she pointed out in defeat, "he would still describe how I ran an illegal shebeen and paint the worst kind of picture of me. The result would be that neither of us would get custody of the children, and all of them would be sent to institutions."

"There's something you've overlooked!" Bastian put in urgently. "Pierre came back because he'd learnt about the money the shebeen is making. He'd be cutting his own throat if he used the shebeen to blacken your character in court. The police here would be alerted and they would close the place down. Sue Pierre for divorce and let him have the damned shebeen!"

She shook her head wearily. "He wants the shebeen, but he knows he couldn't hope to start running it suddenly, without my help. And as for your argument about his not daring to use it against me in court – well, Pierre is no fool. If I were to leave with you and tell him I'm divorcing him, do you know what he'd do? He'd hide most of the stocks of malmsey and turn the customers away tonight with a show of outrage and then he'd go to the police. Later, after the divorce case, he, as the supposed innocent party, would come back here — with or without the children — and ask for the digger's licence to be transferred to his name. And why should the overworked police at the diggings suspect for a moment that *he*, the one who had first drawn their attention to the use to which the kitchen had been put by me, was running the shebeen again? Even if he had to run it less successfully without my help?"

"You can't possibly know all that!" Bastian said angrily.

"And you don't know Pierre." In particular he did not know the hold Pierre had over her through the children, and she couldn't possibly explain it to Bastian. She added wanly, "For the sake of the children, I have to stay with Pierre and drop the idea of a divorce."

"And where does that leave me?" Bastian demanded in a raw voice. "Am I to hover forever on the fringe of your life, with no hope at all of being able to share it one day?"

She stared at him, the truth slowly dawning. "You lied to me, didn't you? It wasn't simply going to be a business association between us, with you doing nothing to risk a scandal."

"Yes, I lied," he admitted without compunction. "I meant to start people talking about the amount of attention I was paying you, in the hope that Annette would be goaded into ending our marriage."

Sabella gave a ragged sigh. She could no more trust Bastian than she could trust Pierre. She discovered that, without thinking, she had led the way to the far end of the claim she had run to peg out and she stood there with Bastian, staring at the useless hole which had grudgingly given up the few diamonds it held and was now no more than another ugly scar on this blighted landscape.

"There's nothing more I could say or do to make you change your mind?" Bastian demanded, breaking the silence.

"No."

"I see. Well, Sabella, do you remember what you told

me that first night I arrived here? You asked me how I could expect Annette to give me children when I've never made any secret of the fact that I don't love her, and so it was no wonder she refused to be treated as a brood-hen. Well, perhaps you were right. Perhaps I never really gave Annette a chance, because my obsession with you always got in the way. So now I'm going to concentrate on trying to salvage my own marriage."

"I wish you luck, Bastian," she said with a generosity she did not feel.

"I'd wish you the same," he responded heavily, "if I had the slightest belief it might do any good." He nodded and walked away from her. She saw him check, and turn to look back at her.

It was a long, intent, unsmiling gaze which held her eyes, and it came to her that this time he really was severing the bonds between them.

To Sabella's surprise and relief, it began to seem that Pierre had no intention of interfering with the way she ran the shebeen. He helped to serve the customers and chatted pleasantly to them, and at the end of the night he did his share in clearing up the room so that it would be a kitchen again in the morning instead of a shebeen.

He made only one intimate approach to her after his return. Thinking of the children, Sabella did not resist. She lay leadenly on the mattress, gritting her teeth and steeling herself to endure a repugnant invasion of her body. But then Katrien, on her mattress in the same room, woke and began to cry, and Pierre did not resume what he'd started once the little girl had been soothed to sleep again.

After that, he made no further advances to her, and when he started going out at night she concluded that he was picking up girls who would be more responsive than his wife. Her only reaction was one of relief.

But after two weeks of his nightly prowling it became clear that whatever else he had been doing with his time, he had also been visiting other shebeens.

With hideous foreboding, Sabella listened as he told her, "This place has a 'sissy' reputation. There are many serious drinkers at the diggings who wouldn't set foot in it the way it is now."

"I made sure that they wouldn't want to set foot in it!"

"Their money is as good as anyone else's, and *they* wouldn't expect frills like dainty sandwiches and stools with pretty cushions on them. If we got rid of the stools and the benches, there would be standing room for many more customers each night."

Furious with herself for having been lulled into a sense of false security, she wanted to fight him tooth and claw. But then she saw the anxious expression on Nantes's face, and watched as Daan went to Pierre's side and clutched his arm, as if to make clear where *his* allegiance lay. Daan, she had realised, feared Pierre as much as Nantes did, but unlike Nantes, he didn't remember Pa at all and Pierre was the only father he had ever known. And she had learnt here at the diggings where life was often raw and violent that children would forgive even the most degraded parents anything and continue to strive for their love. Now, the brother she had brought up since babyhood was pleading with her with his eyes, telling her that while he loved her too, Pierre had a special place in his heart, and begging her to do nothing to make the man turn on him.

"Do as you like," she told Pierre, conceding defeat. "But don't expect me to serve the kind of customers you want to attract."

"I don't, my love. Your nose-in-the-air attitude would put them off their drink." He gave her a calculating, challenging look. "But it's not a bad idea to give the customers something to feast their eyes on while they're drinking, so Ria will help me to serve the wine."

"No!" Sabella cried forcefully. "I won't allow it!"

"She may be your sister, but she's my *daughter*," Pierre pointed out. "And you don't think I would allow customers to do more than look, do you?"

"The very idea is obscene, Pierre!"

He stared at her. "Are you really going to kick up a fuss about nothing, my dear?" His tone of voice, as well as the deepening of fear in Nantes's eyes and the way Daan clung more tightly than ever to Pierre's arm told Sabella that she had no other course but to give in.

After that, she remained helplessly in the background as Pierre turned her shebeen into a replica of the worst at the diggings. But they, at least, did not use a beautiful young woman with the mind of a toddler to attract and excite customers. Night after night Sabella lay awake with Katrien in her arms, listening to the drunken laughter, the occasional audible obscenity, and the regular fights which broke out. Her own customers had always deferred to the fact that there were children in the house, but the rough men now lured to the shebeen had no such inhibitions, particularly as Pierre was adulterating the malmsey, which brought out the worst in them.

She had only two small consolations to which to cling. The ribald suggestions she was certain were being made to Ria would pass completely over her head. Her very handicap was her protection. The other thing for which to be grateful was the fact that Pierre was making so much money that he hadn't pressed her to turn her own savings over to him. They were still in Mr Kowalski's care, and it gave her a measure of consolation to know that, if a miracle should happen and some way presented itself of rescuing herself and the children from Pierre, she would have the money on which to fall back.

But as his new-style shebeen flourished no small consolation could lighten Sabella's growing anguish. Ria was beginning to repeat obscenities picked up from the customers, without having any understanding of why the words were taboo; the boys were hollow-eyed from lack of sleep because the roistering customers did not leave until very late, and Katrien was growing more and more frightened by the nightly noise which she didn't understand.

I can't bear this, Sabella thought with desperation. If only

I had a weapon to use against Pierre, one that would not lead to his beating one of the children . . .

Suddenly, with a flash of inspiration, it came to her that she *did* possess such a weapon. The next morning she rose, leaving Pierre to sleep on as he usually did, and after she had made breakfast for the children she announced that she was going shopping. Taking the yawning, hollow-eyed Ria and the subdued Katrien with her, she set off for Mr Kowalski's office instead.

Because she conversed with him in English neither Ria nor Katrien, even with their limited vocabularies, would be able to pick up any of the words and innocently repeat them in Pierre's presence.

"I expect you have heard," Sabella addressed Mr Kowalski, "that my husband came back."

"Yes." He growled a word in Yiddish which she sensed was extremely derogatory. "Also I have been told how he has changed your fine shebeen, Missus."

"I can't allow him to continue," she said in a low, shamed voice. "It will destroy the children. Mr Kowalski, could I ask you to do something for me?"

"Never before have you been slow to ask something of me!" But in spite of the astringent tone, his expression was compassionate.

She looked straight into his eyes. "Will you arrange for the police to raid the shebeen tonight?"

He nodded slowly. "You have thought of what will happen, Missus?"

"I have. It's the only way. And Mr Kowalski – please don't allow the police to suspect that I have had any hand in arranging for the raid."

"Jacob Kowalski you can trust, Missus."

"Thank you so much. You've been the best – the only friend – I've had at the diggings." She offered him her hand. "I shall call tomorrow to collect my savings."

It took all her concentration, during the rest of the day and the early evening, not to behave in any way which would later be remembered as having been different or significant or suspicious. She treated Pierre with her usual mixture of bitter resentment and scorn, and when the time came for the shebeen to open its doors to customers she asked him, as she always did, whether he could do something *this time* to keep the noise down.

That night she lay tensely next to Katrien, who had at last fallen into exhausted sleep. The raid came at half-past ten, the noise waking Katrien and the boys and sending Ria screaming into the bedroom where Sabella sat up on the mattress and lit a candle. She was trying to calm both Ria and Katrien when Pierre arrived in the room, wearing a look of shock.

She pretended to have noticed nothing unusual about his expression. "Your customers are really surpassing themselves tonight, aren't they?" she hurled at him with a cold fury which she prayed would sound convincing. "What have they done to Ria to put her in such a state? Have you no control at all over those animals you attract to this house?"

"Sabella," he said, ignoring her questions, "you have got to get up – "

"Why? If *you* can't control the drunks out there, why should you expect *me* to be able to do so?"

"You don't understand, damn it!" he exploded. "It's a police raid, and they want to speak to you!"

"Oh? Why me? Tell them it's your shebeen – "

"The digger's licence which allows us to go on living here is in your name! *That's* why they want to speak to you!"

"I see." She made her voice grim. "I really have a lot for which to thank you, haven't I, Pierre?" She pushed the bedclothes aside. "Go and tell the police I'll be with them in five minutes."

She dressed quickly, and took Ria and Katrien to the boys' room, asking Nantes to keep them together. "There's no need to be frightened," she added.

In the shebeen she found that most of the customers had fled and only a minority of very drunk and voluble ones were trying to fight the police, who were wrestling to put handcuffs on them.

The policeman in charge gave Sabella a look that shrivelled her self-respect. "The digger's licence is in your name, Mevrou le Roux," he said curtly. "Even if you hadn't known what was going on in your house at night – which would be impossible to believe – you would still be held responsible."

"I – I see." She tried to look shocked, and as if she hadn't known this from the outset.

"Some of my men will now search the premises and confiscate all money found."

"That's outrageous!" Pierre bellowed. "There's money in the house that has no connection with the shebeen – "

"Too bad. It was a risk you took when you started selling liquor illegally." The policeman turned to Sabella. "As for you, Mevrou, your digger's licence will be revoked and if you are still at the diggings twenty-four hours from now, you will be arrested. Is that clear?"

"I – " She pretended dismay. "Yes, it's clear . . ."

She went to sit down by the table, looking down at her lap so that her inward elation would not show. She had done it; she had beaten Pierre in a way he would never suspect. She heard him protesting as the policemen brought out the money he'd hidden all over the house; he was almost in tears but she felt no shred of pity for him.

The night was almost over by the time the police had destroyed the vats of malmsey they'd found, taken away the arrested customers and completed their search of the house.

Sabella found herself alone in the kitchen with Pierre. "You won't want to saddle yourself with responsibility for the children now," she said. "They're of no further use to you. If you'll drop them, and me, off in Lichtenburg I'll find some way of providing for them."

With a shock, she heard him say, either with assumed injury or because he was lying to himself again, "How can you even suggest that I would want to leave all of you to fend for yourselves?"

"Pierre, face facts – " she began in desperation.

"We'll stay together and start again. We'll use your savings."

"*My savings*." So that was it . . .

"I know you hadn't hidden it in the house, Sabella, because I'd looked. Where is it?"

She stared at him with loathing. "You're not getting your hands on my savings, Pierre! They're hidden where you'd never find them, and I'd sooner forfeit the money than let you have it!"

"A very silly attitude, Sabella." He gave her a calculating look, and went to the inner door, calling Ria's name.

He would never beat Ria, Sabella tried to assure herself as he sat down and waited. *Part of his hellish strategy lies in the fact that the children* know *they are being beaten because of me, and Ria wouldn't understand that . . .*

Her sister entered the room, yawning and knuckling her eyes. "Come here, Ria," Pierre said softly. "Come and sit on Daddy's knee."

The girl obeyed. For all her woman's body, her manner was that of a child as she settled herself on Pierre's knee. Momentarily, Sabella was struck dumb with horror as he unbuttoned her sister's blouse and uncovered one full, rounded breast, cupping it in his hand. "Pretty Ria," he crooned.

Oh God, Sabella thought, recognising her sister's instinctive sensual response. "Pretty Ria," the girl echoed, wriggling with pleasure under Pierre's touch.

Sabella found her voice. "Get out of here, Ria!" she screamed. "Button your blouse and don't come back – do you hear me?"

Chastened, her lower lip trembling, Ria slid from Pierre's knee and he did nothing to stop her from scurrying out of the room, buttoning her blouse as she did so. He looked at Sabella, and his expression said, there'll be other times. Do as I ask, or I'll teach Ria what it's like to be a woman.

"You are disgusting," she whispered. "Beneath contempt. I am not turning my savings over to you, so you can drop any idea of taking me and the children away with you."

"I couldn't force you to go with me, Sabella, but with or without you and the money, I'm taking the children."

He was bluffing, she told herself. With no money or prospects, what use would the children be to him? It had been different, the last time, because he'd been fighting to take over the profitable shebeen. So long as she refused to hand over her savings, Pierre would leave without the children. Once he had safely gone she would ask Mr Kowalski to drive them all to Lichtenburg in time to prevent herself from being arrested.

But if it was bluff, Pierre was nerve-rackingly clinging to it for as long as he could. Sabella remained in the background as the morning wore on, watching him pack all their household possessions on the back of his truck with the help of the boys. Their own clothes and personal belongings were packed too, and only Sabella's ostentatiously left inside the house.

It was only when he ordered the boys to climb on the back of the truck too, and installed Ria and Katrien inside the cab, that Sabella cracked. "Wait," she said through her tears. "I'll go and collect my savings."

Pierre nodded with satisfaction. "I knew you'd see sense. I'll pack your things on the truck."

Oh, she wasn't beaten yet! Hatred and tension had caused her tears, not defeat. She knew he would wait for her, no matter how long she might take. He was only too well aware that if she hadn't left the diggings by tonight she would be arrested. Instead, *he* would be the one to be arrested!

As usual, Mr Kowalski set aside whatever had been occupying him and gave her his attention. "Your money you have come for, Missus," he greeted her.

"No. I've come to ask you for help. I want to use the money, every penny if necessary, to hire a lawyer to – do whatever it is they do to bring charges against someone."

Mr Kowalski listened without interruption as she poured out everything, including Pierre's implicit threat against Ria. "I'm sure there's a law," she ended, "against forcing people to hand over money by using threats. You could also help by telling the police that *I* arranged for the shebeen to be raided to stop Pierre."

"Aai, Missus, my dear," Mr Kowalski sighed, his eyes resting on her with pity. "To hire a lawyer would be throw away your money."

"Why?" Her voice rose. "*You* believed what I told you; I could see that. Why shouldn't a lawyer?"

"What is believed and what is not makes no difference." He went on to explain the realities of the situation to her, and she sat there, feeling more and more beaten as she took it in.

There *was* a law against extorting money under threat, but it didn't apply to married couples. It would count as no more than a domestic dispute – *if* Sabella had been able to prove her story. But she had no witnesses to back up her allegations that Pierre had ever beaten the children or sexually molested Ria. The very fact that he had to all appearances been prepared to take responsibility for the children and drive away with them, even without Sabella's savings, would be in his favour and throw doubt on her story. And against her was the fact that, whatever Pierre might have made of the shebeen after he'd returned, *she* had created it in the first place. Moreover, because the digger's licence had been in her name, the police raid and her eviction from the diggings under threat of arrest would appear on her record, and not on Pierre's.

Defeat bitter in her mouth, Sabella took her savings from Mr Kowalski, kissed him goodbye, and walked to where Pierre was waiting for her. All around her was the noise of washing-and-sorting machines, the sound of shouted profanities, the thud of pickaxe and spade and the rumbling of water-carts. Deep in her own comfortless thoughts, she scarcely heard them.

Pierre smiled as he opened the door of the cab for her and she climbed inside, taking Katrien on her lap. With a look of icy hatred, she handed her savings to Pierre.

He started the motor of the truck, and before long the diggings had been left behind them. "You know, you've always had good ideas, Sabella," he broke the silence between them, as if nothing in the least untoward had happened. "Take that idea of yours to tell everyone I'd gone to drive transport."

He had been the one who'd first put that story about. It seemed that he was conveniently lying to himself again. She listened in sullen silence as he went on.

"I'll take you and the children to Goedgesig, the smallholding near Johannesburg which is jointly owned by myself and my brother and sister. No one is living there at present so we'll be able to move straight in. Then I'll use your savings and buy pineapples on the market and drive out to farms, selling the fruit to farmers."

She had intended to maintain a stony silence but the madness of his scheme forced her to speak. "Why *pineapples*?"

"Just think for a moment, Sabella! Folks on isolated farms would never have seen a pineapple. They would pay through the neck for one."

"Really?" she asked scathingly. "Would *you* pay hard-earned money for fruit you'd never seen before in your life, and have no idea whether you'd find to your taste or not? At a time, moreover, when farmers are hard-pressed because of the drought? You'd end up with a truckload of rotten pineapples!"

"I suppose," he said reflectively, "you may have a point. It would still be worth trying, however, because I know where I can buy pineapples cheaply – "

"Forget about pineapples," she cut in tersely. "You'll *buy* from farmers, not *sell* to them. You'll buy chickens as cheaply as you can and bring them back to Goedgesig. There, we'll work together to pluck and dress them for the Johannesburg market. There'll be a strong demand for ready-to-cook poultry, saving housewives and servants an unpleasant and messy job."

He took one hand from the steering wheel and turned her face to his, grinning at her in jubilation. "You're right! It's a wonderful idea! I've always had a dream to become very rich, Sabella, and with you by my side I know I'll make it come true!"

She brushed his hand away and stared out of the window. Bitterly, she cursed her own ambition, her bright ideas and her perseverance and ability to make them work. *They* were the reasons why Pierre would never again relax his hold over her.

But then, gradually, resolve grew inside her. Pierre had left them once before, when he'd stolen her diamond. The only reason why he had come back had been to take control of the money-making shebeen. And if it hadn't been for the savings he'd known she possessed, he would have abandoned her and the children today.

She would, she determined grimly, use all her ambition and energy in the future to make that large fortune for which he craved. And when she had made it she would barter every penny of it with Pierre in exchange for freedom for herself and the children.

Part Three

1940

13

The sun's heat was fierce and almost paralysing here on the Highveld. The wagon had been drawn off the road and the mules outspanned; a few white-thorn trees provided shade for the wagon on which all their possessions had been packed and among which one had to create one's own little space in which to squat during the long, slow journey.

There was a *spruit* nearby, at which the mules were already slaking their thirst. Daan had taken cans upstream to fill them so that the water could be boiled and left to cool for drinking, and Anton had gone to search for fuel.

Abstractedly, Katrien watched as a chameleon, barely visible against the bark of a tree, flicked out its tongue with the speed of forked lightning and snared a hapless cricket. The cricket, at least, had had no foreknowledge of its fate while *she* was mentally bracing herself for the trouble which had been brewing since this morning.

They had picked up a farmer whose truck had broken down, and were giving him a lift to the nearest village where there was a garage. With their over-full wagon, they'd had every excuse *not* to offer the stranger a lift, and even he had seemed embarrassed at first at having accepted the pressing invitation to share their limited space.

Katrien's glance went to the man she thought of and also addressed as Derrie. It was a corruption of "Daddy" which she had used in early childhood and to which she had deliberately reverted as soon as she became old enough to reason for herself. The word Derrie had no meaning, and to her its use reduced the man who was her step-father and her adoptive father to equal meaninglessness. She had also perfected a way of putting emphasis on the word so that it sounded like a studied insult, but couldn't be pinned down as such. He had long since given up furious attempts to make her change it to "Daddy", telling her she was neither a baby nor a simpleton like her Tante Ria. Katrien would stare at him with calculated innocence and say, "I can't help it; it just comes out that way, *Derrie*."

The reason why he had insisted on giving the farmer a lift this morning was obvious to her. It had presented him with an opportunity to impress the stranger with his kindness and generosity, and also given him someone to whom to tell the story of their many shifts in fortune, in such a way that he always figured as the indomitable hero, forever struggling against overwhelming odds to provide for his family.

Really, Katrien thought, the whole affair had been rather funny in a way because while Derrie was trying to impress the farmer, *he* in turn was giving Mammie the kind of sidelong glances that Katrien, at fifteen, was well able to recognise. Mammie might be thirty-five but she looked at least ten years younger, with her slim figure and dark red curling hair and flawless complexion which came from never going bare-headed in the sun and also because, if she had nothing else to rub into her skin to keep it smooth, she used lard. Trying to impress Mammie, just as Derrie was trying to impress *him*, the farmer had boasted that he was a high-ranking member of the *Ossewa Brandwag* movement. Mammie had grabbed the reins in her own hands, bringing the wagon to a halt, and said tersely, "Get out. Find one of your own sort, another rabble-rousing Fascist, to give you a lift."

Derrie had tried to laugh and turn it into a joke about Mammie having made a stupid fuss about nothing. "What do women understand about politics? You're welcome to a ride on my wagon, friend."

"He is neither welcome, nor a friend!" Mammie had

burst out, too angry to remember the need for caution. "And it's hardly *your* wagon, Pierre! It was paid for with what we managed to salvage after your latest folly. And I say this Nazi gets off it *now*!"

The man had taunted spitefully as he jumped from the wagon, "You'd better watch out or your wife will have you in khaki before you can turn around, and on your way to help the English fight their war!"

"Not a chance, old mate! The fact is, she's taking it out on you because I've decided to join the *Ossewa Brandwag* myself." It had been a great big lie, because apart from the fact that Derrie wouldn't join anything unless he thought he might be able to make money out of it, or impress people, the para-military organisation which had taken its name from the old Oxwagon Guards used by the early Trekkers had been banned, and its members risked internment for the duration of the war. But to add substance to the lie, Derrie had flung out his hand in the Nazi salute and added, "*Heil* Hitler!"

"*Heil* Hitler!" Uncle Anton had echoed, as usual making it clear that his sympathy was with Derrie, and angry with Mammie for having exposed his hero to ridicule and embarrassment.

Since then hardly a word had been spoken by anyone but only poor, beautiful, simple Tante Ria had been unaware of the brewing tension. And now that they had outspanned, Derrie would punish Mammie for making him lose face. His target, Katrien knew, would almost certainly be herself again.

Considering the matter dispassionately, she didn't believe he would beat her. He seldom did so nowadays, because she had trained herself to refuse to cry out or shed tears, but stared at him throughout with hard-eyed contempt. And afterwards, she made a deliberate, defiant travesty of that ritual which seemed to mean so much to him.

"Why did I beat you?" he used to ask her, just as she had heard him ask poor Uncle Nantes or Daan so many times.

"Because you enjoy it, Derrie," she would respond, her chin in the air.

"That isn't the answer!" he would bellow at her.

With a scornful shrug, she would offer him the truth. "Because you really want to hit Mammie, but this way you get twice as much fun."

"*Damn you, I beat you because I love you!*"

"Then I'd rather you hated me instead, Derrie," she would say stonily.

And because he couldn't force her to vary her response or display an emotion other than contempt, he very rarely beat her now. But he found other ways. Oh yes, he was good at finding other punishment; like that time when he'd insisted he'd seen lice on her head and had shorn her hair to her scalp so that she'd had to face the ridicule of everyone at school with her bald head . . .

He was staring at her now with a calculating expression, and she steeled herself not to react in any visible way. "Katrien," he said abruptly, "we passed a farmhouse a way back and I want you to walk there, and ask the people to give you anything they can spare in the way of food for your hungry family. Put on that white blouse of yours; you know the one I mean. It would make them feel generous."

Katrien's heart plummeted into her shoes. Before she could say anything Mammie cried with force, "No! You're not turning her into a beggar, Pierre! We're *not* hungry; we have sackfuls of mealie meal and flour and sugar and – "

"My dear Sabella, it's a good thing I'm here to think ahead for all of us. The more of our supplies we can save on the journey, the longer they'll last us until we can get on our feet again."

"That isn't the true reason, and you know it! I won't allow you to send Katrien to beg for food!"

"And *I* won't do it!" Katrien lifted her chin and stared at him with defiant disdain. "Beat me if you like, but I won't go and beg from strangers!"

Derrie shook his head and gave that smile of his which

298

anyone outside the family would have mistaken for one of charming ruefulness and resignation. With a swift glance to check that Anton and Daan were still out of sight he said, "*You're* not against me like everyone else, are you, pretty Ria? Come to Daddy."

With a mixture of shame, embarrassment and pity, Katrien watched her aunt's beautiful, vacant face take on the look of a toddler being offered sweets. "Pretty Ria," she crooned, hurrying towards Derrie, her hands fumbling with the top button of her dress.

"No!" Katrien and Mammie shouted simultaneously. Tante Ria stopped in her tracks and began to cry, very much like a toddler would have cried if the offer of sweets were being withdrawn.

Derrie's smile became even more charming. "Don't forget to put on the white blouse, Katrien," he reminded. "And if the people at the farm won't help your hungry family, you'll have to walk on to the next one."

Giving him a look of hatred, she went to the wagon and climbed on the back to look among her clothes for the white blouse of shame. Under the privacy of the wagon's half-canopy she changed into it, and she had just fastened the last button when Mammie joined her.

"Here's a tickey, Katrien." She held out the small silver coin. "It's the only change I have. Ask the people at the farm what they can *sell* you for it, even if it's only a few eggs."

Gratefully, Katrien pocketed the tickey. Her pride would not have to be sacrificed, and Derrie had been beaten. But not quite, she amended with bitterness, thinking of the white blouse. The tickey might save her from knocking at the farmhouse door as a beggar, but the blouse would tell its own story before she could even produce the coin.

In the fierce heat, a while later, she felt as if she were struggling to walk through melted toffee. The farmhouse for which she was heading was still on the distant horizon, shimmering and moving in a haze with the sunlight reflecting on its corrugated tin roof like a winking eye.

The same sunlight, she knew, was picking out the faint but unmistakable words BLUE RIBBON FLOUR across the front and back of the blouse which Derrie had forced her to wear. Mammie had tried her hardest to bleach the lettering out of existence both before and after she'd unpicked the cotton flour-bag to make the blouse, but the sun never failed to show them up for all to see.

Katrien's mouth set in a grim line. To her own deep embarrassment her figure had been developing by leaps and bounds during the past months, and it was perfectly true that she was constantly outgrowing blouses. What hadn't been true was Derrie's insistence that they couldn't afford, at the time, to buy another length of material for a new school blouse. Oh no, that had been another of his calculated punishments. He'd wanted Mammie to know that everyone at Katrien's last school would be sniggering at her because the straining buttons across her bosom drew attention to it. Mammie had fought him by scrounging the empty flour-bag from the owner of the general store, but her failure to bleach the letters from the fabric had simply handed him an unexpected triumph.

"Old flour-bag blouse! Old Blue Ribbon tits!" the children at school had chanted after Katrien. So Mammie had started baking batches of cakes and selling them to Mr Sundarjee's general store until she'd scraped together enough money to buy white material from which to make other blouses for Katrien, but Derrie had used veiled threats to make sure the flour-bag blouse wasn't destroyed, so that it could be used for future punishment. At the farm for which she was heading it would make her a figure of fun at best, or an object of pity at worst.

"As soon as we're back at Goedgesig," Mammie had promised just before Katrien set out for the farmhouse, "I'll embroider flowers all over the blouse so that the lettering won't show. I should have done it before."

Goedgesig. Katrien sighed as she thought of that bleak, miserable smallholding to which they had so often been forced to return after Derrie had yet again ruined one of

Mammie's bright ideas and plunged them into another period of poverty.

Of course, there had been something called the Depression which Katrien had been too young at the time to remember, and during which practically everyone other than people like Uncle Bastian had been poor, and even Mammie's bright ideas had been unworkable. But the Depression had long since ended. Looking back, it was hard for Katrien to believe that one moment they would be living in a comfortable, well-furnished house, with Derrie driving a flashy new Chevrolet or Studebaker, and the next both house and car would be gone and they'd be driving back to Goedgesig in a ramshackle truck or a wagon drawn by mules or even donkeys, so that Mammie could rack her brains for another money-making idea. And then it would all start over again, with Derrie doing something stupid to wreck everything.

Like that time when Mammie rented a shop in a small country town from which she'd sold clothing which factory inspectors rejected because they had some small defect or other. Just when that business was on the point of becoming a success Derrie had taken the truck and instead of picking up an assortment of rejected clothing from factories in Johannesburg as he was supposed to do, he'd brought back a full load of ladies' shoes. Because he'd been able to buy them very cheaply, leaving him with money to bet on a horse which naturally failed to win, he had completely missed the fact that the shoes had been a silly, eccentric craze which had been briefly fashionable some years before but had since become totally unsaleable. The small shop had been forced to close, and back to Goedgesig it had been yet again.

So many past ventures; so much hard work and ingenuity on Mammie's part and so much folly and greed on Derrie's . . . There had been the farmhouse, for one, which she had turned into a restaurant, specialising in serving only freshly gathered vegetables grown by Anton and Daan, so busy cooking and waiting on customers that she hadn't

301

realised Derrie wasn't banking the takings but squandering them on crazy schemes of his own instead.

Katrien's eyes filled with sorrowful tears as she remembered another of Mammie's money-making ideas, because *that* one had ended in tragedy. For the first time Mammie had accepted help from Uncle Bastian; not money, of course. She hadn't ever accepted a ha'penny from him; at least not Katrien's knowledge. Instead with capital she had managed to scrape together and keep out of Derrie's rapacious hands she had arranged for them to buy a large farm on the edge of the Bushveld, which was for sale at a very low price because it was virtually impossible to cultivate. The previous owner had found that any crops he sowed were eaten by the plentiful game in the area, and his own domestic stock couldn't compete with the wild animals for pasturage. Mammie's idea was that rich men from Johannesburg would pay for the privilege of being allowed to hunt there. Of course, they could have travelled some distance further and hunted without paying anyone for the privilege, but Mammie had shrewdly gambled on the fact that they would prefer the illusion of roughing it in the bush rather than experience the uncomfortable reality. So the tents set up on the farm had been equipped with truckle-beds and soft mattresses; hot water had been available on demand from the farmhouse, and when the hunters – all of them there on Uncle Bastian's recommendation – cooked their spoils over a camp fire Mammie provided them with the refinements of newly baked bread and fresh salads and endless brews of coffee. At last all had seemed to be going well and Derrie was kept too busy, helping to sow crops to attract a plentiful supply of game to their farm, to squander the profits. And then . . .

Katrien sat down on a giant termite hill and stared at the repellent white ants scurrying around it. Some tribesmen considered their eggs a delicacy, she knew, and the termites even bore the nickname of Bushman-rice . . . It was no use. She couldn't blank from her mind the memory of what happened on that Bushveld farm. She closed her eyes and it was as if the years had rolled back as she relived the events of that fateful day five years before.

Freak weather conditions had set in overnight and in the morning Katrien had to steel herself to wash in the water from the flowered jug which should have been pleasantly tepid, but was icy instead. Afterwards she opened the window to empty the bowl so that she could help Tante Ria, who shared the bedroom with her, to wash as well, and as she did so a blast of cold air stung Katrien's face. Before she closed the window she saw the three hunter-guests from Johannesburg emerging from their tents, blowing on their hands or jamming them into pockets for warmth and looking up at the grey sky as if it had deliberately clouded over to spite them.

They huddled together in conversation and one of them gestured half-heartedly towards the sheltered spot where, on a normal hot Bushveld morning, they would have lit a fire and cooked steaks of venison and played the game of pretending to be intrepid hunters. The two others shook their heads and shrugged, and then Katrien saw them walking rapidly towards the farmhouse.

They would want a breakfast cooked by Mammie, who at this time of the morning would already be slotting in chores like bread-making with the simmering of porridge and the brewing of coffee. But these men from Johannesburg, Katrien felt certain, would not be content with a simple family breakfast of porridge and coffee. She was ten years old, and hers was the only help Mammie and Uncle Nantes had with all the extra domestic work the visiting hunters made, and so Katrien hurried to wash and dress Tante Ria before she went to the kitchen.

Uncle Nantes was stoking the already-blazing fire in the kitchen range and Mammie was pinching off pieces of bread-dough and forming them into rolls which could quickly be baked in time for breakfast. The three hunting visitors were standing as close to the range as they could, talking about city business-affairs.

303

"Katrien," Mammie said without pausing in what she was doing, "crack a dozen eggs into a bowl and get them ready to be scrambled." Over her shoulder she added, "Give the porridge a stir, Nantes."

"Porridge *and* scrambled eggs," Daan exulted, greedily rubbing his stomach.

Katrien refused to call him Uncle, because he was only a few years older than herself. She wouldn't call Anton Uncle either, but not for the same reason. She looked at him now, standing close to Derrie who had butted into the hunters' conversation, and nodding at everything Derrie said as if he were listening to the richest pearls of wisdom ever uttered. Imagine being stupid enough to make *Derrie* one's hero, Katrien thought with withering contempt.

The hunters certainly didn't share Anton's admiration for their host, because one of them interrupted quite curtly as Derrie was giving them the benefit of his opinion on something called stocks and shares, and commanded, "Let's have some coffee, le Roux, and make it good and strong."

That's put him in his place, Katrien thought with satisfaction as she whipped the eggs vigorously. But a little later Derrie got his own back. The men were expressing doubts about taking their guns out that morning because of the cold, and Derrie cut in tauntingly, "Surely you're not going to be put off hunting because the weather is a little fresh?"

"It's more than a little fresh – " one of the men began.

"The wind is bound to drive the clouds away before long and then the sun will be out, as hot as ever, and the wind will drop."

Katrien glanced up from what she was doing. She might only be ten years old, but she could recognise a simple grown-up dilemma when she saw one. None of the men had a fancy to brave the cold air; all of them were casting surreptitious looks of longing at the kitchen range but not one of them wanted to lose face by admitting they would sooner spend the morning indoors.

304

"You're sure the sun will come out soon?" one of them demanded of Derrie as they all sat down at the table to have their breakfast.

"Quite sure," Derrie lied. How could he possibly know what the sun would or wouldn't do? No, it was just that he didn't welcome the prospect of having the men underfoot all morning, treating him like a waiter and pointedly shutting him out of their business-talk.

After the guests had breakfasted they left, without noticeable enthusiasm, to fetch their guns and go out into the surrounding bush. As the morning wore on the clouds didn't lift, the sun didn't come out or the wind die down. Katrien washed the breakfast dishes and put them away, glad of the heat in the kitchen, and expected at any moment that the hunters would come shivering back to the house. But individual pride must have prevented each one of them from being the first to throw in the towel.

She began to scrub the kitchen table, which Mammie had just finished using for her bread-making. Derrie, Anton and Daan hurried inside after having fed and watered the poultry and livestock, and they huddled as close to the range as they could. Mammie had given Tante Ria the simple task of sweeping the floor, and in a corner of the kitchen Uncle Nantes squatted, scouring the porridge saucepan. He was using the small pieces of grit among the wood-ash for the purpose and they made scraping noises as he worked, and suddenly Derrie erupted. Katrien might have realised that *someone* would have to be punished for the slights he had suffered from the hunters.

"*You!* Nancy-boy!" he flung at Uncle Nantes. "Can't you do your women's work more quietly?"

"The p-p-p-pan got b-b-b-burnt," Uncle Nantes managed.

"Then leave it to soak, and stop getting on my nerves!" Derrie glared at him with venom, and everyone held their breath.

Uncle Nantes had always been more of a victim to

305

Derrie's cruelties than the others, and Katrien sensed it was because he showed so clearly that all he felt for his adoptive father was fear. Daan feared him too, but for some reason that Katrien would never understand he loved him as much as he feared him. Katrien doubted that Derrie had any true affection for any of them, not even for Anton who idolised him and aped everything he did or said, but he really hated Uncle Nantes.

More usually, Derrie chose to mask his true feelings but now he lashed out at Uncle Nantes with open viciousness. "It's time you stopped skulking out in the kitchen like a girl, so go out and look for firewood, nancy-boy!"

"The p-p-pan," Uncle Nantes began to explain. "Sabella n-n-needs it – "

"We *all* need firewood more! Go on, get out there and collect some!"

Mammie said with a mildness that Katrien knew was carefully controlled, "We're not short of firewood, Pierre."

"We soon will be if this weather continues. Stop protecting the *bliksemse* pansy, Sabella!" Derrie turned to Nantes. "Get yourself out there – *now!*"

"Pierre, it's bitterly cold outside," Mammie protested, "and Nantes's jersey is threadbare. He has nothing warm to wear."

"Even a nancy-boy wouldn't be hurt by a bit of wind," Derrie snapped. "Do as I say, Nantes!"

As Uncle Nantes rose to his feet Katrien burst out, "You don't have to do as he says at all! You're a grown-up, Uncle Nantes!"

Everyone was staring at herself now, and she noticed a vein throbbing at Derrie's left temple. Mammie's eyes bored into her own, conveying the old familiar warning: don't interfere. You know it always makes things worse if one interferes.

Oh, Katrien knew it well enough. But she loved Uncle Nantes for his gentle nature and his willingness always to help Mammie, and apart from a feeling of outrage that he should still have to suffer being ordered about like a child

306

by Derrie, she hated the idea of his having to brave the cold wind in his thin, worn-out jersey.

"*I'll* go and collect firewood," she announced. "I'll wear my warm jacket."

Derrie gave her an ominously deceptive smile and said, "You stay and help your mother. It will do Nantes nothing but good to do something as *manly* as searching for firewood." He added with malice, "Since you and your mother are so concerned about him wilting in the wind, he can wear Ria's coat."

She saw the flush staining Uncle Nantes's face, and guessed what he was thinking. He was thinking of being spotted by those sophisticated hunters, ignominiously buttoned into Tante Ria's coat with its fake fur collar, and imagining their ridicule. Even so, he took a step towards the door behind which the coat hung from a hook.

Unable to contain herself, Katrien shouted, "Uncle Nantes, stop doing what he tells you all the time! You don't need to! *You* could tell *him* to fly to the devil! You – you could even hit him if you wanted to!"

A terrible silence followed her outburst. It was the first time she had ever forsaken dumb insolence for outright hostility and it was also the first time any of them had questioned Derrie's authority over everyone in the household.

Uncle Nantes broke the tense silence. "I'll g–g–g–go," he announced, and hurried to the door.

"Wear Ria's coat," Derrie ordered, adding with a malevolent smile, "Women's clothing would certainly suit you!"

Uncle Nantes hesitated, and then he lifted the coat from its hook. As he buttoned himself awkwardly into it Katrien knew why he had accepted that particular indignity. He was hoping that by doing so Derrie wouldn't punish her for what she had said and done.

He might have succeeded, but on the other hand Derrie seldom gave advance warning of any punishment to come, and after Nantes had left the house a tense atmosphere hung over the kitchen. It was made worse by the sound

307

of the wind howling like a lost soul around the sides of the house.

Defiantly, Katrien dipped the brush into the bowl of soapy water and continued to scrub away at the kitchen table with quite unnecessary force. Let him do his worst, she thought, and at the same time wished the wind would stop blowing so unnervingly. It was strong enough now to carry the crack of gunshots into the house.

Anton had just stoked the range again when they heard the sound of running footsteps outside. The kitchen door burst open, letting in an icy blast. One of the hunters rushed into the room, his mouth working.

"Terrible mistake," he managed after gulping several times for breath. "The young man – wearing a brown coat – " The hunter stopped, looking at them with tormented eyes. "Caught a glimpse through the bush – thought it was a buck – "

"*You've shot Uncle Nantes!*" Katrien screamed in dreadful understanding.

The man turned to stare at her, his tongue flicking over his lips. "He shouldn't have been there," he muttered tonelessly. "Not stooping behind a bush, wearing a brown coat – not when he knew we were out with our guns . . ."

In spite of the heat baking down on her, Katrien shivered as she recalled so vividly the tragic and ignominious end to her beloved young uncle's life. She had blamed herself for it ever since. If she hadn't interfered, if she hadn't drawn Derrie's vengeful attention to herself, Uncle Nantes wouldn't have tried to deflect that attention by giving in and wearing Tante Ria's brown coat.

But now, suddenly, a different aspect of the matter struck Katrien. There had been no pressing need for anyone to collect more firewood that morning, and Derrie had known the hunters were out with their guns and that the cold snap would make them unwilling to venture far from the house. Unlike Katrien, who had been too young at the time to make the connection, *he* must have realised that

Uncle Nantes, in that brown coat with its fake fur collar, would be at risk. Was it really too far-fetched to believe that Derrie had *hoped* Uncle Nantes would be mistaken for a game animal?

If that was the truth it could never be proved. Had the same suspicion entered Mammie's head at the time? Was that the reason, apart from her grief, why she had refused to have more hunters on the farm? Derrie had sold it at a loss to the first buyer who'd offered for it, and they had returned to Goedgesig yet again.

Wiping the tears from her cheeks, Katrien walked on towards the farmhouse. The burden of her own guilt in the matter of Uncle Nantes's death had been lightened considerably now that she understood the part Derrie had played in it. Even if he hadn't actively hoped the hunters would mistake Uncle Nantes for a buck, even if the possibility had never entered his mind, it was still *he* who had forced Uncle Nantes to wear the brown coat. He was as much to blame as if he had shot Uncle Nantes himself, and Katrien put it at the head of a long list of reasons for hating Derrie.

Poor Uncle Nantes, she thought. He had been a grown man in his twenties when he was shot dead, and quite old enough to have left the rest of them and made a life of his own. But he had stayed, Katrien felt sure, because of his love for Mammie and his wish to lend her whatever help or support he could. Perhaps, too, he had felt himself too inadequate, with his painful stammer and his gentle, meek nature, to make his own way in life.

But Anton – and even Daan now – were old enough to leave and live their own lives. Mammie had tried so many times to persuade them to find jobs and become independent. But then Derrie would say, "And how am I going to keep our heads above water without the help of my two strong sons?" So they had stayed, partly because their schooling had suffered as a result of the family moving so constantly and they weren't qualified for anything except menial labour, but mostly out of loyalty to Derrie.

The moment *I'm* twenty-one, Katrien vowed grimly, I'll be moving out and I'll never see him again. I'm not stupid, like Daan and Anton, and Uncle Bastian will help me to find work. I'll go to night-school and when I've earned enough money I'll rent a place where Mammie and Tante Ria can live with me. Or, no – I'll buy back Mooikrantz and the three of us will farm it . . .

She had never forgotten that beautiful farm which had been the home of her real father, the one who had died before she was born. On one of their many returns to Goedgesig, Derrie had made a detour to visit it and although Katrien hadn't understood the reasons behind it, she had sensed that he'd done so to punish Mammie. Oh, but what a magical place it had seemed to Katrien, with its background of high, echoing hills and the baboons moving from peak to peak, the males showing off, the females clutching their babies to their breasts and the youngsters teasing one another and playing just like human children. There had been trees laden with oranges and a lovely old farmhouse that had instantly seemed like home to Katrien when the farmer's wife invited them inside. Mammie had looked wistful too, and as if she wished herself back there.

One day, Katrien vowed, I'll buy the farm for her, and Derrie won't be allowed to set foot on it. I'll train the baboons to attack him on sight, and Uncle Bastian will call regularly to visit us . . .

The daydream occupied her mind with much-savoured pleasure until she realised that she had reached the farmhouse for which she'd been bound. A dog began to bark at her as she approached the back door, and a middle-aged man wearing an ancient, out-of-shape hat called the animal sharply to heel.

"Well, child," he addressed Katrien, studying her. "What can we do for you? I suppose your family have come to wait for the Commando on Wheels to pass by."

"I – no," she began in bewilderment. "We've outspanned some distance away from here, Uncle. We're moving to a smallholding near Johannesburg."

"Ah. Well, no one knows for sure when the Commando will be passing. Some are planning to camp along the roadside, but I have more important things to do with my time." His eyes had registered the fact that her blouse had been made out of a flour-bag, and she felt herself reddening. "Moving, you said," he went on. "Where are you from?"

"Our last farm was called Kalkdrift, Uncle, out Messina way." Her hand tightened about the silver threepenny coin in her pocket. "I – my step-father sent me to buy a tickey's-worth of food from you."

"I see. Well, come inside, girl-child, and out of this heat."

She followed him into the cool kitchen with a cement floor and a high ceiling from whose beams hung strips of beef biltong wrapped in muslin. A woman entered from what Katrien guessed was the pantry, and who was obviously his wife, and the farmer told her that the child's family had outspanned before carrying on towards Johannesburg district, and that she had come to see what food supplies a tickey would buy for them.

The woman's smile was kind. "A nice mugful of buttermilk for yourself, to begin with," she said. "Sit down. What is your name?"

"Katrien le Roux, Tante."

The woman returned to the pantry for a jug containing buttermilk, and in between sipping the refreshing drink Katrien answered the curious questions with which the couple bombarded her.

"It was all my mother's idea at the start. She has very clever ideas, but – " Katrien stopped. Criticism of her step-father would antagonise these people, she felt sure, because they would take the conventional view that children should not judge their elders. She continued, "We would buy a farm that had been neglected and was on sale at a rock-bottom price. Then we worked together to get the house into a good condition, and my step-father and my uncles tilled the fields and sowed mealies or wheat. As soon as everything looked its best and the seedlings were

311

thriving we sold the farm and bought another rundown one – "

"Ah yes, I understand," the farmer put in, nodding and grinning. "And if there was drought or flooding later to ruin the harvest, it didn't affect your family. You always sold at the right moment. Very clever."

"Yes," Katrien agreed. It *had* been clever, and it had worked every time – until Derrie's greed had once again got the better of him. She went on tonelessly, "But with the last farm, Kalkdrift, my – we made a mistake. We didn't sell at the right time. The harvest was looking so promising, Uncle, that my step-father said we would benefit from it and delay selling until next year's crops had come up and could be seen to be thriving. We'd invested everything we had in Kalkdrift; it was our biggest farm yet. Then – well, the army worms came and we were farmed-out overnight."

"*Army worms!*" her host echoed. "I've heard of them, of course. Thank the Good Lord, I've never had experience of them. No one seems to know what causes them, or how, or why. Tell us about it, child."

She shuddered at the memory. "We woke up one morning, a few weeks ago, and they were everywhere. Inside the house, crawling over everything, blocking out the light from the windows . . . The floors looked as if they were covered with moving carpets of dark brown. They – they *squelched* underfoot with every step one took. And when we'd swept as many of them as we could out of the house and we looked outside, it was – " She shrugged helplessly, unable to convey the true horror of it all. "There were millions and *millions* of them, each about an inch long. It was hard to believe our eyes. There wasn't a spot on the entire farm on which they weren't crawling. By the evening, they'd gone – I don't know where. They disappeared as suddenly and strangely as they'd first appeared although quite a lot of them, of course, must have been eaten by birds. But when they had gone there was *nothing*. Not a blade of grass or a leaf on a tree. No harvest, no grazing

312

for our milk-cows; the vegetables eaten down to the roots and even the bark stripped off the fruit trees. In one day the farm had been turned into a desert. And – there was money owing for improvements made on it, so we had to sell at a huge loss, and now we're on our way to the smallholding my step-father owns jointly with his sister and brother. At least we'll have a roof over our heads there."

"My dear life," the farmer's wife breathed. "It all shows how little control we have over our own fate."

What it showed, Katrien thought sourly, was that greed brought its own punishment. If Derrie hadn't been sharpening his teeth in anticipation of a rich harvest, the army worms would have been someone else's disaster and not theirs.

She watched in growing embarrassment as the farmer's wife began to pack foodstuffs into a basket; mealie meal, flour, sugar, eggs, strips of biltong and a large wedge of cheese.

"That's – that's far too much for a tickey, Tante!" she protested.

"Bless you, child, we don't want your tickey! What would the world be coming to if one couldn't help someone who'd been dealt such a blow as your family suffered?"

Another thought occurred to Katrien, adding desperation to embarrassment. If she went back with such a large amount of food Derrie wouldn't just be sending her in future to beg as a punishment; he would force her to do it regularly because he relished getting something for nothing.

With the half-formed idea of using principles as an excuse to refuse acceptance of all that food, Katrien asked, "Uncle, are you – do you belong to the *Ossewa Brandwag*?" If he did, she could say that Mammie hated the movement, and perhaps some of the food would be removed from the basket.

But the farmer responded vehemently. "Those Nazis? Certainly not! *Your* people aren't *Ossewa Brandwag*, are they?"

She resisted the temptation to claim that they were, for her own feelings on the subject were too strong. "No, Uncle. My god-father, who is also my mother's cousin, is half-English and he wanted to join up when the war started but they said he was too important to be a soldier. He has told us how the *Ossewa Brandwag* have been trying to steal dynamite from the mines to blow up trains carrying soldiers."

"Nazi scum!" the farmer said forcefully. "One of these days I fear they might succeed. I have two sons with red tabs and they'll be in enough danger from the enemy up North without having to worry about being blown up by their own countrymen!"

The red tabs he had mentioned were really orange flashes which the volunteer troops wore on their shoulder-straps, and which meant they were prepared to serve anywhere in Africa. Places of which Katrien had formerly never heard were now on the tongues of everyone – Gilgil, Mombasa, El Wak – and thousands of South Africans were being sent to them either to be trained or to take part in the fighting.

Her thoughts were interrupted when a young man who looked as if he were about twenty, like Daan, entered the kitchen from outside. The farmer introduced him to Katrien as his middle son, Otto, and added with pride, "Like your god-father, Otto is too important to be a soldier. I keep telling him to apply for an 'On Service' badge to show that he has been declared a key man, too greatly needed to help produce food for the nation to join his brothers in the fighting." He turned to his son. "Otto, carry the basket for Cousin Katrien to where her people have outspanned."

The young man smiled at Katrien in a sly, appraising way that embarrassed her as much as the over-full basket did. She had no wish to have him accompany her and besides, she'd planned to "lose" some of the basket's contents along the way. But the farmer and his wife had been so kind and generous that she could only thank them sincerely and accompany Otto from the house.

"You have pretty hair," he remarked, as soon as they were out of earshot of his parents.

She didn't know how to deal with compliments, and didn't welcome one from him. Ungraciously, she said, "*I* don't think so. My mother has lovely hair, dark-red and curly."

"Well, I've always liked my women blonde," he returned with a swagger. "Perhaps it's the Nazi in me."

She gave him a sharp look, and he winked. " 'On Service' badge, indeed," he mocked his father's proud words. "I wouldn't wear *anything* linking me with the Smuts government! If you're going to be staying at the outspan for a day or two, Cousin Katrien, I'll show you what I look like in my *Ossewa Brandwag* uniform."

It was the second time in one day that someone had boasted about his involvement with the banned movement. Katrien wished she could have been as insultingly forthright as Mammie, but apart from the fact that Otto was carrying the food his parents had kindly given her, if she made a fuss they might find out that the son they thought of so proudly as a "key worker" was a secret member of the *Ossewa Brandwag,* and therefore an enemy of his own soldier brothers.

"We're only going to stay overnight," she said at last, and added, "Look, I can easily carry the basket from here. You must have jobs to do on the farm."

"They can wait. To be honest, Cousin Katrien, apart from the fact that you're so pretty I was really grateful for an excuse to get away from the farm. The Commando on Wheels is due to pass by at any time now and I'd like to find out if they've been sighted yet."

"Commando on Wheels," Katrien repeated. His father had mentioned them too, she remembered. "What or who are they?"

Otto made a sound of resentment and disgust. "What they are is a disgrace and an insult to true Afrikanerdom. That traitor, Smuts, has been showing them off throughout the country to encourage more men to join up. The

Commando on Wheels are armoured cars, troop carriers, machine guns, field kitchens, ambulances and I don't know what else. All to be used in the war against the Italians up north and therefore the allies of Germany, which is the natural friend of the Afrikaners. Hitler will win this war and the English will be driven into the sea. Our country will be a republic again, belonging to us and not to our English bosses!"

"I don't know anything about politics," Katrien responded woodenly. They were now approaching the outspan-place and she noticed with relief that Mammie and Ria were alone in the shade cast by the wagon, while Derrie and Anton and Daan were in conversation with several men some distance away. "I'll take the basket now," she went on. "Thank you for carrying it for me. Why don't you introduce yourself to my step-father and my uncles. I don't know who the men with them are – "

"I do!" Otto interrupted with excitement. "They're neighbours, all *Ossewa Brandwag* men. They must have had word that the Commando on Wheels is on its way here."

She took the basket from him and he hurried over to join the men. There was an unspoken understanding between Katrien and Mammie, who said when she saw how much the basket contained, "We'll add the mealie meal, the flour and sugar to our own stock, and I'll hide some of the biltong and cheese."

"The farmer's wife wouldn't take the tickey, Mammie." Katrien held out the coin.

"No, keep it." Again that unspoken understanding between them told her that Mammie had meant: there'll be other times on this journey when you'll be sent to beg. Aloud, Mammie confirmed her message, for she said with a twisted smile, "It will be your pride-tickey, Katrien."

Even though she tried to bite her tongue, Katrien could not prevent herself from bursting out, "Why did you do it, Mammie? Why did you ever marry *him*?"

Mammie's head came up sharply, and she opened her mouth as if to snub Katrien. Then she shrugged instead.

"I was about to tell you that you're far too young even to *think* of asking such a question. And then I remembered that I was a year younger when my mother died and I had to bring Daan and the others up, and I asked myself a lot of grown-up questions. It's a long story, Katrien, and one day perhaps I'll tell you all the details. But for now, the only answer I can give you is that it was necessary at the time."

"Because of all the children you had to care for?"

"Yes, that was the main reason."

Greatly daring, Katrien asked, "Was it also because of Uncle Bastian being married to someone else?"

She watched the colour flooding into Mammie's cheeks even as she tried to laugh. "What on earth makes you ask such a thing?"

"I came into the kitchen once, when I was about twelve. You were there with Uncle Bastian and you were kissing one another."

"We are cousins, for heaven's sake, and cousins *do* kiss."

Not like that, Katrien thought, remembering how she herself had felt as she watched the two of them, unnoticed – shocked, confused, but also wistful. Ever since she could remember she had wished that Uncle Bastian had been her father, and she'd day-dreamed ruthlessly that his English wife, as well as Derrie would die and that Uncle Bastian would marry Mammie so that he could, at least, become Katrien's stepfather instead.

As if to rub out of existence those questions about herself and Uncle Bastian, Mammie went on, "Katrien, I know you hate Pierre. But it would help all of us if you didn't show it so plainly. It's very important to him that people should love him, or at least like or admire him."

"There's nothing to love, like or admire." Katrien glanced at the group of men, which had now been swollen by several newcomers. "Mammie," she burst out, "why do you always let him get his hands on the money *you've* worked to earn?"

Mammie sighed. "Katrien, do you remember that time

317

on Goedgesig when we were so poor that I bought a sewing machine on easy terms from the Indian shop-owner in the village, and I made dresses and men's shirts at home for which the owner paid me a shilling a dress and a sixpence a shirt, and then sold for a dozen times more in his shop?"

"Yes . . ."

"The Indian knew *I* would be doing all the work and paying for the sewing machine. But he wouldn't agree to the transaction unless it was set up in Pierre's name, with all the money handled by him. And that is how it has always been. Every transaction I've made, every idea I've put into operation, has always had to be in Pierre's name. Men do not trust women when it comes to business. They will only do business with other men. Even bank managers would never agree to my opening an account in my own name. It always had to be in Pierre's."

"Well, I think it's stupid and rotten and unfair!"

"Yes, well," Mammie said with a twisted smile, "that just about sums up life in general, my child." She added conspiratorially and consolingly, "I've always managed to hoard some secret savings of my own."

Katrien said nothing. She remembered developing earache one evening after she'd gone to bed and she'd crept into the room Mammie shared with Derrie to wake her up. But although Derrie was fast asleep Mammie had been awake, with a candle burning, and Katrien had watched her going through his wallet. She didn't blame Mammie one bit for stealing back some of the money that should rightfully have been hers . . .

Katrien started. Even though it was as hot as ever, and without a cloud in the sky, she thought she could hear a distant rumble of thunder. Quite a crowd had gathered now, she saw, and were lining the side of the road, Derrie having joined them with Anton and Daan.

"At least when we're back at Goedgesig," Katrien changed the subject, "we'll see Uncle Bastian more often. I wish *he'd* been my father instead of my dead one and then Derrie," she voiced her old dream.

318

Mammie made no comment on that. Instead she said, without looking at Katrien but with her eyes on the crowd lining the roadside, "Over the years I've come to understand some things about Pierre. Things that he keeps deeply hidden inside him and only rarely allows one to know about. It may help *you* to know about them, Katrien. His mother ran away with another man when he was very young, and his drunken father used to beat him. In his child's mind, he saw his father as punishing *him* for the fact that his mother had run away. So, in a sense, when he's punishing me through one of you, I think it's really his mother he's punishing in some hidden part of his mind. And I told you that it's important to him that people should like or admire him if they can't love him. He said something, once when he'd had more to drink than was good for him, to make me understand why."

"Why?" Katrien asked dutifully, not in the least because she wanted to know but because Mammie expected it of her.

"He said that one day, when he's rich and has crowds of friends who admire him and look up to him, he's going to search for his mother and show her what she'd thrown away when she ran off and left him."

Katrien said nothing. She was not in the least sorry for Derrie because of his bad childhood. *She'd* had a bad childhood too, but she couldn't imagine herself ever beating or torturing her children one day because of it.

What had originally sounded like distant thunder was growing louder, and on the horizon a red cloud of dust coloured the air. More people had arrived to line the roadside and Katrien suggested that she and Mammie and Ria should join them. "It must be the Commando on Wheels approaching," she said, and explained what Otto had told her about it.

It wasn't long before the first of the vehicles heading the convoy came into sight. Painted a drab greenish-grey, it led what was literally miles of similarly coloured military vehicles, many bristling with what Mammie said were mortars and were used for firing shells, and other vehicles carrying smartly-uniformed troops on whose rifle-barrels the sun gleamed.

The crowd lining the road was stirred into a frenzy at the spectacle. Many of them cheered the Commando on Wheels, waving their hats or handkerchiefs at them. But just as many hurled insults at the drivers and the troops as they passed, and gave the Nazi salute, shouting, "*Heil* Hitler!" Derrie, Katrien noticed as she cheered herself hoarse, was one of those giving the Nazi salute and so, too, was Anton. Daan neither cheered nor jeered but simply stared at the uniformed men carried along on the convoy.

At last the Commando on Wheels had passed out of sight, leaving only red dust swirling behind it. It also left behind it passions which had been stirred to boiling point, and fights broke out between those who had cheered the convoy and the ones who had hurled insults at it. Mammie took Katrien and Tante Ria by the arm and hurried them away to the wagon, but Katrien turned her head and watched the ugly sight of bitterly divided Afrikaners trying to beat one another to a pulp.

With the noise of the fighting in the background, Katrien helped Mammie to get a fire going so that supper could be prepared. "I hope Anton and Daan are just onlookers," Mammie fretted, "and that they are not getting involved in the fighting."

She'd expressed no concern about Derrie, and Katrien knew why. *He* would certainly remain on the outskirts as an onlooker and Katrien hoped Anton would copy his hero as usual. Daan, she thought, would avoid taking sides with either faction, afraid to commit himself one way or another.

Thinking it might take Mammie's mind of her worries, she asked, "Do you remember the many times I came home from school at Kalkdrift with bruises or a black eye?"

"Yes . . ."

"I pretended I'd got into a fight about the flour-bag blouse. It was hardly ever about the blouse. Most of the

320

children said they and their families supported the National Party and called themselves *Natte*. Some, like myself, were on the side of General Smuts's South African Party and called ourselves *Sappe*. The fights were between the *Natte* and the *Sappe*. They called us swear-word English lovers and because there were more of them they usually won the fights. Some of them," Katrien added scornfully, "were so stupid that they thought the war was between an Englishman called General Smuts and a German called Hitler. None of us had ever even met a German in our lives, and yet those people at school wanted them to win the war because their parents had taught them to hate the English so much."

"It has been like that ever since I can remember," Mammie said sadly. "I wish we could all be one nation – English, Afrikaans, Black, Asian, Coloured, Chinese . . . Instead, we're no more than dozens of different tribes. And this war is splitting even the Afrikaners into divided factions. I *wish* Anton and Daan would come back to the wagon," she added worriedly.

When the setting sun and a sufficiency of spilt blood brought the fighting to an end, they did return to the wagon. Anton had a bruise on one cheek but neither Daan nor Derrie bore any signs of having been involved in the fighting. But Anton liked a brawl for its own sake and would have joined in without any particular allegiance to one side or another, in spite of the Nazi salutes with which he had shown solidarity with Derrie.

That night as she lay curled up in a blanket on the hard earth, trying and failing to fall asleep, Katrien heard Mammie and Derrie talking quietly together.

"I've decided to join the *Ossewa Brandwag*, Sabella."

"You're out of your mind!" Mammie's whisper was harsh with revulsion.

"I've *made up* my mind," he corrected.

"You know it's a banned organisation, Pierre!"

Derrie laughed. "A ban that clearly can't be enforced! All those who gave the Commando on Wheels the Nazi salute this afternoon were members of the *Ossewa Brandwag*. Did you notice any action being taken against them?"

"The troops had obviously been ordered not to react. If there had been policemen present it would have been a different story!"

"Nonsense! I've spoken to several *Ossewa Brandwag* men and not only do they have many policemen among their members, but politicians and even judges. The movement has openly been holding meetings, and no one made any attempt to break them up, let alone arrest the members."

"It would be different at Goedgesig, so close to Johannesburg! A blind eye wouldn't be turned to Fascist meetings there!"

"I'm not going to advertise to all and sundry that I'm a member of the *Ossewa Brandwag*, Sabella! Be practical! Your clever ideas for making money have always involved dealing with farmers, and many farmers belong to the *Ossewa Brandwag*. It makes good business sense for me to join. Besides," he went on, "if a man works hard for the movement and gives time and energy to its cause, he can earn the title of captain, or field cornet, or even general!" Savouring the sound of the words, he added dreamily, "General Pierre le Roux . . ."

"I don't want my family to be involved in any way with those Nazis," Mammie said in a stony voice.

"Don't try to put obstacles in my way, Sabella." The way in which Derrie spoke the words turned them into a threat, and Mammie didn't respond.

General Pierre le Roux, Katrien thought with scorn. She could just see him trying to make a bomb for the detestable *Ossewa Brandwag* and ruining his own efforts by doing something stupid.

On the yearning thought that he might blow himself to pieces with his own bomb, Katrien drifted into sleep.

14

This particular return to Goedgesig, Sabella thought grimly, was turning out to be the very worst yet. Christmas 1940 was over, with nothing in the least joyous having marked it, and she had not yet been able to think of a way of making money so that they could leave this place before Christmas 1941.

Goedgesig! She gave a snort of bitter derision. The name meant "Good Prospect" and whoever had originally bestowed it on the smallholding must either have had a black sense of humour or an excess of optimism bordering on lunacy.

Even allowing for the fact that the herds of goats Pierre's father had kept had continually cropped the grass so closely that soil erosion had set in, causing ugly craters to appear in the earth, the smallholding could never have been anything but a miserable, bleak place. All that thrived in that rocky, impoverished soil were a row of prickly pears, and there was nothing of beauty anywhere to lift the spirit. The landscape was flat and bare apart from a few stunted bushes and clumps of weeds, and the occasional flat-topped thorn tree on which vultures could often be seen perching like hideous symbols of the dying land.

Sabella heaved a defeated sigh. The poverty of this small-holding, which only remained in the joint ownership of Pierre and his brother and sister because it was unsaleable, was not the worst of her problems.

Even before they had completed their long journey to Goedgesig, Pierre had stopped in the nearby village of

323

Uitspan to join the *Ossewa Brandwag*. Anton, deaf to all Sabella's pleas, had accompanied him to do the same; Daan, torn two ways as usual, had stayed on the wagon with Sabella, Ria and Katrien.

"I'm not joining anything," he muttered. "Not the *Ossewa Brandwag* or the Army."

Sabella understood. Unable to please both herself and Pierre, Daan had decided to compromise by not actively displeasing either.

Even in that small village Sabella had been dismayed by the passionate divisions that were tearing the country apart. Those villagers who had cheered Pierre and Anton as they entered the house of what everyone knew was the *Ossewa Brandwag*'s local leader, had called Daan an English-loving traitor for not following their example; the ones who hurled the word "*Nazis!*" after Pierre and Anton had tried to reach up and shake Daan's hand.

Ever since their return to this miserable smallholding Sabella had tried again to persuade her brothers to break away and become independent. "Go to Johannesburg and find jobs! There'll be plenty of vacancies now that so many men have enlisted, and your lack of experience and qualifications won't matter. You'll be given training for jobs – "

Pierre walked in and interrupted with a jeer, "And what sort of jobs do you suppose they'd get, Sabella? Slave-labour in one of the factories owned by a Jew-boy?"

"The only 'Jew-boy' I've known," she retorted passionately, "was a wonderful, compassionate man – what he himself would have called a *mensch*. My brothers would be fortunate indeed if they were to find work with someone like Mr Kowalski!"

"At the last O.B. meeting Anton and I attended," Pierre said flatly, "it was agreed that this country must be purged of the rich Jewish parasites as well as the English. And talking about the O.B., Sabella, I've volunteered to undertake fund-raising in the new year. I know you must have savings squirrelled away – you always do – and I want a share of it.

How would it look if *I* failed to contribute to the funds I've promised to raise?"

"Are you out of your mind, Pierre?" she cried, enraged. "Apart from the fact that I wouldn't, on principle, contribute a penny to the cause of your Nazi friends, we have to think of a way of making a living, and whatever plan I can come up with will need every penny of capital I have!"

"If I started off my fund-raising by making a substantial personal contribution, it wouldn't go unnoticed by the High Council of the *Ossewa Brandwag*. Call it an investment, Sabella, because it would buy us help and goodwill once you've thought up a plan for making money."

"No!"

Ever since then he had been punishing her for her refusal to part with the money which, whatever his excuses, he really wanted as a means of currying favour with the *Ossewa Brandwag* leaders and furthering his aim to earn high office within the movement. Katrien was his target, and he used the implicit sexual threat to Ria if Sabella tried to intervene.

Pierre had a diabolical instinct for sensing what his victim's weakest spot was at any particular moment and then exploiting it. Even she herself, Sabella thought with a mixture of self-reproach and loathing, had not realised how disproportionately sensitive Katrien was about the crop of adolescent pimples which had broken out on her face soon after their return to Goedgesig. But Pierre had, and he went out of his way to draw attention to them whenever friends of Daan or Anton from the village came to call. "Poor Katrien," Pierre would say with affected concern, "I do believe that nasty spot on your chin is beginning to turn into a carbuncle. But then, the ones on your cheeks don't look much better. I think you need a tonic or something to purify your blood."

In desperation, Katrien tried to get rid of the pimples by squeezing them and only made matters worse, which gave Pierre opportunity to insist on daubing gentian violet all over her face. When the pimples had disappeared and the virulent colour of the gentian violet was fading he came up with a new, devilish form of torture.

After returning from a trip to Johannesburg he'd thrown on the table a dog-eared pulp novel with a luridly-coloured cover and said to Sabella, "A friend of mine lent this to me and said it was well worth reading. I'm no reader but I know you are, so I accepted the loan on your behalf."

With her insatiable hunger for any kind of reading matter, Sabella had lost no time in flicking through the novel. It had been published in America, she noticed, and she only needed to read a few paragraphs to realise that its publication must have been illegal, and that it had somehow been smuggled into South Africa, because the novel described in sickening detail perverted sexual acts.

"It's filth," Sabella said, throwing the novel down. "Give it back to your friend."

She ought to have known better, of course. She ought to have kept her mouth shut and pretended to read the wretched novel. But on the other hand, it was only too likely that Pierre had been acting with calculation throughout, that he had been perfectly aware of the book's nature and that he'd wanted Sabella, too, to be made aware of it in advance. Because that evening he handed it to Katrien and ordered her to read it aloud to him.

"Your mother is worried about the amount of school you've been missing," he said, giving Sabella a triumphant look from under his lashes. "Reading aloud will brush up your English, at any rate."

Katrien read the book to him in such a wooden manner that it was possible she didn't understand the contents, but she had always been good at English and one couldn't be certain that she wasn't deliberately fighting back against Pierre. And Daan and Anton, who had never been good scholars and whose English had all but deserted them, had no idea of what it was their "Daddy" was forcing Katrien to read, and wouldn't believe it if they were told. The point was, of course, that *Sabella* understood the filth her daughter was made to read aloud.

326

I have to get her away from here, Sabella thought desperately as she set out for a walk in that comfortless landscape. Quite apart from the mental and emotional damage Pierre was inflicting on her daughter, it was true that she had missed a good deal of schooling. The new term was due to start next week and Katrien was too old to attend the village school in Uitspan, which only took pupils to the age of twelve. She was a clever child and if only she could be enrolled in a school in Johannesburg there was no reason why she shouldn't eventually gain a matriculation pass.

In her desperation, Sabella had broken her own self-imposed rule and written to Bastian, telling him that they were back at Goedgesig and that she needed his help. He had not responded, and to add to all her other troubles, she had to contend with the pain of rejection as one week passed after another and he did not write or call. After all the many times throughout the years when he had failed in his resolve to stay out of her life, it was beginning to seem that *this* time he had found the strength to do precisely that.

Sabella's wandering had brought her to the large black *stad* which had been established long before her first introduction to Goedgesig. She visited it regularly whenever the family took shelter on the smallholding, and she had many friends among the women. One bond which they had always shared was that of poverty.

Naked small children and mangy dogs hurried to meet her, and the women cooking on the communal open fire in the centre of the village of beehive huts showed their teeth in delighted smiles and tore off extra lumps of dough from a dish, flattening them between their palms before placing them on the piece of metal sheeting suspended over the fire and supported by piled-up bricks.

A few moments later Sabella was sitting with the women around the fire, breathing in the mixture of smells of smoke, of fresh straw coming from the interior of the huts and the flat cakes of baking dough which were called *roosterkoek*. Being an honoured guest, she was given the first of the *roosterkoek* as it came off the fire. It was stodgy and had no particular taste to it, and she was grateful for the *magouw*, a sour-porridge beer, which helped to wash it down.

As she and her black friends exchanged news, Sabella made an ironic discovery. *They* were no longer poor. Their husbands, who had worked fitfully as casual labourers in the past, were now holding steady, well-paid jobs in Johannesburg. Factories there had been turned over to the production of shells, boots, uniforms, grenades and countless other commodities demanded by war, and there was work to be had for anyone able and willing to commit themselves to it.

If only Anton and Daan, Sabella fretted with frustration, could be persuaded to break away and apply for one of those jobs going begging. But they wouldn't, because Pierre had conditioned them to remain within his sphere of influence. If no one else in the world loved and admired and refused to see wrong in him, *they* did, and the fact that they were allowing themselves to stagnate instead of making something of their lives didn't bother him at all.

There was another reason why he had bonded them so closely to himself. In the beginning, it hadn't troubled Pierre that he hadn't fathered a child of his own, but as the years went by he began to resent the fact that Sabella had failed to give him children. Naturally, he hadn't entertained for a moment the possibility that the cause of the failure might lie with himself. Instead, he insisted that Katrien's birth must have damaged Sabella in some way that prevented her from having more children. As much to punish her as to feed his own ego he deliberately set out to make Anton and Daan give him their blind loyalty. What grieved Sabella particularly was the fact that he had killed any initiative her brothers might otherwise have developed. They would work hard enough when they were required to do so, but like Pierre they were otherwise perfectly content to mark time and leave it to Sabella to rack her brains for another bright idea to make money.

She sighed, and forced herself to put aside these black

thoughts for the moment. "I've decided to buy a nanny-goat in milk," she told the women of the *stad*. "We've been using condensed milk since our return but the supply is running low. I also need a few laying hens. Have you any for sale?"

After a good deal of excitable rivalry, young boys were despatched to catch hens and round up nanny-goats for Sabella's inspection. In the meantime the women insisted on presenting her with a dozen eggs. Sabella thanked them and hid the remains of her *roosterkoek* inside her pocket to avoid giving offence. It was barely palatable while hot but once it had cooled it became a penance to choke it down. The flat cakes were made by mixing flour and baking soda with sour milk, and she wondered why the women didn't go to a little extra trouble and adapt the griddle of their fire to form an oven so that they could bake the sweet cookies which they loved instead of the invariable *roosterkoek*.

A tingle of excitement shot through her. "If I baked sweet cookies," Sabella asked these women who were now financially so much better off than she, "would you buy them?"

"*Ewê!*" they agreed enthusiastically.

The boys returned with a selection of squawking hens under their arms and reluctant nanny-goats driven before them, and after Sabella had selected a goat and four laying hens she said, "Please send the children over with them, and I'll return tomorrow to pay, and also to sell you some sweet cookies."

As always, when her ideas started flowing she felt exhilarated, ready to tackle the world and with a fresh perspective on her problems. By the time she reached the ramshackle house that sheltered them during hard times, her mind had been made up on several matters.

Sabella was grimly amused, when she returned, to find Pierre searching through her personal possessions. He was looking for her hidden savings, but they were somewhere it would never occur to him to think of searching. The neatly-folded banknotes had been wrapped in cotton wool, and then hidden behind flowers of coloured felt which she had appliquéd on to a cardigan of hers.

"I need the truck," she said calmly. It had been bought with the proceeds of the sale of the wagon and mules, and Sabella had become a competent driver.

"Why?" Pierre demanded.

"I'm taking Katrien to Johannesburg so that she can attend school when the new term starts." Sabella slung the appliquéd cardigan over her shoulders.

"Oh?" Pierre's expression challenged her. "I'm Katrien's legal father and you'd need my permission to take her out of my custody – which I refuse to give!"

"There is a higher authority than yours, Pierre. The law says she has to attend school, and if you stop me from taking her to Johannesburg I'll report you to the School Board. As her legal father," Sabella added tauntingly, "*you* would be the one they would fine for not sending her to school. Since I would refuse to pay a penny towards your fine, you would have to go to prison instead."

The look in his eyes set her heart racing with fear, and she decided that Ria would have to be taken along to Johannesburg too. Hopefully, Pierre might contain his rage, but if he didn't and he vented it on Daan it might be a blessing in disguise. An undeserved beating, after all these years, might shock her young brother out of his unquestioning devotion to his "Daddy".

"And where," Pierre asked in a deceptively silky voice, "is the money to come from to pay Katrien's board and lodging in Johannesburg? From your rich English cousin? It's obvious that he has grown tired of you, Sabella!"

She forced herself not to react to the taunt. "I'll find a way of earning the money to pay her board and lodging, and I'm going to ask your brother Louis and his wife to let Katrien stay with them."

There was nothing Pierre could say to that. He despised his brother Louis, and called him a Bible-thumper, but he was also a policeman and Pierre knew that Louis would be on Sabella's side in the matter of complying with the law and sending Katrien to school.

Sabella went to look for her daughter and told her of her plans. "You like Uncle Louis and Tante Maria, don't you?"

"I've only met them once since I was bridesmaid at their wedding. He preaches a bit but she seemed quite nice." Katrien's expression darkened. "Even if they're not always nice, *no one* could be as horrible as Derrie! And I've been worrying about having nowhere to go to school." Impulsively, she embraced Sabella. "Thank you, Mammie!"

"I should have thought of it before, my love."

It took less than half an hour to pack Katrien's possessions, wipe Ria's face clean, and leave in the truck. Katrien sat in the middle of the cab seat so that Ria could look out of the window. As they rattled along the surfaced road Sabella heard her daughter say in an unsteady voice, "You – you will come and visit me sometimes?"

"As often as I can, Katrien. It may be difficult at first. I have to find a way of making a living."

"What will you do, Mammie? Have you had any ideas?"

"One or two. I'm going to bake batches of sweet cookies tonight, and ice some of them in different colours. Then I'll sell them to the women in the *stad* and charge slightly more for the iced ones. When I've raised enough money I'm going to buy remnants of material and some flock for the stuffing and make small soldier dolls. I'll dress them in khaki uniforms with embroidered buttons and badges and different kinds of caps and helmets. Once I've made enough of them I'll set up a stall by the side of the main road to Johannesburg and sell them to passing motorists."

"That's a brilliant idea, Mammie! Everyone who has a relative in uniform will want to buy one!"

"Let's hope so. After that – well, I haven't yet thought how to invest the takings in a *real* business."

They lapsed into silence. As they reached the outskirts of Johannesburg Sabella saw the public posters for the first time. There were two of them, side by side. One showed a drawing of a man with a surprised expression on his face, his forefinger pointed at himself, and above it was printed in huge letters "WHO, *ME*?" followed by the reply towards the foot of the poster, "YES, *YOU*!" Below that, in white letters against a black background, the message read: "We've GOT to win the war! JOIN IN – *JOIN UP*!"

But it was the second poster that impressed Sabella. The same words appeared on it, but this time the surprised-looking figure was that of a *woman*, and the answer to the question read: "YES, *YOU* TOO!"

"Oh, I wish I was old enough to join up!" Katrien exclaimed wistfully. She touched Sabella's arm. "You'd better make some of those dolls woman soldiers, Mammie."

"Yes." It had taken a war, Sabella thought, but at last women were being recognised as having value in their own right.

Once they had entered the city of Johannesburg Sabella saw evidence of the war everywhere – not only in the shape of uniformed soldiers or airmen but in public notices inviting people to enrol with the Red Cross; posters asking volunteers to knit khaki socks, mufflers, mittens and balaclavas for Allied servicemen; appeals for contributions towards the Gifts and Comforts Fund for the troops. And outside the City Hall, against a large board bearing the slogan "STOP 'EM FRYING – KEEP 'EM FLYING" had been piled an amazing assortment of domestic utensils made of aluminium. Obviously, the metal was needed for the manufacture of aeroplanes. As Sabella drove past in the truck she saw a poorly-dressed woman add a dented but obviously still serviceable saucepan to the aluminium dump. People who could hardly afford it were making real sacrifices for the war effort, she thought angrily, while Pierre was trying to extort money from herself which would be used towards the making of bombs to sabotage it.

Once the city had been left behind she was soon driving through the suburbs. Louis and Maria le Roux lived in Mayfair, which was not far from Westdene and very similar to it in layout and class of population. Now that she was so close to her destination Sabella found herself besieged with doubt and anxiety.

What kind of reception were she and Katrien and Ria likely to get? Louis le Roux had changed since that first time she'd met him on Mooikrantz; he had "found religion" and, unlike his sister Johanna, had forgiven Sabella for being the cause of losing a third-share in the family farm. He had visited them a few times over the years, more as a grimly self-imposed duty than a pleasure, because Pierre mocked him mercilessly both for his conversion to an evangelical sect and for joining the police force. Louis had stopped turning the other cheek when Pierre belittled him in front of his new wife when the two of them had visited Kalkdrift a year before; he'd cut short their stay and the two brothers hadn't been in touch with one another since then.

Would Louis now lump her together with Pierre and refuse to speak to her? If it came to that, would he even be at home? She had no idea what hours he worked.

She stopped the truck outside a modest house and mentally squared her shoulders. Using the pretense that she wasn't certain this was the right address, she delayed to unpick, unobtrusively, some of the stitches around one of the appliquéd flowers on her cardigan so that she could remove the banknotes behind it. She didn't want to risk Ria giving away the hiding place to Pierre.

Once the money had been safely tucked into the pocket of her dress, she opened the door of the truck and moments later she and Ria and Katrien were climbing the steps to the stoep. Her anxieties were laid to rest when Louis himself opened the door to them, and greeted them with a welcoming smile. "What a pleasant surprise! And how fortunate that I'm on night duty this week! Come inside. Is the Lord continuing to bless all of you on Kalkdrift?"

"Unfortunately not," Sabella returned wryly. "A plague of army worms ruined us, and we're back on Goedgesig again."

"*'He that covereth his sins shall not prosper,'*" Louis hinted darkly, obviously seeing the army worms as a divine punishment directed at Pierre. If he knew the nature and extent of the sins his brother covered up, Sabella thought with stark humour, Louis would consider that God had shown regrettable restraint by sending a mere plague of worms.

As they followed him inside the house, Sabella told herself that Louis might be dull and irritatingly ready to preach to one, but at least he was uncomplicated and sincere, unlike Pierre. With his acne-scarred face and balding head, he did not share his brother's good looks either, which no doubt accounted for the fact that he hadn't married until he was well into his thirties.

His wife Maria hurried from the kitchen to greet them. She was ten years his junior, somewhat insipid and self-absorbed, and her company could be wearisome because her conversation tended to be dominated by accounts of what she called her "female problems" of which there seemed to be an extraordinary variety, some of them unknown to medical science.

"I mustn't complain," she replied in a martyred voice to Sabella's conventional enquiry about her health, her expression adding that she had plenty about which to complain if she were given the encouragement. But when none was offered she added, "Come into the front room. I baked a cake this morning and I'll soon have some tea brewed."

While they waited for Maria to rejoin them with tea and cake, Louis asked after everyone including – with pointed Christian charity – his estranged brother. Sabella made conventionally bland replies, since she didn't believe it would benefit her to break the long-established conspiracy of silence about Pierre's true nature at this stage. She said nothing about the *Ossewa Brandwag* either, because if Pierre were to be interned for belonging to it then so, too, would Anton.

As she sipped her tea a while later Sabella came to the point of her visit. "By law Katrien should be in school when the new term starts, but there is none near Goedgesig, as you know, for her age-group. Would you be prepared to have her lodge with you, so that she may enrol at a nearby school?"

They agreed immediately. Louis regarded it as a family duty as well as his duty to the law he served to uphold, and Maria said Katrien would be company for her when Louis worked unsocial hours. "There is an Afrikaans-medium school quite close to us," she added.

"I want to go to an English school," Katrien said, her expression challenging.

But instead of arguing, Louis nodded. "A wise decision, and the English-medium school is no further away than the Afrikaans one. If I hadn't learnt English, with the help of the Lord, I wouldn't have been accepted into the police force, and would still have been trying to scratch a living by raising poultry on Goedgesig."

Sabella came to an agreement with them over the cost of Katrien's board and lodging, and handed over two pounds. Louis gave her a ten-shilling note in change and went to collect Katrien's suitcase from the truck.

"Thank you both so much," Sabella said with deep gratitude as she shook hands with Louis and Maria.

Katrien accompanied Sabella and Ria outside to the truck. Impulsively, her daughter threw herself into Sabella's arms and whispered tearfully, "Oh Mammie, take care – "

Sabella stroked her hair, a painful knot in her throat, because she knew exactly what Katrien had wanted to express.

"Don't worry, my love. He has never done anything to me, and I'll make sure that Ria – " Sabella left her own sentence in the air and kissed her daughter. "I'll come and see you as soon as I can," she promised.

Katrien was still standing there on the pavement, wiping her eyes, as Sabella drove away with Ria. Blinking her own eyes rapidly, Sabella told herself that at least her daughter would no longer be at Pierre's mercy.

She did not return to Goedgesig immediately. There were a few things she wanted to buy for the baking of sweet cookies, like icing sugar and food colouring which, if they were available at all from the village store, would be dearer there than in the city. She found a place in which to park the truck, and with Ria she walked to the shops. Once she had bought what she needed it occurred to her to spend a few pennies at a butcher's shop on bones. After they had been boiled for stock Anton or Daan could take a sledgehammer to them and grind them into meal for the laying hens.

The price of the meat in the shop shocked her. "There is no shortage in this country, or rationing because of the war," she told the butcher, "so why is your meat so expensive?"

"Expensive, Mevrou?" he returned with genuine astonishment. "It's not much more than it has been for the past few years."

"I can't see how the women around here can afford to buy it at all!"

The man smiled. "I don't know where you've come from, Mevrou, but most of the women around here can now afford to buy occasional expensive cuts, and meat every day, instead of stewing meat once a week. Those who have small children and can't go out to work in the munitions factories do piece-work instead in their own homes. Oh yes, they can afford things nowadays that used to be beyond their means!"

Sabella smiled broadly. "How wonderful!" she rejoiced, remembering her own long-ago dream of freeing women, burdened by children for whom they could not afford more than a basic diet and second-hand clothes, by creating jobs they could do at home. The war had done it for her instead.

The butcher was looking curiously at her. "From the sound of it, Mevrou, you're out of touch with life in Johannesburg. Where have you been living that makes you think my meat is expensive? If there's a shop in any suburb that can undercut my price I'd like to hear about it!"

"I *am* out of touch," Sabella admitted. "And I can't remember when I last bought meat from a butcher's shop.

We've been living in the country, and it was the custom for neighbours to join together and buy meat on the hoof from a farmer and share the carcass."

"Ah, well, there's your answer! You weren't only cutting out the middle-man but the meat you bought didn't have to pass government inspection. It all adds to our costs, you see. We have to buy at market from suppliers who naturally want their share of the profit, and the government inspectors who decide whether or not the meat is free of contamination or disease also have to be paid. All of that has to be reflected in the prices we charge customers, otherwise we'd go out of business. As it is, our profit margin is pretty slim."

"I see . . ." The tingle of excitement she experienced told Sabella that she'd found her way of making money. She had to remain silent then and pretend to deliberate over the various joints on sale, for a woman came into the shop. As soon as she had been served and left, Sabella said briskly, "I have a proposition to make to you. I can tell from experience whether an animal on the hoof is healthy or not, and if I were to buy and butcher stock myself I could offer you carcasses at a very much lower price than you're paying at the market. What do you say?"

The butcher pulled at his chin. "It would be illegal . . ."

"But profitable," she tempted him, "and with no harm done to anyone."

"Let's talk some more about it, Mevrou," he invited.

They did so. She explained that it would take her a while to raise the capital to buy stock from farmers, but they discussed in general terms the kind of prices to be paid for various carcasses, and he promised to talk some of his colleagues into joining in the scheme later on, when she would be able to expand.

Her feeling of euphoria was dampened when the butcher said, "You spoke of 'we' at the beginning, Mevrou, so you have a husband, and obviously you can't be planning to do the butchering by yourself. Send your husband to see me so that we can discuss the matter and shake on the deal."

337

Pierre is not going to get his hands on the profits this time, she thought fiercely. She looked the butcher straight in the eyes. "My husband is dead. I live with my brothers on a smallholding. They will help me with the buying of the stock and the butchering."

"I see. Then send one of your brothers to work out the details with me."

The war might have forced recognition of women's worth in their own right, she thought bitterly, but only as far as allowing them to work in factories or at home for a boss. When it came to business, men still refused to deal with any but another man.

Anton, she knew, would never keep her secret from Pierre but Daan might just be persuaded to do so. "I'll come back some time in the future with my brother Daan," she told the butcher. "He is twenty," she added with heavy irony.

It was wasted on the man. "I'll look forward to doing business with him. Good day, Mevrou."

She bundled uncomprehending Ria into the truck and set off on the journey back to Goedgesig. In spite of the sour note struck by the butcher's insistence on dealing with a man, Sabella told herself that she had accomplished much today. Katrien was safe, and she herself had a goal towards which to work . . .

Then the ugly smallholding appeared in the distance and she was assailed by a sudden overwhelming longing for Mooikrantz with its beauty and its majestic hills that grandly pretended to be mountains and replied to one's every call. Inevitably, the thought of Mooikrantz also reminded her of Bastian, and a tightness constricted her throat. How can I blame you, she thought. All those years of useless longing; all that waste. I suppose you've found someone who is free to become your mistress. Why should you be condemned to go on enduring an empty existence with Annette, just because I'm condemned to do so with Pierre?

338

15

The sun was setting when Sabella drew the truck up outside the house. There was no sign of Pierre or her brothers and she decided they must have walked to the village, where Pierre had relatives on his mother's side and Daan and Anton had friends made during past periods when they had sought sanctuary at Goedgesig. The fact that the nanny-goat she had bought from the women in the *stad* had been tethered to a post of the stoep railing, and the four hens were squawking inside the crudely-made coop in which the young boys must have carried them, bore witness to the fact that Pierre and her brothers must have left home soon after she herself did.

The goat would have to be milked and the hens watered and fed, but Sabella decided to put it off for a few minutes longer and drive on to the *stad* to pay the women for her purchases. With Pierre watching her most of the time there were few opportunities to retrieve her money from its hiding place, and he would certainly think it suspicious if she visited the *stad* wearing the appliquéd cardigan during the heat of the day. Telling Ria to get back into the truck, she unpicked a few stitches of another of the felt flowers and removed a banknote, and then she drove to the *stad*.

It was completely dark when they returned to the housee. She would have to milk the goat and feed the hens by the light of the truck's headlamps. Telling Ria to come and help her, she entered the house, feeling her way to where matches and a candle were kept in the room which was kitchen, pantry and parlour all in one.

Her hand had just encountered the candle when she heard the sound of a match being struck, and a moment later the room was illuminated by the powerful light of a spirit lamp. Its brilliance gave Pierre, who was stooping over it, the look of a satyr.

He moved the lamp to the centre of the table, and smiled. "You've kept me waiting a long time, my love. What was the reason for your sudden second trip?"

The thought of him hiding in the house, earlier, set the short hairs at the nape of her neck tingling. What was in that devilish mind of his now? She tried to speak evenly. "I went to thank the women in the *stad* for sending over the goat and the hens. I have to see to the milking and feeding – "

"I've already done all that, Sabella. I didn't want anything to delay our – shall we call it a reconciliation or a reunion? No – let us call it a new adventure!"

As he came towards her she backed away. "Where are Anton and Daan?" she demanded, tentacles of fear spreading through her. He had never before threatened her directly . . .

"Spending the night with friends in the village," she heard him answering her question. "I didn't want them intruding on our privacy. Ria, of course, doesn't count."

A sexual advance – which he had not made to her in a long time – was obviously part of what he had in mind. No doubt he intended to take her brutally and humiliatingly. Well, it was better to face it and get it over with. "I'll go into the bedroom," she said shortly.

"Oh no." By now his steady advance towards her and her own retreat had forced her against the wall. His hands went to the buttons of her dress, and as they did so her sister cried with the excitement and jealous rivalry of a small child claiming her own share of a special treat, "Pretty Ria too! Pretty Ria too!"

"Not this time," Pierre murmured, smiling at Sabella. "This time pretty Ria will have to be content with watching."

"No!" Sabella cried, her skin crawling. "Ria, get out of here!"

"She stays," Pierre countermanded. He added, without turning his head, "You hear me, Ria?"

A dry heave of nausea cramped Sabella's stomach and throat. "Please – our bedroom – " she whispered.

His hands were cradling her exposed breasts, forcing a whimper of envy from Ria. He said against Sabella's cheek, "The bedroom is so boring. I was thinking of that scene Katrien read from the American book – you know the one where they use a table and ropes – ?"

"*Jesus.*" The anguished sound was wrenched from Sabella. She remembered the scene only too well in all its depraved perversion. And this was what Pierre had chosen as her punishment, with Ria looking on . . .

Blindly, Sabella began to fight him, lashing out at him with hands and feet. But he was too strong for her and soon she was trapped impotently in his hold, and found herself being pulled towards the kitchen table. As he forced her to lean backwards over it his hand went to one of the appliquéd flowers which now hung by only a few threads from her cardigan. "What a shame," he said with mock regret. "I've ruined your pretty jersey." He made a show of concern by going through the motions of trying to press the flower back into place.

Sabella saw his eyes narrow as he realised that the appliquéd flower lay flat against the knitted fabric of the cardigan, and did not stand out in relief as the others did. He began to rip away one of the flowers and when he'd found the banknotes it had been hiding all thought of perverted sexual acts had obviously fled from his mind.

He almost tore the cardigan from her body, and ripped feverishly at the appliquéd flowers. She was trembling too violently to make any attempt at stopping him.

"You cunning little bitch!" he exclaimed, when he'd counted the last of the banknotes. "There's enough here to put a deposit on a car, *and* make a contribution to the *Ossewa Brandwag* that will get me noticed by the leaders!"

Sabella found a ragged semblance of her voice. "Pierre – no. It's all we have to fall back on. Katrien's board and lodging has to be paid. We have to eat . . ."

"There is still ample food left over from the supplies Katrien was given by farmers on the way here, and my Bible-thumping brother's conscience wouldn't allow him to throw Katrien out in the street if her board and lodging isn't paid. In the meantime, Sabella, I know you'll find a way of making more money for all of us – you always do." He gave her his most radiant smile. "I think I'll buy a Pontiac this time."

He would tell the most convincing lies about his ability to keep up the repayments, she knew with impotent hatred, and when the hire-purchase company pressed him for the money he would turn to her and use another satanic plan to extort sufficient cash to stop them from repossessing the car. He had milked her dry and would go on doing so – and for what? Just so that he could make an impression on the *Ossewa Brandwag* leaders with his flashy Pontiac and his generous contribution to their evil cause.

"At least leave me the truck," she said stonily.

"Oh, you're welcome to the truck." He blew her a kiss, crammed the banknotes into his pocket and walked out of the kitchen, whistling.

If only Anton hadn't blindly followed him into joining the *Ossewa Brandwag*.

But her brother had, and therefore the only weapon she possessed against Pierre had been rendered unusable. Sabella stood there for a moment, her clenched fists pressed against her eye-sockets, mentally cursing him and the treacherous fate that had led her to bind all of them to him in the first place.

Then she began to assemble the materials she would need to make sweet cookies for sale to the women in the *stad*. As so often before in the past, she had to concentrate on the basic need to survive.

In the weeks that followed, Pierre was hardly ever at home. He would make occasional flying visits to the smallholding in his smart Pontiac car and brag about the successful schemes he had dreamt up for raising funds for the *Ossewa Brandwag*, and about the important connections he was forging with elevated members of the movement. His smart new clothes and the occasional contribution of fresh meat and vegetables he made to the staple diet of mealie porridge at Goedgesig bore evidence that not all the funds he raised went into the coffers of the *Ossewa Brandwag*. He was recklessly indiscreet, too, and from his boasting Sabella learnt with dismay the extent to which the subversive organisation had infiltrated practically every official body in the country.

If she hadn't been so worried about Anton, she would have rejoiced more heartily in the infrequency of Pierre's visits home, and the fact that he was enriching himself at the expense of sources other than her own pitiful earnings. Anton, too, was away on *Ossewa Brandwag* business for long periods at a time, but he rode a powerful motorcycle with which the movement must have provided him, and he refused to talk about where he went and what he did.

Pierre had joined the Fascist movement for self-seeking reasons but Anton, Sabella admitted unhappily to herself, was committed to its cause. And Daan, refusing to join anything or seek a job, hung around the smallholding doing next to nothing.

Sabella sighed. She was busy cutting up material for the making of her soldier dolls; she had spent last evening as usual in baking batches of sweet cookies and icing some of them and after breakfast Ria had carried them in a basket to be sold to the women in the *stad*. Having delivered the cookies Ria would spend most of the day there, playing with the children who didn't seem to find it odd that this grown-up white woman liked joining in their games. When it was time for her to go home the women in the *stad* would fill a draw-string pouch with coins in payment for the cookies and then they would pin it securely to Ria's dress so that she wouldn't lose it.

That was the extent of the help Sabella could rely upon in

her struggle to make money merely to keep them in food. Her vision blurred as she worked. How Nantes would have thrown himself into sharing the doll-making with her . . .

Thoughts about her dead eldest brother were interrupted as her youngest, Daan, came in from outside, carrying a pailful of milk. "I've turned the goat loose to graze," he told Sabella, "and when I've fed the hens I think I'll walk to the village. There's nothing to keep me hanging around here," he added with discontent in his voice.

She looked at him, the baby she had brought up to become an aimless young man, trapped between loyalty to herself and devotion to his "Daddy", too afraid of committing himself even to show a normal, healthy interest in girls – unlike Anton, who took his pleasures without conscience wherever he found them and then moved on.

"Daan," she suggested, without much hope, "wouldn't you like to stay and help me?"

"*Making dolls?*" he countered with derision. "No thank you, Sabella! If it had been possible to grow anything on this place I'd have taken a spade and dug over the soil. But I'm not going to make dolls – even if they are soldier dolls and not girl-baby dolls."

"I wasn't going to ask you to help with making them. But I have about half a dozen of them completed and dressed, and I thought you might take the truck and park beside the main Johannesburg road and sell them. You could set them out on the back of the truck, with a large cardboard placard behind – "

"Oh no! Thank you very much! Can't you just imagine the abuse I'd get from passing motorists? Jan Smuts's supporters would want to know why I'm selling soldier dolls instead of being in uniform myself, and the *Ossewa Brandwag* lot would call me a traitor. Both sides would stop to beat me up, and not to buy dolls!"

Sabella had to concede that he was probably right. Only a female would be able to get away with selling soldier dolls in this hopelessly riven country.

"I'm going to spend the day with Neels Conradie," Daan

added, and she thought his choice of companion said far more about her brother than his refusal to help with the matter of the dolls. Daan was carefully avoiding visits to old friends who belonged to the *Ossewa Brandwag* or who planned to join the armed services or who had applied to join and been turned down. Neels Conradie had contracted polio as a child which had left him crippled, and therefore he was of no use to either the armed forces or the *Ossewa Brandwag*. With him, Sabella knew, her brother would not have to defend his own lack of commitment or justify himself. With him, there would be no fear of controversy or abuse.

A neat piece of fence-sitting, Daan, Sabella thought sadly as her brother slouched out of the house and she continued her painstaking work on the dolls.

Inevitably, her mind returned to the subject of Nantes, who hadn't lived long enough to face the decision as to where *his* political loyalties lay. Then it came to her that she had already lost one of those children for whom she had sacrificed so much, and she couldn't escape the question: had she been right to make those sacrifices?

If she had allowed her brothers and sister to be taken away from her instead of fighting so hard to keep them, Nantes would not now be lying in a lonely grave at the edge of the Bushveld. Ria wouldn't have been corrupted by someone who used her sexuality – which she herself did not have the mental power to understand – for his own vicious, warped ends. And Daan – yes, it couldn't be denied – Daan would not have been turned into a spineless weakling with no initiative or motivation of his own. As for Anton . . .

She dropped the piece of material she had been trimming and her hands clenched together in impotent fists. She forced herself to recall a snatch of conversation she had overheard when Anton and Pierre chanced to visit the smallholding on the same day.

"I've agreed to do it because you asked it of me. Of course, I'm also thinking of our nation and our fatherland,"

Anton had added, "but mostly because I want you to be proud of me, Daddy."

"I *am* proud of you. I want to shout it to the rooftops – well, to the highest ranks of the *Ossewa Brandwag*, at any rate – that my son has been specially picked out for the Cause."

Sabella had thrust the overheard conversation from her mind, afraid to examine its implications. Even last week, when she'd called at the village store and listened to the whispered rumours among the customers, she had shut her mind to the possibility of a connection. There had been a daring raid on a police station in Pretoria, the rumours said, and most probably with inside help from some of the police themselves. Guns and ammunition, which had been confiscated from the general public under laws specially passed at the outbreak of war, had been stolen. Even though the raiders had been masked and hooded they had without a doubt been *Stormjaers*, and in the tension of the raid two of them had been referred to by name – Labuschagne and le Roux.

Anton's surname is van Renselaar, Sabella had told herself with a kind of defiant despair, refusing to allow herself to remember another snippet of that conversation between her brother and Pierre. It forced itself on her consciousness now.

"You're going to make a name for yourself," Pierre had told Anton, and added, "I just wish that name had been le Roux, and not van Renselaar."

To Anton, a wish of Pierre's was as good as a command. Sabella could no longer hide the truth from herself. Anton was calling himself le Roux now, and he had allowed Pierre to persuade him to become a *Stormjaer*, a member of the extreme military wing of the *Ossewa Brandwag* which modelled itself on the Nazi Storm Troopers.

One dead brother, Sabella's desolate thoughts pursued her; one who is a Nazi, a criminal and a thug; and another who is totally without guts. Was it all my fault that things turned out as they have?

No easy answer came to her, but she was struck by an ironic thought. For the very first time since she'd married Pierre, she could leave him without fear of being punished for it through others. Nantes was dead; both Ria and Anton were over age and Daan would also come of age within a matter of months. Pierre had no legal jurisdiction over Anton or Ria any longer and he would soon have none over Daan. If her youngest brother should decide to climb off the fence and join her instead of staying with his "Daddy" he would be free to do so. And Pierre was enjoying himself far too much, being important in the eyes of the *Ossewa Brandwag* and in his own, for Sabella to believe that he would fight for custody of Katrien if she herself were to leave him.

She smiled wryly at the grim humour of her situation. What she was making from selling cookies to the women in the *stad* could be counted in pennies, and if she was lucky her soldier dolls might sell for a shilling each. At this rate it would take years before she would be able to afford to rent a house in Johannesburg where she and Ria and Katrien could live together. When Pierre took her savings, her long-term plan to butcher stock and sell the meat illegally had had to be abandoned, and all she could hope for now was to earn enough to continue paying Katrien's board and lodging, and buying food to keep herself and Ria and Daan from starving. Oh yes, freedom was still an unimaginable dream for herself . . .

The sound of an approaching motor cut into her thoughts. *Pierre.* She considered bundling the evidence of the soldier dolls she was making out of sight, and then decided against it. If Pierre had been genuinely committed to the cause of the *Ossewa Brandwag* he might have used threats to stop her selling the dolls, but the most she had to fear from him was that he would ridicule her plan to earn money in this way. Calmly, she went on stuffing flock inside the completed body of a doll.

She didn't deign to look up until the light from the open back door had been blocked out for a moment or two. And when she did, the doll slipped from her suddenly-trembling hands and her heart began to pound with all the bitter-sweet tumult of a young girl's. Bastian stood there, the light from outside casting a silver nimbus about his streaked fair hair, one green and one light brown flecked with yellow eye fixed intently upon her.

She stood up slowly, resisting the longing to run to him and fling herself into his arms. "Well, Bastian," she said in a toneless voice, "I suppose I should count your visit as an honour after all this time."

"I would have come sooner if I'd been able to." He, too, spoke with constraint, as if his long absence from her life had turned them into little more than strangers. "May I come inside, Sabella?"

"By all means," she returned formally, and gestured to him to sit down by the table. He picked up a dressed soldier doll and examined it.

"It's exquisitely made, but what is it for, Sabella?"

"For selling," she responded in sardonic, staccato bursts of explanation. "To earn money. To buy food. To survive."

His sun-darkened face, still unlined apart from a slight crinkling at the outer corners of his eyes, deepened in colour as he flushed with anger. "I had no idea matters were this bad," he said roughly. "I've told you, I came as soon as I could. What has that incompetent crook of a husband of yours done *this* time that you're back here once again?"

Briefly, without expression, she told him about the plague of army worms. "And where is le Roux now?" Bastian wanted to know. "For that matter, where is everyone?"

Sabella thought swiftly. "Daan has gone to see a crippled friend of his in the village. Ria is playing with the children in the nearby *stad* and Katrien is at school in Johannesburg, lodging with Pierre's brother and sister-in-law."

"How is she?" Bastian asked, his voice softening.

"I haven't had a chance to visit her, but I'm sure Louis

348

le Roux would have let me know if she weren't well and happy."

"And Pierre le Roux and Anton?" Bastian asked the question she was dreading.

"They are away, visiting farms, exploring plans for a business idea I've had." Please God, she prayed silently, don't let either of them choose today of all days to arrive home, because it wouldn't take a genius to realise that the only business they're interested in is *Ossewa Brandwag* business . . .

"Why didn't they take the truck?" Bastian asked, surprised but apparently not suspicious.

"They're using a wagon and mules, because the truck is too expensive to run," she lied.

He accepted the lie, and changed the subject. "Your letter said you needed my help urgently. It's a question of money – ?"

"It *was*. Put your wallet away, Bastian. I've solved the problem that forced me to pocket my pride and write to you."

"Listen to me, damn it!" he burst out. "I wasn't in Johannesburg when your letter arrived at my office. I was attending meetings with various people, among them General Smuts. The country would be thrown into financial chaos if there should be disruption in the mining industry, and so it was vitally important to make the mines safe against any possible action by subversive organisations. Or perhaps you don't believe there are such things as saboteurs in this country?"

"I believe you," Sabella said quietly and colourlessly, thinking of Anton.

Bastian was silent for a moment, and she had the impression that there was something else he wanted to tell her, but didn't know how to begin. Or perhaps he wasn't quite certain that he could trust her . . .

"This business idea of yours," he broke the silence abruptly. "What is it?"

"I – well, to buy healthy small stock from farmers,

349

butcher it ourselves and sell the carcasses directly to Johannesburg retailers."

"I suppose you know it would be illegal?" Bastian commented.

"Running a shebeen at the diggings was illegal too," she reminded him, her chin lifting.

He stared into her eyes for a moment and she knew he was remembering that long-ago night when they had slept together on the floor of her shebeen in such bitter-sweet intimacy and innocence. He looked away and changed the subject. "My mother has been ill and in hospital. That was another reason why I was prevented from going to my office where your letter was waiting."

"I'm sorry to hear about it. Is your mother quite well again now?"

"Not really. At least – " He stopped, and picked up the soldier doll again, turning it over in his hands. Without removing his gaze from it he continued, "I'd better tell you the whole story."

But he did not do so immediately and to Sabella, watching him, it seemed that he was casting his mind back to the beginning of whatever it was that had happened to his mother.

Bastian had been attending a meeting, together with members of the Mines Engineering Brigade, at the home of the Prime Minister. No uninformed stranger would have guessed for a moment that the sprawling, comfortable but totally unassuming house set on the Doornkloof farm was the home of General Smuts and his wife. Their style of living, Bastian thought sardonically, would have dismayed Annette if she had been included in the invitation. He must remember to tell her that Mrs Smuts, or Ouma as she preferred to be called, more often than not wore her husband's woollen socks instead of stockings, and that her idea of dressing for dinner was to wrap a piece of lace about the neck of a plain black dress that reached to below the calf in defiance of modern fashion.

The meeting had just begun that morning when a telephone call interrupted it, and because he was nearest to the instrument General Smuts answered it himself instead of waiting for an aide to do so. "Meetings can always be rearranged," the others heard him say. "This one certainly can. I'll send him home at once." When he replaced the receiver General Smuts looked at Bastian and said, "That was your father. Your mother has been taken to hospital after a suspected stroke. You'd better go and pack."

Ouma insisted on giving him *padkos*, sandwiches and slices of cold fruit tart to eat on the road, and within a short while he was driving to Johannesburg. Edgy with worry and a build-up of fatigue, he would have preferred to go straight to the hospital but he had with him secret papers which could not be left even in a locked car. He would have to go home first and put the papers away in the safe.

As he turned his car into the drive of the house in Parktown he tried to put anxiety about his mother to the back of his mind and thought, instead, how much he disliked the place. It had been Annette's choice, and he had never cared sufficiently to insist on stamping his own mark on it. So the formal flower-beds, the neatly-trimmed shrubs, the manicured lawns that defied anyone to stretch out and lounge on them had nothing at all to do with him.

The front door was opened to him by the butler, Jackson. Of course it was not the Zulu's real name, but Annette would never dream of taking the trouble to pronounce the man's tribal name, and when Bastian had tried to do so in the beginning she had told him firmly to stop confusing the servants, who belonged to her domain.

Everything, Bastian thought sourly as he stepped inside the house, belonged to Annette's domain, and reflected her personality. The expensive furniture was too beautiful for comfort or for making the place into a home. The way in which the curtains had been carefully chosen in colours to pick up those of the upholstery, whose colour in turn blended with those of the rugs on the floor, all added up to such self-conscious good taste that it inspired a sense of anarchy in him and made him long to commit an act of deliberate vandalism. Good Lord, even the pictures on the walls and the cut flowers in their bowls had been chosen specifically because their colours toned and blended with those of the furnishings.

At that moment Annette herself appeared, presumably from her bedroom. Just like the house, everything about her was expensive and in calculated good taste. He had, Bastian realised suddenly, never seen her with her fair hair less than perfectly sculpted to frame her rouged, powdered, lipsticked face. She chaired, or served on, every fund-raising committee dedicated to helping the war effort, but Bastian knew that to her the greatest, secret calamity of the war lay in the fact that once her hoard of imported cosmetics had been exhausted, she would have to use the inferior home-produced powders and paints.

"You've come home," she greeted him, "because of Mater."

"Yes. What is the latest – ?"

"Pater telephoned from the hospital. Apparently it isn't quite as serious as they'd first thought. They believe she suffered a cerebral haemorrhage."

"I'm just going to lock these papers away," Bastian said, "and have a quick wash, and then I'll drive to the hospital."

"You'll have time for a bath," Annette told him, "because I still have several telephone calls to make before I shall be ready."

"You don't have to come," he said shortly. "Mother will understand. She knows you're hosting the dinner party in aid of the Air Raid Heroes Fund – "

"Oh, I shall find someone else to stand in for me. Mater and Pater must come first. I wouldn't *dream* of not going to the hospital with you."

Swallowing his irritation and impatience, Bastian left the room. He knew she would be telephoning all her friends to tell them about her mother-in-law because it would enable her to slip in something like, "I'm also concerned about poor Pater, the Right Honourable Peregrine, and I feel I must lend moral support."

He'd wanted to rush to the hospital to find out for himself what had happened to his mother and how she was faring, and it was doubly irksome to have to wait for Annette when he knew she was using the opportunity to give her social status an extra polishing. By leaving out his surname her references to his father made his political title sound more like a hereditary one than ever, and was probably accepted as such by her more ignorant friends. It had always grated on Bastian's nerves, too, that she insisted on calling his parents "Pater" and "Mater". He knew the reason for her snobbery and pretentiousness, and it did nothing to endear her to him. She was deeply ashamed of the fact that her own father had been a totter in London, a dealer in second-hand junk, before he married his housemaid sweetheart and left to seek and find his fortune in South Africa. Annette considered her parents "common" and saw as little as possible of them.

She was just putting down the telephone when Bastian rejoined her, having bathed and changed his clothes. "I'm leaving now," he said shortly, "whether you're ready or not."

She was ready, and they set off for the hospital in his car with scarcely a word spoken between them. Later, when Annette's elegant high heels clicked as they walked along the endless corridors of Johannesburg General Hospital, he thought of telling her that Ouma Smuts never wore anything but the plainest black shoes with no heels to speak of and a strap across the ankle. But then he caught sight of his father, standing in the doorway of one of the private wards and beckoning to him, and there was only room in Bastian's mind for concern about his mother.

"I wanted to prepare you," his father said. "The doctors tell me they think she'll make a complete recovery in time. But the stroke she suffered, or the shock of finding herself suddenly overtaken by something she didn't understand, or the medicine they've given her – or perhaps a combination of all three – has left her mentally confused. Don't be upset if she doesn't recognise you, or can't remember things."

Bastian nodded, and followed Annette who had already swooped on the patient in bed. "Oh Mater, dear!" she exclaimed.

"Go away!" His mother's voice was unexpectedly strong, even excitable in spite of being slightly slurred. "I'm not your Mater!"

Bastian stooped over his mother and kissed her cheek. He noticed that her eyes had an unnatural, almost feverish brightness and that one side of her mouth was slightly dragged down. "Hullo, darling," he said softly. How old she looked, he thought, and then realised that, like his father, she was in her seventies.

Her smile accentuated the drooping of her mouth. "You must forgive me, because I can't quite place you, but I know you're someone very dear. It will come to me." Her tone turned conspiratorial. "Can you get me out of this place? Perry is being very disagreeable and refuses."

"Now, Mater, everything that is being done is for your own good," Annette chipped in.

"I'm not your Mater!" Bastian saw the side of his mother's mouth that was not affected by the droop begin to tremble. "I'm no one's Mater. And since the operation . . ." Her eyes took on a look of confusion. "Perry, am I here for the operation?"

"No, dear." He sat down by the bedside and took her hand, and Bastian noticed for the first time that it was slightly clenched and obviously paralysed. "Don't fret. You'll soon be – "

"Then I must have had the operation already." Tears gathered in the corners of her eyes. "No babies for us . . ."

"What nonsense, my love. There's our son Sebastian." Although his father spoke calmly, Bastian thought he detected an underlying note of alarm in his voice.

"Ah yes, Sebastian!" She looked beyond her husband,

at Bastian. "Did you ever meet him? I'm sure you must have done so. What a dear little boy he is. So clever, and such good manners. No one would ever suspect that he isn't — "

Mercifully, Annette interrupted what she obviously took to be mindless rambling. "Mater, dear," she said patronisingly, "I think you ought to get some rest now."

"And *I* think you should wash that painted face of yours, whoever you are!" Eliza Grant returned with asperity. "And stop calling me Mater!"

Bastian's father rose, signalling to him and Annette to do the same. "I'm going to ask them to give you something to help you sleep, Eliza dear. I'll stay with you until you wake up."

"Thank you, Perry. You've always been so good to me. Yes, well, you *were* naughty during the war, but that's all forgiven." She beckoned to Bastian, and confided in a loud whisper, "She was a Boer girl, you know. The wife of an enemy. But there, I did get something out of the affaire for myself, because she let us have Perry's son to bring up as our own. *Sold* him to us, really, but then the Boers are a strange lot."

There was utter silence in the room after she had spoken. Bastian's father pressed a bell to summon a doctor, and after a moment she broke the silence, her mind darting to a totally different topic. "I do so feel for the poor Princess of Wales. The death of one's first-born must be a terrible thing. As if she has not already endured enough with that husband of hers . . . Tell me, have they buried the Duke of Clarence yet?"

At that moment a doctor hurried into the room, and Bastian's father said, "Could my wife be given something to make her sleep? I feel she has been overtaxed by her visitors."

The doctor examined Eliza and nodded, and after some coaxing she submitted to an injection which had an almost immediate sedative effect.

After the doctor had left, satisfied that Eliza was asleep,

Annette began to speak. "So," she said in a hard voice, "quite a few family skeletons have come rattling out of the cupboard, haven't they?"

Bastian gazed steadily at her. "If you feel that you no longer wish to be married to someone you've discovered to be half Afrikaans, and illegitimate into the bargain – "

She interrupted him with a harsh laugh. "Oh, you'd like that, wouldn't you? No, Sebastian, I wish to continue exactly as we have before. Indeed, I am *insisting* that my life should not be changed in any way – *ever*."

"Could you," his father put in wearily, "please go and discuss your marital affairs in private, at home?"

"No, Pater dear, because they affect you as well." There was a triumphant glitter in Annette's eyes. "I want you to be aware of the fact that if Sebastian were ever to leave me for another woman, I would not meekly accept the humiliation of being the abandoned wife. I would fight back by claiming that I had thrown him out because I'd just discovered the scandalous truth about his birth."

"You are talking about blackmail, of course." The contempt in his father's voice echoed that which Bastian was feeling.

"I prefer to think of it as consolidating my own position," Annette returned, unruffled. "But to make quite certain that Sebastian would never be tempted to upset the *status quo*, I am insisting that a legal contract be drawn up, by the terms of which I would get everything – his shares in the Grant Mining Corporation, his invested capital, the marital home – *everything*, in the event of his leaving me for another woman. Oh yes," she added with malice, "I shall also want possession of that farmhouse you bought between Johannesburg and Pretoria, Sebastian, the one in which you spend most of your weekends. In other words, if you left me you would walk out of our marriage without a penny to your name."

As Bastian had been speaking Sabella had listened with growing astonishment at the ruthlessness with which

356

Annette was clinging to her marriage to a man who did not love her any more than she loved him.

"I would walk out tomorrow and let her have everything," Bastian continued with chilly hatred. "Even Father said he was prepared to run the risk of a scandal ending his political career. But there are other risks neither of us dare take. Mother has recovered from her stroke; she has absolutely no memory of what she said while she was mentally confused, and the doctors have warned us that she must live quietly from now on and avoid any stress or shock because there is a high chance of it bringing on a second and fatal stroke."

"And a public scandal *would* produce that kind of shock," Sabella said slowly. "Surely Annette must know that?"

"She does. It merely strengthens her hand. She says that if Mother did die as a result of a public scandal, it would be on my conscience and not hers." He paused. "There is another reason, apart from the danger to Mother, why I dare not lay myself open to a public scandal. I shouldn't be telling this even to you, Sabella, but General Smuts has asked me to work for the government in an unofficial and secret capacity."

"As a spy?" she asked bluntly.

He shrugged. "As someone who listens and observes and forms a link in the chain of Government Intelligence. General Smuts knows about my birth and background; I insisted on telling him myself. But if I'm involved in a public scandal, with my name in the newspapers and on everyone's lips, I would be an embarrassment to the government, and I would have to be relieved of the special duties General Smuts has asked me to undertake. And since I've been prevented from joining up and taking part in the fighting," he added with passion, "I *want* to help the war effort in any other way I can. So, even though she doesn't know it, Annette has a further hold upon me. I loathe and despise her, but I have to live under the same roof with her while my mother is alive and the war continues."

How dearly life could make one pay for one single

mistake, Sabella thought. Bastian's mistake in rushing into marriage with Annette; her own in marrying Pierre. There was not even a remote possibility, now, of herself and Bastian ever sharing their lives, because even if his mother died and could no longer be affected by scandal, Sabella could never allow him to beggar himself by walking out of his marriage to Annette . . .

A sudden thought struck her, and she frowned. "But Bastian, Annette has never known about you and me, and she couldn't have found out suddenly, because we haven't seen one another for so long. So why did she suddenly go to such lengths to make sure you wouldn't leave her? Why *should* she have feared you might be planning to leave her?"

Bastian gazed at a spot above Sabella's head. "She – paid an unexpected visit to the farmhouse where I spend most weekends. She found me there with a girl."

Sabella stared at him in blank shock. She forgot that she had been telling herself he deserved some happiness, that she couldn't blame him if he'd found someone who was free to become his mistress.

Gripping the edge of the table, she stumbled to her feet with such a jerky movement that she sent her chair toppling over. Her arm described an arc in the air and the palm of her hand connected with Bastian's cheek in a blow that made his head jerk back.

"You miserable lecher!" she shouted at him. "Oh, you – you filthy damned *adulterer*!"

The last word had come out in a sob and she dropped her head in her hands, swaying backwards and forwards as she wept with rage and loss and a sense of bitter betrayal.

Sabella felt his hands gripping her shoulders. "Listen to me – "

She twisted away from him. "D–don't touch me! Keep your d–dirty hands for – your *girl*, your mistress!"

He swore, and reached for her, turning her roughly so that they faced on another. Even in her own pain and grief she recognised the anger in his eyes. "She is not my mistress. I have no mistress. She was just a girl, one of several over the years."

"*And you think that makes it better?*" she all but screamed at him.

"I'm not trying to make it sound better, or worse! I'm stating a fact. God Almighty, Sabella, I've loved you for sixteen years, and where has it got me? Apart from the time I spent on Mooikrantz with you, there has been the occasional furtive kiss when we've managed to be alone together for a few minutes. Was I supposed to comfort myself with those memories?"

"I have had to," she said with bitterness.

"Oh yes? You may not love the man you married, but I'm not stupid enough to imagine that there has been no physical relationship between you, and if you think I haven't suffered agonies of jealousy at the knowledge . . ." Bastian shook his head as if he were trying to clear it of unwelcome thoughts. "I'm not a monk or a saint, Sabella. I'm married to a woman who wants nothing from me but my money, the respectable status of being my wife in name, together with the social advantages of being my father's daughter-in-law! A woman who regards sex as a boring duty to be endured if it can't be avoided altogether. I stopped seeking her grudging favours many years ago, and I can't have you, so what did you expect me to do? Spend the rest of my life in frustrated celibacy? Did it never cross your mind that I might take occasional comfort, grab the illusion of love, from someone else?"

She wiped her eyes with the backs of her hands. "It crossed my mind," she admitted in a wretched whisper. "It's just – I didn't expect it to hurt so much to hear it being confirmed."

He caught her in a fierce embrace, his mouth seeking hers, and the years fell away. She was nineteen again and he twenty-three, with not a thought for anyone else or the possible consequences of their actions.

But there *had* been consequences, the thought intruded

into her mind as his hands continued to caress her treacherously responsive body. "Bastian, no," she said quietly, pushing him away from her and doing up the buttons of her dress which he had undone.

"You see?" he grated with an angry laugh, and mimicked, "'*Bastian, no!*' We are alone together for the first time in many, many years, and still it's '*Bastian, no!*' So don't judge me, Sabella, the next time someone else who means nothing to me says eagerly, '*Bastian, yes!*'"

"You fool." Her voice was flat. She leant against the table and went on in a monotone. "Pierre hankers after a child of his own. He utterly dismisses any possibility that he might be incapable of fathering one. If I didn't go on saying 'Bastian, no,' and I became pregnant, I would have no choice but to arrange matters in such a way that Pierre would believe the child to be his own. And how would you feel about *that*, Bastian?"

His answer took the form of a muttered obscenity. She went on remorselessly, "Apart from your feelings in the matter, I have my own to consider. Pierre has kept me tied to him through all these years by using the hold he had over my brothers and Ria and Katrien. But the boys and Ria have grown up and the times are changing rapidly. I haven't made the fortune for him which Pierre always hoped I would. What if something happened to make him decide that I'm not an asset to him, but a liability? What if he met a rich war widow, for instance, and wanted a divorce, and bartered custody of Katrien for that of the baby – *your* baby? Or fought me for custody, and won?"

The ferocity of Bastian's expression told her that she had been right, throughout all those years, to keep from him the knowledge that Katrien was his child. And if he'd known, in addition, that Pierre punished herself through the children . . . Sabella shuddered at the thought.

Bastian drew her towards him again, but gently this time, with a kind of hopeless resignation that she found overwhelmingly sad. Bastian had never been resigned

360

before; his instincts had always been to fight against all odds. But the odds had become too impossible.

"What a mess," he muttered against her hair. "Between the two of us, what a mess we've made of things . . ."

"Yes."

He traced the outline of her face in a lingering caress, and then touched his forehead to hers. "Those girls," he mumbled, "every one of them, Sabella, has had some quality that reminded me of you. And – it made it possible for me to pretend for brief moments, each time, that she *was* you."

She fought the searing pain of jealousy, and then tried to hide it behind a self-mocking smile. "Should I thank you for that two-edged compliment, Bastian? Well, never mind . . . Now, unlike those girls who reminded you of me, I'll have to go on with my doll-making, because this evening I must bake sweet cookies to sell to the women in the *stad*. There's coffee on the stove; pour some for yourself if you want to."

He shrugged the offer of coffee aside and said roughly, "Let me help you. Accept an allowance from me – "

"No," she interrupted with intractable finality.

He sighed, and sat down to watch her working on the soldier dolls. "How do you intend selling them?" he asked after a while.

"By offering them to passing motorists on the main Johannesburg road. I'll display them on the back of the truck."

"They're far too beautifully made for such hit-or-miss marketing, Sabella! I have a better idea." His lips twisted in a sardonic smile. "We'll use Annette to get the very highest prices for them."

"*Annette!*" Sabella echoed.

"I've told you, she serves on or controls every fund-raising committee in Johannesburg. I'll get her to auction the dolls at one of her society jamborees. Think about it, Sabella – apart from being beautiful objects in themselves, these are *soldier* dolls, and patriotic fever has never been

361

higher among the moneyed classes. I'll work out an agreement with Annette that a quarter of the cash raised should go to a war fund and the rest will be yours. In no time," he added with an ironic lifting of an eyebrow, "you'll have the capital you'd need to start supplying retailers with illegally butchered meat."

Sabella looked at him with suspicion. "Why on earth should Annette be prepared to put herself out for me? Or for *you*, come to that? I don't want disguised charity from you, Bastian – "

"Don't be silly," he cut her short. "Annette wouldn't be doing it for me or for you. She'd do it because she'll recognise the quality of the dolls. The fact that they are hand-crafted and not mass-produced will add to their snob appeal. Annette is no fool, and she'll realise immediately that auctioning the soldier dolls for a percentage would add enormously to her unofficial reputation as the Queen of the Forces' Funds!"

Although Sabella could accept most of his argument, she remained suspicious. "If *I* had just driven my husband into a corner by blackmailing him, and he came to me with any kind of proposition, I would be extremely wary!"

"True. That's why I'll get my father to approach her in the matter. I'll ask him to tell her the dolls are made by someone in his constituency. She'd love that; it would give her the opportunity of mentioning her father-in-law, the Right Honourable Peregrine Grant. Trust me, Sabella, and let me take the dolls you've completed so far."

"Very well." She stood up and found a cardboard box into which to pack them. As she handed it to him she said quietly, "Bastian, don't call again, will you? Keep in touch by post."

"Why, Sabella?"

She looked into his eyes, and then glanced away. "Because no matter how hard I might try not to, I'm going to brood about those *girls* who remind you of me. And if you should call again and I'm here alone, I might not have the strength to say, once again, '*Bastian, no.*'"

"And I might not have the strength to remind you to say it," he agreed in a low voice. He put the boxful of dolls on the table and drew her to him, kissing her with almost savage passion. Then he put her away from him, took the dolls and left without a backward glance.

She stood there for a long while, staring into space. By asking him to stay away from her she had probably pushed him back into the arms of one of his *girls*, and it was a bitter thought with which to live. But it had been the right decision, because apart from the need to keep temptation at bay, she couldn't risk him being at Goedgesig on a day when Pierre came driving home in his flashy Pontiac, or Anton roared up on his *Stormjaer* motorcycle. Bastian worked for Government Intelligence and it would be his duty to report their links with the subversive organisation.

As she sat down, finally, to resume work on the dolls it struck her with black humour that while Bastian's wife was busy, devoting her energies to raising funds for the war effort, her own husband was doing the same thing for the people whose aim it was to sabotage that effort.

16

However much Pierre raised for the *Ossewa Brandwag* before he creamed off a proportion for his own enrichment, Annette certainly deserved her title of Queen of the Forces' Funds which Bastian had said society had bestowed on her. Only a week passed before Sabella received word from the post office that a registered letter was waiting there for her collection and signature. It contained a brief note from Bastian, asking her to send a parcel of other dolls she might have completed, and enclosing thirty pounds in banknotes.

Thirty pounds! she kept reminding herself in astonishment as she drove home in the truck. Her share of seven auctioned dolls, and she had already completed four more. If she could earn thirty pounds for seven dolls, then there was no need for her to butcher stock and sell the meat illegally . . .

Her business acumen caused her to see, almost immediately, the flaw in that argument. If she made too many of the dolls, she would devalue them. Who would want to buy a soldier doll if every Tom, Dick and Harry owned one? No, the clever thing to do from now on would be to send Bastian one doll at a time. That would not only push up the price at auction but it would maintain the rarity value of the dolls. And in the meantime she must get started on her scheme to butcher meat for the market. But first she would have to win Daan over to her side.

That evening, as she and Ria and Daan ate their supper, Sabella deliberately began to reminisce about the distant past. "Do you remember, Daan, how you and Ria used to go and visit Tante Bessie when we lived on Mooikrantz? She had a mulberry tree and the two of you used to come home with your hands and faces black from the juice."

"I remember a fat old lady," he returned with indifference, "but nothing about mulberries."

"You must remember the baboons, and the way the young ones used to play just like human children." If she could stir his memories of the days before Pierre came into their lives, she thought, it might tip the scale of his divided loyalties in her favour.

But almost as if he had known what was in her mind, he said, "All I remember about Mooikrantz is that Daddy used to bring us chocolates." He added wistfully, "I wish he would come home. It's so boring here with him and Anton away and with nothing for me to do."

Sabella swallowed her disappointment and her secret hurt, and decided to build on what she'd been offered. "You and I will soon have plenty to do, Daan. I told you that Uncle Bastian's wife was going to try and sell my soldier dolls. Well, she did so, and I have enough capital to start a business with your help. But first I want you to promise to keep it a secret from Pierre. Will you?"

"I couldn't promise to do anything behind Daddy's back," Daan replied stubbornly, and added, "I wouldn't do anything behind *your* back either, Sabella."

She stifled a sigh. This would take skilful handling. "It's for Pierre's own sake that I want to keep it a secret, Daan. You know how – how generous he is. If he knew we were running a profitable business, he wouldn't be able to stop himself from wanting to give most of those profits to the *Ossewa Brandwag*. Now, whether you secretly support that organisation or not, the war is going to end some day and once the Nazis have been defeated and the world is sane again – "

"I'm not sure the Nazis *will* be defeated, Sabella," Daan put in. "I listened to Neels Conradie's wireless set the other day, and they said that German troops have crossed over from Italy to North Africa."

"And I read the newspaper headlines while I was in the village today," Sabella countered, "and learnt that British troops, reinforced by South African volunteers, have invaded Italian Somaliland."

Daan said nothing, making it impossible to tell which side he secretly supported. "Whoever does win the war," Sabella went on, "it *will* end one day, and when it does, I want to have earned enough money to make sure that we never again have to live on Goedgesig. Think of what a pleasant surprise it would be for Pierre when he discovers that there's money in the bank, Daan, and a flourishing business for him to take over!"

Her brother was silent, obviously weighing up the matter. At last he said, with a gleam in his eyes, "And it will have been *me* who helped build up the business, and not Anton! Daddy would be grateful to me, and proud of me too."

"That's right." Sabella listened to the falsely bright note in her own voice, and thought sadly: where have you gone, Daan; what happened to that baby I brought up and took into my bed when he cried and comforted when he was frightened? How could Pierre have become as important to him – if not more – as myself?

"What kind of business are you planning, Sabella?" she heard him ask.

Briefly, she explained the scheme to buy stock and sell meat to suburban Johannesburg butchers. "I have already spoken to a butcher in Mayfair about it and we could go and see him tomorrow, and visit Katrien at the same time. Then, as soon as we've made all the arrangements, you could take the truck and visit farms to buy our first pig or sheep, or even both if you could get them for the right price."

"But how can we keep it a secret from Daddy, Sabella? I mean, he might well make a visit home at a time when we're in the middle of butchering."

"I've thought of that. We'll pretend it's just an isolated occasion. We'll say I've managed to raise a little capital and

366

it's just a way of tiding us over. After all," she couldn't resist adding, "Pierre *has* left us alone here to shift for ourselves or starve."

"He brings meat and vegetables and other things whenever he comes home!" Daan flared up in Pierre's defence.

Sabella forbore to point out that Pierre brought food home on his infrequent visits because he himself liked to be well-fed, instead of subsisting on mealie porridge. Instead, she said pacifically, "Yes, well, by butchering pigs and sheep we'll be able to eat meat quite regularly. We'll keep the offal for ourselves and buy vegetables at the village shop. Now, are you with me in this, Daan?"

He nodded, and as she cleared away the dishes Sabella felt in better spirits than she had been in a long while. Quite apart from negotiating with that butcher in Mayfair tomorrow, she would be seeing her beloved daughter again. There had been no contact between them since Katrien had gone to live with Louis and Maria le Roux, because neither of them had been able to afford postage stamps. But this, like many other matters, would now be remedied.

Early the next morning Sabella drove the truck, with Daan and Ria sharing the cab seat, from the smallholding to Johannesburg. As she negotiated the busy city streets, she coached Daan in what he should say to the butcher.

"We'll call on him first, because Katrien will still be at school. We didn't introduce ourselves formally, but the name printed above his shop door was Visagie. Don't let him beat you down on prices, Daan, because he'll still be getting the meat for a very much lower price than he'd have to pay at market. And don't forget to tell him that you're able to spot any sign of disease in small stock." She hesitated. "By the way, when I first spoke to him I told him I was a widow. I thought it would make him more sympathetic towards me. If Meneer Visagie learnt that I'd lied he wouldn't trust either of us."

"I'll remember not to mention Daddy," Daan promised.

The visit to Meneer Visagie went entirely according to Sabella's plans. She banked down her resentment at being forced to stand there as a near-silent witness while the verbal transaction was hammered out between Daan and the butcher, as if she had no more intelligence than poor Ria.

After they had left Meneer Visagie they bought the equipment they would need for butchering stock, and then set out to visit Katrien.

Sabella was dismayed at the change in her daughter. She seemed subdued and withdrawn, and hardly spoke at all but allowed Maria le Roux to dominate the conversation with her news that, despite all her many "female problems", she was expecting a baby. Naturally, no other woman had ever had to endure as many permutations of pain and discomfort as she. "Louis is over the moon," she sighed, "but of course, he has no idea of what I'm going through. Why, some mornings I can hardly drag myself out of bed!"

Sabella made all the required responses but her attention was fixed on Katrien, who was serving tea. Was it merely Louis's preaching and Maria's endless martyrdom to her "female problems" that were wearing her down, or was something more serious amiss?

Sabella did not get a chance to speak to Katrien privately until it was time for them to leave, and her daughter accompanied them outside. Sabella drew her close and asked quietly, "What is the matter, my love?"

"I don't know what you mean, Mammie. Why should anything be the matter?"

"You look – well, you don't look happy."

Katrien drew away. "The people at school – they don't like me. They call me a Nazi-lover because I used to go to an Afrikaans-medium school."

Sabella chewed at her lower lip. "Would you like to leave, and enrol at the Afrikaans school?"

"It wouldn't help," Katrien said resignedly. "*They* would only call me different names for having been to an English school."

Because there was no other comfort she could offer her

daughter, Sabella pressed a pound note into her hand. "Don't spend it all at once. Buy stamps so that you'll be able to write to me, and if matters don't improve at school, let me know."

Katrien nodded. "Don't worry, Mammie. I expect the people at school will grow tired of calling me names. And thank you for the money."

Mentally cursing the gulf between English and Afrikaner which had been turned into a yawning chasm by the war and was causing her daughter unhappiness, Sabella began the return drive to Goedgesig with her brother and sister. The irony was that many more Afrikaners were fighting the enemy alongside the British than were trying to sabotage the war effort, but it made no difference to entrenched attitudes. Katrien would go on being called a Nazi-lover by her English-speaking classmates.

The cheap alarm clock on the kitchen dresser showed that it was just past four in the morning. Sabella sat on her haunches on the floor, dazed with fatigue and swamped by despair as she looked at the sides of pork lying on clean sacks.

In two hours' time Daan would get up, ready to drive the pork to Meneer Visagie's shop and unless a miracle happened that would be the end of their enterprise. One look at the sides of pork would tell the butcher that he was dealing with incompetent amateurs who'd had very little practical experience of butchering stock.

With the money Sabella had given him, Daan had managed to buy two sheep and a pig, and the butchering of the sheep had presented few problems. The main one had been that, because of the heat of the autumn sun, the butchering had to be done at dusk and the carcasses delivered at dawn so that the meat would arrive fresh at the butcher's shop.

Why, Sabella wondered bitterly, could a pig not be like a sheep, with a fleece that came away with hardly any difficulty? She had two hours left in which to make the sides of pork presentable and she had run out of ideas of how to do it.

She had envisaged no problems when she'd first begun to hack away at the coarse hair with a sharp knife, assuming that she would be able to cut it off level with the hide. How wrong she had been! The rough black bristles that were left were now too short for a knife even to make contact with them, and the only possible way she could think of removing them would be to pull each hair out individually with a pair of tweezers. And that was obviously out of the question.

Tears of weariness and defeat filled her eyes. This – this *mess* with its hide that resembled a man's three-day-old stubble would just have to be shared with the women in the *stad*, because the carcass could not possibly be offered to Meneer Visagie in this state. He was expecting a delivery of pork, and their failure to fulfil an order at this probationary stage of the enterprise would spell their ruin . . .

Stubble! The simile returned to her mind and she considered the inspiration that had struck her. A slow, tired smile spread across her face and she rose, lighting the primus and setting water on it to boil. Then she took the lantern and went to the room which Pierre shared with her on those odd nights when he was at home.

In common with many other members of the *Ossewa Brandwag*, he was growing a full beard and side whiskers, and he only used his safety razor to trim his moustache when he came home. He had always considered his razor so sacrosanct that he'd never allowed her brothers to borrow it. With no qualms at all, she took it from a drawer, together with a packet of blades and a tablet of shaving soap.

It did not take her long to work up a rich lather on the hide of the first side of pork, and then she began to shave off the stubble. She grinned tiredly to herself. Not only had she solved the problem of fulfilling their contract with Meneer Visagie, but oh – it was going to give her such secret pleasure, the next time Pierre trimmed his moustache, to know that his precious razor had last been used to give a close shave to a pig!

Their enterprise flourished after that initial problem had been solved. Sabella was too bone-weary to react strongly when Anton came roaring home on his motorcycle just after the last animal had been butchered. He dismounted, his smile and the gleam in his eyes almost fanatical. "The Germans have invaded the Greek island of Crete!" he cried jubilantly, adding almost by reflex action, "*Heil* Hitler!" and giving the Nazi salute.

Sabella regarded him with tired, disillusioned eyes. A burly, good-looking young man, her brother had developed to the full the physical aggression she had always tried to stamp out in him. But if Pierre, she thought bitterly, hadn't talked him into joining the brutish *Stormjaers*, he might have turned out differently.

"I worry about you, Anton," she said, shaking her head. "I worry about what is to become of you one day."

"Well, you needn't. The Afrikaner nation is rising up against their oppressors, and when *we* are the masters I shall have earned the right to be among the leaders!"

"Or in gaol," she suggested sombrely, "because I don't believe your Fascist heroes will win."

"You don't understand anything, Sabella. You're a woman." He looked at the meat lying on the kitchen table. They were the parts of the carcasses which were unsalable; the heads, chitterlings, lights and in the case of the pig, its liver, because there was no commercial demand for it. Sabella had been about to pick out what they themselves could consume and send the remainder to the *stad* to be shared among the women, with the vultures getting what was left over. In exchange for the meat the *stad* friends of Sabella's treated the sheep fleeces for her, and she sold them in Johannesburg.

She began to explain to Anton that she and Daan had undertaken to butcher the animals for a farmer in exchange for the unwanted by-products, but he was not in the least interested in where the meat had come from, or why. "I'd like some of that liver fried for my breakfast," he said. "Then I'm going to sleep all day because I have important business to see to after nightfall."

The "important business", Sabella thought as she threw a large piece of liver into the frying pan, was almost certainly sabotage. She remembered the tough small brother whose neck she used to scrub, and again the question pierced her: where did you go? What happened to the young Anton who used to be scared of ghosts and fought poor Nantes's battles for him?

As the weeks passed, the money Sabella and Daan earned grew impressively. This time she did not make the mistake of trying to find an ingenious hiding place for it at home where Pierre might sniff it out. She had gone with Daan when he was driving the last of a batch of carcasses to Johannesburg, and while he delivered meat to the butchers in Mayfair she went to a bank and asked for an appointment with the manager.

To her surprise, no obstacles were put in her way, and she was shown into his office. His name was Mr Hartley and he was a tall, distinguished-looking man whom she judged to be in his early forties. "Please sit down, Mrs le Roux," he invited cordially. "How may I help you?"

"My husband is on active service," she lied without shame, "and I'm earning money by raising crops on our smallholding. I want to save what I can towards the day when he comes home."

"That is very commendable of you. You are planning, perhaps, on expanding – ?"

"Oh no. I – I just wondered if you would allow me to open an account in my own name, so that I may deposit the money I'm saving."

"My dear Mrs le Roux!" The bank manager smiled broadly. "Of course we would be most happy to look after your savings for you, and there is no reason in the world why the account should not be in your name."

No, she thought cynically, understanding what had not been spelt out. If she'd wanted to expand, as he'd mentioned, and make her mythical crop-raising into a business, she would have been shown the door. It was only when a woman wanted to run a business in her own name that banks shut their doors in her face, afraid she might fail and get into debt. Allowing them the use of her savings was a different story altogether.

Mr Hartley had a bank book issued in her name, and she deposited the money she had brought with her. As a valued depositor instead of a potential debt-ridden failure she was escorted to the door where Mr Hartley shook her hand warmly.

Each time she called to deposit money in the bank after that, Sabella also visited the household of Louis le Roux to see Katrien, but her daughter continued to keep her at an emotional arm's length.

"I'm fine, Mammie, honestly." Obviously trying to demonstrate how "fine" she was, she added, "I came top of the class in History last week."

"Oh, good! Are you happier at school now, Katrien?"

She answered the question obscurely. "I've made friends with a new girl."

"I'm so glad. What is she like, your friend? What's her name?"

"Norma King. She's – she looks coloured, Mammie. She lives with her aunt, and her two cousins, who started at school when she did, say Norma is a throwback."

"I see." Sabella did, indeed, see. Katrien's expression had told her that Norma King was shunned by the others at school, including her cousins. But had Katrien befriended the girl because of her own hatred of unfairness and intolerance, or was it a case of two outcasts clinging together for mutual support?

"Tell me some more about Norma," Sabella invited.

"There's nothing more to tell, except that she's nice, and we go about together. Our class is to visit a soap factory next week," Katrien added, almost as if she were desperate to find *some* topic on which to communicate with her mother.

"And there's nothing else you'd like to tell me, Katrien? I worry about you so much . . ."

Her daughter's eyes slid away from hers. "Don't worry about me, Mammie. There's no need." But when Sabella tried to embrace her Katrien drew away and faked a fit of coughing.

Sabella sighed, and climbed back inside the truck. How could she fail to go on worrying about her daughter?

If she had allowed Mammie to embrace her, Katrien thought as she lay in bed that evening, the truth would just have come spilling out of her like water from an overflowing river during a cloudburst. And Mammie had enough worries on her mind without Katrien adding to them. Besides, what would be accomplished if she *did* tell the truth? She'd have to go back to Goedgesig and to the old situation of being a weapon through whom Derrie could punish Mammie at will.

Katrien turned over in bed. She could hear Maria snoring loudly and unrhythmically in the bedroom where she was sleeping alone, because Louis was on night duty. Katrien was certain that most of the complaints Maria was forever adding to her long litanies of suffering were brought on by the many different pills she took. She only had to read about some new pill or powder and she would send Katrien to buy it for her. Those pills and powders, apart from any other effect they might have on her, were almost certain, too, to be the cause of her inability to wake up in the morning. How Katrien dreaded those mornings when Maria couldn't be woken up, and Louis was on early duty and needed to have his breakfast by five o'clock . . .

But he's on night duty this week, Katrien reminded herself. You have a whole week, and anything might happen in that time. A policeman's job is often dangerous. He could be stabbed during a robbery, perhaps . . .

She forced herself to cling to that hopeful thought, and at last drifted into sleep. She was woken up, less by any sound or movement than by some warning sixth sense. Her heart almost exploded in her chest when she opened her eyes and saw him kneeling beside her bed. He was still in his police uniform, apart from his helmet which lay on the floor, so he must have come straight from duty and into her bedroom. In the grey light of dawn she saw him moistening his lower lip with his tongue.

"Katrien," he said softly, "the Lord spoke to me during the night."

"Go – go away," she stuttered, sitting up and clutching the bedclothes around her. "Leave my room – "

"The Lord spoke to me as clearly as I'm speaking to you now, Katrien," he went on. "He told me of your secret, lustful thoughts and of the way you touch yourself when you're in bed. He spoke to me, Katrien, and ordered me to touch you in those places, to make you aware of the evil of what you do. So come now, let us both obey the Lord, and throw those bedclothes aside – "

"*I'll scream for Tante Maria!*" Katrien cried, jumping from the bed to evade his groping hands. But he knew as well as she did that even screams would not make Maria wake up.

"Katrien, Katrien!" As he advanced upon her he quoted, "'*Hear counsel, and receive instruction, that thou mayest be wise in thy latter end. There shall no evil happen to the just . . .*'"

Her hand had found the doorknob. With relief so overwhelming that she almost fainted, Katrien heard the sound of the letter-box on the front door rattling. "I'm going to run outside in my nightdress and bring the postman in here!" she threatened.

Louis shook his head sadly. "You would expose yourself in near-nakedness to a stranger? Ah, Katrien, there is a great deal of the Lord's work needing to be done with you." But he picked up his helmet and she dashed into the corridor, halfway to the front door, to make sure that he would leave her bedroom. When she saw him going into the kitchen she sped back to her room, wishing it had been possible to lock its door. He had never come to her room before . . .

She dressed quickly in her school gym-slip and blouse. With Maria still snoring her head off and Louis at large, Katrien was not going to risk going into the bathroom in nothing but her nightgown. She would undress and wash herself and then get dressed again.

But Louis had anticipated her. He was already inside the bathroom, and when she opened the door he smiled at her. " '*Come, eat of my fruit,*' " he quoted softly, his fingers at the buttons of his fly.

She banged the door shut, and after stopping only long enough in the kitchen to grab a piece of half-stale cheese, she walked to school with trembling legs.

Because it was so early she had the cloakroom to herself and she was able to wash after a fashion and brush her teeth with her fingers. Fortunately, she always kept a comb in the pocket of her gym-slip and so could bring some order to her hair.

Without tasting it, she nibbled at the piece of cheese. I don't know what to do, she thought. If it's no longer safe when Louis is on night duty, what *am* I to do?

She was not really surprised when the cloakroom door opened and Norma came in, even though it was still far too early for anyone to need to be at school. Norma had her own troubles at home, but neither of them ever referred to their respective troubles, let alone spelt them out. They just knew, instinctively, that they were victims who needed each other's support.

"Hullo," Katrien said, giving her friend a wavering smile. "Want a piece of cheese? It's a bit hard."

"Thanks. You can share my sandwiches at lunch-time." Norma had noticed that Katrien hadn't brought a lunch-box, just as Katrien had noticed that Norma had been crying. Those cousins of hers again, of course, taunting her about her crinkly hair and coffee-coloured skin . . .

Katrien hooked her arm through Norma's. "Let's go and

sit on the grass and talk about when we're twenty-one," she said.

That was what they lived for. To be twenty-one, and no longer kept in subjugation by their elders, powerless in the grown-up world.

17

As Sabella had known it would, the day inevitably came
when one of Pierre's fleeting visits home coincided with
their butchering of a sheep. It was now winter, so that
they could work during the day without fear of the meat
turning bad before they could deliver it in Johannesburg,
and the sheep was the last of their latest purchased stock
to be butchered. There was no evidence anywhere that the
sheep didn't represent one of a few isolated transactions,
and Sabella's bank book was safely hidden in a tin buried
in the ground of the hen-house and covered with planks.

"Whenever I have enough money saved from selling
cookies in the *stad*," Sabella explained to Pierre, "Daan
goes to buy a sheep or a pig cheaply from a farmer, and
we sell the meat to Johannesburg butchers."

"Very enterprising of you," Pierre commented. He
seemed to have put the matter out of his mind, because
he went on to tell her and Daan about the important people
he had been meeting and the influential friends he'd made.
His speech, these days, was sprinkled with slogans and
platitudes and she guessed it was *Ossewa Brandwag* jargon
which he had learnt by heart and which had become so
much a part of him that he wasn't aware of using it.

Just when Sabella wasn't expecting it, he demanded to
know how much they stood to make from the sale of the
butchered sheep carcass, and before she could dart him a
warning glance, Daan told him.

Pierre rubbed the side of his nose, his expression calculating. "That should be enough to buy another sheep

and a pig," he said. "It has given me an idea. We're conveniently situated here, within easy reach of wealthy Afrikaners in Johannesburg – people like doctors, lawyers, bank managers – the very kind of people we want to recruit into the *Ossewa Brandwag*. They are also the kind of people who would dig deeply into their pockets for the Cause. So I'm going to organise a *braaivleis*, Sabella, to be held on Goedgesig as soon as the cold weather ends. I want you to save what the sale of the meat fetches, and when the time comes buy that sheep and pig with the money. We'll butcher them the day before the *braaivleis* and barbecue them over a large outdoor fire."

"No," she said flatly.

He gave her his deceptively sweet smile. "I'm going to organise the *braaivleis* all the same. I think you'll find the money from somewhere, nearer the time, to buy the stock."

He can't threaten me any more, she told herself. Katrien was safely in Johannesburg and he seemed to have developed a revulsion for Ria, and would push her away when she tried to embrace him, so it was unlikely that he would use a sexual threat against her. No, Sabella decided, Pierre's power to punish her through others had spent itself.

And so she continued her normal business with Daan's help, buying stock and butchering it and selling the meat, and all but forgot about Pierre's plan to have a *braaivleis* at Goedgesig for his *Ossewa Brandwag* colleagues and sympathisers, and for which he expected her to supply the meat.

It came as a rude shock, therefore, when he arrived home unexpectedly one beautiful spring day just after Daan had returned from a buying trip with the usual two sheep and a pig, and said, "Ah, good! I knew you wouldn't let me down, Sabella, and I see you've even produced a bonus of a second sheep. The *braaivleis* has been organised to take place three days from now. I'll help Daan to butcher the animals and cut up the meat while you bake bread and cakes to offer our guests. No doubt you'd have to go to Johannesburg to buy ingredients – "

"I wouldn't give the time of day to your Fascist friends, Pierre," she interrupted angrily, "let alone bake for them! And those animals have been promised to Johannesburg butchers. In fact," she lied, "they were bought with money advanced by the butchers, and Daan and I will be paid for getting them ready for the retail market!"

"I'm sure your butcher friends will understand," Pierre returned smoothly.

"They won't be asked to, because the meat is going to them as arranged!"

Her heart gave a thud of fear as he turned his most dazzling, dangerous smile on her. "I know what it is, Sabella. You're overtired. It's high time you had Katrien here to help her poor mother. She has just turned sixteen, so the law allows her to leave school. I'll drive to Johannesburg right away to fetch her."

Fool, Sabella berated herself. How could you have forgotten that until Katrien comes of age, he'll always have a weapon to use against you?

"You win," she said with sullen hatred.

"Yes, I knew I would," he smiled. "You'd better take the truck and go to Johannesburg right away, Sabella, because apart from buying what you'll need to bake cakes for the *braaivleis* you would also have to explain matters to your butcher friends. I'm sure you'll think of something convincing."

"I hope," she said with venom, "that Daan made a mistake this time, and at least one of the beasts is diseased. I hope the meat is as tough as leather and chokes your Fascist friends!"

She walked towards the truck, because it really *was* necessary for her to visit the butchers who would be expecting delivery of carcasses, and explain to them that this time she had been prevented from supplying them.

It was late afternoon by the time she had made all the rounds, but even so she delayed her return home by visiting the house of Louis le Roux. He was in the front room, dressed in his police uniform as if he had just come off duty, and lying on the sofa was Maria with her pregnancy well in evidence and an expression on her face that suggested she had been interrupted in a long description of her "female" woes.

"Where is Katrien?" Sabella asked.

"Doing her homework. I'll call her – " Louis began.

"Not immediately. Here – " Sabella handed him bank-notes and loose silver. "This is an advance payment of three months' board and lodging."

"Why in advance, Sabella?" he asked in a pained voice. "We have always trusted you in the past."

"The thing is – Pierre might try, one of these days, to bring Katrien home now that she has passed her sixteenth birthday. I don't want that. She should carry on with her schooling. I want you to promise that you'll refuse to let him inside the house or tell him the name of her school."

"You may safely put your trust in me, Sabella," Louis assured her.

"The very idea!" Maria exclaimed indignantly. "I *need* Katrien to be here when Louis is on night duty! I wouldn't be able to manage without her! Really, I don't understand how your husband can be so selfish – "

At that moment Katrien entered the room, and she had obviously overheard much of the conversation, for she said, "One of the neighbours could come and stay with Tante Maria. If you need me at home, Mammie, I don't mind leaving school."

"*I* would mind you leaving school, Katrien."

Sabella had to say goodbye soon afterwards, and Katrien saw her to the truck. "Mammie," she said soberly, "if Derrie wants me at home, then I know the reason for it. And – and I'd rather he did something to me than – than to Tante Ria."

"He won't, my love. He never pays attention to Ria these days." Sabella took from her purse the five crisp, new pound notes she had specially withdrawn from the bank earlier that day. "These are for your birthday, Katrien. I'm sorry it's a little late."

"Thank you, Mammie." The response was thoughtful rather than ecstatic, and given with downcast eyes, and when Sabella kissed her daughter she sensed an instinctive withdrawal.

The sun had set by the time she reached home, and from the darkness came the squealing of the pig and the bleating of the sheep. Sabella fought an impulse to free them from the pens in which they had been enclosed and allow them to escape, rather than have them fed to the hated *Ossewa Brandwag* members.

When she entered the house she found that Pierre and Daan were eating supper of scrambled egg and bread. Something in her brother's expression caught her attention, and she asked sharply, "Where's Ria?"

"She has gone, Sabella." Pierre's voice was calm, but his eyes held a look which suggested that he was preparing to justify himself.

"Gone where?" Sabella demanded, caught between bewilderment and terror. "Gone how?"

"Now look, Sabella, it was for her own good. She couldn't have gone on running wild. And how would it have looked if she'd been here to pester people during the *braaivleis* with her baby talk? I mean, apart from her being an embarrassment to us as a family, the *Ossewa Brandwag* share Herr Hitler's belief that people like Ria should be – well – got rid of, and I *am* an important active member as well as the official host at the *braaivleis* – "

"You bastard!" Sabella screamed, cutting through Pierre's rambling argument. "What have you done with my sister?"

He shrugged, and this time he made no attempt to justify his action. "I've had her committed to a mental institution."

First Nantes, and now Ria. The thought pounded in Sabella's brain as she climbed into the truck, early the next morning, to drive to Johannesburg. She had just started the motor

382

when she saw Daan coming towards her. Last evening he had barely spoken but he'd looked sombre and uneasy.

"Sabella," he said, and stopped.

"Yes?"

"I – I didn't know what Daddy was planning to do about Ria. He told her he was going to take her for a drive."

"And how do you feel about him having locked your sister away?" Sabella asked in a hard voice.

Daan's eyes slid away from hers. "I – well – if they treat her kindly . . . And they might be able to do something to make her normal . . ."

"Oh, go away, Daan," Sabella said wearily. "Go and settle yourself comfortably on the fence."

"I don't know what you mean – "

"Don't you? Please stand aside; I want to be on my way."

"I hope you'll be able to get Ria back, Sabella," Daan blurted out, but she noticed that he looked over his shoulder as if to make sure that Pierre hadn't overheard such a disloyal outburst.

I *will* get her back, Sabella thought fiercely as she nosed the truck along the rutted track that led to the main Johannesburg road. I'll explain that Pierre had no right to do what he did, and if necessary I'll tell the people at the institution that he had her committed because of his membership of the *Ossewa Brandwag*. If I have to gamble Anton's freedom against Ria's, I'll do so. *She* didn't ask to be locked away in a mental institution, but Anton became a member of the *Ossewa Brandwag* and a *Stormjaer* of his own free will . . .

Their members are everywhere, she remembered, and clenched her hands tightly around the steering wheel. In this divided land almost anyone could be a traitor, a secrete *Stormjaer*, a committed officer of the *Ossewa Brandwag*. They were in the law courts, in the police force, and elsewhere, so why not among key staff inside a mental institution?

I'll get her back, Sabella vowed again. I'll explain that

she does not belong in a mental institution, that she isn't mad or dangerous, that her poor brain simply got stuck at the age of three. Oh God, please let me get Ria back . . .

Sabella had to stop the truck several times to ask directions of passersby to the institution whose name Pierre had given her with a gesture of bored indifference. At last she reached it, and its outside was as depressingly grey and forbidding, dotted with small barred windows, as she imagined its interior must be.

"I want to speak to whoever is in charge of admissions," Sabella told a girl in uniform as soon as she had entered the building. She was shown into a room furnished with a desk, filing cabinets and two chairs. After she had been waiting for a while a middle-aged woman entered, also uniformed, but with an air of authority about her.

"My sister, Ria van Renselaar, was committed to this place yesterday," Sabella began without polite preliminaries. "My husband made sure I would be out of the way so that he could bring her here. He had no right to do so. I've come to take her home."

"I'm sorry, Mrs le Roux." The woman reached into a wire basket on the desk and took out some papers, running her gaze briefly over them. "Your husband brought with him a document, showing that he had adopted your sister and was therefore still her legal guardian since she will obviously always need a guardian in some shape or other. He also brought a letter from your family doctor, recommending that she be committed to an institution such as this – "

"We don't have a family doctor!" Sabella interrupted triumphantly. "My husband must have forged the letter – "

"It was genuine, Mrs le Roux. We check these things very thoroughly. Perhaps I misunderstood your husband about the matter of Doctor Haasbroek being the family doctor, but the letter was no forgery. Doctor Haasbroek's credentials are impeccable."

Sabella had never heard of a doctor by that name. An *Ossewa Brandwag* member, the knowledge flashed into her mind, and she felt overwhelmed for a moment by the mounting evidence that Pierre had been planning, cold-bloodedly and for some time, to have Ria committed.

"Apart from a guardian's authority and a recommendation by an independent doctor," she heard the woman go on, "we don't commit anyone unless one of our own doctors confirms that such a course of action is desirable. And I'm afraid that our Doctor Graham *did* confirm it."

"She – she isn't mad," Sabella managed through trembling lips. "She isn't a danger to anyone – "

"She is a danger to *herself*, Mrs le Roux. A grave moral danger."

"I don't understand you," Sabella said blankly.

"She – well, I'm afraid she made blatant sexual overtures to your husband in the presence of myself, of Doctor Graham, and of a very embarrassed junior nurse."

"Oh." The enormity of Pierre's treachery almost paralysed Sabella. When she found her voice she cried passionately, *"He taught her! He invited what she did!"*

The woman shook her head. "Mrs le Roux, I can assure you that he did nothing of the sort. He said in a most kind, compassionate voice: 'You must go with the nice lady, my pretty Ria.' And she – well, she responded by unbuttoning her blouse, and – I'm sorry, but I have to spell it out to make you understand – she not only offered herself to him but caused him deep embarrassment by catching hold of his hands and trying to force him to fondle her breasts."

The unspeakable monster, Sabella thought numbly. First he had corrupted her defenceless sister and then he had used the fact of her conditioned, uncomprehended corruption to destroy her. And all because he hadn't wanted her embarrassing, flawed presence there while he entertained his *Ossewa Brandwag* friends at a *braaivleis*.

She thought of telling the woman that her sister had been taught, by Pierre, to respond with sexual excitement to the words "Pretty Ria". But how could she do that, without also explaining convincingly why she hadn't taken steps, herself, to stop what Pierre was doing? How was it possible to explain her husband to a woman who had clearly perceived him as a charming, caring, compassionate guardian acting only for Ria's own good?

At last, Sabella merely asked, "Could I please see my sister?"

"I'm afraid not, Mrs le Roux. It would unsettle her too much at this stage."

"You – you mean that she is crying, that she hasn't stopped crying since she was left here?"

"She *is* in an overemotional state, yes. Leave her with us for a few months, Mrs le Roux, so that she may become used to the routine here. I'll write and let you know when you may visit her." The woman's voice was kind, but firm and final.

Sabella couldn't remember, afterwards, leaving the building and walking to the truck. She climbed into the cab and rested her head upon the steering wheel as she wept. First Nantes, and now Ria too. Oh Ma, oh Pa, she thought in agony, I didn't keep my promise. It has all gone so wrong, and I've lost two of the children I swore to care for in your place . . .

At last she had no more tears left to shed and she sat up, steel entering her soul. Pierre would pay for what he had done, Oh, he would pay dearly . . .

As soon as she had driven away from the grounds of the institution she stopped the truck to ask directions to the office of the Grant Mining Corporation. It was a large, imposing building, and at first it was difficult to associate Bastian with it. But as Sabella crossed the marble floor to where a girl sat behind a desk, she found herself wondering involuntarily: is *she* one of them, those girls with whom Bastian finds comfort? Is there anything about her to remind him of me?

Then the girl supplied the answer to Sabella's unspoken question by looking at her with pitying curiosity, and she knew what this pretty, fashionable young girl with her skilfully made-up face must be seeing: someone no longer in the first flush of youth, who wore a faded print dress and whose hair was a tangle of untidy curls, her eyes swollen by weeping.

"May I help you, madam?" the girl asked doubtfully, as if she could not imagine how someone like Sabella could have found herself inside the Grant building other than by mistake.

"I want to see Mr Sebastian Grant," Sabella said.

The look of pitying curiosity on the girl's face changed to one of stiff outrage. "I am afraid Mr Grant does not see anyone except by appointment."

"I believe he'll see me. Tell him Mrs Sabella le Roux needs to speak to him urgently."

The girl hesitated, and then she turned to what Sabella supposed must be a switchboard and a moment later she was saying, "Mr Grant's secretary? I'm sorry to trouble you, but there's someone here called Mrs Sabella le Roux who wants to see him. I'm sure he'll be too busy, but I thought I'd better check with you first. Yes, I'll wait." After a few seconds of silence she said with astonishment, "I see," and looked at Sabella. "Mr Grant's secretary is coming down to show you to his office."

The strangeness of making her first-ever visit to Bastian's place of work had temporarily blurred the raw edges of Sabella's pain and rage, and when his secretary stepped from a lift and came towards her, she couldn't help wondering again: is *she* one of the girls he told me about?

But a short while later Sabella had been ushered inside Bastian's office, and his familiar face and figure blinded her to all the trappings of success and money which surrounded him, so that her mind was once again filled with desolation at Ria's fate and the bitter desire for revenge.

"Sabella!" Bastian exclaimed, leaving his desk and hurrying to take her in his arms. "You've been crying. What has happened? Tell me."

"Pierre has had Ria committed to a mental institution," she said bleakly.

"*What?* He had no grounds – "

387

"Oh, he believed he had," she cut in, her voice corrosive with hatred.

"Sit down, and tell me everything," Bastian commanded.

"I've come to inform on my husband, Bastian, but before I do so I want you to promise immunity for Anton. Pierre joined the *Ossewa Brandwag* months ago, and he encouraged Anton to join as well, but I believe Pierre's arrest will shock my brother into leaving it."

Instead of looking stunned at the information, as she had expected him to, Bastian leant forward across the desk and took her hand in his. "Sabella," he said gently, "tell me from the beginning how and why Pierre had your sister committed."

"He is organising a *braaivleis* which is to be held on Goedgesig tomorrow night. It is to be a joint recruiting and fund-raising event for the *Ossewa Brandwag*." Her voice took on a raw note. "He deliberately got rid of me so that I wouldn't be there to stop him, and then he drove Ria to the mental institution. He had a letter in his possession, written by an *Ossewa Brandwag* doctor who has never even set eyes on Ria, recommending that she be committed. And all because the *Ossewa Brandwag* members don't believe that people like poor Ria should be allowed to offend the sight of *normal* people like themselves!"

"We'll have her discharged, Sabella," Bastian promised vigorously. "I'll call in the help of the best doctors in the country – "

"It wouldn't do any good." Sabella spoke in a small, shamed voice now. "Pierre – for years it has amused him to encourage Ria to – to exhibit the sexual attraction she feels for him . . . Don't look like that, Bastian! She may have a child's mind, but her body and her instincts are those of a woman. And she – she tried, in front of witnesses at the institution, to get Pierre to fondle her naked breasts. So there is no hope at all of getting her discharged. They say she needs the protection of the institution for her own moral safety. But Pierre, the contemptible bastard, *conditioned* her to act as she did! By saying two words, "Pretty Ria", he *knew* she would unbutton her blouse and offer him her breasts. He had taught her to do it, after all!"

Bastian made a sound of revulsion. "Why didn't you tell me this a long time ago?"

"What good would it have done?" she returned dully. "I thought I would always be around to protect her. And now," her voice hardened, "now I want to destroy Pierre. I want him in gaol. But first I want your promise that Anton won't be involved."

"Sabella." Bastian stopped, and shook his head in a gesture of futility and regret. "I have known for a long time that both Pierre and Anton belong to the *Ossewa Brandwag*. If we were to have all known members of that organisation thrown in gaol or interned it would cost the country a fortune."

"So – I've come here for nothing," she said, the rank taste of defeat in her mouth.

"I'm sorry. You see, apart from the sheer size of the *Ossewa Brandwag* movement presenting a problem when it comes to enforcing the ban against them, we have high hopes that they will lead us to someone we really do need to capture very urgently. Have you ever heard of the *Stormjaers*?"

"I – believe so," she said, without meeting his eyes.

"They started as a militant wing within the *Ossewa Brandwag*. Most of them are just hot-heads who present no real threat, but there is a hard core of extremists among them and many in the *Ossewa Brandwag* have become increasingly disenchanted with them and inclined to disown them. But while they remain linked, several *Ossewa Brandwag* leaders are secretly working with us, trying to flush out the men we are really after."

Anton is one of them, instinct told her. Aloud, she said, "Are you telling me that there are spies among the *Ossewa Brandwag* who are informing on fellow members?"

Bastian's lips twisted in a hard smile. "My dear Sabella,

389

there are spies and counter-spies everywhere in this country of ours."

"Those men you're after," she said, thinking of Anton, "are the ones who have been committing acts of sabotage?"

"Yes, but there is more to it now than the odd home-made bomb lobbed inside an empty public building during the night." Bastian hesitated. "There is a man named Robey Leibbrandt, a South African who spent several years in Germany, where he was cultivated by Hitler. He is known to have slipped back into this country now, and his mission is to assassinate General Smuts. That hard core of extremists among the *Stormjaers* of whom I told you have taken Leibbrandt's somewhat melodramatic but deadly Blood Oath and are calling themselves National Socialist Rebels. They have committed themselves to the plot to assassinate General Smuts. *They* are the people we are after, as well as Robey Leibbrandt."

"I see. This man, Robey Leibbrandt – does he have a special slogan of his own?"

"Why do you ask?" Bastian stared curiously at her.

"I just wondered," Sabella said, trying to sound convincingly indifferent. "After all, every political movement in this country has its own slogans. If he does have one, I could keep my ears open for it tomorrow night at the *braaivleis.*"

"As a matter of fact, Robey Leibbrandt's slogan is: '*Die Vierkleur Hoog!*'"

The Republican Flag High! Oh yes, she thought grimly, now I know exactly how I'm going to destroy you, Pierre.

She and Bastian talked for a while longer. Without holding out much hope, he promised to see if there might be some loophole by which Ria could be discharged from the institution, but Sabella knew in advance that he would fail. Pierre had done his work too well, and now he was going to pay for it.

She twisted her hands together and rested her chin on them, saying with intensity, "Bastian, I can't bear to see

Pierre getting away scot-free after what he has done! Even if there is no possibility of his fellow members and himself being arrested for holding a rallying *braaivleis* tomorrow night, I want him to be embarrassed, to be frightened, to look a fool. I want the police, at the very least, to break up the event. Indeed, I feel they *should* break it up, because there are many people in the Goedgesig district, fellow Afrikaners whose menfolk are fighting with the Allied troops up north, and who loathe the *Ossewa Brandwag*. Violence would almost certainly break out if they got to hear about the *braaivleis*. So I want to contact the police and ask them to turn up in force. But the trouble is that Pierre has often boasted the police force is riddled with *Ossewa Brandwag* members and sympathisers, so I don't know which particular police station I could trust. If I telephoned the wrong one I might find policemen turning up to join in the violence on the side of the *Ossewa Brandwag* instead of keeping the peace."

"I know the very man to contact," Bastian said. "I'll telephone him – "

"No," Sabella put in quickly. "I don't want you to involve yourself! It might set someone wondering and lead to the link between us being discovered. Just give me the man's name and his telephone number, and I'll speak to him."

Bastian looked at her for a moment, then shrugged and said, "Very well. His name is Captain le Grange and I'll write his telephone number down for you. You could contact him from my office."

"Thank you, no." She searched her mind for a plausible excuse. "I have a few things to buy while I'm in the city, and it would give me time to decide exactly what I should say to Captain le Grange. I want to embarrass Pierre as much as I can. I'll telephone the policeman from a tickey-box."

Bastian didn't argue, but wrote down a telephone number for her and kissed her a lingering goodbye. It was a kiss of such deep understanding and love that it brought momentary, fresh tears to her eyes. She brushed them away and hurried from his office and out of the building.

It didn't take her long to find a tickey-box. She fumbled in her purse for the silver coins, the only ones the public telephone system could take, and then dialled the number Bastian had written down for her. She was told that Captain le Grange was at present engaged in another telephone conversation, and asked to hold on. Her nerves on edge, she fed tickeys into the slot at intervals, but at last a voice said, "Captain le Grange speaking. May I help you?"

Sabella took a deep breath. "I can't tell you my name," she began, "but there is a smallholding called Goedgesig, about twelve miles north of Johannesburg. Tomorrow night a *braaivleis* is to be held there for – "

"For the purposes of recruiting members, and raising funds for the *Ossewa Brandwag*," the disembodied voice finished for her.

"Oh. You know about it – "

"I've received information, yes. Am I, by any chance, speaking to Mrs Pierre le Roux?"

She was too taken aback to respond for a moment. Then she stammered, "I – don't know anyone by that name and I – I can't tell you mine." *Bastian*, she thought. While she had been waiting to speak to Captain le Grange, Bastian had been in conversation with him. Perhaps concern for her safety had prompted Bastian to take direct action, or perhaps he had simply been ensuring that Captain le Grange wouldn't have her fobbed off when she herself telephoned him.

Her voice strengthening, she went on, "Captain le Grange, will you and your men be arriving during the *braaivleis*?"

"Indeed we will, madam." The polite title had been given an ironic inflection, telling her that the police officer knew precisely to whom he was speaking.

"Well, Captain le Grange," Sabella said, "may I suggest that your men don't confine themselves to keeping the peace and perhaps making a few token arrests. It would be worth their while to make a thorough search of the house. Could you arrange that?"

"Most certainly – madam. Thank you for the suggestion."

She replaced the receiver, and walked to where she had parked the truck, her mind busy.

After Anton's last visit home, a few days ago, she had washed and ironed the dirty clothes he'd left behind him, and when she had put them away in his drawer in the chest which he shared with Daan, she had found the letter.

At the time, it had been just one more detail to add to her worry over Anton. She was glad that she hadn't realised its significance earlier, for it would have driven her half-crazy with anxiety.

The letter had been so short that she could remember it word for word. "Dear le Roux," it had begun in Afrikaans, "just a brief note to express my gratitude for your help in the cause of getting vital material across the Mozambique border. God be with you. *Die Vierkleur Hoog!* Leibbrandt."

She hadn't wanted to think about it at the time, but the "material" smuggled across the Mozambique border into South Africa couldn't have been other than explosives or weapons. She had replaced the letter and had tried not to wonder where Anton had travelled to this time on his powerful motorcycle or what he might be doing.

A grim smile touched her lips. Tomorrow evening, when Pierre was busy welcoming his *Ossewa Brandwag* friends as they arrived at Goedgesig, she would remove the letter from among Anton's possessions and tuck it inside the pocket of one of Pierre's pairs of trousers.

I can hardly wait, Pierre, she thought vengefully, to listen to you trying to explain away such a damning letter found in your possession. When you seduced my brother into becoming a *Stormjaer* and calling himself le Roux so that you could bask in his reflected glory, you couldn't have dreamt that it would all explode so disastrously – and deservedly – in your face . . .

18

The police raided Goedgesig at nine o'clock the following night.

Even though she was alone inside the house, slicing bread for Pierre's guests to eat with their barbecued meat, Sabella had schooled herself to keep fixed on her face the expression of sullen resentment she had been wearing all day. But when she heard the unmistakable sound of the police cars drawing up, her facial muscles relaxed in a grin of triumph and she hurried to the window to watch.

Oh, what a sweet sight, she rejoiced. A few moments ago *Ossewa Brandwag* members had been strutting about arrogantly in their "uniforms" which consisted of trousers held up by a wide belt and tucked into leggings, a bandolier strapped across the chest and a wide-brimmed hat with one side tilted upwards to the crown, so that the men resembled as closely as they could the burghers who, at the turn of the century, had fought in the Anglo-Boer War. But now they did not look in the least like burghers as they ran ignominiously towards their cars or trucks or horses, colliding with one another in their frenzy to flee before the police could identify or arrest them. In their panic they were totally unaware of the fact that the dozen or so policemen who had arrived were idly standing by, watching them with derisive amusement.

Within the space of minutes, the large fire which had been built for the *braaivleis* illuminated only the figures of Pierre and Daan and the policemen. Most of the policemen returned to their cars and sat there, waiting, while three of

394

their colleagues talked to Pierre and Daan. A short while later Sabella could see the five men approaching the house and she arranged her own expression into one of nervous bewilderment.

As soon as the men entered she recognised the accusation in Pierre's eyes. *You bitch*, it said. *This is your doing.* But he had obviously decided that if he was to be brought down he would drag Sabella with him, for he said with the urgent intimacy of a co-conspirator, "My dearest, someone informed on us. Captain le Grange here says they received an anonymous telephone call about the *braaivleis* being held here tonight."

His glance had gone to a man of middle years, whose bearing was one of authority, his eyes sharp and intelligent. Sabella studied Captain le Grange with surreptitious interest. His expression was polite, and if he still suspected that it was she who had made the anonymous telephone call, he did not show it.

"I didn't see them arresting anyone," she told Pierre. "Do they intend arresting you because you organised the *braaivleis*?"

"No," Captain le Grange answered for her. "Not for organising the event, Mrs le Roux. But if my men should find evidence that anyone in this household has been involved in acts of sabotage or subversion, that would put a different complexion on things."

"Oh. That sounds as if you intend searching the house?"

"I'm afraid so. We'll try to inconvenience you as little as possible. I should like you, Mrs le Roux, and your husband and your brother each to partner one of us so that there'll be no question, in the event of incriminating evidence being found, that it could have been planted by a member of the police."

"You'll be wasting your time," Pierre said with a scornful shrug as he went off with one of the policemen, while Daan accompanied another. Her brother had said nothing at all since he'd entered the house with the other men.

Sabella found herself paired with Captain le Grange.

"What, exactly, are you looking for?" she asked, since it seemed the obvious question to put in the circumstances.

"We don't know, Mrs le Roux." He paused, and added smoothly, "Perhaps *you* do?"

She gave him a guileless look. "If you don't know, why on earth should I?"

The search was extremely thorough. Strong torch-light reinforced that given off by the lanterns suspended from the ceiling beams as mealie meal was tipped out of sacks by le Grange, then flour and sugar, which was only funnelled back into the containers after having been minutely inspected. The cold ashes were raked out of the kitchen range and then the stove itself was taken apart and every conceivable hiding place searched.

Captain le Grange was just beginning to clear everything out of the kitchen dresser when Daan and his accompanying policeman entered the room. Daan looked as if he were about to burst into tears, but the policeman said triumphantly, "We've found it, Captain!"

"Let me see." Captain le Grange took the letter from his subordinate, holding it by an edge between thumb and forefinger as he read it, and Sabella forced herself to make her expression one of tense bewilderment.

"It seems a little unnecessary to ask," Captain le Grange commented, "but where did you find it?"

"Inside a pocket of a pair of trousers hanging in a wardrobe. The wardrobe was in the bedroom young Mr van Renselaar told me is the one occupied by his sister, Mrs le Roux, and her husband when he is at home. For obvious reasons, Mr le Roux himself is overseeing the search of the room occupied by Mr van Renselaar and his brother."

"Call them in here," le Grange ordered.

While they waited, Sabella decided to ask the question any anxious wife would put in a situation like this. "What is the letter about, Captain? And who wrote it?"

"Let us just say," le Grange responded, "that the letter is of an incriminating nature. Ah, here is your husband now." The captain held the letter out so that Pierre could identify it and – coincidentally – read it. "You don't have to say anything at this stage, Mr le Roux, but it is fairly obvious that this letter was addressed to yourself."

"I've never seen it before in my life," Pierre said slowly, his voice dazed.

"And naturally, you have never heard of Robey Leibbrandt?" Captain le Grange suggested with irony.

"I've *heard* of him, of course. Who hasn't? I've never met him, let alone helped him to bring anything in from Mozambique!" Pierre's voice turned shrill with panic and anger. "The letter is a forgery, and your man *must* have planted it when Daan wasn't looking!"

"Handwriting experts will soon establish – " Captain le Grange began, but at that moment Pierre grabbed the letter from him and began to tear it to pieces. With lightning speed the two policemen rushed forward and held him in restraint while le Grange picked up the scraps of the letter.

"I was about to add," the captain told Pierre serenely as he straightened up, "that fingerprint experts would also establish whether or not you had ever handled the letter. But what you've just done will make it pointless to call in such experts, and when the letter has been patched together it will be offered in evidence against you. I must add that your attempt to destroy the letter will be seen as an admission of guilt."

A moment of total silence followed, with Pierre looking stunned by the realisation of his own folly, and Daan more than ever as if he were about to burst into tears. Sabella tried to remove any vestige of expression from her face. The question of fingerprints had never entered her mind, and she could only thank whatever benign providence had moved Pierre to act as he had. There would be no question, now, of anyone else's fingerprints being taken – prints that would have been found to match her own on the letter and also Anton's, but not a single one of Pierre's.

Moving with the jerkiness of a clockwork toy whose spring was running down, Pierre accompanied the police to where their cars were lit up by the still-burning out-door fire. Sabella stood watching through the window and thought with stony unforgiveness and not a trace of guilt: that's for poor Nantes, Pierre, for corrupting Anton, for turning Daan into a gutless puppet, and for every act of cruelty towards Katrien. But most of all it's for what you did to Ria.

"Sabella," she heard Daan's voice, hoarse and shaky, and turned. Her brother stared at her with wet, accusing eyes. "That letter had been written to *Anton*. He was so proud of it that he showed it to me, and if Daddy had been here he'd have shown it to him as well."

"The letter was addressed to someone called le Roux," she stated flatly. She would never, she vowed, admit to a single soul during her entire life that she had planted false evidence and plotted Pierre's arrest for something of which he was innocent.

"You know as well as I do that Anton had been calling himself le Roux for some time!" The accusation in Daan's eyes hardened. "You found that letter among his things, and you put it inside one of Daddy's pockets. And you arranged for the police to come and search the house."

"You're talking nonsense. Anyone in the district who opposes the *Ossewa Brandwag* and who knew about the *braaivleis* could have alerted the police anonymously. As for the letter itself – if Pierre was innocent, why did he try to destroy it?"

"He acted in panic. You betrayed him, Sabella, and I don't think I'll ever be able to forgive you for it."

"If, as you say," Sabella put to him, "the letter had been addressed to Anton, then why didn't you tell that to the police?"

Daan's glance flickered away from hers. He didn't have to give her an answer, because she knew it in advance. He had been too afraid to climb down from his safe position on the fence and commit himself.

"Anton will come home, and tell the police himself," Daan answered at last. "He explained to me once that there's a secret network by which messages are passed from one *Stormjaer* to another. It won't be long before he learns about what has happened, and he'll come and confess. He'd do anything for Daddy."

Sabella knew her brother was right. She could only pray to that capricious God who sometimes listened but more often ignored her pleas that no one would believe Anton's confession. She lay awake that night, worrying about the glaring probability she had so totally overlooked when she planned Pierre's downfall.

The next morning Daan was terse with her, speaking to her only when it was necessary. He refused to take the truck and visit farms to buy more stock for butchering, saying instead, "I'm going to drive to Johannesburg and see if they'll allow me to visit Daddy. There'll be things he'll need."

I've lost you too, Sabella thought sadly, as she watched him leave. Even if you never climb down from that safe fence of yours, I know you'll never be my baby brother again either.

Later she heard a motor approaching the smallholding, and frowned. The hum of its engine was too smooth for it to be Daan and besides, it was hardly likely that he would have changed his mind about going to Johannesburg and turned back. Perhaps Captain le Grange was calling on her to take a statement, she decided, and she squared her shoulders, mentally preparing herself to lie and eventually commit perjury.

But her visitor was Bastian. He must have come because Captain le Grange had told him about the result of the police raid. With a fast-beating heart, Sabella went outside to meet him. Would she be able to hide her secret from Bastian, and lie her way out of what she had done?

She joined him where he had stopped to stare at the ash and pieces of charred wood left over from last night's *braaivleis*. The vultures had long since swooped to devour every scrap of left-over meat. "You – heard?" she questioned Bastian tentatively.

He nodded. "Captain le Grange telephoned me early this morning and told me what had happened. Some sixth sense prodded him into searching the house."

Sabella was giving mental thanks to the police officer for having kept to himself the fact that an anonymous caller had suggested a search of the house, and that he suspected it to have been herself. Then she chanced to look at Bastian.

His unmatching eyes were telling her, as clearly as it was possible to convey a message without words, that he knew she had been planning Pierre's arrest even as she sat in his office, that he didn't condemn her, and that the matter would never be referred to between them.

A surge of love for him flowed through her as their eyes locked. At last he ended the unspoken, intense communication between them by breaking the silence. With heavy irony, he said, "According to le Grange, your husband was immediately accorded celebrity status at Marshall Square gaol as word reached the inmates – and not a few of the warders – of his connection with Robey Leibbrandt."

"Pierre has always wanted to be regarded as a hero," Sabella shrugged, "but he'll obviously reject this particular claim to fame at his trial – "

"He won't be tried in open court, if at all," Bastian interrupted. "Under the emergency powers, he'll be held without charge for a period while they question him, and then he'll be sent to one of the internment camps. Or, of course, they'll release him if they should decide he is innocent."

Sabella digested this information with mixed feelings. She hadn't relished the thought of a trial, with herself having to give false evidence under oath, but the alternative – that Pierre might be released – would be bitterly unwelcome, particularly if it happened as a result of Anton confessing to his own guilt.

It must have been the telepathic communication that existed between them that made Bastian say, "There's little chance that they'll decide Pierre is innocent. He damned himself when he tried to destroy that letter."

Impulsively, she put her arms about his neck, feeling the hardness of his body as she moulded herself against him, and parted his lips in a deep kiss. He held her in a fiercely-responding embrace for a moment, and then pushed her away so roughly that she almost lost her balance.

"Damn you, Sabella," he said in anger and frustration. "Just because it's not possible for matters to develop into a '*Bastian, no!*' situation, with Katrien in the house, you offer me the kind of temptation that's hard for any man to resist, let alone one who loves you!"

"I'm sorry. You're right; it was unfair of me . . ." Her voice trailed off and her eyes narrowed. "What did you mean about Katrien being in the house?"

"Well, I hardly imagine she'd have gone off in the truck with your brothers!"

"No, of course not. I don't know what you're talking about. Why should – "

"Are you saying," Bastian interrupted sharply, "that she didn't arrive home yesterday?"

As the full sense of what he had been saying struck her, terror snaked through Sabella and she asked through suddenly frozen lips, "Isn't she – with Louis and Maria le Roux?"

"No." Anxiety etched lines on Bastian's forehead. "She left Johannesburg for Goedgesig yesterday morning. I wanted to bring her home myself, but she showed me five pound notes and insisted she would rather take the train to Uitspan village and walk from there." He added, "She promised to come straight home. I had no reason to suspect she wouldn't. She had more than enough money for the fare." He made a thwarted, angry sound. "If it had not been for the money, I could have *forced* her to accept a lift home from me."

Thoughts had begun to scrabble through Sabella's brain, reminding her of chickens running senselessly from one end of a coop to the other in frantic efforts to solve the riddle of finding a way out. Katrien was not safely under the roof of Louis and Maria le Roux. She had promised to take the train to Uitspan yesterday morning, but she hadn't arrived at home. Why? *And where was she?*

Sabella felt Bastian taking her arm, and heard him say, "Let's go inside."

One foot before the other, she tried to encourage herself, fighting the swirling dizziness which threatened to suck her into its centre. Just place one foot before the other and you'll make it . . . Even so, she needed Bastian's arm about her, steadying her and propelling her towards the house.

He made her sit down by the kitchen table. "Now hold on to yourself and don't panic." She heard his voice, which struck her ears as if it were being distorted and shredded by fierce gusts of wind. "It *was* only yesterday morning that she called to see me. It's not as if she has been missing for days. With hindsight, I believe she must have decided to stay overnight with a friend, because I'd mentioned the *braaivleis* Pierre was organising for his *Ossewa Brandwag* cronies. It's obvious that she felt she couldn't face it, and decided to take the train today. She will almost certainly turn up here any moment now."

Sabella gripped the edge of the table so that the sharpness of the wood bit into her palms. "Katrien – went to see you," she repeated, a part of her mind thinking how stupid she sounded, like a child unable to grasp a simple mental sum.

"Like mother, like daughter, I thought at the time." Bastian was, she knew, deliberately trying to make his voice sound light and reassuring. "I was flattered. Each of you arriving in turn at my office to ask my help and advice."

"Bastian." Sabella's voice came out so strong and calm that she could barely believe it was herself speaking, this woman who was cracking into pieces inside. "Bastian, stop treating me like a child. *Why* did Katrien go and see you?"

"She was unhappy at school, and didn't know what to do about it – "

"No. There had to be more. Much more."

Bastian was silent. There was a deeply troubled note in his voice when he did decide to speak. "She made me promise not to repeat what she'd come to tell me."

"*She's missing, damn you!*" Sabella screamed, her control slipping away.

"Not missing; just late." But Bastian's correction lacked conviction.

"Why did Katrien go to see you? If she had any reason at all to want to come home, she had more than enough money for the train fare as you've pointed out yourself. I gave her the five pounds only a few days ago. Tell me why she went to see you!"

"I gave her my promise – " Bastian began.

"*She* promised *you* that she would come home, and she hasn't! *Tell me why she went to see you, Bastian!*"

Slowly, reluctantly, with deep emotion of some kind blurring his voice, he obeyed. "She was desperate to get away from the home of Louis le Roux, and she begged to be allowed to lodge with Annette and myself instead. I was forced to explain to her that Annette would never agree to it, and I urged her to go home."

"Desperate," Sabella repeated. "She was *desperate* to leave the house where she was lodging. Why? Did they mistreat her? Was Maria using her as a skivvy?"

But it had been far worse than that. As Bastian broke his promise to Katrien and recounted what had passed between the two of them, Sabella's reaction wavered between shock, self-blame, horror and a creeping disgust, and then back to the impotent terror of not knowing where her daughter was now.

Bastian was unable to spare her anything as he recounted how Louis le Roux had subjected Katrien to sexual abuse ever since she had gone to live under his roof.

"It started with him passing remarks which could also have been taken for those of a concerned adult towards a young person in his care," Bastian said. "He would make comments like: 'Are you sure you're dressed warmly enough, Katrien? There's a cold wind blowing outside.

Tell me what you're wearing underneath your gym-slip and blouse.' That kind of thing." Bastian broke off and muttered an oath. "Then it progressed to touching her – once again in such a way that he could claim an innocent show of affection if challenged. Katrien just didn't know what to do about it, whom to tell, or even if there really was anything worth telling."

"I can understand why she didn't tell Maria," Sabella said painfully. "But why didn't she tell *me* when I called to see her?"

"She decided that you had enough worries without her adding to them. And the incidents, at the beginning, sounded so trivial whenever she rehearsed them in her mind. Then Louis's wife became pregnant and started spending most of the day in bed, and slowly the abuse became more overt. Katrien told me that when he was on early duty it became her task to get up at four in the morning to cook his breakfast because Maria was taking so many pills and potions that she couldn't wake up before noon. And this was when Louis began exposing himself to Katrien, rubbing up against her, forcing her to touch him. When she threatened to tell Maria he smiled and said the Bible was full of texts about false witnesses and lying tongues, which made it plain that he would successfully deny everything if she went to Maria."

"Oh God," Sabella whispered, remembering how she had noticed the change in Katrien and blaming herself for not forcing her daughter to confide in her.

Bastian's voice took on a rasping note. "He also told Katrien that there were many different ways to bring sinners to salvation, and that he was acting as an instrument of the Lord by making her aware of the temptations of the flesh."

"The – slimy, disgusting hypocrite . . ." Sabella ground out.

"Indeed. On the one hand the poor child had Maria complaining that every day might be her last because of her pregnancy which, from the sound of it, is like no other pregnancy the world has ever known. On the other hand Katrien had Louis threatening her, preaching at her and frightening and confusing her. She didn't know where to turn."

"She could have turned to me," Sabella muttered. "But I was too busy, wasn't I, making money, doing deals, to do more than put the change in Katrien down to the fact that she was growing into a woman. I should have known instinctively."

"Should you?" There was unexpected anger in Bastian's voice. "Should you *really* have known by some kind of maternal instinct that Louis le Roux was making it clear to Katrien that when his wife went to hospital to have her baby, it would be her Christian duty to comfort him in bed? Should you have guessed that he was telling her she could only find salvation by yielding to the temptations of the flesh and afterwards praying for forgiveness? That he was claiming it was his duty as a lay-preacher to bring her to salvation in that way?"

The harshness of Bastian's voice, combined with the horror of what he had been saying, finally broke Sabella. She bowed her head over the table and began to weep. He rose and stroked her hair, and then he pulled her to her feet and held her. "Wash your face," he commanded after a while, "and we'll drive to the railway station in Uitspan and watch the Johannesburg trains as they arrive."

She nodded, and obeyed. But when they were on their way to the village, she asked tensely, "Shouldn't we go and see whether Katrien changed her mind and decided to stay where she was until Maria had to go to hospital?"

Bastian shook his head. "Katrien had already burnt her boats. She'd brought all her belongings with her when she called at my office. She'd left the house after Louis had gone on duty and before his wife was up. Katrien would have had to face too many awkward questions if she'd gone back."

Sabella nodded, and pressed her fingers against her throbbing temples. Something else occurred to her. "Did you tell Katrien about Ria? Because I can easily imagine her camping in the grounds of the institution until she's allowed to see her – "

"No," Bastian dashed that hope. "I judged it best that she should hear about it from you."

Sabella lapsed into fear-ridden silence. As they drove along the dusty main road of the ugly village of Uitspan part of her mind was aware that she and Bastian were the focus of everyone's attention. There couldn't be anyone left for miles around who remained unaware of the fact that Pierre had been arrested for helping Robey Leibbrandt in his mission to assassinate the Prime Minister, and while some were delighted at his downfall, just as many people sympathised with Pierre, and all of them were wondering what his wife was about, being driven in an expensive car by a well-dressed, handsome stranger. She didn't care. Desperate anxiety about Katrien and the anguished sense of having failed her daughter left room for nothing else.

Bastian parked at the side of the track from where they would have a view of everyone alighting from a Johannesburg train. Sabella's stomach muscles tensed and her mouth turned dry at the sound of the first train approaching, and when it stopped and none of the few passengers who stepped out onto the platform was Katrien, despair swept over her.

And so it went on for the remainder of that dreadful day. She and Bastian rarely spoke, but it was a silence of shared anxiety and unexpressed terrors. Once, Bastian broke it by asking, "Is there any possibility at all that someone might have – well – been a threat to Katrien *after* she'd arrived at the station, and before she could walk home?"

"None. Everyone here knows everyone else, as well as all their business, and if Katrien had stepped off a train here I would have heard of it within the time it would have taken her to walk home."

They relapsed into silence again, waiting for the next train. At last, when the sun had set, Sabella spoke with fierceness born of despair. "Did you give her more money,

Bastian? Enough money to enable her to – to do something stupid?"

"I did not!" His voice roughened. "She came to me in desperation to ask for a safe haven. Do you really think I would have been crass enough to offer her money instead?"

"No," Sabella conceded dully. "I'm sorry." She heaved a ragged sigh. "There's no point in waiting any longer. Katrien won't be coming now."

Bastian started the engine of his car in mute agreement, and drove the short distance back to the smallholding. The truck was drawn up outside the house and there were lanterns burning inside. Bastian opened the passenger door for Sabella, and said, "I'll be back early tomorrow morning. We'll start the search in Johannesburg." He touched her cheek in a gesture of comfort and love, and she put up a hand to lay it briefly on his.

After he had driven away she turned to enter the house. The sudden throught struck her that Daan might have come across Katrien wandering the Johannesburg streets and brought her home, and Sabella almost ran inside the house.

But it had been a forlorn and far-fetched hope. Her brother was alone, eating a fried egg sandwich he had made for his supper. "I've milked the goat and fed the hens," he said, and then frowned with frustration. "They wouldn't let me see Daddy; they wouldn't even agree to pass on to him the cigarettes and matches and razor blades I'd bought for him. I hope they'll tell him, at least, that I tried. I hope he won't be thinking I never even bothered." Daan added, on an afterthought, "Where have you been all this time, Sabella?"

"Katrien is missing," she said in a strained voice.

"What do you mean, missing? She's with Uncle Louis – "

"No." She went on to tell him what had happened.

When she had finished, he blurted out, "I don't believe it!"

"Do you mean that I'm lying, or that Bastian is lying, or

407

that Katrien lied? Or all three of us?" There was an edge to Sabella's voice which she could not control.

Daan frowned. "Well – I think Katrien must have imagined it all, or exaggerated some little thing that happened. I don't believe Uncle Louis would have done things like that."

"Because 'Daddy' is his brother, I suppose?" Sabella lashed out, her nerves ragged. She ought to have known better than to trust any relative of Pierre's, she thought bitterly. In their different ways, each brother was as corrupt and warped as the other . . .

"Well, yes, but only partly," she heard Daan's reply to her snide question. "Uncle Louis has a wife of his own, Sabella, and soon they're to have a baby and become a family, so why should he even think of wanting to do any of those things to Katrien or any other girl?"

Sabella stared at her brother as if she were seeing him for the first time. How could she have failed to recognise Daan's total lack of sexuality? She'd put his indifference to girls down to the fact that he'd been too busy trying to please Pierre to pursue the opposite sex, but it had never been as simple as that. Daan was like Hendrik used to be . . . No, that wasn't true either. In Hendrik's obsession with cleanliness, which had been his way of atoning for the guilt he had inherited from his mother, he had seen sex as the ultimate in dirtiness. But Daan's sexuality was like – like a newly-formed apple which had been blighted by an unseasonal sharp frost before it had had a chance to grow to maturity, so that it remained withered on the bough. And that was Pierre's fault too, and by association her own.

"Oh Daan," she said brokenly, dropping her face in her hands. "I'm sorry, I'm so sorry . . ."

She felt his hand on her shoulder, and heard him say awkwardly, "Don't cry, Sabella. It *was* very wrong of you to do such a terrible thing to Daddy, but I know why you did it. You should have trusted him, you know. He was hoping that the place where he sent Ria might find a way of curing her – "

"You don't understand." Sabella looked up, wiping her eyes. "You simply don't understand anything."

His intense frown told her that he was trying very hard to do so. "You meant you were sorry for believing such things about Uncle Louis," he said at last, his face clearing. "I'll go and see him tomorrow; I'm sure Katrien has gone back there – "

"No, she hasn't," Sabella interrupted, her voice sounding as defeated as she felt.

"Then I'll try again to get them to let me visit Daddy. He'll know what to do. He'll know where we should search for Katrien."

Sabella simply looked at him, this brother of hers whom she had formerly thought of as merely lacking in guts. The lack in him was so immeasurable that she couldn't even put a name to it. In a way he was a little like Ria, who had been born with a brain that was destined never to progress beyond the age of three. But Daan, who had been born normal, had been conditioned to retain the stunted development of a boy of eleven or twelve.

Sabella said good night to him and went to bed, knowing in advance that she wouldn't be able to sleep. *Where are you, Katrien?* The agonising question re-echoed in her mind. Bastian had talked about her spending the night with a friend. But to Sabella's knowledge, her daughter had made only one friend at school, Norma King, who lived with her aunt and whose own cousins shunned her because the colour of her skin and her crinkly hair shouted their family secret to the world. Perhaps their parents were less unkind; surely they must be, or they would not have taken Norma to live with them? But what if they weren't, and they resented the girl so much that they would refuse to shelter her only friend?

If it came to that, would *any* friend's parents agree to shelter a runaway schoolgirl?

19

Dawn streaked the sky with a flamboyant range of colours that seemed to mock the ugliness of the smallholding and the blackness of Sabella's despair.

Nothing could dissuade Daan from once again taking the truck to Johannesburg in an attempt to be allowed to visit Pierre in gaol. In the slim hope that Katrien might arrive at Goedgesig during the day, Sabella wrote a note to her, explaining that she and Bastian had gone to search for her, and left it propped up on the kitchen table.

When Bastian arrived he looked as if he, too, had spent a sleepless night. He caught Sabella's hands between his own and held them in a tight grip for a moment and then released them, saying, "The school first, I think."

"Yes."

They spoke hardly at all as he drove to Johannesburg. War aeroplanes streaked overhead like large but welcome birds of prey, and when the city had been reached Sabella noted automatically that beyond her own narrow but fear-ridden world the war was escalating. "GERMANS ADVANCE ON LENINGRAD," the posters screamed above the newspaper stands. She tried to think of all those mothers whose lives were blighted by this cruel war because their sons, little older than Katrien, were also missing and possibly dead, but it brought her no comfort.

At the English–medium school in Mayfair, the headmistress received Bastian and Sabella with polite curiosity. "I'm sorry I haven't visited you before to introduce myself," Sabella said. "I am Katrien le Roux's mother, and Mr Grant is her god-father."

The headmistress shook hands with them. "I take it that Katrien is sick," she said. "She has never been absent before. I do hope it's nothing serious."

"She isn't sick. She – " Sabella swallowed. "I'm afraid she has run away."

"Oh dear." The woman's distress was tinged with guilt. "I knew she wasn't very happy at school. Children can be so cruel. It was her Afrikaans name, coupled with the fact that she had previously attended only Afrikaans-medium schools. Her excellent command of English, strangely, seemed to deepen the resentment of the other pupils against her – "

"She did have one friend here, didn't she?" Sabella put in. "A girl called Norma King. Could we please speak to her?"

"I'm so sorry, Mrs le Roux. Norma left school as soon as she reached her sixteenth birthday, about three weeks ago."

"Oh." Sabella clutched the arms of her chair as she fought threatening faintness.

She heard Bastian say, "Could you please let us have Norma King's address? She might have been sufficiently in Katrien's confidence to know where she was likely to go once she had made up her mind to run away."

A short while later, armed with a scrap of paper on which the address had been written, Bastian supported Sabella back to his car and they drove the few blocks to the house of Norma King's aunt, Mrs Thomas.

She was a small, squat woman with sharp deep-set dark eyes like currants in a bun, and the lines about her mouth gave her face a bitter, hard-done-by look. As soon as she was asked about Norma she confirmed the impression given by those lines.

"That ungrateful girl! For sixteen years, Mr Grant, I have treated her like one of my own and do you think she repaid me with a little gratitude? Do you think that would have been too much to ask?"

"If we may talk to her – " Sabella began.

But Mrs Thomas had decided to address herself solely to Bastian, and she ignored Sabella. "She was my younger sister's only child. When Norma was born her father refused to believe she was his child, and he walked out on them. My sister couldn't face life on her own with a half-caste baby. A throwback, that's what Norma is. Way, way back in the family one of our ancestors married his black housemaid, but there'd been nothing like that since, and we'd all thought the strain had been bred out of the family. And then, out of the blue, there it was back – in Norma. Well, my poor sister killed herself."

"Oh," Sabella said faintly.

Mrs Thomas accorded her a moment's attention. "You may well say 'Oh.' So there was this baby with coloured skin and crinkly curls, and no mother or father to care for her, and I was forced to take her in. My mother wouldn't hear of her being sent to an orphanage and of course she stood no chance of being adopted by anyone. It was a great sacrifice, bringing her up, because it meant that my family had to live with the embarrassment of Norma. We, who had always been respectable, and English! I mean, it wouldn't have been so embarrassing for an Afrikaans family, because no one expects better from *them*. But to us she was a cross and a – "

"A cross!" Sabella could not stop herself from interrupting with heat. "Because she happened to *look* different, even though the same blood runs in her veins as that running in yours! It could so easily have been one of your own children who'd been born a throwback!"

Mrs Thomas, caught off guard, gave her a look that was totally revealing. Then, ostentatiously, she turned her back on Sabella.

"I'm sure you've done your best for Norma, Mrs Thomas," Bastian said pacifically, giving Sabella a warning glance. "If we may have a word with her – "

"Well, you can't. Just when she was old enough to be taken out of school and begin to repay a little of what she owes me, she cleared off! She hung around here, sulking, refusing to take a job in one of the factories where they employ coloured girls, and finally she just packed her things and left while I was out doing the shopping. Didn't even have the decency to leave a note, thanking me for what I'd done for her in the past!"

Bastian exchanged a significant glance with Sabella. "When did she leave, Mrs Thomas?"

"Day before yesterday."

Sabella took a deep breath. "My daughter also disappeared the day before yesterday, Mrs Thomas. Did Norma say or do anything to make you suspect that she'd planned to run away with a friend?"

Mrs Thomas gave her a sharp look. "So that's why you're here! I thought you might have been from Children's Welfare."

"No," Bastian took over the initiative. "*Did* Norma give any clue that she might be planning to go away with someone else?"

"I told you, she left without so much as a note."

"Where do you think she is now, Mrs Thomas?"

The woman looked him up and down. "Put yourself in the place of a coloured-looking girl who thought she was too good to go and work in a factory for coloureds. So what else is there?"

Bastian frowned and said nothing, and it was left to Sabella to form the question the woman was so obviously expecting. "What else, Mrs Thomas?"

"The streets," came the blunt reply, but once again those sharp, deep-set eyes gave her away.

Sabella cleared her throat to speak, and then decided against it. They took their leave of Mrs Thomas and returned to Bastian's car. "What a poisonous woman!" he exclaimed as they drove away.

"I couldn't help feeling sorry for her," Sabella admitted.

"*Sorry!*" Bastian echoed in disbelief.

"That story about the sister who'd killed herself and the mother who had refused to have Norma sent to an

413

institution – it was a lie. If the girl had truly been an unwanted burden Mrs Thomas's reaction would have been: good riddance! No Bastian, that long, bitter story was a well-rehearsed mask for the true feelings of a mother."

"You believe she is Norma's mother, and not her aunt?" he asked in astonishment.

"I'm sure of it. But poor Norma, the throwback, had to be disowned for the sake of the rest of her pure-white family. In our wretchedly unfair society the Thomas family could only cling to respectability by rejecting Norma and pretending she wasn't really one of them."

"But they kept her, and brought her up – "

"In their hearts, I'm sure her parents love her. But the only way they could save face was to distance themselves from her by claiming she was the orphaned child of a non-existent sister, and instead of becoming outcasts they earned people's admiration for having saddled themselves with such a 'burden'." Sabella made a sound of pity. "That woman is secretly as terrified for her daughter as I am for Katrien – " She broke off, and clutched Bastian's arm with a trembling hand. "The – what she said – about going on the streets. Do you suppose – ?"

"No!" Bastian forcibly rejected the unformed question. "Not Katrien, certainly. Lord, Sabella, she ran away because of what Louis le Roux was planning to do to her! Do you suppose for one moment that she might consider such a thing?"

Sabella drew a deep, uneven breath. "No. You're right." Clinging to small comforts, she added, "It's a little less frightening to know that Katrien isn't entirely alone, and that the two girls are together."

Bastian hesitated. "We can't be totally certain of that, Sabella. It might be a coincidence that they disappeared on the same day. If *you* lived in a household like Norma's and believed you were a dreadful burden and embarrassment to your family, and you didn't want to be forced into doing monotonous work in a factory, wouldn't you also reach the point where you'd want to run away?"

414

"So – you don't believe the two girls are together?" Sabella's voice shook.

He drew her against him and held her close. "They may be. Let's hope it's so. But don't let us become blinded by the assumption that they are together, because it might rule out other places in which to search for Katrien." He let Sabella go and added grimly, "Louis le Roux next."

"I want to speak to him alone, Bastian. I want you to wait in the car."

"Why?"

"Because you might make a violent scene."

"That's a mild description of what I have in mind," he said ominously.

"No! Whatever Louis has done, his wife is innocent, and pregnant, and I don't want to risk her going into early labour. So let me speak to him alone."

Grudgingly, Bastian agreed, and stayed behind the wheel of his car when they reached the house to which Sabella had directed him. Her heart beating sickeningly, she climbed the steps to the stoep. What if Louis were on duty? How on earth could she sit there for hours, and not let Maria guess what had happened to make Katrien run away?

But Louis answered the door, a Bible in one hand, not a flicker of guilt or apprehension on his face. "Come inside, Sabella," he said heavily. "We've been expecting you to call."

She followed him into the sitting room, where Maria was reclining on a sofa. She heaved herself into an upright position when she saw Sabella, and exclaimed, "If you've come to ask us to have that ungrateful daughter of yours back, the answer is no!"

"I would like to speak to Louis in private," Sabella said in a strained voice.

"There are no secrets between us," Maria declared grandly and with total inaccuracy.

"I want to speak to him in his capacity as a policeman," Sabella lied. "It's to do with Pierre – "

"We already know that he has been arrested and is being held in Marshall Square gaol," Maria said.

Louis touched the top of her head lightly. "I think, my dear, it might be best if I heard Sabella out in private. As a policeman, there may be something I could do to make Pierre's lot easier."

With exaggerated awkwardness and a great deal of groaning, Maria rose and lumbered across the room, saying in a suffering voice, "I'll put the kettle on for tea."

As soon as they were alone, and before Sabella could speak, Louis said, his fingertips self-importantly making a temple of his hands, "I have to admit to you that even *I* will be able to do very little to help my brother now that he has confessed. I'm not condoning what he did, Sabella, but – "

"*He has confessed?*" she repeated with astonishment, everything else temporarily wiped from her mind.

"Yes, indeed. And it's rather late in the day for you to concern yourself about what happens to him, since it's widely known that you were the one who arranged for the police to raid Goedgesig! Regardless of what he has done, Sabella, the Bible says this of a wife's duty toward her husband: '*She will do him good and not evil all the days of her life* – '"

"Don't you preach to me, you pious little toad!" Sabella cried. "I didn't come here about Pierre; he deserves to be where he is and *you* deserve to be in gaol with him! What you did to my daughter has made her run away, and I want to know if you have any idea where she might have gone!"

Louis held up a hand, his composure not shaken in the least. "When your daughter left here Maria and I naturally assumed that she had gone home. Indeed, we have been expecting some kind of apology from you on her behalf – "

"Apology!" Sabella almost choked on the word. "You – you hypocritical pervert! You told Katrien, practically in so many words, that when Maria goes into hospital

416

you intended to rape her – and *that* was after months of increasing sexual assaults upon her – "

"Really, Sabella, you would do well to guard your tongue! You are obviously repeating lies told to you by Katrien, and I shall forgive you on this occasion, because you are clearly not yourself. The truth is that Katrien was a very lazy young woman who resented having to do a share of the housework. She resented it more and more as Maria's pregnancy advanced and my wife was forced by her condition to ask Katrien to take over certain other duties – "

"Such as getting up at four in the morning," Sabella hurled at him, "and cooking your breakfast, which gave you the opportunity of exposing yourself to her and forcing her to touch you!"

"Sabella, Sabella!" Louis shook his head with saintly forbearance. "The heart of the matter lies in the fact that Katrien is a lazy girl who resented getting up at *any* hour of the morning, let alone the occasional times when she was asked to rise early and make breakfast for me. My, oh my! The times I have said to her: '*Go to the ant, thou sluggard; consider her ways, and be wise.*' But no, with Katrien it was always a case of, as the Bible has it: '*Yet a little sleep, a little slumber, a little folding of the hands to sleep.*' I cannot express to you the sorrow and the disappointment I feel at the news that Katrien has so wickedly attacked my good name to cover up her reason for running away. Indeed, had she not been a family connection of ours I would have thought seriously of taking some action for her to be punished and sent to a reformatory. I am not only a policeman, Sabella, but a lay-preacher too, and as such my unblemished reputation is very precious to me!"

Sabella struggled against the impulse to attack him physically. He watched her with a complacent piety that told her he knew as well as she did herself that there was no scrap of proof that he had sexually assaulted Katrien or threatened to seduce or rape her, and that even if Katrien were found it would still be the word of a schoolgirl against that of a policeman and a lay-preacher.

Sabella looked away from him and said tonelessly, "Please tell me if you have any idea where Katrien could have gone."

"How would I know, Sabella? A girl who is capable of thinking up such wicked lies – how could anyone possibly guess what else might be going on inside her impure mind?" He added maliciously, "As her mother, as a wife who has thrown her own husband to the wolves, *you* must be more capable than anyone else of divining the way in which Katrien's mind works."

Sabella stood up, her hands clenched into fists. "Wherever Katrien is," she said acridly, "she couldn't possibly be in greater moral danger than when she lived under the same roof as a slimy, filthy-minded, pious hypocrite like yourself!"

Louis shook his head sadly at her. "'*These things doth the Lord hate*,' Sabella," he quoted. "'*A lying tongue, an heart that deviseth wicked imaginations, feet that be swift in running to mischief and a false witness that soweth discord.*' The words are particularly apt about both Katrien and yourself. I shall pray for the two of you."

Sabella turned and ran from the room and from the house, for to have stayed would have led to an undignified and pointless physical scuffle between the two of them.

She remained incoherent with rage even after Bastian had started the car and they were driving away from the house. "Hypocrite!" she stammered. "Lecherous pig . . . Pervert! Hiding behind the Bible . . ." And then she burst into tears.

Bastian left her to cry out her fury and sense of impotence and her increasingly desperate worry about Katrien. But after a while he stopped the car and got out, and his surprise action stemmed the flow of her tears. She watched blearily as he entered a café and when he came out again he was carrying a cardboard box full of purchases.

"Buttered bread rolls, sliced sausage, cheese, fruit and

milk," he said. "I don't suppose you've eaten anything during the past twenty-four hours, and I guessed that you wouldn't want to lunch in a public restaurant. We'll have a picnic somewhere."

They found a spot, just outside Johannesburg, where blue-gum trees cast their shade upon patchy grass, and they ate their impromptu meal there. Sabella was surprised to discover how very hungry she had been, and she felt sufficiently strengthened, afterwards, to tell Bastian about her interview with Louis le Roux.

"He had been expecting me," she finished, "and had his story well rehearsed. He made my flesh crawl. Oh, Bastian, he should be made to pay – "

"Shh." Bastian placed his forefinger across her lips. "Give yourself a few moments' peace, Sabella. You'll drive yourself into a breakdown if you don't." As a deliberate diversion he threw a half-eaten bread roll to a hovering bird and asked, "What is it called? Do you know?"

Sabella glanced at the bird with its red breast-feathers and its cheekily tilted tail. "It's a *Piet-my-vrou*."

"Why is it called that? It doesn't make sense. It means 'Piet my wife,' but Piet is a man's name."

She smiled. "I know. But listen to it singing to its mate that there's food for the taking. Do you hear it? *Piet-my-vrou! Piet-my-vrou!*" she mimicked the bird.

"Mmm . . . To my English ears, it seems to be calling, 'Pick my bow! Pick my bow!'"

Sabella's briefly-lightened mood deserted her, and she said sombrely, "Everything comes back to the differences in our society, doesn't it? From our opposing ways of interpreting a bird's call, to *Stormjaers* plotting to blow up troop trains, and Katrien being ostracised at school for being Afrikaans, and her friend Norma for looking coloured . . ." Sabella shook her head, and suddenly remembered something else. "Louis le Roux told me Pierre has confessed that Robey Leibbrandt's letter *was* written to him!"

Too late, she realised her mistake in putting such emphasis on that one word. Whatever Bastian might guess about her own actions, he couldn't possibly know that the letter found among Pierre's possessions had, in fact, been written to Anton. She felt whatever colour might have been left in her face fading from it altogether. "I mean – " she began, trying to amplify what she'd said and the way she had said it, but Bastian stopped her by taking her hand in his.

He lifted it to his mouth and kissed her work-roughened palm. "I know what you mean," he said quietly.

She gazed into his eyes. Yes, of course he knew. Working with Government Intelligence as he did, it was inconceivable that he wouldn't have known Anton was a *Stormjaer* and a member of the National Socialist Rebels, that he had taken Robey Leibbrandt's Blood Oath, and that he was calling himself le Roux.

Bastian deliberately changed the mood between them by saying cynically, "Your husband found himself cast as a hero among the Fascists in gaol, and he enjoyed the adulation so much that he willingly confessed to links with Robey Leibbrandt. No one will ever be able to take that away from him now."

Yes, Sabella thought with an ironic twist to her lips. For years Pierre had been relying on her to make him the fortune he needed so that he would achieve importance and stature. She hadn't provided that fortune, but she *had* given him the importance he craved – by having him arrested for a crime he hadn't committed. With his ability to believe his own lies, it was only too probable that he had convinced himself, by now, that he *had* been one of Robey Leibbrandt's right-hand men.

Then the thought of Katrien re-entered her mind, leaving room for nothing else, weighing her down again. "Bastian, do you think the two girls could have taken jobs in one of Johannesburg's factories?"

"I doubt it. Norma King resisted the pressures of her so-called aunt to go and work in a factory, and if the girls *did* run away together it's not likely that they would have been able to get work in the same factory. Katrien might have been accepted for the job of helping to make munitions, but Norma, with her half-caste appearance, would have been absorbed into one of the factories employing coloured workers. Still, I'll have enquiries made at all the factories and the youth hostels. But, as I warned you before, Sabella, we must not rule out the possibility that it might have been pure coincidence that the two of them ran away on the same day."

Sabella spoke in a small, defeated voice. "What you're also saying is that even if they did run away together, they would have been parted by this society of ours which won't allow a white girl and one with the looks of a half-caste to cling to one another for safety and comfort."

"Yes." Bastian still had her hand in his and now he twined his fingers through hers in a gesture that said: we are together in this, it's my pain and anxiety as much as yours. Aloud, he asked her, "Is there anywhere you know of that Katrien particularly liked, a place to which she might have returned? One of those farms or villages where you previously lived, and where she had made close friends? Remember, she had five pounds, and she could have travelled quite a distance with a sum of money like that."

How bitterly Sabella now regretted that generosity of her own birthday present to Katrien. She shrugged the thought aside and considered. "I can't think of anywhere. We lived such a nomadic life and there was never time for any of us to make close friends . . . *Mooikrantz!*" she exclaimed, interrupting herself. "Pierre once made a detour to take us there, and Katrien fell in love with it on sight! She often said how much she would like to live there!"

Bastian rose, pulling Sabella to her feet as well. "Tomorrow morning we'll set out for Mooikrantz." He held her for a while, and the comfort and strength of his embrace filled her with a surge of optimism. Katrien would be at Mooikrantz.

He drove Sabella home to Goedgesig, and left her there. She found Daan moodily cleaning out the hen-house. "They still wouldn't allow me to see Daddy," he volunteered, and added on an afterthought, "Have you found out anything about Katrien, Sabella?"

"No," she said, and added mentally, but tomorrow I shall. She *will* be at Mooikrantz. I can so easily imagine her taking the train to Stilstroom, and then begging a lift to the farm, and asking the present owners to let her work for her keep because Mooikrantz had once been her family's home . . .

Cheered by the certainty that Katrien would be found safely on Mooikrantz, Sabella was able to pick up the pieces of her life and begin to plan for the future. "You must take the truck soon, Daan," she said, "and buy stock for us to butcher for the Johannesburg shops."

"But Daddy – " Daan began.

"Will still need the capital we're saving for him for when the war ends," Sabella lied. There was no point in telling Daan that Pierre had confessed to a crime he hadn't committed, and no point, either, in letting him know that she intended vanishing with half of the money and with Katrien, long before Pierre would be free and in a position to get his hands on everything she had worked so hard to earn and save. She would divide the money equally between herself and Daan, for he had worked equally hard, and what he chose to do with his share would be his own affair.

"I doubt if farmers who are members of the *Ossewa Brandwag*, or who sympathise with them, would sell stock to us," Daan continued to look on the black side.

"Then we'll buy from farmers who oppose the *Ossewa Brandwag*," Sabella told him briskly.

"There's something else you haven't thought of," Daan pointed out, almost triumphantly. "The *Ossewa Brandwag* people around here hate you now, and they'll pay you back for what you did to Daddy by telling the police that you're illegally supplying meat to Johannesburg butchers!"

"Nonsense!" Sabella dismissed the prediction with scorn. "They have no idea that what we've been doing is illegal.

You didn't know it before Meneer Visagie explained that all meat sold through retail outlets is supposed to have been passed by government inspectors. Stop being such a Jeremiah, Daan, looking for trouble where none exists."

"Well, if you say so," he gave in. "But I'll wait a few days, in case they allow me to see Daddy after all."

Sabella thought sadly of Pa, and wondered what he would have made of his last-born's slavish devotion to the totally unworthy man who had adopted and ruined him. But thinking of Pa offered nothing but discomfort, for it reminded her of how she had failed both him and Ma where her other brothers and sister were concerned. She put the thought behind her, and began to prepare supper so that she would be able to go to bed early.

That night optimism and exhaustion allowed her to sleep soundly, and she woke up in the morning feeling refreshed and confident. She washed herself with water boiled on the kitchen range and put on her best print dress, and she had just finished brushing her unfashionably curly red-brown hair when Bastian arrived to collect her for the drive to Mooikrantz.

"I'm sure that's where we'll find Katrien," she shared her conviction with Bastian as they set off. "She has probably told the owners that she's an orphan and alone in the world."

Bastian made no comment, and she lapsed into silence, watching the countryside alter as they reached the rocky outcrops which meant that they would soon be driving through Stilstroom. Sabella remembered the very first time she had come this way with the children, and how frightening and strange everything had seemed, and now it felt like going home.

She laughed as a group of four *meerkatte* suddenly stood upright on their hind legs, turning their questing heads from side to side, and when she caught sight of several springbuck leaping in the air Nantes's voice returned to her from the past, explaining, "What they're d-d-doing is called *p-p-p-pronking*." Tears blurred her eyes and she wiped them surreptitiously away. She could not cry forever for Nantes.

People in the village of Stilstroom recognised Bastian and herself, and waved to them as they drove past. "The village seems half-deserted," she commented.

"Probably because it *is* half-deserted," Bastian said. "So many of the younger men have either joined up, or else they have moved with their families to Johannesburg where work is suddenly available to men and women alike, even when they have few skills. There has been an exodus from small farms as well, for the same reasons."

As he spoke he turned the car off the main road where the giant blue-gum trees grew, and there it lay before them – Mooikrantz, with the jagged hills towering over the farm-house and the fields. Bastian stopped the car suddenly.

"I've – never been back before," he said, his voice hoarse. "I've wanted to, but never had the courage. It – it haunts me, Sabella. As time has gone by the past has haunted me more and more."

"Tante Wilhelmina?" she asked gently. "Your true mother?"

"Partly." He stared straight ahead, his hands clutching the steering wheel. "The far-away memory of being made to leave with a strange lady who wore a dead dog around her neck . . . And then coming back, and finding you here, my cousin, my life-time's love . . ." He turned in his seat and reached for her, holding her in a hard, painful embrace. "I can't face going further, Sabella. The house contains too many memories. The times we spent together, the stolen moments, the impossible dreams and then the killing of all hope. Only concern for Katrien could have brought me this far, but even for her I can't go on. You'll have to go alone and walk from here."

"No." She clutched his hands tightly in hers. "This – this is probably the worst possible time to tell you, and I don't suppose you'll ever forgive me. You have to come with me, Bastian, because – because Katrien is your daughter."

She felt him react as if a bolt of lightning had passed

through him. The pupils of his oddly-coloured eyes were dilated as he stared at her. *"Mine?"* he whispered.

"My marriage to Hendrik was never consummated. He died without knowing that I was pregnant, and I allowed everyone to take it for granted that he had fathered the baby I was expecting." Sabella's mouth began to shake. "You can – hate me, curse me, cast me off entirely – but you must help me to – bring your daughter home. It's your duty – as well as your right."

He said nothing, and it was impossible to read his expression. After what seemed an eternity he withdrew his hands from Sabella's and switched on the engine of the car, but his driving was erratic in a way that had nothing to do with the potholes in the unmade-up track as he steered the car towards the farmhouse.

From their ledge on the hills the baboons barked excitedly, almost as if they had recognised Sabella as an old friend and were welcoming her back. A young woman appeared on the stoep and watched them with curiosity. Bastian got out of the car and opened the door for Sabella, but he said nothing at all and it was still impossible to know what he was thinking.

Sabella's eyes darted everywhere for signs of Katrien as she climbed the steps of the stoep and held out her hand to the young woman. "My name is Mevrou le Roux," she said in Afrikaans, "and this is my cousin, Bastian Grant. You are – ?"

"Mevrou Lena Marais," the woman introduced herself. "Please come inside."

Even in her preoccupation with Katrien, Sabella was aware of the ghosts as they stepped over the threshold into the front room of the farmhouse. *That* was where Hendrik's coffin had rested and Tante Bessie – long since dead – had wanted her to kiss his lips and the falsely charming Pierre had stopped her. Just along the corridor was the room which had been Tante Wilhelmina's, and in which Katrien had been conceived . . .

"If you wouldn't mind coming into the kitchen," Lena Marais said, "I could make coffee and offer you a slice of *melktert*."

Since she was already leading the way to the kitchen there was little Sabella and Bastian could do but follow her. And oh, how those ghosts were multiplying and crowding around them . . .

"Mevrou Marais," Sabella said abruptly and urgently, "I'm looking for my daughter Katrien, and I feel sure she would have come here, offering to work for her keep – "

"*Here?*" the woman interrupted with a snort of bitter laughter. "Why on earth would a young girl want to come to this dead-and-alive place?"

Sabella felt as if her heart were a blown-up paperbag which had suddenly been burst by a clenched fist. "She – this was her family home once," she insisted desperately. "She *must* have come here. She's sixteen years old, with streaky blonde hair like – like my cousin's, and green eyes – "

"No one like that has been here," Lena Marais said flatly. "If it comes to that," she added with bitterness, "apart from yourselves, no one has set foot on Mooikrantz for months. I've been left here to rot while my husband is busy playing soldiers up north. I didn't want him to join up; as a farmer he could easily have been given an 'On Service' badge to show that he was a key worker, but he wouldn't listen."

Her grievances continued to spill out as Sabella drank coffee she didn't want, and made an occasional vague sound, while Bastian continued to say nothing at all and hid his feelings behind an impenetrable mask. However unresponsive her audience might be, Lena Marais was determined to keep them captive for as long as she could.

She described how she and her husband had been married soon before the declaration of war, and how it had always been his decision to farm while she had hankered after life in a town or a city.

"During all the years when I was growing up on a farm," she went on sourly, "I promised myself I would

426

escape to an easier life one day, some place where people outnumbered animals. And what happened? Here I am again, on another farm, with hardly any help and the only neighbours too old to get about and come visiting! Well, I'm not putting up with it for much longer. I'm writing to my husband and telling him that unless he allows me to put the place on the market I'll just walk away from it and let the baboons take over!"

At last Sabella could endure no more, and she stood up, cutting through a renewed list of grievances. "Thank you for the coffee, Mevrou. I'm – sorry we came here on a fool's errand."

"Have some more coffee," the woman urged, obviously desperate for company, but Sabella refused with thanks while Bastian simply turned to the kitchen door. It occurred briefly to Sabella to give her address to Lena Marais in case Katrien should still decide to come to Mooikrantz, but then she rejected the idea. Katrien would either have come here immediately, or else it had not even occurred to her to do so. When she left Bastian's office that morning with five pounds in her pocket she must have had a definite destination in mind, but it hadn't been Mooikrantz after all.

Still in total silence, Bastian began to drive away from the farm. When the blue-gum trees had been reached and Mooikrantz was hidden from sight by them, he stopped the car and drew it up into the shade of the trees.

Sabella braced herself for the full force of his fury, but it didn't come. His elbow was on the steering wheel, his chin resting on his hand and he stared ahead of him. Her own despair at finding that the hope to which she had been clinging with such certainty had had no substance transmuted itself into rage instead.

"Say it, Bastian!" she hurled at him, cutting through the silence. "Ask me how I dared to lie, and keep it from you that Katrien is your daughter until now, when she's missing! I was a widow, and pregnant, and then I learnt that you had married Annette. When you forced your way back into my life you were so reckless, so uncaring of the

427

consequences of your actions that I couldn't risk telling you the truth about Katrien. You would have used her as a weapon in your campaign to make me live in sin with you, no matter who might be hurt by it! And if all else failed, I knew you would have fought me for custody of Katrien!"

"Yes," he said, turning his head towards her, and she saw the brightness of unshed tears in his eyes. "Yes, I would have fought you – *then*. But now – dear God, if we were to find her tomorrow I wouldn't even be able to acknowledge her as my daughter, because the shock of it might cause Mother to have another stroke, which might kill her. Believe me, I've been forced to understand why you kept it a secret from me. But – "

He stopped, and put his hands to his face. "She came to me, *my daughter*," he went on, his voice blurred and tormented, "because she was desperate. And all I did was offer to drive her to Goedgesig. The fact that she hadn't gone straight home, but instead had come to see me should have warned me that she hated or feared Pierre le Roux. She asked for my help and I failed her . . ."

Sabella reached up and drew his head down to her breast, stroking his hair as if he were a child in pain. "You did what you thought was best at the time. Indeed, what else could you have done? Even if you had known she was your daughter you wouldn't have had the legal right to make any decision about her future. So stop blaming yourself, Bastian. Instead, take comfort from the fact that when she found herself in a desperate situation, *you* were the one to whom she thought of turning."

He sat up and took her hands, holding them palms downwards against his heart. "Yes." His voice roughened with emotion. "Thank you for my daughter, Sabella. Thank you for being wise and strong during all those years when I was reckless and hot-headed and couldn't see beyond the need to be with you." He brought her hands to his mouth and kissed each fingertip in turn. When he spoke again his voice was iron-hard. "I'm going to find her, Sabella. I'm going to find our daughter."

428

He set the car in motion again and as he drove Sabella back to Goedgesig he talked about his plans for searching for Katrien. The police would be kept out of the matter, both of them agreed. Apart from the fact that the overworked police were not likely to waste much effort on finding a girl who had obviously disappeared of her own free will, there was the danger that if it became an official matter and the police *did* find her, she might be sent to a reformatory. Instead, Bastian would engage private investigators and every factory, every shop or office that might have given employment to a girl of sixteen with no skills or qualifications would be targets in the search for Katrien. "The five pounds you had given her would have been enough to pay for a month's board and lodging in advance, and left her with sufficient change for such things as tram fares. I'll find her," he reiterated.

When he dropped Sabella on Goedgesig he declined her invitation to come inside, and then said abruptly, "Could you let me have the adoption certificate naming Pierre as her father?"

"He waited until after her birth, and then adopted all the children at the same time, so the names of my brothers and sister are on it as well. Why do you want it, Bastian?"

"It might help to find her – " He stopped, and shook his head with a rueful grin which did not hide the look of yearning in his eyes. "No, that's not true. I want to find out if there is any legal way in which she can stop being the adopted daughter of Pierre le Roux." His tone hardened. "I may not be able to acknowledge her as my own, but at least I could try to stop him from having any future control over her."

Since it was something Sabella also passionately longed for, she hurried inside the house and collected the adoption certificate Pierre had handed her sixteen years ago as if he were presenting her with the moon. And in her folly and ignorance at the time, she had felt that he *was* handing her the moon . . .

She shrugged the futile thought aside and hurried to give

the certificate to Bastian, who was waiting in his car. She watched him driving away at speed, impatient to begin the search for Katrien, and heard Daan's voice from behind her on the stoep.

"They said I could see Daddy tomorrow, Sabella!" he told her excitedly.

She was still wondering whether she should break it to him that Pierre had made a confession of guilt when Daan went on, "There's a letter for you on the kitchen table. I stopped by the post office on the way home. It's from Katrien."

Her heart hammering, she flew into the kitchen. The postmark on the envelope was that of Johannesburg, which didn't mean much. With shaking hands Sabella opened it and withdrew a single sheet of paper.

"Dear Mammie," Katrien had written, "I'm sure Uncle Bastian will have told why I had to leave the house of Louis le Roux. I know I made Uncle Bastian promise to keep it a secret, but I also know you would have wormed it out of him.

"Please, dear Mammie, don't worry about me. You'll understand why I couldn't do what Uncle Bastian wanted, and go home. I knew if I did, Derrie would just carry on using me whenever he wanted to punish you. I've never minded any of the things he did to me nearly as much as I minded you having to stand by and suffer without being able to do anything about it. Don't be angry with me, and please don't forget me, because when I'm twenty-one and Derrie won't have a say over me any more I'll fetch you and Tante Ria and we'll go and live on Mooikrantz together. Your loving daughter, Katrien."

Please don't forget me . . . Sabella cradled her head on her arms and wept for her daughter who had run away for the most unselfish of reasons, who would not have felt the need to run away at all if it hadn't been for Pierre. Sabella also wept for that naive, unworldly dream of Katrien's of rescuing her mother and her aunt from Pierre when she came of age, and somehow installing them on Mooikrantz.

430

Sabella wiped her eyes and reread the letter to check that there were no clues which she had overlooked. But there was nothing at all to give any indication of how Katrien meant to survive until she reached the magic age of twenty-one. If only it had been possible to let her know that Pierre was behind bars, and Ria in a mental institution . . .

The raucous sound of a motorcycle approaching cut through Sabella's thoughts and she put Katrien's letter in her pocket and waited for Anton to arrive. Daan came to join her, and Sabella saw the indecision in his eyes and knew the reason for it. Should he side with Anton during the coming storm, or with Sabella? She knew that, when it came to it, he would do neither.

The aggressive sound of the motorcycle died, and moments later Anton entered. He seemed to have grown in height and in physical strength since Sabella had last seen him. Ignoring Daan, he glared at her with hate-filled eyes.

"You treacherous cow!" he said malevolently. "I'd like to kill you! You stole a letter which had been written to me, and planted it among Daddy's possessions, and arranged for it to be found. I shall never forgive you for as long as I live!" His mouth worked, and his eyes glazed over with tears. "I went to Marshall Square to confess and give myself up so that Daddy would be set free. And do you know what he has done? To save me, he confessed to something of which he is totally innocent! And *that's* the kind of man you betrayed!"

"Anton, listen to me!" Sabella cried. "Your 'Daddy' didn't sacrifice himself for love of you! He confessed because he found himself being treated like a hero! I've no doubt he'll come to regret it, but at the moment he is revelling in being regarded, by fellow Fascists among the prisoners and warders, as a man who helped Robey Leibbrandt – "

"Shut your filthy, lying trap!" Anton bellowed at her. He moved past her and said over his shoulder, "I'm collecting my things. I never want to spend another night under the same roof with you!"

Sabella sat down heavily. Daan had fulfilled her expectations by keeping aloof during the exchange but now he began to weep. When he was able to speak he stammered, "If – if Daddy had confessed they – they will keep him interned for as long as the w-war lasts – "

"No, they won't!" The interruption came from Anton, who stood in the doorway with his possessions crammed inside a haversack. "We National Socialist Rebels will see to that!" He clicked his heels together and gave a salute which was similar to that of the Nazis but somehow subtly different, and cried, "*Die Vierkleur Hoog! Heil* Hitler!"

He picked up his haversack and made for the back door. Before he reached it Sabella asked urgently, "What did you mean, Anton, about the National Socialist Rebels seeing to it that Pierre won't be interned?"

Anton looked through her and addressed Daan. "Tell that traitorous bitch who used to be my sister," he said curtly, "that Daddy will be helped to break out of gaol. The husband whose boots she isn't fit to clean will soon be a free man."

As Sabella listened to the roar of his motorcycle a moment later she thought bleakly, I've truly lost them all. Oh Pa and Ma, forgive me . . .

20

Anton's boast that Pierre would be helped to escape from prison had not been an idle one, because only a few days later Bastian called at Goedgesig to tell Sabella and Daan the news.

"It happened during the night, and even though it can't be proved, there is no doubt that warders actively helped with the escape. We're supposed to believe that Pierre knocked out two warders, took the keys from one of them and let himself out. The truth is that it was all well planned and carefully staged, and Pierre was almost certainly met by *Stormjaers*, National Socialist Rebels who waited for him outside Marshall Square."

"Oh." Sabella tried to look and sound as if the news had come like a bolt from the blue, but a moment later Daan rendered any such effect pointless.

"Anton *said* Daddy would be helped to escape!" he cried jubilantly.

"Ah yes, Anton." Bastian's voice was quite neutral. "I'm afraid he has made something of a fool of himself – "

But Daan was not interested in his brother. "Daddy will find a way of arranging for me to meet him! I know it!"

"Hardly," Bastian dampened his indiscreet enthusiasm. "The betting is that he is at this moment on his way to being smuggled into Mozambique."

"Then he'll have written to me!" Daan exclaimed. "I'm going to the post office right away!"

When he had hurried outside, Sabella asked with a frown, "Why Mozambique, Bastian?"

"Pierre's stock rose sky-high while he was in gaol, because Robey Leibbrandt had a letter smuggled inside to him, expressing his warm thanks for Pierre's past support and calling him a martyr to the Cause whose work won't be forgotten when the new South African Republic is born." Sabella's astonishment must have shown, for Bastian went on evenly, "The letter was a gesture of bravado on Leibbrandt's part, a way of cocking a snook at the authorities. He must have learnt from his followers that Pierre had confessed to smuggling arms or ammunition across the border, and there are so many men who have taken the Blood Oath that Leibbrandt cannot possibly remember all their names. But that personal letter from him to Pierre means that your husband is considered important enough to be escorted over the border, and he'll be sitting out the war inside the German Consulate in Lourenço Marques, living in luxury and being fêted as a friend of the Führer."

Oh yes, Sabella thought as she digested the information, Pierre would be in his element. He would have all the status and the respect he had craved for so long.

Then she remembered something else. "What did you mean, Bastian, when you said Anton had made a fool of himself?"

Once again Bastian's voice held no expression as he explained, "Apparently, Anton went and confessed that the letter found in Pierre's possession had been written to himself. No one believed him, and his confession earned him a great deal of resentment among the supporters of the National Socialist Rebels in gaol. They saw it as an attempt to claim Pierre's role of hero for himself."

"I see. But – that hardly amounts to having made a fool of himself . . ."

"If the letter really had been written to Anton then his confession did him no good at all with the higher ranks of the National Socialist Rebels among the *Stormjaers*. If, that is," Bastian added smoothly, "he ever was one of them. Having drawn so much official attention to himself with his

434

confession, he'd be of little further use to them, because his movements will be monitored from now on. Once again, of course, assuming he had ever belonged to them in the first place."

Sabella looked at Bastian with love and gratitude. He had taken a circuitous route to assure her that he was not only arranging for a blind eye to be turned to her brother's past activities and involvements, but that Anton would be so closely watched in future that he would no longer be able to be used in plots of subversion or sabotage. With bitter irony, she acknowledged to herself that Anton would blame her further for the fact that he was being pushed out into the cold by his former compatriots.

She changed the subject by telling him about Katrien's letter, thankfully adding that he wouldn't be able to understand it since it had been written in Afrikaans. The time was not yet right for Bastian to learn how Pierre had used his daughter when he wanted to punish Sabella. "I know you would have told me," she added, "if your men had found any clues yet."

"Give them time." Bastian hesitated, and then went on, "I have other, unwelcome news for you, Sabella. I visited the mental institution to see if I could have Ria released on the grounds that the adoptive father who had arranged for her to be committed was in prison on serious charges. They sent for Ria, and she recognised me. Then they – insisted on a test . . ."

"What kind of test?" Sabella asked with foreboding as his voice trailed off.

Reluctantly, Bastian said, "They asked me to call her Pretty Ria. I did, and she – well, she reacted in the same way she had with Pierre. They said – and one can't really blame them for it – that she would not be safe in the outside world."

Sabella swallowed, and looked down at her hands. In such a short while the foundations of her own world had crumbled. Anton hated her, poor Ria would never

435

be allowed to come home again, and Katrien was God-knew-where. And all because of Pierre who, instead of being punished, would be living in luxury in the German Consulate across the border and treated as a hero.

Bastian rose, and pulled her to her feet. "I love you," he said with intensity, "and one day, I swear it, we'll be together – you and I and our Katrien." He kissed her with deep passion and then left her.

It was hard to see how he could possibly fulfil that rash promise, she thought dolefully. Even if Katrien were found, even if Bastian's mother died and could no longer be harmed by scandal, and Sabella herself divorced Pierre, Bastian would have to beggar himself if he walked out on his marriage to Annette. And how could she, Sabella, allow him to make such a tremendous sacrifice?

Daan returned from his trip to the post office. There had been a letter waiting for Sabella but it was not from Pierre or from Katrien, but from Louis le Roux. Liberally sprin-kled with quotations from the Bible, its message was never-theless clear. He and his sister Johanna had decided that in view of Sabella's treachery towards their brother, she was no longer welcome on their jointly-owned property, Goedgesig, and they were demanding that she leave it by the end of the month. After that date she would be regarded as a trespasser and would be dealt with accordingly.

She handed the letter to Daan to read. It was no use trying to pretend to herself that this was not another blow. Bleak and comfortless though the smallholding was, at least it had been rent-free and had enabled her to make money by butchering and selling meat. She stared into space, contemplating her uncertain future. She would have no trouble in finding employment in one of the factories in Johannesburg but *that* was not what she'd had in mind, all those years ago, when she had dreamt of proving her own value in the market place.

"Where will we go, Sabella?" she heard Daan ask with anxiety in his voice.

"We? *You* aren't being asked to leave. I'll give you half the money I've saved, and you could go on living here, buying stock and butchering them for the retail shops – "

"I don't fancy living on my own."

Sabella looked at him. He didn't want to cleave to her because he was her baby brother, but because he felt too inadequate to face a future in which he would have to take decisions and make commitments. "Daan," she said wearily, "the only alternative would be for us to rent a house in Johannesburg, and take jobs in factories."

"We could find work in the same factory," he suggested hopefully.

She sighed. "I'll take the truck tomorrow, and search for a house to rent in one of the suburbs."

Posters were everywhere when she drove through the city of Johannesburg the next morning, and all of them screamed: AMERICA DECLARES WAR ON GERMANY AND ITALY. Surely, Sabella thought, it must mean that this wretched war would soon be over, with America adding her might on the side of the Allies.

But whether or not the end of the war was now in sight, she found to her dismay as she drove through adjacent suburbs like Westdene, Newlands, Brixton and Mayfair that rented accommodation had become virtually non-existent. Not one single "to let" sign was to be seen anywhere. It was not difficult to work out the reason. As more and more small farmers had given up the land and migrated to Johannesburg to take advantage of the available jobs offering regular wages, they had also snapped up the houses for rent. Several of the more modern houses had built-on garages, and she saw evidence that people were sub-letting their vacant garages, and whole families were using the cramped space as living accommodation.

In the end Sabella decided that her only hope lay in paying an agent to find a house which she and Daan could rent. But the agent shook his head. "I'm sorry, madam. I don't have a single property on my books. If you would be prepared to *buy*, however – " He left the suggestion in the air.

"I couldn't afford that."

"There are several properties going for rock-bottom prices," he enticed her. "And remember, buying a house. means you'd be making an investment, instead of paying monthly rentals which disappear forever into the pockets of a landlord."

She decided there would be no harm in allowing the agent to drive her to see the houses for sale. It was immediately obvious why they were being offered at such apparent bargain prices.

"None of the houses you've shown me is habitable!" she told the agent angrily.

He shrugged. "The owners had previously let them to tenants, but hadn't spent money on upkeep, and the buildings have been condemned. But any one of those houses would make a good investment for the future, madam."

"I need a house in which to live *now*. None of those houses could even be repaired, because you know as well as I do that most building materials are unobtainable because of the war!"

"Well, yes, and that's why the houses are going for a song. I still say they'd make a good investment, but – " The man spread his hands. "I'll keep an eye open for rented accommodation for you, madam, but frankly, I'm not hopeful. If a house does become available these days, a new tenant hears about it on the grapevine before the owner has time to put a 'to let' sign up."

Sabella drove back to Goedgesig, depressed and tired. Tomorrow, she thought, she would try some of the southern suburbs and see if there was anything available for rent there.

As she lay in bed that night, unable to sleep because of the many anxieties and problems that crowded her mind, she thought of those derelict houses she had inspected during the day. One of them needed its entire roof replaced; another's doors and window-frames had rotted so badly that pieces of board had been nailed across them. A wall was in the process of collapsing in another, and one could be described as little more than a pile of builders' rubble . . .

She sat upright in bed, the old familiar exhilaration surging through her. Of course! That was the answer! Why hadn't she seen the possibilities earlier?

After a night during which she had been far too excited to do more than fall into a light doze from time to time, she rose and removed her bank book from where it was hidden underneath the hen-house. When she had washed and dressed herself in her most presentable clothes she snatched a hasty breakfast, told Daan that she intended searching further for a house to rent, and drove to Johannesburg.

She went straight to the bank in which she had deposited her savings, and asked to see the manager, Mr Hartley. He received her with courtesy but also with slight surprise which made it clear that he was not accustomed to receiving calls from females except when they were opening an account to deposit their savings.

Sabella had been rehearsing her story throughout the night. "You know something of my circumstances, Mr Hartley. You know that I have been living on a small-holding and saving money from whatever I managed to produce against the time when this war ends and my husband returns home."

"Yes." Mr Hartley waited.

"The smallholding was not owned by us but by members of my husband's family. Their own circumstances have now changed and they want to move to the smallholding themselves. I visited the less expensive Johannesburg suburbs around here yesterday, hoping to find a house which I could rent, but as you are probably aware, there is a severe shortage of such property."

"Indeed yes, Mrs le Roux." He was clearly wondering when she would come to the point of her visit.

"As you know, I have more than a hundred pounds

on deposit with your bank," Sabella said, recklessly disregarding the fact that Daan was entitled to half of that money. Since her brother refused to stand on his own feet, his share of the money would be used for their common good whether he liked it or not.

"I am aware of the total in your account, Mrs le Roux. If you would like advice about investing it – "

"Not advice, no. But I *do* want to invest it and I need your help, Mr Hartley. You see, when I found there were no 'to let' signs anywhere I applied to an agent, who advised me that in today's circumstances I would do better to buy a property instead of hoping for rented accommodation. But in spite of being on sale at rock-bottom prices, the houses which he took me to see were all uninhabitable. I believe I could beat the prices down even further because of the scarcity of building materials – "

"I'm sorry, Mrs le Roux, but you've lost me entirely. Of what use would it be to you to buy a derelict house in which you could not live, and which you could not renovate because of a lack of building materials?"

"Not *one* house, Mr Hartley," Sabella said eagerly, leaning forward in her chair. "To begin with, I'd like to buy two houses. I would then have the one in the worse condition carefully dismantled by a gang of labourers, and use its bricks and other building materials to repair the second house. If we can't get hold of cement we'll use *dagha*, which as you may know is mainly clay and water. That would give me one good, habitable house plus a vacant building-stand as an investment for when the war ends and new houses can be built. But I don't want that to be the end of the matter. As soon as I have a house in good repair I wish to buy more derelict ones and repeat the process, selling at a profit or letting each renovated house. The building-stands left vacant could then be developed when the war is over and – and my husband has been released."

"Released?" the bank manager repeated.

Sabella arranged a suitably anguished expression on her

face. "He is a prisoner-of-war, Mr Hartley. When he eventually returns home, after all he has been made to suffer, I want the business to be running smoothly for him."

"Mmm . . . I see. You wouldn't be here unless you wanted a loan. The war has forced us to alter our attitudes and we do now consider lending money to the weaker sex for the purpose of starting a business, but invariably for a *ladylike* business – "

"Like a nice little hat-shop?" Sabella put in with heavy satire, scenting rejection.

The satire had passed Mr Hartley by. "Precisely! Your idea is a sound one, Mrs le Roux, and while I congratulate you on it I have to say that my superiors would not authorise lending money to a female to start a business in what is essentially a man's world."

"If my husband had not been a prisoner," Sabella said with the bitterness of defeat, "and he had been able to come home on leave, you would have granted *him* a loan even while knowing that *I* would be running the business during his absence and making the repayments!"

"That is so, yes, but – "

"But because he is a prisoner-of-war he is being further penalised through your refusal to make me a loan!" Tears of anger and frustration filled her eyes.

Fortunately, Mr Hartley failed to recognise the true reason for the tears. He said hastily, "Please don't be distressed! Give me a few minutes to reconsider the matter." He stood up and began to pace his office floor, occasionally pausing to stare out of the window. Sabella sat very still, almost holding her breath as she waited tensely.

At last Mr Hartley sat down opposite her again. "I believe I can authorise a loan, provided the business – which would of course form the collateral against the loan – is registered in your husband's name, Mrs le Roux."

She looked down at her hands so that he would not see the fury in her eyes. "I understand," she forced herself to say evenly.

"You would merely be acting as his agent, his manager. It is the only way I could have the loan authorised by my superiors. Your husband's name is – ?" He waited.

Sabella was thinking swiftly. The newspapers were seriously affected by the shortage of newsprint, and with so many war stories jostling for space in the reduced editions it was highly unlikely that there would have been a report of Pierre's arrest and escape. Besides, such a story would have been seen as a propaganda boost to Robey Leibbrandt and his subversive rebels, and would almost certainly have been kept out of the newspapers.

"My husband's name is Pierre Jakobus le Roux," she said at last, since it would have been impossible to lie, because Mr Hartley was bound to ask to see their marriage certificate. "The initials alone would look more businesslike," she added, just in case some future purchaser or tenant of hers might know the real Pierre Jakobus le Roux.

"P.J. le Roux," Mr Hartley mused, writing it down and considering it. "It always looks better and inspires confidence if one could add something like 'and son'. Do you have a son, Mrs le Roux?"

"No," she said, her heart twisting at the reminder of her lost daughter. "My husband has two sons," she added. "My brothers, whom he adopted legally when they were children. One of them will be helping me with the business and the other is – on active service."

Mr Hartley asked for the full names of Anton and Daan, and having written them down, mused, "P.J. le Roux & Sons. Yes, that looks and sounds very well. Come and see me again, Mrs le Roux, when you have found the two initial properties you've decided to buy, and negotiated a favourable price. And, of course, you will have to recruit a gang of labourers you can trust."

Smiling broadly, she shook hands with Mr Hartley and left his office. She already knew how to recruit a trustworthy gang of labourers. The women in the *stad* who were her friends would help her find the men she needed from among their own male relatives.

Her step was lighter than it had been for a long time as she hurried to the truck so that she could go and inspect more closely the first of the two derelict houses she intended to buy.

Sabella's business in the name of P.J. le Roux & Sons flourished almost from the day it first started to operate. Her cheerful, willing and able gang of labourers demolished one of the derelict buildings with hardly a brick broken in the process, or a window pane scratched. Daan drove the truck carrying the materials to the second house, where Sabella oversaw the repairs and renovations. By the time she had to leave Goedgesig the house was ready to move into, and there was a vacant plot of land in the same suburb which she would be able to sell for development after the war. She had left a forwarding address at the post office in Uitspan village, in the hope that Katrien might write to her again.

Surely, Sabella thought with yearning, there would be a letter or a card from her daughter at Christmas? But nothing arrived, redirected by the village post office, and on Christmas Eve she asked Daan to drive to Uitspan to see whether a last-minute communication had been received from Katrien.

But he returned empty-handed, and the only news he brought was the fact that he'd heard paperboys in the city calling out the headlines: Robey Leibbrandt had at last been caught and arrested.

Of course Sabella was glad that a man so evil and dangerous was behind bars, but the silence on Katrien's part cast its shadow over everything else. Where was she, and what was she doing that she could not even send her own mother a letter or a card at Christmas?

On Christmas Day itself Sabella and Daan went to visit Ria in the institution, and even though her sister recognised them and fell eagerly on the small presents they had brought, she soon lost interest in her visitors and wandered away like a bored toddler. She had adapted to life there, and the people among whom she lived had become far more important to her than the sister who had brought her up or the baby brother she used to copy. Ria had to be coaxed by one of the staff even to come and say goodbye to Sabella and Daan.

When they returned to their house in Brixton, where Sabella planned to roast a chicken for Christmas dinner, they found Anton waiting outside. He no longer had the motorcycle, but a rusty bicycle was propped against the railing of the stoep.

"Please come in and join us for Christmas dinner, Anton," Sabella invited, with undisguised supplication in her voice.

He gave no sign that he had even heard her, and his eyes swept blankly over her as if she were invisible. "Daan, I'd like to have a word with you," he said.

As she let herself into the house she heard Daan ask eagerly, "Have you any news of Daddy?"

Bleakly, Sabella thought: I have truly lost every one of them now, even my own daughter. Daan is only with me because he is afraid of being left on his own.

Later, she heard from him that Anton had a job as a tram conductor and lived in lodgings. The fact that his *Stormjaer* motorcycle had been withdrawn by the leaders and that he'd been forced to find a full-time job told her that he had been relegated to the fringes of the subversive organisation. She was glad that he would no longer be speeding around the country on a motorcycle, carrying out dangerous missions for the National Socialist Rebels, but it pained her deeply that he hated her too much to speak to her or acknowledge her, let alone eat Christmas dinner in her company.

On New Year's Eve Bastian called to see her, bringing news which lifted the blackness from her spirits and set them soaring. "My investigators have tracked down a girl called Katrien le Roux who says she is nineteen but might well have lied about her age. She is with the South African Military Nursing Service, a probationer at a training hospital in the Cape. I'm leaving today to see her."

444

"Oh, I wish I could come with you," Sabella said wistfully. "But as soon as the New Year holiday is over Daan and I must get to work with our labourers on the two houses we've just bought. I want to pay off the bank loan as soon as I can."

"You could have borrowed the money from me," Bastian said accusingly.

"You know I have always refused to take money from you." Sabella gave him a curious look, because instinct told her that he was using the issue of a loan to play for time, and that he had other, less comforting news to impart.

At last he began, "Sabella – " and stopped, seeming to be picking the right words in his mind. "There's something you have to know."

"Yes?" She waited tensely.

"I took that adoption certificate to a lawyer, as you know, because I wanted to find out whether Pierre le Roux could forfeit his rights as Katrien's adoptive father. My lawyer has identified the document as a fake."

She stared at him in disbelief. "But – that's impossible. Pierre even brought the lawyer who handled the adoption to see me, and he made me sign consent forms and had my signature witnessed – "

"Do you happen to remember what he looked like, this lawyer?"

Sabella frowned in concentration. "All I can remember is that he had a bad cold at the time. His eyes were runny and he looked flushed with fever."

"His flush and his runny eyes had come out of a bottle," Bastian said bluntly. "He was a man called Darcy who had been disbarred for misusing clients' funds. He was also an alcoholic, and at the time he would still have had access to official forms. He was precisely the kind of man Pierre le Roux would have known and cultivated. I would guess that he paid Darcy the price of a bottle of brandy for that fake adoption certificate."

Sabella stared at him in blank shock, unable to take in, as yet, the full implications of what he had told her. Then one of them occurred to her, and she said urgently, "Promise that you won't tell Daan – or Anton!"

"Why not?"

"It would destroy them. Promise to tell no one else that the adoption was a charade!"

Bastian did not argue or comment, but promised to keep the news secret. He brushed the curls away from her forehead in the way a parent might try to convey comfort and compassion, but the expression in his eyes was not remotely parental. "Anyone would have been fooled by that fake adoption certificate, Sabella. Anyone but a lawyer who realised there should have been one for each child, and who researched Darcy's background."

She nodded mechanically, but after he had left her to begin his journey to the Cape in search of Katrien, Sabella told herself bitterly: I should have guessed the truth. Employing a lawyer, going through the courts to adopt five children would have cost a good deal of money, and when did Pierre ever spend money on anyone but himself? I should have suspected something when he and that so-called lawyer made all those excuses to explain why it wasn't necessary for me to attend the court . . .

Then the enormity of the revelation struck her with full force. All those years during which Pierre had kept her in subjection, threatening to claim custody of his "adopted" children if he left him – all that misery and suffering he had put the children through whenever he wanted to punish her . . . Oh God, what a fool she had been! What an utter waste she had allowed him to make of her life, and all because she had been taken in by a lie.

In the days that followed, as she waited for Bastian to return from the Cape, her mood alternated between the happy certainty that he would be bringing Katrien with him, and bitter hatred of Pierre for the way he had tricked her. As soon as she had paid off the bank loan, she thought savagely, she would start proceedings to divorce Pierre. And then she would immediately have her business reregistered in the name of Isabella le Roux & Daughter.

She would pay Daan his share and allow him to go on working for her if he was still too weak to stand on his own feet. But it would be on the strict understanding that he never mentioned his "Daddy" within her hearing again . . .

In the meantime, her labourers completed renovations of one of the last two houses she had bought; she let it out at a good rental and bought two more derelict houses at bargain prices. If she could sell the one to be renovated at a profit instead of letting it, she would be in a position to pay off the loan to the bank and so free herself from the need to shelter behind Pierre's detested name. She would still have sufficient capital to continue her business, and there would be a growing number of vacant stands to be developed once the war ended.

But the war showed no signs of ending, even with American help. Daily, the newspapers carried reports of new battles and of horrendous raids on England, and in South Africa society was still split between those who supported the war effort and others who did their best to sabotage it.

Anton continued to call and wait outside the house to speak to Daan, but he never acknowledged Sabella by word or glance. And it was through Anton that she received the latest news about Pierre.

"Daddy is a real hero, Sabella!" Daan announced, his eyes bright with worship. "The Germans are sending him on missions across the border to take messages or – or other things to people who are working for their side!"

"A hero?" Sabella returned harshly. "What he is doing can't be called anything but treason!"

When she considered the news more dispassionately later it struck her that no matter how he might cover it up, Pierre must be a very reluctant "hero" indeed. He had never had strong political convictions; his priority had always been that of self-interest but he'd also been unable to resist boasting and then convincing himself of the truth of those boasts. His total belief in his own lies must have made a deep impression on his German hosts inside the Consulate in Lourenço Marques, and they had taken his tales of valour on trust and decided to send him on dangerous missions. He would, she thought sourly, much rather have continued in idle, safe luxury inside the Consulate, spinning tales of past heroic exploits.

I hope someone shoots him dead on one of his missions, she thought with unashamed malevolence.

And then she heard Bastian's voice coming from the stoep, and everything else fled from her mind. She ran to meet him and to be reunited with their daughter, and stopped in her tracks. There was no sign of Katrien; Bastian had been talking to Daan.

Bastian hurried towards her, taking her hands in his. "Oh, God, Sabella," he said helplessly, with pity and pain. "I'm sorry . . ."

Her mouth shook. "It – wasn't Katrien?"

"Not *our* Katrien," he answered in a low voice. "Another girl, who happened to have the same name."

It was too cruel a blow. She felt her knees buckling, and the next moment Bastian had caught her in his arms and was carrying her to the sofa in the sitting room. He knelt beside her. "I'll find her, Sabella. I swear it. I'll never give up the search."

"Pierre is to blame for everything," she said dismally. "As soon as I've repaid the bank and I don't owe the manager an explanation I'm going to start proceedings to divorce him."

"No, Sabella," Bastian interrupted. "That would be unwise. Oh, you have more grounds for a divorce petition than you'd need, but it would mean you'd have to name your husband in court as Pierre Jakobus le Roux."

"So?" she asked, bewildered.

"You've become a successful businesswoman, Sabella. The name of your company, P.J. le Roux & Sons, sounds pretty anonymous. If you started divorce proceedings you would have to identify those initials as standing for Pierre Jakobus. And Pierre Jakobus le Roux is not only an escaped prisoner but he is making a name for himself as a German collaborator. His supporters would vilify and probably harass you for divorcing their hero, and those who detest him would fight shy of buying or renting your properties. They wouldn't want to be connected in any way with a woman who was once the wife of Pierre le Roux."

"So," she said bitterly, "I'm to remain tied to him for the remainder of my life?"

Bastian dropped a gentle kiss on her mouth. "No. Just until the end of the war."

"If I paid off the bank loan, and changed the name of the business – " she began.

"Once again, you'd have to identify Pierre by his full name," Bastian interrupted. "My advice to you would be to lie low until the end of the war – by which time you should be sufficiently secure to withstand anything, and political emotions will no longer be running so high."

She had to acknowledge the sense of what he had been saying. The people to whom she had been selling or renting houses were equally divided between those who had relatives serving with the forces, and those who supported the *Ossewa Brandwag* or other subversive organisations. By divorcing Pierre while feelings ran so high, she would alienate both factions. It hadn't occurred to her that what Pierre was doing could affect her so closely and damagingly.

And so she left matters as they were, and mourned for her lost daughter, and threw herself into work. Since there was no practical point in paying off the bank loan she used her accumulating funds instead to hire a second gang of reliable labourers, and the property she owned in the name of P.J le Roux & Sons began to constitute a small empire. So much bookwork now had to be done that she bought a suburban office building, and she would have felt a greater sense of achievement if the letters spelling out the name of her business on the plate-glass window had not stood for Pierre Jakobus le Roux, whom she loathed with passionate intensity, and his two "sons" – one of whom continued to

449

behave as if she didn't exist while the other had developed no more backbone than he'd possessed before.

She was sitting alone in the office one morning, making entries in the ledgers, when the door opened and Bastian stepped inside. "I've brought someone to see you, Sabella," he said with a smile. "Norma King."

"Oh!" Her heart gave a tremendous jump. "Katrien's friend! Norma must know where she is, or you wouldn't have brought her – " Sabella's voice died away as the door opened once again and Katrien stood there, smiling tentatively at her.

Sabella's emotions were too complex for her to react immediately. She stared at the girl who was her daughter, and yet so different from the way she used to be. She wore the uniform of the Women's Auxiliary Army Service, and her streaked blonde hair, where it showed underneath her jaunty little cap, had been cut short and swept away from her face. She looked totally grown-up and mature for her seventeen years.

The next moment the two of them moved simultaneously, and flung their arms about each other as they began to weep. "Oh Mammie," Katrien sniffed, "I'm sorry. So very sorry you worried about me . . ."

"Not even a letter, Katrien," Sabella reproached tearfully. "Not so much as a card in all those months . . ."

"But can't you see, Mammie, that I daren't write? The postmark would have given away where I was. If I'd known that Derrie had gone – " Katrien stopped, shrugging and fumbling for a handkerchief.

Sabella turned to Bastian. "How did you – And why did you say it was Norma King?"

Katrien answered for him. "When we ran away together, Mammie, we decided we'd be less likely to be traced if we switched names. I wrote a letter, pretending to be Norma's father and giving his consent, and she did the same for me. Then the two of us lied about our age and went to the headquarters of the Women's Army Defence Corps to enlist. We'd hoped to be able to stay together, but Norma

450

was taken into the SAMNS, the military nursing service, and I was sent to join the WAAS. Of course, everybody wanted to join either the WAAF or the Women's Naval Service, because they're so much more glamorous, so I suppose that's why nobody bothered to ask too many questions about Norma and myself and just sent us to where recruits were most needed – "

Sabella interrupted, staring at Bastian. "The Katrien le Roux you went to see in the Cape – she was really Norma King?"

"Yes. I didn't want to tell you, and raise more hopes that might be dashed, until I had tracked Katrien down. Norma could only tell me that Katrien was with the Women's Auxiliary Army Service but she didn't know where she was doing her training. The two of them had lost touch after they were separated."

Sabella found that Katrien was watching her with wide, apprehensive eyes. "Mammie, you won't make me leave the WAAS, will you? I love the work. I'm learning to maintain and service ambulances, and later on I'll be taught to drive one. Please don't make me leave!"

Sabella chewed at her lower lip. It was not just Katrien's physical presence to which she wanted to cling; there was no telling how long this war might last and how events might escalate. What if Katrien were to be sent up north one day as an ambulance driver, in the thick of the fighting?

"Please, Mammie," Katrien begged. "I'll spend every leave with you. I'll write every week. I've already asked Papa, and he said the decision must be yours."

"I don't know – " Sabella stopped, her eyes widening as she stared at her daughter. "*Papa?*"

Katrien moved to Bastian's side and hooked her arm through his, and the look on his face was one of immeasurable pride and love. "He told me everything," Katrien said. "I won't call him Daddy, because it sounds too much like Derrie, so I'm calling him Papa." Her eyes glowed, and she pressed closer against Bastian. "Ever since I was little I've wished he was my real father, and when he told me he *was* it felt as if a fairy godmother had waved a magic wand!"

Sabella looked into Bastian's eyes. "That – was most unwise," she said, shaken.

He spoke in a quiet voice. "News reached me at the hotel in Durban where I was staying, before I went on to the WAAS training base, that my mother had suffered another stroke. No, it wasn't fatal," he added in answer to Sabella's unspoken question, "but apart from partially paralysing her it has left her with a permanent mental impairment so that she is unable to distinguish between the present and the past. My father has resigned his seat in Parliament to devote his time to her."

What he had really been telling her, Sabella knew, was that Annette could no longer harm his parents with her blackmailing threats. But Sabella also remembered that if Bastian left his wife he would walk out without a penny. She said evenly, "It would be best if the fact that you are Katrien's father remained a secret between the three of us."

He nodded. "I have to leave now. I must pay a visit to my parents. It will be your decision, Sabella, whether or not Katrien stays in the WAAS."

As soon as she had kissed him goodbye Katrien begged with intensity, "Mammie, *please* let me stay! It's such important work, and I'd do anything else you ask of me!"

"I don't understand how they ever allowed you two girls to join up without asking to see your birth certificates," Sabella stalled.

"Oh, they did!" Katrien confessed. "But both Norma and I pretended they must have been delayed or lost in the post, and the SAMNS and the WAAS were so desperate for recruits that they stopped nagging us about them after our interviews. Besides," she added, "I'd bought some make-up and high-heeled shoes and stockings with the five pounds you'd given me, and we wore our best dresses, so that we looked so grown-up that no one ever suspected we were under age."

452

"You certainly sound an accomplished little cheat," Sabella said severely. "I don't see how I could possibly allow you to go back, Katrien, as Norma King and a good three years older than you really are!"

"Papa has already straightened all that out," Katrien informed her blithely. "He made me confess everything to Captain Monica Norris, who gave me a great ticking off, but then she said that as I had shown an aptitude for the work and they were short of competent recruits she would bend the rules and have me back as Katrien le Roux, but only if I brought with me a letter of consent from you, Mammie. Please say you'll write one!"

"Well," Sabella capitulated, "since you say you're so happy there, I suppose you'd better be allowed to stay with the WAAS."

"Oh, thank you, Mammie!" Katrien embraced her like an exuberant puppy. "I have three days' leave before I have to go back. We'll spend every minute of the time together." Her expression changed to one of uncertainty. "But I suppose you'll be too busy – "

"No, Katrien," Sabella corrected in an unsteady voice. "I'll never be too busy for you again." She freed herself from her daughter's clinging embrace and added with a smile, "I'll close the office and we'll go and have an early lunch."

"You must be terribly rich, Mammie," Katrien exclaimed with awe when Sabella led her to the Packard she had recently bought for her own use. "You always did have clever ideas. Papa told me how you've been buying old houses and using the building materials from some to repair and sell the others."

"What else did he tell you?" Sabella asked quietly as she drove to a restaurant on the outskirts of Johannesburg.

"Oh, you know, everything. About Derric being taken to gaol and escaping, and that horrible Louis throwing you out of Goedgesig . . . ." Katrien's voice caught. "And – about poor Tante Ria being sent to a mental institution. Is she very miserable there, Mammie?"

"No, Katrien. I think she is as happy as it's possible for her to be." Sabella hesitated. "That wasn't what I meant when I asked you what else Bastian told you."

"I know," Katrien confessed. "You meant – about the two of you." She touched Sabella's arm. "He explained that the two of you fell in love when you were both very young, but were never free to marry one another. I'd guessed, a long time ago, that you loved each other. And you know, Mammie, I'm old enough to understand how it must have been for both of you."

Sabella decided to change the subject. "Tell me everything you've been doing since you ran away."

Katrien wriggled in her seat in the well-upholstered car, and happily began to obey. As she listened to her bubbling, enthusiastic daughter Sabella gave mental thanks for the fact that what she had suffered at the hands of Pierre and then his vile brother Louis had clearly left no psychological scars.

Katrien's three days of leave seemed to speed by. Bastian visited them on the first two evenings and ate dinner with them, and he could not hide his joy and pride as he watched his daughter. But because of Daan's presence, none of them referred to the relationship.

Daan, Sabella noticed, was not in the least interested in hearing about Katrien's experiences in the WAAS. The only subject which he wanted to discuss with her was Pierre, and it was not a subject she welcomed, so that a certain coldness developed between the two of them. And when Anton paid one of his visits, without setting foot inside the house but leaning on his rusty bicycle outside to talk to Daan, he barely acknowledged Katrien's existence.

"Mammie, don't you think Daan and Uncle Anton are both strange?" she asked Sabella.

"I don't know what makes you say that," Sabella lied. They *were* strange, but they were also lost, and not just to herself. They were lost to the kind of young men they might have become if it hadn't been for Pierre's influence.

"I can't explain." Katrien frowned. "Daan told me that you had Derrie falsely accused of a crime he hadn't committed. *Did* you?"

"No," Sabella lied again, unflinchingly.

"I wouldn't have blamed you if you had. Do you know what I'd wish for most in the whole world, Mammie?"

"No, my love. What?"

"That Derrie would blow himself up with one of those bombs Daan boasts he smuggles across the Mozambique border for the *Stormjaers*, and that Papa's wife would drop dead so that the two of you could get married."

"That's a shocking thing to say, Katrien! In the first place, if Pierre *were* to blow himself up he would become a martyr in the eyes of all those Fascist groups. To put it mildly, it would put me, as his widow, in a most horribly embarrassing position. And to wish dead a woman you don't even know – "

"I've met her," Katrien put in. "She's really awful, Mammie."

"How could you have met her?" Sabella demanded with a frown.

Katrien looked guilty. "It was the one thing I left out when I told you what had happened since I ran away. After Papa – Uncle Bastian as I called him then – said I couldn't live with them instead of with Louis and Maria, because his wife wouldn't agree to it, and that I should go home, I decided to visit his house and speak to his wife instead. I found the address in the telephone directory. I was sure that if I explained to a *woman* what Louis had been saying and doing to me, she would understand and allow me to live with them. So I went to their house – it was terribly grand! – and she was just about to climb into the back of a car which had a man in uniform at the wheel. She saw me and she looked at me as if I were a piece of dirt she'd accidentally stepped in and said, 'Kindly go away at once. You are trespassing on private property.' I knew then that it would be pretty hopeless, but even so I said politely, 'I wanted to speak to you, Mrs Grant.' And she gave me a kind of cold, sneering look and said: 'I cannot imagine a single topic I might possibly wish to discuss with a child from the slums.' Then I grew angry, Mammie, and I said to her, 'I've read in the newspapers that you collect money for charities – ' I was about to finish the sentence and say, 'but you don't seem like a charitable person to me.' But she didn't give me a chance. She looked more than ever as if I were a piece of dirt and said, 'I don't hand out charity to beggars. If you don't leave at once I shall have the dogs set on you.'

"So then I left," Katrien went on, "and I waited outside Norma King's house until her aunt went out shopping, and I persuaded her to run away with me and enlist in one of the services. But Papa's wife really is a horrible person, Mammie, and it must be miserable for him to have to live with her."

Sabella decided to change to a more neutral topic of conversation. It was the last evening of Katrien's leave and Bastian had left them to spend it together, since he would be driving their daughter back to her training base in the morning. She drew Katrien out about her friends in Natal, and watched the blush creeping into her daughter's cheeks when she mentioned one particular boy she had met, a young sailor on shore-leave. I was your age, Sabella found herself thinking, when I first met your father, and barely older when I fell in love with him . . .

In the morning, when Bastian called for Katrien, she clung to Sabella and promised to write every week, and also to let her know when she would next be able to get leave.

"I'll call to see you tomorrow evening when I get back from Natal," Bastian told Sabella before he drove away with Katrien.

She tried to pick up the threads of her business again, but her mind continued to stray to other matters as she worked on the ledgers in the office. Katrien had always been an excellent mimic, and Sabella remembered the way she had aped Annette's voice. It had been that of an arrogant, cold-hearted woman. She worked hard and publicly for charity, but as Katrien had said, Bastian's wife did not have a scrap of charity in her heart. "*It must be horrible for him to have to live with her . . .*" Small wonder, Sabella thought painfully, that he sought occasional comfort and warmth from an eagerly compliant girl.

She stared into space for a while, and then she attacked the ledgers again, but this time it was not simply for the sake of bringing the books up to date. She made calculations and considered options, and by the end of the day she had worked matters out carefully in her mind.

On the evening of the following day, just before Bastian was due to call upon her, Sabella inspected her reflection in the mirror. She had made her very first visit to a hairdresser that morning, and her curls had been subdued into sculpted waves framing her face. She wore a new dress, one of the modern short-skirted frocks in an attractive print of sprigs of cornflowers on a white ground. She thought, with neither vanity nor false modesty, that she did not look at all like a woman who had passed her thirty-sixth birthday. Her figure was still slender, her bosom rounded above a slim waist, and there was no trace of grey in her hair.

Satisfied with her own appearance, she went into the front room where she had set a bowlful of roses in the centre of the table which she had first spread with a white cloth. Daan had responded to her broad hints and had gone to the bioscope to see the latest Gary Cooper film.

When she heard the familiar sound of Bastian's car stopping outside she went to the door. He bounded up the steps of the stoep, and stopped in his tracks when he saw her.

"Sabella, you look – *beautiful*," he said on a sharp intake of breath. "And not a day over twenty , ,"

"Hullo, Bastian." She held out her hands to him, and drew him inside the house. This time she did not put up the usual barriers which limited any physical contact between them to a brief kiss or a caress. Without inhibitions, she moved into his arms, locking her hands behind his head,

457

drawing his mouth down to hers. It had never needed much to kindle the passion which went hand in hand with their deep love for each other, and the reckless intimacy of her kiss brought a flaring response from him. He slipped his hands into the side-pockets of her dress so that he could mould her body more closely to his own.

He lifted his head, a bemused question in his eyes. "Sabella – what happened to '*Bastian, no*'?"

"A woman has the right to change her mind," she said demurely. She took his hand and drew him inside the front room. "I've prepared salads, and roasted a chicken to be eaten cold. I thought we would have a celebration dinner – afterwards."

"*Afterwards?*" His voice was intimate, his eyes gleaming at her.

She felt herself blushing. "Yes – but – not just that. Sit down, Bastian. First of all, I want to make you a proposition."

He grinned. "It's some time since a beautiful woman made me a proposition . . . You have my eager, undivided attention, Sabella." He sat down and she took a seat facing him.

"Bastian," she began, "I would never have dreamt of allowing you to leave Annette to live with me if circumstances hadn't changed so drastically. Not only has she lost the power of hurting your parents by causing a scandal, but if you walk away from your marriage now, I am in a position to compensate you in some way for what you would have to lose financially."

He leant towards her, watching her attentively. "Please explain, Sabella."

"I've made calculations, Bastian, and I would show you the figures if you'd like to see them. But to put it briefly, I'm in a sufficiently secure position financially to buy a house for us in one of the better suburbs. Daan and Anton could then share this one. As more and more houses fall into disrepair because of the shortage of building materials, I'll buy them up and expand the business. When this war does end the returning troops will create a bigger demand than ever for houses and the vacant stands alone could bring us a small fortune – "

"You said 'us', Sabella," Bastian put in. "Do you see a role for me in the running of the business?"

"Of course," she responded eagerly. "You could be in charge of the office – "

"Answering the telephone, collecting rents from your tenants, issuing receipts?" He stood up, his hands gripping the edge of the table, and for the first time she became aware of the cold rage he had been concealing. "Have you any idea, Sabella, just how insulting the proposition is you've just been making me!"

"I – I don't understand you – "

"Obviously not! I've loved you for almost twenty years, and during all that time you've refused to accept a penny from me!"

"That's not true!" she burst out.

Bastian ignored her and continued his tirade.

"In your pride, you preferred to live in near-starvation and even in squalor rather than take money from me! God above, you even denied me the right to provide a few of the things my own daughter needed and for which you couldn't pay!"

He banged his hand so hard on the table that the bowl of roses in the centre shuddered for a moment before steadying itself. "For more years than I care to remember, Sabella, I begged and schemed and plotted to share your own poverty, but you fought me in every way. If you had still been poor I would gladly have joined you in poverty now, but by your own admission you would never have me on those terms! No, you've become wealthy by your own efforts – always having rejected offers of help from me – and you've 'made calculations' as you so delicately put it, to see whether you can afford me or not! You have the bare-faced gall to suggest that I should walk out of my marriage with nothing and allow myself to be kept by you! Even more insultingly, you're offering to create

459

a meaningless job for me in your business, a job you've been doing in your spare time!"

"I – you make it sound – " she began in dismay.

"I make it sound precisely what it is," he grated out. "Disguised charity – most crudely disguised, moreover – when you, in your pride, were always suspiciously on the look-out for disguised charity from me! How arrogant you've become, Sabella! You imagine pride to be your own exclusive preserve!"

He looked down at her with cold disdain. "Your insulting 'proposition' has helped me to make up my mind about something I'd previously meant to reject. General Jan Smuts has asked me to stand as a candidate in the by-election for my father's vacant seat in Parliament. I didn't want to do it, because being a safe seat for the South African Party I'd be bound to win, and it would mean continuing with the charade of my marriage to Annette. But better an empty charade, Sabella, and a career in which I'd be able to take pride, than being your kept man and pretending to be earning my way by answering your office telephone!"

He held out his hand to her as formally as if he expected never to see her again. "Goodbye, Sabella." He confirmed the impression. "I'll keep in touch with Katrien, and I hope you'll be generous and fair-minded enough to allow her to spend some of her time on leave with me."

He left without a backward glance, and Sabella sat there, staring at the bowl of roses in the centre of the table. Slowly, anger began to replace the stunned disbelief in which she had been wrapped. She had acted in good faith and with the best of intentions. How dare he throw her offer back in her face like that? And to accuse *her* of arrogance . . . Good Lord, he had always been the most arrogant man she'd ever known! It was the English blood in his veins, of course; the English streak in him that insisted *he* should always be the giver of largesse and that help from others was demeaning to himself.

Her anger did not sustain her for long. That night she lay in bed, weeping tears of bewilderment, regret and loss. She had put her proposition clumsily, that was all. She should have placed less emphasis on the fact that he would be coming to her with nothing, and concentrated on making him feel that they would, together, be working towards a prosperous future. She should have offered to put him in sole charge of the business.

Her mood gradually swung to one of optimism. Bastian had threatened, so often in the past, to abandon her and cut her from his life and he had never succeeded in keeping to it. By tomorrow his anger would have cooled and he would call to see her.

But he didn't call, either the next day or on the ones that followed, and when she read a brief statement in a newspaper that he had been selected as a candidate for election to the parliamentary seat made vacant by his father's resignation, she knew with chilly certainty that this time he had really meant what he'd said.

Even if he were to want to change his mind in the future, he would be unable to do so. How could the Right Honourable Sebastian Grant, MP, possibly link himself with the wife of Pierre le Roux, who was known to have conspired with Robey Leibbrandt and others in a plot to assassinate Prime Minister Jan Smuts? The wife of a man who was now notorious for collaborating with the Germans?

21

As always when she was deeply unhappy, Sabella threw herself into a frenzy of work, buying, renovating and selling more houses. But even work could not smother the growing recognition that Bastian had been right, and that she *had* become arrogant through prosperity.

I always wanted to know what my value would be in the market place, she thought, and now I know. I'm growing richer and richer, and at the same time I have nothing worth having. I've lost the brothers and sister for whom I sacrificed so much, and even Katrien is only on loan to me. If she should want to marry her English sailor at the end of the war and go and live in London with him I couldn't and wouldn't want to stop her. I've lost Bastian, and when I've divorced Pierre at the end of the war it will make very little difference to my life. I shall be rich, and alone, and lonely.

Not that the end of the war seemed remotely in sight. Each day the Roll of Honour in the newspapers grew longer and longer as the names of South Africans – Afrikaners as well as those of British ancestry – who had given their lives in fighting the enemy, were published. Side by side with those Rolls of Honour there often appeared news that hinted at sabotage. Communications had been disrupted by faulty telephone wires, and one had no difficulty in reading between the lines that those wires had been deliberately cut. News of a train's derailment almost certainly meant that sticks of dynamite had been laid on the tracks. Robey Leibbrandt was waiting for the death sentence to be carried out, but his recruits of rebels had been well trained by him in subversion.

My country, Sabella thought, is as big a mess as my own life . . .

Foeitog! The slang word had been Ma's favourite expression of scorn towards any form of self-pity, and it popped unexpectedly into Sabella's mind. She smiled unwillingly. Yes, *foeitog* indeed. There was nothing she could do about her country's mess, but instead of feeling sorry for herself she could do something to improve the quality of her life.

She came to a sudden decision. Since she *was* rich she would start indulging herself. She would fulfil the fantasies of her girlhood. It might not be much, but at least it would be a beginning. At least it would be a form of fighting back.

Locking the office door, she climbed behind the wheel of the Packard and drove to the city, parking as close as she could to the department store of James Paradise & Company.

How the memories came flooding back as she stepped inside the store. Hardly anything had changed since that first day when she had gone to apply for a job as a lift girl. The management had always been conservative and not even the lifts had been modernised, so that the same latticed gate was closed by a girl wearing an updated version of the bias-cut dress and jaunty hat which Sabella remembered so well. She also remembered Bastian stepping into her lift with Annette, and both of them behaving as if she herself were invisible. She banished the inevitable stab of pain it brought to the back of her mind, and made a point of smiling warmly at the girl who was now operating her own old lift.

Sabella threw discretion and thrift to the wind as she went from one department to another. She bought petti-coats and camiknickers in pure Jap silk or crêpe de Chine; dresses of printed or plain linen and silk foulard with well-defined waists and padded shoulders to create the modern tapering silhouette. The elegant high-heeled shoes she bought in different colours naturally needed to be teamed with stockings of pure silk at three shillings and sixpence a pair, and she agreed recklessly with the salesgirl that it would be a false economy to buy less than a dozen pairs. She chose several shallow-crowned hats in woven straw, some trimmed with wispy veils, others with silk flowers or dyed feathers. She spent so lavishly that it was necessary to make several trips to the parked Packard with her purchases. She saved her visit to the store's beauty salon for last.

After she had had her hair trimmed and styled she confessed frankly to the cosmetician, "I've never used make-up and I'm not sure what I should buy."

"I shouldn't be telling you this, but – very little, madam." The girl studied her with professional admiration. "You've clearly looked after your skin so, apart from vanishing cream, you'd be better off leaving your face pretty much as it is. The war has put an end to cosmetics from London or Paris, and our own home-produced lipstick and powder are really rather awful. The lipstick is like putty and only available in a harsh, bright red that flatters hardly anyone."

"I thought it was a new fashion!" Sabella exclaimed. "It makes most women look like red-beaked finches!"

The girl laughed. "At work I'm forced to wear the products we sell, but when I'm going out I always wash it off and then I soften and dilute a little lipstick with vanishing cream and brush that on my lips. I also use a small amount of it as rouge instead of the ghastly pink pressed-powder I'm forced to sell. Let me show you what I mean, madam."

She began to work on Sabella's face. It was truly amazing, the difference a hint of colour on her full lips and just below her high cheekbones could make. A few feathery strokes with a brown pencil added emphasis to her eyebrows and Sabella smiled inwardly as she remembered those arched, symmetrical, thinly-plucked brows which had seemed so desirable and unattainable to her in her youth.

When the cosmetician had finished her demonstration she mentioned that they still had in stock some phials of French scent but that it was very expensive. Sabella bought one and then, on impulse, asked for a second phial. "After all, you were honest enough not to persuade me to buy unflattering cosmetics," she smiled.

She made a point of once again taking her own old lift down, and when it had reached the ground floor she waited until all the other customers had left. Then she slipped one of the phials of expensive scent into the hand of the lift girl, whose mouth became an "O" of astonished delight. "In memory of another lift girl, many years ago," Sabella explained with a smile, and then hurried out to the Packard.

Her expensive new wardrobe, her hairstyle and her touches of make-up helped to boost her morale, even if there were only the odd few male tenants to be impressed by the way she looked.

But the new image she had created for herself also helped to prop up her courage when she received a peremptory summons to go and see Mr Hartley, the bank manager. She had kept the interest payments on the loan scrupulously up to date and so, she thought with a fast-beating heart, there could be only one reason why Mr Hartley wanted to see her. He had discovered the lies she had told about Pierre when she secured the loan.

Could those lies invalidate the whole of her business enterprise, she wondered uneasily as she dressed for the interview. She tilted a flower-trimmed hat to one side of her head, and pinned a matching silk flower to the shoulder of the emerald-green silk foulard dress whose hem stopped just below the knee, showing her shapely legs in their silk stockings. After a discreet application of scent, she set off in the Packard to keep the appointment with Mr Hartley. She might end up by being defeated, but at least she wouldn't give him the satisfaction of looking it.

Stern-faced, he was waiting for her in his office. The stern look fell away almost instantly and he stared blankly at her at first, and then with undisguised admiration. He made a visible effort at becoming the banker, the dispassionate professional, once more.

"Mrs le Roux," he said, "I've asked you to see me because your personal account has been overdrawn by almost thirty pounds."

"Oh." *Was that all?* She almost smiled in relief.

"It was so unlike you," he continued, "that I wished to speak to you before taking any action in the matter. I thought there was a possibility that someone might have been forging your signature on cheques, but – " his professional manner slipped slightly as he studied her – "I fancy that I understand what has happened. You went on a spending spree."

"I'm afraid so," Sabella confessed. "I allowed myself to be carried away."

And the result is enchanting, his expression said in another unguarded moment. With his professional mask fixed in place once more, he spoke briskly. "I suggest that you take one of two alternative courses of action. Either transfer a lump sum from the business account to your personal one to clear the overdraft, or else vote yourself a substantial increase in the salary you draw as the company's manager. Indeed, you could do both."

"I don't think so," Sabella decided. "A higher salary would only encourage my newly-discovered streak of extravagance. No, I'll authorise a transfer of, say, forty pounds from the business account to my personal one. That will cover the overdraft and leave me with ten pounds until my next month's salary."

He nodded, and handed her a form to fill in and sign. When she had done so and was about to leave, he said abruptly, "Mrs le Roux, would you give me the great pleasure of dining with me this evening?"

She stared at him, astonished, and watched the flush spreading across his face. "I – I'm sorry – " she began.

"Please let me explain," he put in quickly. "My situation is not unlike your own. My wife was born and brought up

466

in Germany and she has nephews fighting for the Führer. Like other Germans in this country, she has been interned for the duration of the war. She is as much a prisoner of war as your husband is."

"I see," Sabella said, looking down at her hands so that her expression would not give her away.

"We have no children," she heard him go on, "and I try to keep myself busy by taking work home. But there's no denying that life is lonely. So – if you feel we could be platonic friends, and share each other's company occasionally – "

Why not, she thought, and smiled at him. "Thank you, Mr Hartley. I should like to have dinner with you tonight."

He beamed at her. "Thank *you*. And do you think you could call me Neil?"

It did not take many dinners for Sabella to discover that, with the best intentions in the world, their friendship was no longer platonic on Neil Hartley's side. She also discovered that Mrs Hartley had not been interned merely for being German-born, but because she was vociferously pro-Nazi, and that Neil was simply waiting until she had been freed before he asked her for a divorce. Since he had confided in Sabella about his wife, she decided to tell him the truth about Pierre. His advice to her was the same as Bastian's had been – to do nothing which would link her business with the name of Pierre Jakobus le Roux, but to wait until the end of the war and then pay off the bank debt and rename the business, appointing herself managing director.

Why can't I fall in love with him? Sabella asked herself as she drove to her office after spending the morning looking at possible houses to buy. Neil is good-looking, charming in a quiet, unassuming way and very kind. Even though he has never said so in words I know he loves me, so why can't I feel anything for him other than friendship?

Because he isn't Bastian, the obvious answer rose to mind, and she sighed. It had been Bastian first, last and forever, and there was nothing in the world she would ever be able to do about it . . .

The office telephone was ringing as she unlocked the door and she hurried to pick up the receiver. Daan's voice reached her, sounding strange and jerky. "Sabella – could you come home? Right now." He replaced the receiver at his end before she could respond.

Frowning, she locked the office again and climbed into the Packard to drive home. Daan should not have been at home so early in the afternoon, and she wondered if he had given one of the gang of labourers cause to down tools, and now expected her to sort out the mess of his making. The new truck which he now drove was parked outside the house but she noticed with a puzzled frown that Anton's rusty bicycle was propped up against the front wall. And yet there was no sign of him, and it could only mean that he had decided, after all this time, to set foot inside the house.

As soon as she entered through the front door Sabella heard the sound of weeping. It came from the sitting room and she hurried to investigate. It was Daan who was crying, his face covered by his hands, his shoulders heaving with grief. Anton stood behind him and it was clear that he, too, had been shedding tears. There was only one reason she could think of that would reduce both her brothers to tears, and yet she asked with foreboding, "What has happened?"

Because Anton would not answer, Daan removed his hands from his face and stammered, "D-Daddy is d-dead."

Sabella stood motionless, totally untouched by grief or regret. All she could think of were the disastrous repercussions of Pierre's death. She had once spelt them out to Katrien, and now they were about to come true. Shot by an Allied agent, blown up by a bomb – whether by one of his own or a booby-trap set for him – however he had met his violent death he would become a martyr, a dead hero whose name would forever be revered by the Fascists in this country. And as his widow she would be forced to share the notoriety of that name.

468

By all the laws of nature, she thought, Pierre should have turned out to be an average, ordinary Afrikaner. With so little formal education, a drunken father and a runaway mother he should have ended up as one of life's failures. He *had* been a failure in the sense that he'd never really achieved anything other than inspiring the myth that would follow his own death. No, he would certainly not be remembered as having been a failure. Because of his charm, which had enabled him to present himself to people in the light in which he'd wanted them to see him, and by his ability to lie to himself, he had projected himself as the stuff of which heroes are made.

She frowned. Like his father, he had been violent, but *his* violence hadn't been sparked off by drink or even always by anger. It had been cold and calculating and secret. It had been used as a weapon to manipulate and control people . . . Yes, that was the clue. Pierre had had no real substance, and yet he'd been able to control people and make them believe in him, simply because *he'd* believed in the lie that was Pierre le Roux.

He had caused so much harm, Sabella brooded, ruined so many lives, and inspired devotion in some whose lives he had ruined so that they would never even recognise what he had done to them. All because he'd been driven by his Big Dream to make money in order to achieve prestige and power. And for what? For the underlying need to impress the mother who had abandoned him and who had probably died years ago.

Sabella couldn't help wondering whether Adolf Hitler also had a mother somewhere whom *he* wanted to impress.

She broke the long silence. "How was Pierre killed?"

"He d-died," Daan answered tragically, "of m-measles."

Sabella stood there for a moment, stunned. Then she repeated, "*M-measles!*" stammering almost as badly as Daan, but for very different reasons. "Ordinary or G-German?" and then she could no longer hold it back, the hysterical laughter which had bubbled up inside her at the ludicrous anti-climax of it all. Pierre le Roux, collaborator and saboteur, had not died gloriously for the Cause but of a children's disease! There would be no subversive monuments to him; no martyrdom or folk worship of a dead hero. Indeed, the cause of his death must have been a bitter propaganda blow to the people he had served, because Sabella wouldn't be the only one to make the connection with German measles and turn his death into a cruel joke. Yes, Pierre's name would be allowed to sink very rapidly into obscurity, only the harm he had caused living after him . . .

"*You callous bloody bitch!*" Anton's voice reached her in the very first words he had spoken to her since he'd learnt of Pierre's arrest. She gave a final hiccup of laughter and looked into his red-rimmed, hate-filled eyes. "You're going to be laughing on the wrong side of your face in a moment!" he added with a snarl.

She sat down. "Look, I'm sorry. I shouldn't have laughed. It was just – *measles*. The very last thing I expected to hear."

"Shut up and listen!" Anton rapped at her. "You set up your business in the name of P.J. le Roux & Sons. Every single house you've bought, including this one, the office building, the invested capital; *everything* is in that name. Well, P.J. le Roux – Pierre Jakobus," he added, his voice trembling, "our Daddy, is dead. And we, Daan and I, are his sons. You have never had any official standing in the business, Sabella, other than as Daddy's agent and manager. Now we, Daddy's sons, are taking over and we no longer require your services. You can keep the Packard, which is also owned by the company, in lieu of severance pay. Oh yes," he added with vengeful triumph as he saw the expression on her face, "I've taken professional advice. I know an Afrikaans solicitor and I went to see him this afternoon. He telephoned your bank manager and got all the details from him."

Neil, Sabella thought with a feeling of unreality, must have been trying frantically all afternoon to reach her by telephone . . .

"The solicitor," she heard Anton go on, "is arranging to repay the bank loan immediately on our behalf because I'm not prepared to have Daddy's memory besmirched by having it said that he was a prisoner-of-war who'd fought for the British. But the point is, Sabella, that the solicitor says you have no rights and Daan and I now own the business." He gave her a cold, hard grin. "And we want you out of here – *now*."

She rose slowly, and looked at Daan, who had stopped weeping and was wiping his face with his handkerchief. "I've packed your suitcases for you, Sabella," he said, meeting her eyes squarely.

Daan had climbed down from the fence at last, the thought percolated through the numb shock filling her mind.

Bastian accorded her the courtesy of agreeing to see her immediately, instead of forcing her to wait at the reception desk of the Grant Mining Corporation under the curious gaze of the girl behind the desk.

As his secretary ushered her into his office, he stood up. How little he had changed, she thought involuntarily, from that tall young man whom she had first encountered in the corridor of a court of law, with his striking, unmatching looks and his air of unconscious arrogance.

"Please sit down, Sabella," he invited with polite formality. "I've been expecting you. You've come to seek official confirmation of Pierre's death."

She neither denied nor endorsed the statement, but asked, "Is it true that the cause was measles?"

"There were complications, but the basic disease was measles. You will obviously want, as soon as possible, official proof of your widowhood – "

"That wasn't why I called," she interrupted, and went on to tell him that her brothers had taken over her business and forced her to leave her home. "I wanted to tell you what had happened because Katrien was due to come home on

471

leave next week, and as I have no idea where I'll be living at the time I thought it might be best if you were to contact her – "

"Sabella!" Bastian interrupted, his polite veneer gone, his expression outraged. "*You* worked to create that business! Your brothers have no right to it at all!"

"Apparently they have. It's funny – I thought trouble, if it ever came, would be from Pierre, but I told myself I'd have plenty of warning and time to prevent him from taking the business over. It never entered my mind that my brothers might be able to stake claims of their own. They have taken professional advice and it seems that, as Pierre's 'sons', the sons referred to in the business that bore his name, they are perfectly entitled to take over and throw me out. I was never, officially, anything more than Pierre's agent and his manager."

"The point is that your brothers are *not* Pierre's sons!" Bastian said with heat. "They are neither his natural sons nor his adoptive sons! Have you forgotten that the adoption certificate was a fake?"

"No," she said quietly.

He made a sound of exasperation. "Fight them! Go to court and produce the fake document!"

"I can't. They loved Pierre and they revere his memory. God knows, he didn't deserve it, but that's the way things are. He robbed them of everything but their blind belief in him. If I take that away I might as well kill them."

Bastian studied her. "So, in order to leave them in their fool's paradise – and incidentally enrich themselves – you're going to allow them to take from you what you've worked so hard to achieve?"

"I did them enough harm by marrying Pierre," she said quietly. "I can't rob them of the one thing they hold most dear – their belief that Pierre loved them and adopted them as his own sons. I can't do it, Bastian."

He studied her for a long moment. "You're a fool."

"I know. But there it is."

He shook his head. "Still the old Sabella, then – the

Sabella who puts others first and makes impossible sacrifices. I thought prosperity had taught you to put yourself first."

She flushed painfully. "I – want to apologise for – I *was* arrogant when I – "

He made a gesture with his hand, dismissing her incoherent apology. "It no longer matters." He changed the subject. "What are your plans now?"

She attempted a smile. "For tonight, I shall have to find a room in a hotel. Tomorrow I'll have to search for lodgings, somewhere with extra space for when Katrien comes on leave but which won't make too great a hole in my personal savings. I'll have to look for a job as well – "

"Your first priority must be a room for tonight," Bastian interrupted. "Have you any particular hotel in mind?"

"I've never stayed in one in my life," she confessed. "I'm not even sure how to go about asking for a room. I mean, as a woman on my own, they might think – "

She stopped, her breath catching at the sudden warmth in Bastian's smile as he studied her. But he did not comment, as she had expected, on her changed appearance. All he said was, "I'd suggest the Carlton Hotel. I'll go with you to make a reservation."

She had more than a suspicion that the Carlton would be far too expensive for someone in her present position, but she was too grateful to have the matter taken out of her hands to do more than nod.

She followed him from his office and waited as he told his secretary, "I shan't be back, so please deal with any calls that come in, Miss Day."

Outside, Bastian slid into the passenger seat of the Packard and said, "Would you mind driving to Fox Street first? I've remembered an urgent call I have to make."

She had so many thoughts to occupy her mind as she waited outside the address in Fox Street to which she had driven him that it did not strike her, at first, that his call was taking a considerable time. But at last he emerged from the rather nondescript building and said, "I think I ought to take over the driving from here, Sabella."

She agreed, and didn't question the suggestion until she began to realise that, instead of driving her to the Carlton Hotel in the city, he was making for the suburbs. "What is going on, Bastian?" she wanted to know.

"I have another call to make at home." He drew the car to a halt in a quiet, tree-lined suburban street. "I don't want to arrive too early, so we'll waste a few minutes here."

"What is going on?" she demanded again.

"I have some business to sort out with my political agent, Tony Barrows. It was his office I visited in Fox Street, and I fixed up a meeting with him at home. If I'd booked you into the Carlton Hotel immediately you would have had time lying heavily on your hands before you could go down to dinner, so I thought I would attend to my own business first. You don't mind, do you?"

"No," Sabella lied, for she *did* mind quite badly. She had no wish whatever to sit in the car outside the house which Bastian shared with Annette and wait while he discussed political strategy with his agent.

Bastian tooted the horn as a blue Studebaker overtook them, and switched on the engine. "That was Tony. My business with him won't take very long, Sabella."

She said nothing. Looking out of the window, she thought how beautiful the houses were here, how unlike anything she had ever bought and renovated and resold. These houses did not simply have gardens; they were surrounded by large, impeccably kept grounds in which at least one more good-sized house could have been built

Bastian swung her Packard into the drive of one of the houses. Parked beside the blue Studebaker was a gleaming Oldsmobile which must obviously belong to Annette. Sabella wished she had known she would have to spend so much time waiting for Bastian, because she would have bought a newspaper and immersed herself in its pages instead of being forced to sit here and look at the home he shared with Annette.

"Get out, Sabella," she heard him say calmly.

"*What?* I don't w – "

"Please." He had come round to the passenger side of the car and opened the door, and his hand was very firmly on her arm.

"I don't want to meet Annette – " she began to protest.

"I can't leave you sitting in the drive. Whatever would people think?" There was a note of irony in his voice that troubled her, and for the first time she began to suspect that there was far more to his delay in taking her to the Carlton Hotel than he had led her to believe.

He was propelling her so determinedly towards the front door of the house that she could only have stopped him by making a scene. And already, she realised, several black servants were watching them with curiosity, even though the one in uniform who had opened the front door for them was trying to arrange an impassive expression on his face.

As they entered Bastian began, "Thank you, Jack – " and stopped. Then, with an emphasis that brought both surprise and pleasure to the face of the black man, he said, "Thank you, Dingiswayo. The others are in the drawing room?"

"Yes, Mr Sebastian."

Sabella found herself being inexorably steered through beautiful, expensively furnished but coldly unwelcoming inter-connecting halls to a drawing room which seemed more designed for looking at than occupying.

It *was* occupied, however, by a dark-haired young man and a fair-haired woman whom Sabella had no difficulty in identifying as Annette. She rose from the sofa and addressed Bastian angrily. "What is this nonsense that Tony has been telling me, about tonight's political rally having been cancelled?"

"It's not nonsense. It *has* been cancelled."

"Why?" Annette demanded. She had shown no interest in or curiosity about Sabella, perhaps because she had assumed her to be a secretary or a behind-the-scenes political worker.

"Because I'm no longer standing as a candidate in the by-election," Bastian said calmly.

Underneath the expertly-applied rouge – which was certainly not the home-produced kind the cosmetician had described to Sabella – Annette's face turned almost puce. "Are you out of your mind? The seat is yours for the taking! I *demand* that you go ahead with the rally! All my friends are to be there – "

"I'm sorry, Annette, that your dream to be Mrs the Right Honourable Sebastian Grant will never become reality," Bastian interrupted suavely. He put his arm about Sabella's waist and drew her closer to him. "Annette, I'd like you to meet my cousin. My *Afrikaans* cousin, Sabella le Roux."

"Oh." Annette made no attempt to disguise her distaste and shock. But after a moment she took an almost visible hold on herself and turned to Tony Barrows, giving him a parody of a smile. "My husband's little unfunny joke – "

"Too late, Annette," Bastian broke in. "Tony knows the whole story – and also that *you've* been aware of it for a considerable time. He also knows that I've come here this afternoon to tell you that I'm leaving you, and want a divorce."

Sabella felt almost as shocked as Annette was looking. "You're out of your mind!" Bastian's wife shrilled at him. "You've had some kind of brainstorm! Tony, for heavens' sake, *do* something!"

"I'm sorry, Annette. Sebastian won't be shifted from his decision. I am here because he insisted that he would only give me the official story to be handed to the Press if I came to the house."

Bastian spoke calmly. "I know that you have a lot to do, Tony, what with cancelling tonight's rally and also finding an alternative candidate, so I'll try to make all this as brief as possible." He faced his wife. "You'll give me a divorce, because I plan to make it impossible for you *not* to do so. You see, if you deny me a divorce, Annette, the story Tony will give the Press will be that I've withdrawn from the by-election because I intend living with my Cousin

476

Sabella, whom I have loved for most of my adult life, and by whom I have a daughter who was fathered before I married you."

"Bastian!" Sabella exclaimed furiously. "How dare you! How – "

"My darling Sabella," he cut in with a warm, slow, deliberately misunderstanding smile. "Surely you aren't ashamed of our lovely daughter Katrien?"

"Of course not! But – but I forbid you to carry out this – this – "

"This act of folly!" Annette finished for her. She gave Sabella a long, up-and-down look. "You may be Afrikaans, but you're certainly not poor, and you will know, of course, that if Bastian leaves me he'll walk out without a penny. You would hardly welcome him on those terms."

"I'd welcome him on *any* terms – " Sabella began heatedly, and stopped, angry with herself for having walked into such a trap.

Bastian caught her hand in his, imprisoning it as he continued to address his wife. "The fact that the Press would be told about my Afrikaans cousin would mean, of course, that the secret of my birth would also come out. Tony, if *you* don't tell the Press, in those circumstances, that Annette has known the truth about my illegitimate birth for a considerable time, then *I* shall do so." He turned back to Annette. "You would look an utter fool and a fraud in the eyes of your society friends, my dear."

"You – you *bastard*!" she spat viciously at him.

He shrugged. "That is indeed what I am, and I'll make sure the world knows it if you deny me a divorce."

"What if I did agree to a divorce?" she asked sullenly, after a moment's silence.

"If you telephone your lawyer now, and tell him that you are suing me for divorce on the grounds of my admitted adultery, the Press will simply be told that I've withdrawn from the election because I didn't want to embarrass the

477

government by inviting adverse publicity. Now, which is it to be?"

She glared at him for a moment, and then she moved to pick up the telephone, and they listened as she dialled.

Sabella felt a little as if she had been run over by a steamroller. She heard Annette talking to her solicitor on the telephone, informing him with venom in her voice that she was throwing her husband out of the house and asking him to start immediate divorce proceedings.

Bastian nodded when she replaced the receiver and took Sabella's arm. "Come and wait for me in the Packard while I collect my things."

Sabella began to recover some normality of reaction when they found themselves outside. She stopped in her tracks. "How could you have done such a thing, Bastian?" she demanded angrily. "Without consulting me, and then humiliating Annette in such a public fashion – "

"It was the only way, believe me. She would never have given in if I hadn't sprung it on her in public. And I didn't consult you because I knew you would refuse to cooperate."

Sabella shook her head. "I *am* refusing. I can't let you go through with it. I can't let you make such a sacrifice – "

"No?" He spun her around, his eyebrows raised. "Is sacrificing everything *your* exclusive preserve? You're being arrogant again, Sabella!" Then he laughed, an exuberant, joyful sound. "*Sacrifice!* I feel like someone who has been let out of prison!" He bent his head to kiss her.

"You were very sure of me, weren't you?" she asked afterwards, staring up at him.

"Of course," he answered simply. "Haven't you and I always been sure of one another, no matter how many separations and quarrels came between?"

He was right, she admitted to herself later as she waited in the car for him to collect his belongings. They had always been sure of one another, and he had always sworn that one day, by some means or other, they would share their lives.

But who would have thought that he would fulfil his promise because of one flawed man's death by the children's illness of measles . . .

The Carlton Hotel was even grander than Sabella had imagined, and no one looking at the luxury of the suite to which she and Bastian were shown would have guessed that a war was raging elsewhere in the world.

"No," she heard Bastian say as he tipped the uniformed man who had carried their suitcases into the room. "We shan't be coming down for dinner. We'll order something in our suite – later."

Sabella blushed, hoping she was the only one who had recognised the significance of that last word. Bastian closed the door firmly and moved towards her.

"We're going to be very poor," he said, cupping her face between his hands. "Better make the most of all this luxury, because we're not likely to experience it again."

"It was foolish of you," Sabella chided as she began to unbutton his shirt, "to have spent money on booking such expensive accommodation."

He grinned, his hands slipping down to her throat as he began to undress her in turn. "It would have mortified Annette if her friends had got to know that I'd committed adultery in any but a first class hotel!"

Sabella giggled, and moved into his arms, feeling his naked skin against her own again after so many years. She found that his body was as familiar to her as if there had been no lapse between now and the last time she had run her hands lovingly over it.

He picked her up in his arms, and carried her towards the luxurious bed. As he drew her against him he asked, "Where shall we go, you and I – and Katrien? Where shall we make our home? Would Mooikrantz suit you?"

"*Mooikrantz!*" she breathed, her eyes wide. "We couldn't afford it, even if it should be for sale – "

"We can afford it." He bent his head to kiss her breasts with lingering attention. When he lifted his head again he added, "I bought the farm from that disgruntled Mevrou Marais last year."

Sabella stretched out her arms to receive him and to make him part of herself again, just as she had once done on Mooikrantz – where it had all started, and where it was to continue under the benevolent shelter of the high, echoing hills.

Epilogue

Bastian insisted on helping Sabella down from the rocky ledge on which they had been sitting, watching the antics of the baboons. She laughed, pushing him away. "I'm pregnant, not crippled!"

He pulled her against him. "What a remarkably fertile pair we are, you and I. Don't you think we ought to call the baby Carlton if it's a boy?"

As if in appreciation of the joke, a large male baboon barked raucously. Sabella slipped her hand inside Bastian's and together they stood and looked down at Mooikrantz.

Ezekeil and M'dala had kept the farm going ever since Bastian had bought it in a deeply emotional gesture. Now he and Sabella were married, he was determined to become a skilled farmer himself, and the seedlings were beginning to show in the fields while the early oranges were almost ready for picking. With their pooled savings, she and Bastian had bought a small flock of sheep and half-a-dozen cows but Sabella thought she would like to keep chickens too, once the baby had been born and while it was still too dependent to allow her to help with the heavier work.

But in spite of the stock they had bought and the promising seedlings in the fields, Mooikrantz would never be more than a very beautiful but modest farm, allowing them to live in reasonable comfort. They could sell the Packard and replace it with a second-hand truck and use the rest of the proceeds to buy Tante Bessie's farm from her heirs, were it not for one thing.

Periodically, a coded message would arrive for Bastian.

Then he would take the Packard, kiss Sabella goodbye and disappear for several days. He never explained where he had been or why, and she never asked, but she did not need to have it spelt out to her that he was still working for Government Intelligence. All she knew for certain was that he received no payment for what he did, and she could only pray, each time he left Mooikrantz in the Packard, that what he was about to do would not be physically dangerous.

But because he needed the fast car, and because his absences left Ezekiel and M'dala short-handed, buying Tante Bessie's farm was not a practical proposition.

She and Bastian never argued about the matter, but there was another practical proposition on which they were in constant disagreement. She returned to it now as they watched young baboons playing a game of dare. Each would scamper as close to the edge of a precipice as their courage would allow, and occasionally one would pretend to push another over the side. Frightened and squealing, the young baboon would escape from its tormentor and run to its mother, who was invariably nursing another sibling at her breast.

"You see, Bastian," Sabella pointed out gently but significantly, "it's part of nature that young ones should have playmates, instead of growing up as lonely, only children."

"We're not going over all that again, Sabella," Bastian said firmly. "I'm not prepared to risk your health by your giving birth to another baby after this one."

"The doctor says there's no risk, and you know it. He says I'm in excellent physical health, and that I could have two or even three more children after this one. Why won't you accept that?"

"Doctors don't know everything," Bastian muttered.

"Neither do husbands!" Sabella moved to stand in front of him in a challenging attitude. "I don't want our baby to grow up as an only child – "

"It wouldn't be an only child. It would have a sister, Katrien."

"Who is a generation older, and with her own life to live!" She changed her tactics. "Bastian, *you* grew up as an only child, and you've told me how disadvantaged that made you feel. Surely you don't want this baby of ours to grow up feeling the same way?"

His eyes slid away from hers. "Sabella, Mooikrantz wouldn't be able to support a large family – "

She interrupted him with an angry laugh. "It has supported a large family in the past. Oh, not in luxury, certainly, but perfectly adequately! I can see what it is, Bastian – you're harking back to the flesh-pots you had to give up. You can't take the thought of your children having to wear hand-me-downs and being denied expensive treats like holidays. You'd sooner have one miserable, lonely son or daughter with no one to play with but constant new clothes and shop-bought toys than two or three, making clay-oxen together by the river and sharing happiness, companionship and the occasional treat – "

"Damn you!" Bastian cut in, grabbing hold of her shoulders. "I hanker after no flesh-pots! Do you *really* believe I don't also long for the large family I'd always dreamt of having?"

"Then why – "

"I have to think of Katrien. It's true that Mooikrantz could adequately support two or three children, Sabella, but there would never be money left over to provide an insurance for them. And I can't allow the possibility that Katrien might have to be that insurance."

"I don't understand you – " Sabella began.

"Don't you? You should! Nothing in life is certain, Sabella, and the fact that you're thirty-seven and I'm forty-one is not in our favour. What if we had those two or three more children both of us want, and something were to happen to you and me? Katrien would be in exactly the same position in which you were trapped. She would become another you, Sabella. Another young woman sacrificing her life, denying herself the chance of making a free choice when it comes to marriage or a career, always having to

485

put her brothers and sisters first. *That* is what I cannot risk."

Sabella was silent. How could she possibly argue with him when she reviewed her own useless sacrifices? She had decided to let bygones be bygones when she married Bastian in a registrar's office, and had written to Daan and Anton, inviting them to the ceremony. They hadn't replied. She and Bastian had visited Ria in the institution, and she had been as petulant as a three-year-old because they had interrupted a game she'd been playing with another inmate.

"No," she heard Bastian go on. "If I'd been in a position to make financial provision for three or four children so that they would never be a burden on anyone or have to be sent to orphanages, I would welcome a large family. But I'm not in such a position, and so there will be only this one baby."

Sabella reached up and kissed him. "I understand," she said quietly. "You should have spoken to me openly about this before." She changed the subject by adding briskly, "We'd better go home now. I still have to make up beds for the girls." Katrien had managed to arrange for her leave to coincide with that of Norma King, with whom she had re-established contact, and the two of them would be arriving tomorrow.

Bastian put his arm about Sabella's thickened waist and insisted on helping her down the gentle slope. Suddenly, he stopped and pointed to the young baboons, who had found a new game. Like mischievous children, they were picking up pebbles and throwing them down at an indignant-looking *meerkat* in a dip below. Instead of running away, the *meerkat* alternated by dropping on all fours to present a smaller target and then standing on its hind legs again, staring at the young baboons in a how-dare-you attitude. Sabella almost expected the animal to put its front paws on its hips to show the young baboons that it treated their antics with contempt.

"I'll give them a taste of their own medicine," Bastian said with a grin, and began to aim pebbles at the baboons.

486

"*Stop!*" Sabella cried shrilly.

"I haven't hit one yet, and even if I did, the animal would scarcely feel it," he laughed, drawing back his arm to take aim.

She caught at his arm, trying to wrest the pebble from his hand, and in his surprise he dropped it.

She was on her knees, frantically scrabbling through the many loose pebbles strewn around. They had a smooth, washed appearance, suggesting that a river had once run here and had changed its course hundreds or thousands of years ago. Now it had become a footpath . . .

"Have you gone mad?" she heard Bastian ask in astonishment. She didn't reply, or pause in what she was doing. Ah, here it was . . . Good Lord, *there* was another, a little distance away . . .

Still on her knees, the two pebbles clenched in her hands, she began to laugh. The hills threw her laughter back at her, joining in the glorious irony of it all. And, yes, the celebration.

There would be future insurance and to spare for the large family she and Bastian would be raising.

It was almost as if the hills had been waiting for her to grow up and gain experience so that she would be able to recognise their bounty.

"You're wonderful!" she shouted, her throat tilted back, her arms thrown wide.

"Wonderful . . . wonderful . . . wonderful . . ." the hills replied.

There were diamonds on Mooikrantz after all.

ENTHRALLING HISTORICAL NOVELS

	Christina Laffeaty		
☐ 51582 1	Far Forbidden Plains	£3.99
	Audrey Howard		
☐ 52494 2	The Mallow Years	£4.99
	Audrey Howard		
☐ 56236 6	Shining Threads	£4.99
	Judith Merkle Riley		
☐ 51611 3	A Vision of Light	£4.50
	Brenda McBryde		
☐ 55350 2	Hannah Robson	£3.99

All these books are available at your local bookshop or newsagent or can be ordered direct from the publisher. Just tick the titles you want and fill in the form below.

Prices and availability subject to change without notice.

HODDER AND STOUGHTON PAPERBACKS, PO Box 11, Falmouth, Cornwall.

Please send cheque or postal order for the value of the book, and add the following for postage and packing:
UK including BFPO – £1.00 for one book, plus 50p for the second book, and 30p for each additional book ordered up to a £3.00 maximum.
OVERSEAS INCLUDING EIRE – £2.00 for the first book, plus £1.00 for the second book, and 50p for each additional book ordered.
OR Please debit this amount from my Access/Visa Card (delete as appropriate).

Card Number ☐☐☐☐☐☐☐☐☐☐☐☐☐☐☐☐☐☐

Amount £ ....

Expiry Date ....

Signed ....

Name ....

Address ....

....